SCATTER

Hearts of Heroes 1

SCATTER

Hearts of Heroes 1

Molly J. Bragg

Desert Palm Press

Scatter
(Hearts of Heroes - Book 1)

By Molly J. Bragg

©2022 Molly J. Bragg

ISBN (book) 9781654213265
ISBN (epub) 9781654213272

Desert Palm Press
1961 Main Street, Suite 220
Watsonville, California 95076
www.desertpalmpress.com

Editor: Kaycee Hawn
Cover Design: Jeanette Eileen Widjaja

Printed in the United States of America
First Edition February 2022

Acknowledgement

I would like to acknowledge Beck Use, L. I. Pettigrew, Kelly Fitzsimons, Isca Irangwe, Nisha Ward, and the friend known only as Jane. Without them, this book might never have been finished. I'd also like to thank Vikki Ciaffone for her hard work helping me get the novel ready for submission, my wonderful editor Kaycee Hawn for not only editing with a light hand but having a turnaround time that boggles the mind, and Lee Fitzsimmons for giving me a chance to share my work with the world.

Dedication

This book is dedicated to all the people who didn't have superheroes who looked like them growing up

Chapter One

"MOM, FOR THE HUNDREDTH time, no. I can't tell you anything about my new assignment," Danny said, trying her best not to roll her eyes as she was driving along one of the most accident-plagued stretches of highway in the state of Florida.

"If you won't tell me, then how do I know you're not beating confessions out of innocent people in some CIA black site?"

"First, because I'm a Deputy US Marshal."

"Don't remind me. I can barely stand the shame. My daughter, wearing a badge. I have no idea where I went wrong."

"Second, because however ashamed you are of me, I am still your daughter," she said. "I put on the badge because I want to help people."

"You can't help people from inside a corrupt system, Danny. You have to tear it down and start over."

"Maybe, Mom, but until you find the matches to burn it down, I can do my best. That means that sometimes, I have to keep secrets."

"Even from your mother?"

"Especially from my mother. Do you know how embarrassing it would be if I were doing Witness Protection and my crazy ACLU lawyer mother kicked in the door with a court order demanding the release of the witness?"

"So you're doing Witness Protection!"

"I never said that. I just suggested a scenario in which you could humiliate me. You know, like when you sued my high school."

"They were discriminating against you."

"I remember, Mom, and I'm hanging up now. I'm almost at work."

"Okay. I love you. Be safe."

"I love you too. Try not to sue my boss."

"You'd have to give me his name first."

"Bye," Danny said, hitting the 'end call' button before her mom could reply. She loved her mom, she really did, but Deputy US Marshals and pot-smoking hippie civil rights lawyers went together like gasoline and matches. It didn't help that she knew her mom would have preferred her to have been a bit more like her sisters, but Danny had always wanted to be a cop.

She was a good one, too. Or she liked to think so. Her superiors certainly seemed to think so. She'd spent the first four years of her career on a fugitive retrieval team, and now she'd been promoted to 'Metahuman Emergency Response Team Support,' or what most people called 'Superhero Duty.' And not just for any Superhero group, either. She'd been assigned to Focus. A Tier Three asset.

Honestly, she was a little nervous about that. Focus wasn't your run-of-the-mill Superhero. Tier Three Assets were the heroes who got the call for situations that threatened the entire planet. Heroes like the Olympus Six, Ice Dragon, The Gentleman, Clockwork, and Quickstep. They were the most powerful metahumans on the roster, and Focus was one of the most powerful of the Tier Three Heroes in the US. Maybe one of the most powerful in the world. She was the sixth-longest serving Superhero out there, with an active period just a hair shy of thirty-two years. She was also extremely gay. Danny had had a crush on her since she was five years old. She'd had a poster of Focus kissing her former sidekick Scatter on the wall of her bedroom from the time she'd come out to her parents at thirteen up until she graduated from college. She also had a bad habit of turning into a babbling idiot around pretty girls.

She pulled off the Interstate, taking the exit for downtown Pontian, all the while telling herself that she was the junior-most member of Focus' support team. The chances that she'd actually get to interact with the hero her first day on the job were pretty slim. She would just show up, report to the Officer in charge, and probably spend the day setting up her locker, getting entered into the system, and doing other boring shit. Which was a good thing. She could get used to being around a literal ageless lesbian goddess before she actually had to speak to her.

God, she was definitely going to make a fool of herself.

***

"Here's your temporary pass card, ma'am. Your escort should be here shortly."

Danny took the swipe card and clipped it to her belt, then looked around the entryway. The thick steel walls and heavy doors looked more like they belonged on a bank vault than in the lobby of a Marshal's station. There were armored machine gun nests with electric miniguns or air-cooled Browning .50 caliber machine guns. She was a little surprised there weren't rocket launchers.

The place felt a little overdone to her, but then, she'd only ever been in one throwdown with a Super, and he'd been a low level hydrokinetic. A couple of beanbag rounds to the gut had finished things before they could really start. She doubted that the kind of people who could go toe-to-toe with someone like Focus would be taken down so easily, so maybe the arsenal and the armor weren't overkill.

She turned at the sound of boots on the tile floor and saw a short woman, maybe five-foot-four or so, with vaguely middle eastern features, headed towards her. She couldn't quite place the woman's country of origin, but Danny had a lot more experience with picking out East Asian than West Asian features. The woman was beautiful, though. She looked more like a dancer or a model than a cop, and if she hadn't been carrying what looked like a cut-down AR in a hip holster and had a Marshal's badge clipped to her belt, Danny would have taken her for support staff, or a civilian.

The woman stopped in front of her and smiled, and Danny stamped down on the urge to do something stupid, like babble or ask for her phone number, because damn, she was gorgeous. But she was also a co-worker, so definitely a no-fly zone, something which helped keep Danny from making a fool of herself.

"Danielle Martin?" the woman asked.

"Yes, but please, call me Danny."

The woman smiled and held out her hand, and Danny had to work to keep from sucking in a breath, because wow. "Deputy Marshal Lori Ahmad."

Danny shook her hand. "Nice to meet you."

"Likewise," Lori said. "Come on. Let's get you to the boss. It's already been a day, and she's only on her second cup of coffee."

Danny winced as she fell in behind Lori. "What's going on?"

"We've got some wannabe Supervillain pulling tech robberies all over town, but we can't do a damn thing about it since we've got a fucking Kaiju swimming around the bay."

"There's a Kaiju in the bay?" Danny asked, more than a little shocked. "I didn't see any evacuation traffic as I was going in."

"You came in on Interstate 2?"

"Yeah."

"We run the Kaiju evacuations along I-95. Kaiju tend to come straight inland, so it's safer to run the evacs along a North/South route."

"What's the status on the MERTs?"

"Focus is out in the field, along with Beta, Gamma, and Delta Squads. Since Alpha is a person short until we get you on the clock, we've stood down. The city's two Tier Two teams, the Ironclads and the Myrmidons, and all four of the local Champions teams are down at the docks, but honestly, against a full-blown Kaiju, they're mostly limited to aiding evac. Pontian doesn't attract a lot of heavy hitters when it comes to Superheroes. The local chapter of the Black Panthers has the only heavy hitter we've got besides Focus, but they're insisting on holding South Shore in case the Kaiju tries to come ashore there."

Danny nodded. It made sense, given the reports she'd read on the city. Most of Pontian's black population was concentrated in South Shore and the surrounding neighborhoods, and while the Black Panthers worked with the Marshals when they could, they weren't part of the official hierarchy. Plus, after a few incidents where a Super battle had been deliberately steered into low-income black neighborhoods, the Panthers were perfectly willing to tell the Marshals to get fucked if there was even a chance that they might be out of position when the people they were there to protect were in danger.

"Who's the local Panther leader?" Danny asked. "I know I read it in a report, but honestly, I've been through so much information in the last week, it's kind of blurring."

"Yeah. I remember what it was like when I got assigned, and honestly, Pontian's a lot to deal with. The local Pack Master is codenamed Kipengele. Means Element in Swahili. She's an elemental kinetic. Does Earth, Air, Fire, Water, Fauna, Electricity, Heat, and Cold. Has 'all cops are bastards' tattooed on her right bicep."

"Bet she's fun to work with," Danny said.

"Given that her twelve-year-old son was killed by a cop, she's honestly a lot more co-operative than you'd expect, but once she makes a decision, there's no moving her."

"Yikes," Danny said.

"Yeah. Bastard who did it is a Captain in the local PD these days."

"Jesus. No wonder she's salty."

"Right?"

"Can I ask a question?"

"Sure."

"How the fuck did I make Alpha Squad? I expected to be on the reserve if I even got assigned to field duty at all."

Lori stopped and turned toward her. "You don't know?" she asked.

"No," Danny said. "When they told me I'd been promoted, I thought I was getting my own fugitive retrieval team. Then they told me I was coming here. I've never done Superhero support before, and I didn't put in for a transfer. I figured it was because our last capture turned out to be an unrecorded meta, but even if that was it, there's no way that should put me on the primary support team for a Tier Three asset."

"Well, you're not wrong about that," Lori said. "But if you don't know why you made Alpha squad, then I have a feeling the boss is not going to be happy."

"Why?"

"You'll see," Lori said as she started walking again.

Danny followed with a sinking feeling in her gut.

*　*　*

Danny's first thought when she laid eyes on Deputy Marshal Carmen Perez was that this assignment was some kind of joke. It was bad enough that Lori, who was apparently her squad mate, looked like a model, but she just had to have a boss who looked like the centerfold in Hot Butch monthly, too. Short, spiky brown hair shot through with blonde highlights, muscled arms sticking out of the short sleeves of her navy-blue polo, one of those cut down ARs in a hip holster, and a voice that sounded like it belonged on stage in a blues bar filled with cheap cigarette smoke and cheaper whiskey.

She was definitely too gay for this job.

Fortunately, Perez wasn't paying any attention to Danny, and didn't notice her miniature gay meltdown. She was too busy barking orders.

"I don't give a damn what PPD says. The Panthers are backing up the District Four Champions, and I need more bodies in District Three, so you tell that arrogant jackass that he can either move his men, or I will start by arresting him for reckless endangerment of civilians during a metahuman crisis, and keep arresting people in his chain of command until I find someone who will follow fucking orders."

"Yes, ma'am," someone responded, as Lori snorted and shook her head.

"That's the boss," Lori said.

Danny didn't comment. Instead, she looked up at the bank of twenty-seven ultra-high-def screens that made up the status board. A full third of it was showing footage of the bay, where Danny could see a giant shape swimming just under the surface, with enormous spines breaking the surface like the dorsal fin of the shark in Jaws. She expected its entire body to breach the surface at any moment, but nothing happened, and the longer she watched, the stranger that got.

Kaiju were deep sea dwellers. They grew to enormous sizes, and people were terrified of them, but mostly, they were harmless because as deep-sea dwellers, they mostly stayed way the fuck down at the bottom of the ocean. Kaiju attacks had started after the Castle Bravo test off Bikini Atoll back in 1954. The science geeks weren't sure if the bomb had woken them up, or if the radioactive fallout had caused something to mutate, but it didn't really matter to most people. What did matter were the attacks, and attacks were a bit like a Category Five hurricane. Sometimes you get two or three in a year. Sometimes you went a decade and a half without a single one. They were more dangerous than hurricanes because you usually only had at most a few hours warning, but less dangerous because they never wandered very far inland.

The odd part was, when Kaiju did attack, they almost always went straight for land. The fact that this one was swimming in circles around the bay didn't make any sense at all, but that was definitely what was happening. Danny stood there, watching as it made three laps around the bay, and watched as the zone of projected landfall that was on one of the screens slowly followed it in circles around the city.

"Do we have any idea what attracted it to Pontian?" Danny asked.

"No," Lori said. "We don't have any of the usual Kaiju bait. No whaling vessels, no leaking oil tankers, no navy bases with nuclear powered ships, no nuclear reactors. Dumping in the bay has been illegal since that one hit Miami back in '92, so there's no toxic waste in the water. We don't even use mermaid repellent on the beaches, so there's not much chance it was driven here deliberately."

"Any chances it followed a supercargo that lost a few containers?"

"Possible," Lori said. "But if that's it, why hasn't it hit the docks?"

"I don't know," Danny said.

"That seems to be going around today."

"Status change!" someone yelled. "Kaiju is changing course. It's...It's headed back out to sea."

"What the fuck?" someone asked.

"Collins, get me a drone in the air. I want it tasked to follow that bastard until it goes deep. Williams, tell PPD and emergency services that we'll hold the evacuation until the Kaiju is out of visual contact and off coastal sonar. Once we lose contact, if we lose contact, I'll give the all clear to let people go back to their homes. Lopez, re-task the Myrmidons. See if they can find our sticky-fingered Supervillain."

"What about the Ironclads?" someone asked. Danny assumed it was Lopez.

"Leave them where they are. Ironsides is less likely to panic and fuck something up if the Kaiju does another 180," Perez said in an annoyed tone. "If anybody needs me, I'll be in my office."

Danny took it from the tone that anyone who needed her should probably find a way to not need her if they wanted to keep their head, which made it a little unnerving when Perez turned and looked right at her.

"You two, with me," Perez said.

Lori started after Perez, and Danny followed, wondering if it was too late to take her mom up on the offer to send her to school to learn to be an acupuncturist.

***

Perez's office was bigger than Danny expected, but the size had more to do with function than ego. The front wall of the office was curved glass, which gave her a full view of the situation room below, and the back wall was a miniature status board, carrying the same information as the one in the situation room. The office had two desks. One faced forward towards the windows and was relatively bare. The other faced the miniature status board and had a keyboard, a mouse, three additional monitors and an assortment of other electronics. The wall opposite the door had a small armory locked behind thick sheets of bulletproof glass, with everything from swords to assault rifles to two single use rocket launchers.

As Perez crossed the office, she reached down and unholstered the cut-down AR on her hip and dropped it into a holster mounted on the forward-facing desk, then she unceremoniously dropped into the chair and grunted as she gestured to the two chairs on the other side of the desk. Lori unholstered her own AR and dropped it into a holster on the right arm of one of the chairs as she sat down. It was an easy, practiced motion, like she'd done it several times a day for years, which Danny figured she probably had. Danny dropped into the other chair and waited.

Perez opened a drawer in her desk and pulled out a liter water bottle and a bottle of migraine pills, the kind that was a mix of aspirin, acetaminophen, and caffeine. She dumped a couple of the pills in her hand, popped them in her mouth, and chased them with half the bottle of water. She then dropped the bottle of pills back in the drawer, leaned back in her chair, closed her eyes, and started rubbing her temples.

Danny glanced over at Lori, who had an amused smirk on her face. Lori turned to her and gave a small shake of her head.

"Stop it," Perez said.

Danny turned back to Perez, who still had her eyes closed.

"I didn't say anything," Lori said.

"You know I hate being handled," Perez said.

"Yeah, we both know that's not true."

"Are you sure you want to test me when I have a gun in easy reach?"

"You always have a gun in easy reach. Hell, I bet you shower with that .50 caliber Desert Eagle."

"Don't be stupid. I only bought that piece of shit to impress girls with it. I shower with the Model 500."

Lori snorted. Perez opened her eyes and smiled just a little.

"You okay?" Lori asked.

"Yeah," Perez said. "Just...not looking forward to the fallout from this one. I'll have the mayor screaming down my throat by lunchtime about unnecessary evacuations and wasting taxpayer dollars."

"If that thing had come ashore, and you hadn't evacuated, hundreds of thousands of people would be dead."

"I know that, and you know that, and it doesn't change a damn thing. Fucking politics." Perez turned to look at Danny, and Danny had to fight not to squirm under the scrutiny. It was odd. She had stared down hardened criminals without flinching, but there was something in Perez's eyes that was just a bit unsettling.

"So, you're Danielle Martin," Perez said.

"Yes, ma'am," Danny said. "I prefer Danny, though."

"Then Danny it is," Perez said. "So, Danny...you care to tell me how you know Focus?"

"Um...I don't."

"You don't?"

"No, ma'am."

"Never met her even casually?"

"No."

"You didn't run into her on vacation and have a fling, or get drunk with her in Vegas and get married or some shit?"

"Uh...no, ma'am. I've never met Focus. Or if I have, I'm not aware of it. Since her civilian identity is unknown, I can't rule out that I met her out of uniform."

"Do you know anyone who might have some sort of connection to her?" Perez asked.

"Maybe," Danny said. "My mom is a lawyer with the ACLU. I know she worked on a few cases involving Superheroes back when she was first starting out, but that was before I was born, so I'm a bit fuzzy on the details."

Perez frowned.

"Do you have any idea of why she might have requested your assignment to this unit?" Perez asked.

"No, ma'am."

"Danny, are you familiar with the power classification system we use?"

"Yes, ma'am. I memorized it last week."

"And are you aware of how Focus is classified?"

"Yes, ma'am. She's a Class Six Multi-Talent Alpha Juliet Uniform."

"And explain to me exactly what that means."

"Class Six means her power level is beyond what we can measure. Multi-Talent means she has more than one metahuman ability. 'Alpha' for anonymous, meaning we do not know her civilian identity. 'Juliet' for Jack of All Trades, meaning she has a broad enough power set that she can deal with almost any hostile metahuman without assistance. 'Uniform' for unknown, meaning we don't know the full scope of her powers."

"And do you know where Focus ranks in terms of power levels for known metahumans?"

"Yes, ma'am. A Class Six power level puts her firmly into the category of Tier Three assets, meaning she is one of the people we call when the world is in danger of meeting a sudden and unexpected end. As far as Tier Three assets go, she's estimated to be in the top ten in the world, but no one is sure because we can't measure her power level."

"And tell me, do you know what happens when an asset who is that powerful makes a request?"

"I'm guessing we fill it," Danny said.

"Good guess," Perez said. "Though a more accurate way to put it is, they get whatever the fuck they want, as long as it's legal and we can actually provide it. Do you know how many requests Focus has filed in the thirty-two years she's been working with the Marshals?"

"No, ma'am," Danny said.

"Three," Perez said. "The first was in 1998. David Moore, the first Officer in Charge of her support team reached mandatory retirement. She requested her handler Cecile La Saint be given the Officer in Charge role. Easy enough. It made sense. She knew La Saint. They worked well together. No one worries about a request that makes sense. The second request was three years ago. La Saint reached mandatory retirement. At which point, Focus requested me for this job. No one knows why. I wasn't her handler. I wasn't even a squad leader. I was the lead sniper. People worry about requests that don't make sense. You get that, right?"

"Yes, ma'am," Danny said.

"The third request was a few weeks ago. One of our Marshals on Alpha squad had a close call, and decided they were done. It happens sometimes. This isn't a safe job, and he has a wife and kids to think of. He turned in his badge and went to play rent-a-cop somewhere. Normally, when that happens, we promote someone from Beta to Alpha, and someone from Gamma to Beta, and so on. Except this time, Focus requested you by name to fill the empty slot on Alpha squad. Which doesn't make sense. And requests that don't make sense make people worry." Perez leaned forward. "To be clear, Deputy Marshal Martin, I am people. Do I look like I need to be worrying about anything aside from Supervillains and Kaiju attacks?"

"No, ma'am."

"That's right. So, I'm going to ask you one more time. Do you have any fucking clue why Focus requested you by name?"

"No, ma'am. None whatsoever."

Perez let out an exhausted sigh. "Fuck." She turned to Lori. "Take her and get her in the system, and then pull her gear. I want her on the range by lunch, and make sure she doesn't break her wrist. I can't have Alpha team stood down if I'm going to have fucking Kaiju attacks."

Lori nodded and stood up, drawing her AR out of the holster on the chair and fitting it back into the speed holster on her thigh in one fluid motion.

"Come on, Danny. Let's get out of Grumpy's way."

Danny stood up and they started towards the door, but before they could take more than a couple of steps, the door opened, and Focus stepped through it..

Chapter Two

HER TENDENCY TO TURN into a gibbering idiot around pretty women aside, Danny tended to think of herself as fairly level-headed. Her mom was the quixotic civil rights lawyer who spent her time trying to move mountains. Her sister Max was the social worker out to save everyone, and her other sister Sam was the one who was trying to turn abandoned warehouses into organic farms in the middle of San Francisco. Danny had always thought of herself as more like her dad. Practical and rational, and yeah, maybe easily led by a woman flashing a bit of cleavage, but no one was perfect.

She liked to think of herself as level-headed, but when Focus stepped into the room and their eyes met for a moment, just a moment, Danny believed in soulmates and love at first sight. She looked into those gorgeous, inhumanly vivid, cobalt blue eyes and it felt like coming home after a long day. It felt like peace and calm. It felt like all was finally right with the world. She was overwhelmed with longing and relief and joy and anticipation.

She looked into those eyes, and it was like seeing someone she'd longed to hold in her arms for decades. It was the moment before you stepped into a hug, when you couldn't feel their arms around you yet, but you knew they were coming. It was the moment before the kiss, when your lips parted and you just started to lean in and the moment was full of possibility. It was the moment just before you crawled into bed with the love of your life and fell asleep in her arms. It was the moment you slotted the last piece of a puzzle into place.

She couldn't breathe. She couldn't move. She couldn't look away. She wanted more than anything to reach out and pull the woman in front of her into her arms and kiss her like the world was about to end. It had been so long, and she'd been so alone, but here she was, close enough to touch.

"Focus?" a voice called out, and the eye contact was broken. As soon as it happened, Danny felt like a part of her had been ripped away, and it burned so badly that Danny's knees buckled. Strong arms caught her as she fell, and she looked up to see a vision. Those same blue eyes as before. Full lips that looked pillow soft. Golden blonde hair that seemed to shine like burnished metal. A jawline that could cut glass. Impossible beauty, a breath away.

"Gotcha," Focus said, her voice soft and gentle as she lifted Danny back to her feet. It took a moment for Danny to steady herself, but once she did, Focus smiled at her. "There you go."

"Thanks," Danny said.

"Are you okay, Martin?" someone asked, and Danny finally remembered they weren't alone. She turned to see Perez on her feet, a worried expression on her face.

"She's fine," Focus said. "That was my fault."

"What do you mean?" Perez asked.

"It would seem our Danny here is just a teensy bit empathic," Focus said, holding up her thumb and forefinger so close they almost touched.

Perez turned to Danny. "You're a meta?"

"No, ma'am," Danny said. "At least, I don't think so. I've never been tested."

"Easy, Deputy Marshal," Focus said. "I didn't say she was a meta. I said she was a bit empathic. It's a naturally occurring ability in baseline humans." Focus turned back towards her. "I apologize."

"What just happened?" Danny asked.

"I'm more than a touch empathic," Focus said. "It's not an ability I use often because it can be a bit overwhelming, but I was using it today to help track the Kaiju in the bay, and I hadn't completely closed off the empathic connection because I wanted to be able to sense it if it came back. I didn't think anything of it because we only have one other empath on the team, and I knew I wouldn't run into them. When our eyes met, you probably caught a bit of my emotions. It wouldn't be something unusual for you, but because of my empathic abilities, it would be a bit like if you've got a pair of headphones on, and someone walks in and cranks the dial all the way up."

"That's..." Danny stopped. She was about to say that wasn't what happened, but honestly, she didn't want to explain what did happen to Perez or Lori. "That's a good way to describe it," she said.

Focus flashed her another one of those smiles, then turned to Perez. "I have some information about the Kaiju. I spotted it right away, but I didn't want to broadcast it, even on a secure channel."

"Why not?" Perez asked.

"Because it's something that could be weaponized," Focus said.

"Ahmad, take Martin down to medical. I want her checked and a meta-analysis done. If she is actually a meta and we put her in the field without approval, there'll be hell to pay."

"Yes, ma'am," Lori said. She turned to Danny. "Come on. Let's go see the vampires."

Danny didn't want to go. She wanted to stay and talk to Focus about what had just happened, but that didn't seem to be an option, so she let Lori lead her out of the office with one more mystery on her plate.

**

No one was quite sure where the meta gene came from. Scientists knew it was unique to humans, and dated back at least a hundred and twenty thousand years, but beyond that, the origin of the gene was a mystery. They did know that until 1908, the activation of the gene was a fairly rare phenomenon. It was widely assumed that legends of heroes like Hercules, Achilles, and Beowulf were based on historical meta humans. The modern surge in meta gene activations had started after an alien spaceship had exploded over the Podkamennaya Tunguska River in Yeniseysk Governorate, Russia. The 'Tunguska Event' was the start of the age of Superheroes.

In the hundred and thirteen years since, a number of tests for the meta gene had been developed, but Danny's mom was paranoid about anything to do with the government and had carefully avoided having her or her sisters tested. Which was why Danny was now sitting on an exam table in a plain looking exam room, downing her third bottle of orange juice and munching on a protein bar while Lori sat in a chair playing a game on her phone.

"I can see why you call them vampires," she said between bites.

"That was nothing," Lori said without looking up. "They took a whole pint from me once."

"What for?"

"We get exposed to all sorts of weird shit. I think that time they were afraid I was going to turn into an alligator. Or maybe it was a crocodile. Honestly, I don't know the difference."

"Has that actually happened?" Danny asked.

"No," Lori said. "But my ex-boyfriend did get turned into a giant turtle."

"Are you serious?"

"About having an ex-boyfriend, or about him getting turned into a turtle?"

"Both?"

"Yes. He's one of the photo techs on the forensics team. He touched something he shouldn't have. You learn pretty quick not to touch things around here."

"Noted," Danny said.

"I bat for both teams, if you're wondering," Lori said.

"Not my business," Danny said.

"It will be."

"What?"

"We're partners, so we'll be all up in each other's business."

"Oh."

"That a problem?"

"No. I just hadn't realized."

"No reason you should," Lori said. She locked her phone and put it away. "Can I ask you a question?"

"Sure," Danny said.

"Did you really get a look inside the ice queen's head?"

"The ice queen?"

"Yeah. Focus."

"Why do you call her that?"

"Because she is," Lori said. "Seriously, I have been on this detail for six years. I've seen people come. I've seen people go. I've seen shit that would make most people pee their pants. I've seen things that reduced some of the hardest bastards I've ever met to tears. None of it affects her. Out in public, she's nice enough. She shakes hands, she hugs kids, she signs autographs, she's gone to the Pontian Pride festival every year for the last twenty-eight years. Even in here she's polite enough. She knows everyone's names. She keeps up with their kids and spouses and stuff, but she's just cold. There's no warmth. She doesn't seek anybody out. Always eats alone. No one knows anything about her. Her first name, where she's from, how she got her powers, why she became a hero. She doesn't tell anyone anything."

"Seriously?" Danny asked. "She seemed friendly enough to me."

"Yeah, which I don't get. You got more of a response out of her in thirty seconds than anyone else on the base has gotten out of her in the entire time I've been here. So, what's the deal?"

"I don't know."

"What did you see inside her head?" Lori asked.

Danny thought about it for a minute, about the rush of feelings that overwhelmed her, and the moment of...pain wasn't the right word. When she thought back on it, it felt more like grief. So, the moment of grief she felt when the connection broke. Even now, when she poked at the memory, it felt like she'd lost something irreplaceable. The thought of trying to put that feeling into words was unbearable.

"I don't think I should talk about it," Danny said.

"What?"

"What I saw...it felt private. I don't think she meant for me to see it, and I don't think she'd want me to talk about it."

"Please tell me you're kidding," Lori said. "She's one of the most powerful Superheroes on Earth, she's a freaking gay icon, she's gorgeous, and no one knows a damn thing about her. Then you come along, and you get a look in her head, and you're not gonna share?"

"Afraid not," Danny said.

Lori let out a deep sigh. "Fine," she said. "So, what about you? You gay or bi?"

"How do you know I'm not straight?" Danny asked.

"You literally swooned when you met Focus," Lori said. "And that was before the mind whammy."

"I did not swoon."

"You swooned," Lori said.

"I did?"

"Yeah," Lori said. "We can pull the security footage from Perez's office if you doubt me."

"No," Danny said. "I think we can skip the humiliation."

"So, answer the question."

"Gay," Danny said.

"Damn it!" Lori snapped.

"What?"

"I was hoping you were bi."

"Why?"

"Because we're still one person short of a softball team. The lesbians have three teams, and even the straights have a team, but us poor bi ladies can't scrape together enough players."

"Sorry."

"You should be."

***

After receiving the test results and finding out that no, she was not, in fact, a metahuman, and a quick pee break to take care of the seven bottles of orange juice she drank while waiting, Danny followed Lori to the quartermaster's office. There she was measured, issued fifteen uniforms, three thigh holsters for one of the cut down ARs everyone seemed to carry, three new tac vests, three US Marshal Windbreakers, and a handful of other bits and pieces. There was at least three of everything, including the duffle bags to put it in. She watched as all of it was inscribed with her name and badge number and then carefully packed in the bags. She slung one over each shoulder. Lori slung the third one and led her towards the armory.

"Why three of everything?" she asked as they walked down the hall.

"We prefer you come and go in civvies. Leave your work kit here. Sometimes though, you get called about directly to a hot site when you're not at work, so we give you enough kit to keep duplicates of everything at home and in your vehicle. Everything is stamped with your name and badge number because we offer full laundry service. There are bins in the locker room. You just drop your dirty uniforms in them, and they'll be laundered and returned by the next morning. There are separate bins for normal dirt and grime, and blood and gore. Do not drop a bloody uniform in the regular bin. If your uniform is damaged, destroyed, or exposed to unknown contaminants, we will issue replacements."

"Does that happen a lot?"

"Enough that we cover it instead of making you buy your own gear," Lori said as she led them through the door to the armory. "Our budget comes out of Metahuman Affairs instead of Justice. There are perks."

"Good to know," Danny said.

"Hey, Lori," a short, red-headed man behind the counter called out.

"Hey, Matt. I need a full issue for our newbie here."

Matt looked at Danny. "You worked MERT support before?" he asked.

"Nope. I was fugitive retrieval."

"Oh, you're in for a treat," he said as he turned to the computer sitting on one end of the counter. "Badge number?"

Danny gave him her badge number and he keyed it in, then he asked her a couple of other questions before disappearing through a door behind the counter.

"Have you ever fired an AR pistol before?" Lori asked.

"A few times," Danny said. "Always seemed more like a range toy than anything useful."

"Yeah," Lori said. "I used to feel that way too."

Before Danny could say anything else, Matt came out of the back pushing a cart. There were six molded plastic gun cases on it. Three were large enough to hold full-sized rifles, and three were smaller, but big enough to hold the cut-down ARs. Matt put one of the smaller cases on the counter.

"Standard issue battle rifle is a select fire AR-10 pattern. I'm going to assume you know how to use one of those, but this is something you probably haven't seen before." He popped the case open. "This is a bufferless AR-15 pistol chambered in 300 Blackout. The recoil system has been moved from the buffer tube to the bolt carrier group to allow a shorter weapon, and we slap on a five-inch barrel. The accuracy is shit at anything over a hundred yards and it kicks like a motherfucking elephant on PCP, but if you shoot someone with this, they will, by God, know they have been touched."

"Wait, you're issuing 300 Blackout side arms?" Danny asked.

"No," Matt said with a wink. "Of course not. That would make all the little Congress Critters shit themselves. We're issuing 300 Blackout personal defense weapons. As a US Marshal, you are, of course, still responsible for purchasing and maintaining your own duty weapon. We use the same Glock 22s as the rest of the Marshal service, though if you want to upgrade to one of the new G5s, we do have a discount program worked out with a gun store a couple of blocks over, and they hold back some of their stock just for us."

"I'll keep that in mind," Danny said.

"Good. Now comes the fun part. Let's get your paperwork filled out."

***

By the time Lori led her into the cafeteria for lunch, Danny was pretty sure she'd signed away her soul, her first born child, and maybe the book rights to her life. She also had enough weapons in her locker and the trunk of her car to invade a small country. She was a little surprised that they had her keep her rifle in her locker instead of the armory, but Lori had explained that it was a speed thing. It was faster for a squad to file through the locker room and grab their already-issued weapons than to go to the armory and sign out gear. Danny saw the logic behind it, but it made her a little nervous that they needed to move that fast.

There was a lot that was different about this assignment. For one, the office seemed to function more like a military base than a Marshal's office. Then there were the people walking around in brightly colored costumes, or in one case, floating around. Hell, there was a guy wearing what Danny was pretty sure was power armor sitting in one corner of the cafeteria.

"You get used to it," Lori said as they got in line.

"What?"

"The weird. You get used to it. It takes time, and every once in a while, you will have a moment where you go 'how is this my life,' like when your boyfriend picks up an ancient Egyptian medallion and spends a week as a sea turtle, but most days it's just part of the job."

"I'm not sure I want to get used to people turning into turtles," Danny said.

Lori shrugged. "You'll last or you won't," she said. "Either way, just try not to get dead."

"That, we can agree on."

"First lesson in not getting dead. Don't get the fish. The French fries are fine. The Salisbury steak and the meatloaf are delicious if you don't mind mystery meat. If you do mind mystery meat, the chicken and the wings are both good."

"What about the pizza?"

"God, the pizza is to die for. They use whole milk cheese."

"Nice."

When they got to the front of the line, Danny got two slices of pizza, an order of onion rings, honey glazed carrots, and at Lori's insistence, something called collard greens. She was a little surprised when there was no register.

"Food's free?"

"Yeah," Lori said. "The cafeteria is open 24/7. You can eat as much as you want."

They grabbed a table near the door, and Danny reached for the hot sauce, splashing a bit on her pizza.

"You're going to want a splash of that on your greens, too," Lori said. Danny took her advice, still a bit dubious about the collards.

"This is the weirdest assignment I've ever had."

"I know," Lori said. "It runs more like an army base than anything else. Truth is, they probably should have given this gig to the army, but Posse Comitatus and all that. The FBI has been trying to take over since Hoover, but absolutely no one thought giving that fascist asshat access to metahuman assets was a good idea, and by the time he did everyone a favor and died, both the Department of Metahuman Affairs and the Marshal service had dug in their teeth and neither one has shown any sign of letting go. Now, try your greens, because if you side-eye them one more time, I'm going to shoot you."

Danny laughed and got a fork full of collards. She honestly expected them to taste like grass, based on the way they looked, but they were delicious. Rich and earthy and flavorful, with a hint of smoke from the pieces of ham cut up in them, and a bit of a kick from the hot sauce.

"Oh, wow," Danny said.

"They're good, huh?" someone asked.

Danny turned towards the sound of the voice and found Focus standing beside her.

"Mind if I sit?" Focus asked.

"Um...uh...no! No, of course not," Danny said. "Go ahead."

Focus took the seat next to Danny and set a large bowl of noodles on the table with a pair of chopsticks sticking out of it. She smiled at Danny, and Danny felt her heart skip a beat.

"I hope the doctors weren't too rough on you."

"No," Danny said. "They only took eight vials of blood."

"Oh. Only eight vials. I suppose that's not too bad. I hear if you get slimed in the field, they take a whole pint."

Danny felt a smile tugging at the corner of her lips. "I had heard that," she said. "I guess they don't want anyone else turning into a turtle."

"You heard about that?" Focus asked.

"Yeah."

Focus shook her head. "Poor Osborn. He was fine once we figured out how to break the curse, but I can't imagine living in a kiddy pool for a week."

Danny laughed, and Focus smiled a little wider.

"I remember the first time I ever had collards," Focus said. "I'd been in the field all day, and I came home and my girlfriend...well, she wasn't my girlfriend yet, just my roommate, but she had made me dinner. There was cornbread and collard greens and pan-fried chicken, and chocolate cake and macaroni and cheese. It was such a sweet gesture, and I just about broke down when I saw it."

"Why?" Danny asked.

"We'd been fighting. Well, no, that's not true. The truth is, I had been a complete bitch to her."

"You?"

"I know," Focus said. "I'm supposed to be a hero, right. But I'll let you in on a secret. I'm a bit of a hermit."

"She must have forgiven you if she ended up being your girlfriend," Danny said.

"She did," Focus said. She reached out and picked up her chopsticks and started stirring her noodles. "When she first showed up, I didn't really want a roommate, but I kind of had to take her in since it was my fault she didn't have anywhere to stay. Suddenly I have this gorgeous, incredible woman living with me, and I was trying to do the right thing and keep my hands to myself, but I ended up hurting her, and I was terrified that I was going to come home and find her gone. That I'd messed up so bad she'd never speak to me again. Instead, I came home and found her putting dinner on the table."

"So, everything worked out?"

"It did. That was actually the night we finally got together."

"Was that Scatter?" Danny asked.

"It was," Focus said wistfully. "God, I miss her."

"What happened to her?" Danny asked. She'd always wondered, but the Marshals had never issued any sort of official statement. They'd just removed Scatter from the list of active Metahumans the day after Christmas in 1992 and refused to comment on her whereabouts.

Focus looked up from her noodles. "She had to go back home, and I had too many responsibilities to go with her. You should eat before your food gets cold."

Danny turned back to her plate, and picked up a piece of pizza, taking a bite as she watched Focus start eating.

"What are you eating?" Danny asked when Focus had finished chewing her first bite.

"Peanut butter and spaghetti," Focus said.

"I'm sorry. I don't think I heard that right," Danny said. Focus laughed, and Danny was sure her heart was about to pound its way out of her chest.

"Sorry," Focus said, but the amusement in her voice didn't make her sound the least bit sorry. "They're sesame peanut noodles. They're one of my favorites. My girlfriend came out of the shower one morning and saw me dump a huge spoon full of peanut butter into a bowl, stir it for a minute, and then add a pot of noodles to it, so after that, she always teased me about eating peanut butter and spaghetti. I got the lady who runs the cafeteria to add it to the menu for me back in '92. You should give them a try sometime."

"Maybe next year," Danny said. "I'm not really adventurous when it comes to food."

Focus laughed and shook her head before going back to her noodles, and Danny went back to her pizza. She actually tasted it this time and Lori was right, it was fantastic.

That thought made her freeze as she realized Lori was still at the table with them. She turned slowly towards her partner, who was looking at her and Focus like they'd both grown a second head.

Lori mouthed, "What the fuck?"

Danny shrugged and went back to her lunch.

Molly J. Bragg

Chapter Three

"WHERE THE FUCK IS your girlfriend?" Lori yelled as they both dove behind one of the stone barriers Kipengele had raised in the middle of the street. They just barely made it before the air above them was filled with fire.

"She's not my girlfriend," Danny said as she checked to make sure neither of them was on fire. Once she was sure they weren't, she risked a look over the top of the barrier.

She'd been in Pontian six weeks, had been cleared for field duty for four weeks, but this was the first time she'd seen Kipengele in action, and she had to admit, the woman was impressive as hell. Not as impressive as Focus, but Kipengele was holding her own against three of the dragonkin they were fighting, while the rest of the Panthers, as well as the Ironclads and the Myrmidons, were barely holding their own, grouped up three against one. Kipengele had three massive blocks of stone floating in the air, using them as shields, and every time one of the dragonkin tried to breathe fire at her, the stream of flame bent and shot straight up into the air. She was using the water drawn from a nearby fire hydrant to put out anything any of the dragonkin set on fire, and had the entire battlefield surrounded by a dome of lightning to keep them contained so the battle couldn't spread.

As impressive as it was, Kipengele was showing signs of fatigue. Danny could hardly blame her. They'd been at this for two hours, slowly corralling Genetwist's pack of monsters from all over South Shore. The terrorist for hire had released the dragonkin at a political rally for a candidate for the upcoming Governor's race, and Danny shuddered to think what would have happened if the Panthers hadn't been there providing extra security.

"Seriously, though, where is Focus?" Lori asked.

"Last I heard she was trying to find Genetwist's hideout," Danny said. They'd been out of comm contact since the lightning shield went up, and honestly, there wasn't a lot Alpha squad could do. The dragonkin were bulletproof, fireproof, electricity proof, immune to pepper spray, and could take punches from Ironsides and Achilles, and even energy blasts from Yamato.

They needed Focus, but they couldn't call for her.

"Incoming!" Danny yelled as one of the dragonkin picked up a car and lobbed it at her and Lori's position. She ducked back down behind the barricade, praying the stone held as she waited for the impact.

It never came.

"You ladies need some help?"

Danny looked up to see Focus floating above them, a huge grin on her face. She glanced over the barricade to see the car suspended in mid-air. She turned back to Focus.

"We've got it under control, but if you want to help with the cleanup, by all means."

Focus winked at her, and let the car drop as she dove into the fray, snatching up dragonkin here and there and throwing them inside a glowing blue bubble in the center of the battlefield, one they couldn't escape from. Pretty soon, all fifteen of the dragonkin were locked in the translucent cage, and Focus set down next to Kipengele. Danny and Lori scrambled out of cover and moved closer so they could hear the conversation.

"Sorry it took so long to get here," Focus said.

"We contained the matter," Kipengele said. "I'm just glad you were here to end it. Did you find the man responsible?"

"Genetwist is in custody," Focus said. "Whether he'll give up his employers is another matter."

"Msomaji could extract the information," Kipengele said.

"I'll ask Carmen, but you know what she'll say."

"Telepathic scans aren't admissible in court," Kipengele said, disgust evident in her tone. "We could solve the matter ourselves."

"But then you'd be a criminal, and who would protect your people?" Focus asked. "I don't want to see that happen."

"I know, sister, but you know why this happened. It feels like the course of history has reversed itself. The Klan and the Neo-Nazis marching in the streets with the police protecting them. Politicians winning elections on bigotry and hatred. Paid assassins gunning for our leaders. It all feels familiar enough that I'd say you should start with the FBI when you hunt for Genetwist's employer. It would hardly be the first time they got their hands dirty."

Danny winced a little at that.

"We will find who did this," Focus said. "I promise you."

Kipengele seemed to relax a bit at that. "Thank you, sister."

"And Kipengele…"

"Yes?"

"Keep Msomaji handy. Even if human courts won't accept telepathic evidence, the Dragon Council isn't quite so narrow minded, and they are not going to be happy about a human cloning dragonkin."

Kipengele gave Focus a smile that was downright predatory. "Now, that is a good thought," she said.

"I thought you'd like that," Focus said.

Kipengele turned away from Focus, and Danny thought she was about to call out to the Panthers, but before she did, Danny stepped up.

"Kipengele," she said.

Kipengele turned towards her, none of the friendliness that had been on her face when she spoke to Focus present as she looked at Danny.

"Yes?"

"Thank you," Danny said.

"What are you thanking me for?" Kipengele asked.

"You saved our lives today," Danny said. "The barriers you raised. Lori and I would be dead if you hadn't done that, so thank you. I know that doesn't mean a lot coming from someone like me, but I promise you, I won't forget it."

Kipengele stared at her for a moment, then nodded and walked away without another word.

"Same old Kipengele," Lori said. From anyone else, it might have sounded angry, but Danny could hear something close to affection in Lori's voice.

"Are you okay?" Focus asked.

Danny turned to her and nodded. "Oh, yeah. The fire breathing was a bit of an adventure, but we did okay."

Focus smiled, but Danny could see the worry in her eyes. "I'm sorry I couldn't get here faster. It took ages for the IT team to trace the control signal back to its source."

"You did fine," Danny said. "Oh, hey. That reminds me." Danny opened one of the pockets on her tac vest and pulled out a box of Reese's Pieces. She held it out to Focus, whose eyes lit up. She took the box from Danny and then pulled Danny into a crushingly tight hug.

"Thank you!" Focus said before she let go. She looked down at the box. "How did you know?"

"I saw you eating peanut butter M&Ms out of the vending machine at work, and they're okay, but everybody knows Reese's Pieces are better."

Focus smiled ear to ear as she tucked the box of candy into one of the pouches on the belt of her costume. "Thank you," she said again.

"Will the Dragon Council really be interested in what happened here?" Danny asked.

"Oh, yeah," Focus said. "Tarantasio might even wake up from his nap when he hears about this."

"Who?" Danny asked.

"Tarantasio," Focus said. "He's…well, not a fan of humans, to put it mildly."

"Are any of the dragons?" Danny asked, curiosity getting the better of her. "Besides Ice Dragon, I mean."

Focus laughed. "You'd be surprised how many dragons like humans."

"Well," Lori said, "We are crunchy, and we do taste good with ketchup."

Focus grinned as she looked at Lori. "I wouldn't worry too much about that. The only dragon in Pontian is Jewish, and humans aren't kosher."

"What?" Lori asked.

Focus didn't answer her. She turned back to Danny. "I've got to go. I need to get our friends here to containment."

"Go ahead," Danny said. "And thanks for the save earlier."

Focus smiled again. "Always," she said.

Danny watched as Focus floated up off the ground, the blue bubble full of dragonkin following her. She gave one final wave, then shot off towards the horizon, dragonkin in tow.

"Not your girlfriend my ass," Lori said.

Danny started to say something but decided against it, because honestly, some days she wasn't so sure herself.

***

"Here is your ridiculously expensive beer," Lori said as she set the bottle of Kasteel Rouge down in front of Danny.

"I can't help it if some of us have taste," Danny said. She picked the beer up and took a pull, savoring the cherry flavor.

"Some of us drink real beer," Lori said.

"Budweiser is not beer," Danny said.

"Says the girl drinking that fruity Belgian shit."

"Do I need to order a Guinness just to shut you up?"

"Oh, please. Like that would actually shut me up."

"A girl can dream."

Lori smiled and leaned forward. "Speaking of dreams…"

"Oh, here we go."

"Have you sealed the deal yet?" Lori asked.

Danny groaned and leaned back against the back of the booth's seat. "I am not sleeping with Focus."

"Okay," Lori said.

Danny narrowed her eyes, because it wasn't like Lori to give up that easily. "That's it? Just…okay?"

Lori shrugged. "You said you weren't, and I believe you."

"You do?"

"Yeah, but can I ask a question?"

"Sure."

"Why the fuck not?" Lori asked.

"Lori…"

"Seriously, Danny. I've seen puppies that were subtler about their affection than Focus is. Half the time I spend lunch wondering if she's going to mount you right there at the table."

"Stop," Danny said. "I mean, she's friendly—"

"Friendly? Jesus Christ, Danny. That woman has the biggest fucking lady boner I have ever seen, and it's pointed straight at your pink parts."

"Don't talk about her like that!" Danny growled.

Lori shook her head. "God, you're just as bad."

"I'm just trying to be her friend."

"You brought her candy in the middle of a mission."

"You're not going to let this go, are you?"

"You're my partner," Lori said. "I go out there and put my life in your hands every day. I need to know what's going on with you."

"Why?" Danny asked. "Why is it so important that you know this?"

"Because I don't want to get eaten by a giant snail because you're too busy thinking with your ovaries."

"That's not going to happen."

"Really?"

"Really."

"Tell me something," Lori asked. "Has it occurred to you to wonder why the bar directly across from the station is the only bar in town that carries your favorite beer?"

"Not really," Danny said.

"Well, it did occur to me, so I asked. The manager said Focus came in and asked to have it added to the menu."

"Maybe she likes it, too."

"You know, I asked. She's never set foot in here before or since. Told the manager it was for a friend."

Danny frowned. She'd never mentioned liking Kasteel Rouge to Focus. At least, not that she could remember.

"It's weird, right?" Lori asked.

Danny shrugged. "A little."

"So, you want to tell me what's going on, or do we have to keep going round and round?"

Danny sighed. "I honestly don't know," she said.

"Do you think it has something to do with that mind meld the first day?" Lori asked.

"No," Danny said.

"You sound awfully sure of that."

"She asked for me by name before the 'mind meld'."

"Good point," Lori said. "So, what are you going to do?"

"Nothing," Danny said.

"Nothing?"

"Yeah, nothing."

"Danny..."

"Lori..." Danny sighed. "Look, it's not hurting anything, okay? She's lonely. She wants a friend, and for whatever reason, she's picked me. I don't see what the big deal is."

"Friend? Danny, that girl does not want you as a friend. She's probably sitting at home shopping for engagement rings as we speak."

"No, she's not."

"Look, Danny, I get it, okay. Beautiful girl suddenly starts paying a lot of attention to you. She sits with you at lunch, she brings you presents—"

"She didn't get me any presents!"

"Oh, yeah? Then what about the fruit she brings you every day at lunch? Or the way she just shows up with your favorite coffee? Or that she brought you your favorite truffles from Godiva on your birthday? Something strange is going on with her, and you, my friend, are tits deep in it. Don't you want to know what the hell it is?"

Danny shook her head. "Just leave it alone, okay?" she said before taking another sip of her beer. The look on Lori's face told her that the conversation wasn't over, and if she were honest with herself, she knew

Lori was right. Something very strange was going on. The thing was, she didn't want to know what it was, because Lori was right. She liked the attention. She liked it a lot. And she had a feeling that when she found out what was going on, everything was going to change, and she wasn't sure it would be for the better.

***

Danny was turning over the conversation she'd had with Lori at the bar the night before in her head. More than anything, she wished she could go back and duct tape Lori's mouth shut so they never had the conversation, because now that they had, what Danny thought of as her cop brain was turning the 'problem' over and over in her head as she made her way from the locker room to the briefing room for morning roll call. She'd known it was weird for Focus to have just sort of latched on to her the moment she joined the team. It was even weirder that Focus had asked for her by name.

The thing was, Danny liked the way Focus was treating her. It made her feel special, which wasn't something she had a lot of experience with. She'd never had much luck with girls. She'd dated a girl named Helen in high school, who'd summarily dumped her the night before graduation because she 'wasn't really looking to do the long-distance thing.' Then, in college, she'd dated Claire. That had ended when she'd come home from class early and found Claire fucking a member of the girls' basketball team. Then there'd been FBI Special Agent Amber Williams, who'd made Claire and Helen look like wonderful girlfriends by comparison. So, yeah. Danny had been enjoying having a pretty lady not only pay attention to her, but actually treat her really, really well.

But now, all she could do is think about all the things that were out of place. The fact that Focus had asked for her by name. The emotions that she'd felt when her and Focus' minds had touched. The way it had felt like Focus had been waiting for her, specifically. The little gifts. Every day at lunch some exotic fruit Focus was sure Danny would like. Papaya, soursop, pawpaw, roasted breadfruit dipped in fresh coconut milk, passion fruit, dragon fruit. Then there was the coffee and the chocolate, and the fact that she seemed to love to just sit and talk. The way she smiled at Danny like Danny had hung the moon.

None of it made sense.

"Danny, wait up!"

Danny turned around to see Focus rushing down the hall towards her, carrying a small plastic food container and smiling that smile that always made Danny's heart flutter.

"Morning," Danny said.

Focus' smile got a little wider as she held out the container. "I brought you a little something."

Danny took the container and peeked inside. There was a huge slice of some kind of cake. It looked a bit like cheesecake, but it was topped with chocolate and the cheese layer was a light brown color.

"It's peanut butter cheesecake with chocolate ganache icing," Focus said.

Danny closed the container and looked up at Focus.

"I wanted to thank you for yesterday," Focus said.

"It was just some candy," Danny said.

"Yeah, but I burn through a lot of calories when I use my powers, so it helps," she said.

"Well, I'm happy to be of service." She glanced down at the container. "But what is it with you and peanut butter? Peanut butter noodles, peanut butter candy, peanut butter cake. And don't think I haven't seen you sneaking peanut butter ice cream when no one was looking."

"Why, Deputy Marshal Martin, if I didn't know better, I'd think you liked looking at me," Focus said.

Danny nearly swallowed her tongue. Not only was it the single most flirty thing Focus had ever said to her, but the tone, the look on her face...Focus was definitely flirting with her. Focus, her favorite Superhero, the woman she'd had a crush on since she was five years old, the gay icon, one of the most powerful women in the world, was flirting with her.

God, she needed to say something. What should she say? What should she do? Oh, God, she was way too gay for this. Or too stupid for this. God, why did she have to be such a disaster around women? Why couldn't she be cool? Why couldn't she have confidence and swagger? She really needed to say something before Focus decided she didn't like the flirting.

Except, by some miracle, Focus seemed to understand. She reached out and rested a hand on one of Danny's and her smile softened.

"Breathe, Danny," she said.

Danny took a deep breath and let it out slowly as Focus rubbed her thumb over the back of Danny's hand.

"It's comfort food," Focus said.

"What?"

"Peanut butter. It's comfort food."

"Oh. Lots of peanut butter sandwiches as a kid?"

"Sort of. Keep a secret?"

"Sure."

"On my home planet, we had a tuber called Izambane. It was a little mealy on its own, but if you mixed it with Umnquno oil, you got something that had a taste and texture pretty much exactly like peanut butter. It's the first food I found on this planet that tasted anything like the food from home, and every time I eat it, it makes me feel connected to the place I came from."

"Why did you leave?" Danny asked.

Focus's smile got a little wider. "That's a story for another time," she said. "We've got a briefing to get to."

Focus took her hand away, and for just a moment, Danny felt like a piece of her was missing, but the feeling faded as she took another breath, and she followed Focus to the briefing room.

**

"What are you reading?" Lori asked.

Danny looked up from her eBook reader and saw Lori with her cell phone in hand, her thumbs moving quickly as she played whatever game it was that usually occupied her attention. She thought about it for a couple of seconds, whether she actually wanted to let Lori know her reading habits, and decided that no, she definitely did not want to put up with the incessant teasing that would come if she admitted that her library consisted almost entirely of lesbian romance novels.

"Porn," Danny said. A handful of the other members of Alpha squad chuckled or snorted. Lori looked up at her for a second, then shook her head and went back to her game. Danny just smiled and went back to her book.

It had been a week since what Danny had come to think of as the cheesecake incident, and her cop brain was still nagging her about Focus, still asking questions, but she was deliberately ignoring it and going out of her way to find other things to occupy her mind. Every time her cop brain pointed out something odd or weird, Danny just tried that much harder to convince herself it didn't matter.

She knew she was being stupid. Lori was right. She should be trying to figure out what was going on, but she honestly didn't want to. She liked Focus. She liked her a lot. She liked when Focus paid attention to her. The flirting had continued, but only when they were alone, which meant not often. She and Lori spent most of their time at work together, but Focus seemed to have a talent for catching Danny in those rare moments when she was alone, and those moments were always the highlight of Danny's day.

Which was why she was so irritated that Alpha squad was in the hot seat today. The hot seat wasn't a particularly bad job. They basically sat in a room with their gear next to them their whole shift and did fuck all while they waited for a call. There was a bathroom right off the ready room, and they could order delivery from the cafeteria. Hell, even the furniture was comfortable.

The only complaint was, she had to spend the whole day in a room with eleven other people, so there was zero chance Focus would stop by. Zero chance of any flirting, or of seeing that smile she was quickly becoming addicted to. Zero chance of feeling her heart flutter when Focus touched her. Zero chance she would finally be brave enough to ask Focus out.

Zero chance she would hear some secret from Focus' past that she was duty bound to report to high ups but would carry to her grave. Focus was an alien. Her home world was called Umhlaba. She'd been on Earth for 219 years.

She probably knew more about Focus than anyone else in the Marshals, but she was missing the important things. She didn't know her name. She didn't know why she'd left her home world. Didn't know why she'd come to Earth. Didn't know why she was a Superhero. It was like Focus was teasing her with peeks behind the curtain, and Danny didn't know why. All she knew is that she wanted to tear the curtain aside and see everything.

The room turned red, and Danny was halfway to her feet before she even realized the alarm was going off. She drew her AR pistol from the holster attached to the chair and dropped it into the speed holster on her leg in a practiced motion, pulled on her tac vest, clipped it to her web belt, then zipped it up. She grabbed her helmet and her rifle as she filed out the door with the rest of the team and headed for the three waiting SUVs.

She slid into the front passenger's seat and took Lori's rifle as Lori got behind the wheel.

"We have a tier two threat level incident at the Federal Reserve Bank. Focus is on route. You will follow and provide assistance," Perez said over comms.

"Do we have an ID on the hostile?" Danny asked.

"Target is known Supervillain, codename Gammawave."

"Shit," Lori said, and Danny couldn't help but agree.

* * *

By the time they reached the bank, Focus and Gammawave were already fighting, and from what Danny could see as she and Lori hunkered down behind their SUV, it was brutal. Gammawave was a radiokenetic, which meant he could control the electromagnetic spectrum. The thing was, unlike most radiokenetics, he could control the entire spectrum. Everything from ultra-low frequency radio waves all the way up into hard gamma. And he loved playing with hard gamma.

Focus was conjuring force-fields to block the blasts of radiation he was throwing at her and the cops, while hitting him with blasts of pure kinetic energy that he couldn't redirect. The cops were mostly hiding, trying to avoid getting cooked by the radiation, while Gammawave's gang were loading money into an armored car.

"We need to end this before someone gets killed," Danny said.

"Agreed," Lori said.

"I have an idea," Danny said.

"What is it?"

"Rocket launcher."

"I like this idea," Lori said. "Gammawave?"

"The armored car," Danny said. "If they can't get away with the loot, maybe they'll just make a run for it."

"I like this idea less, but Perez will love it. You grab the launcher. I'll get clearance."

Danny ran to the back of the SUV and grabbed one of the M136 rocket launchers, then rushed back to where Lori was.

"Yes, ma'am," Lori said. She turned to Danny. "We're a go."

Danny pulled the safety pin and shouldered the weapon, quickly working through the firing procedure and taking aim at the engine block of the armored car Gammawave's gang was loading.

"Ready," Danny said.

"Fire in the hole!" Lori yelled, and Danny pulled the trigger. The rocket sailed across the distance and slammed into the armored car, blowing a hole through the entire engine.

"*Yes!*" Lori shouted.

Gammawave screamed and turned away from Focus, zeroing in on Danny and Lori, and Danny could see what was about to happen, clear as day. She dropped the launcher and shoved Lori away from her, just as Gammawave cut loose. The beam of gamma waves hit the Suburban first, which probably saved Danny's life, at least in the short term, but the energy that bled through was still enough to knock her back several feet, and when she hit the ground, it felt like she had the worst sunburn of her life.

"*Danny!*" someone screamed. Maybe several someone's. She wasn't sure. There was too much pain. Everywhere her clothes touched her skin, it felt like fire. Her lungs burned and her eyes stung and God, she wanted it to stop.

She coughed, and her mouth filled with blood. She tried to roll over, to clear her mouth, but there was too much pain and she started to choke on the blood.

"Easy," someone said, and she felt herself pushed on her side. She coughed again, and the blood spilled out of her mouth.

"Get out of the way," someone said. A hand touched her, and she wanted to pull away from the pain it caused, but then she felt a cool sensation, like ice spreading out from the touch. It was comforting, but it was heavy, dragging her down into darkness and sleep.

* * *

The first thing she was aware of was the sound of beeping. Regular, steady beeping. The second was the feel of someone holding her hand. It took time and effort for her to pry her eyes open, but she found herself in a dimly lit room, and she slowly looked around, only to find Lori sitting next to her and holding her hand. It took a second to realize it in the dim light, but Lori's eyes were closed.

"Hey," she said, her voice coming out dry and rough. It was enough to wake Lori up, though. She jumped slightly and looked down at her.

"You're awake!" Lori said.

"Water," Danny croaked.

Lori let go of her hand and grabbed a large travel mug filled with ice water. She uncapped the straw and held it so Danny could get it in her mouth. Danny took a long drink, sighing in relief as the water washed away the dryness in her mouth. She kept drinking, and it felt like she must have drained half the mug, but when she finally let go and Lori set it back on the table, she could barely see any change in the water level.

"Where am I?"

"You're at the station," Lori said. "We're better equipped than any of the local hospitals."

"What happened?" Danny asked.

"What do you remember?"

"Fight with Gammawave," Danny said. "I got hit."

"Hit my ass," Lori said. "You got your stupid ass killed is what you did."

"I'm feeling pretty spry for a dead girl."

"You took three times the lethal dose of gamma, you idiot."

"But I'm still here."

"Yeah. Thanks to your girlfriend," Lori said.

"What?"

"Focus," Lori said. "She did something. Fixed you up. I don't know. All I know is that by the time we got you back to the base, you were mostly fine. Your electrolytes are off, you're dehydrated as hell, and they've put enough iodine in you to run a salt factory for a year, but no one can figure out how you're not dead."

"Where is she?" Danny asked.

"She's in a kill debrief," Lori said.

"What?" Danny asked. That didn't make any sense. Focus had one of the lowest kill counts of any active heroes. She was known for it. In thirty-two years, she'd only killed six hostiles, and three of those were modified animals.

"When Gammawave hit you, she put him down."

"How?"

"Don't worry about it," Lori said. "Just rest, and we'll see about getting you home."

"Lori, how did she do it?"

"Danny..."

"Tell me."

"I didn't see it," Lori said.

"But you know."

Lori turned away. "Yeah," she said. "I know."

"What did she do?"

"She picked the armored car up and dropped it on him," Lori said.

"Shit."

"Yeah. The forensics team was still picking him out of the wreckage, last I heard."

"Has she ever lost a Marshal before?"

"A few times," Lori said. "Thirty-two years, shit happens, you know."

"Did she react like that?"

"I don't know," Lori said. "Last time she lost a Marshal was 2010, I think. Before my time."

"I should go see her."

"No," Lori said. "Look, Danny, right now, Perez doesn't want you anywhere near her, and honestly, I think that's for the best."

"Why?" Danny asked. "If she's that upset because I got hurt—"

"Exactly," Lori said. "Look, the truth is, if it had been anyone other than Focus out there, Perez probably would have given the kill order instead of clearing us for the rocket launcher. Gammawave had killed way too many cops and Marshals for us to fuck around with him. But it was Focus out there, and for her to kill him without a kill order in place...people are scared, Danny."

Danny lay back on the bed and closed her eyes. She understood. She did. Bright costumes and silly names aside, metahumans were terrifying. The idea of someone as powerful as Focus going off course had to make a lot of people nervous, but Danny couldn't see it. All she could see when she thought of Focus was the woman who sat with her at lunch, talking and laughing about food and music and movies and TV shows. The woman who brought her fruit and chocolate and cheesecake. The woman who flirted with her when they were alone and touched her so gently.

She felt something touch her, but she didn't open her eyes. The touch wasn't physical. She wasn't quite sure how she knew that, but she did, and she leaned into it almost instinctively. For just a moment, she felt a whirlwind of emotions. Terror, guilt, rage, grief, despair, but also relief. So much relief. Longing, too. Then the emotions were gone, and just the touch remained, like a caress, before it disappeared as well. She knew it was Focus. It felt too much like what had happened that first day to be anyone else, and she knew what she needed to do.

She opened her eyes and looked over at Lori. "Get the doctor," she said. "I want to get out of here."

***

Danny sat on her couch, working on her third jug of Pedialyte as she watched Tommy Lee Jones chase Harrison Ford across the country. She'd seen the movie more times than she could count, practically had it memorized, which made it good background noise when she mostly just wanted to turn her brain off. The doctors had let her go home, but she was on a week of medical leave, and she already hated it. She never did well with enforced down time. She didn't even feel that bad. A bit like she was on the tail end of a massive hangover, but the Pedialyte and the aspirin were taking care of that. She just wanted to go back to work in the morning.

She jumped a bit when her phone rang, startled by the unexpected noise. She picked it up and sighed when she saw her mom's number. She really wasn't up to another round of nagging about her job, but then, it was her mom. She couldn't exactly decline the call. She swiped to accept and lifted the phone to her ear.

"Hey, Mom."

"Oh, thank God! You're alive."

"Um...why wouldn't I be?"

"You tell me," her mom said.

"Mom, you're the one calling me."

"It's all over the internet. A Marshal got killed during a bank robbery this afternoon, and one of those Superheroes went nuts and started killing the bank robbers."

"Oh, for fuck's sake." Danny sighed. "Mom, that's not what happened."

"There's a video," her mom said.

"Yeah, and does the video show the Marshal getting loaded into an ambulance, or a hearse?"

"The video doesn't go on that long. It just shows the Marshal getting hit with some kind of laser beam, and then Focus picking up an armored car and dropping it on top of the person who fired the beam."

"Well, I promise you, the Marshal is fine."

"How do you know? Were you there?"

Danny closed her eyes and tilted her head back, resting it on the back of the couch. "Because I'm the Marshal, Mom."

"*What?*"

"I'm the Marshal that got hit," she said.

"Are you okay?" her mom asked. "No. Of course not! You got shot! I knew this would happen. I'll be on the next flight out. Which hospital are you in? Who's your doctor?"

"Mom, slow down," Danny said. "I'm not in the hospital. I'm in my house. I'm sitting on my couch. The Suburban I was hiding behind took most of the blast. I'm a little banged up from getting thrown around, and I got a bit of a burn from the heat of the explosion. Aside from that, I'm fine."

"Fine? They said you were coughing up blood."

"They also said I was dead. And yeah, I did cough up some blood. I bit my cheek when I hit the ground, but the doctors would not have let me go if there was anything wrong with me."

"I'm still coming out there."

"Mom, no," Danny said. "I'm fine. Honestly. I've taken worse hits in the field. I know the video probably looks bad, but I'm fine. I swear."

"Are you sure?" her mom asked, and Danny could hear the fear in her voice, so she took a deep breath, and told as much of the truth as she dared.

"It was close, but I got lucky, and my team took care of me once I was down. I'm sorry I didn't call you and tell you, but I spent most of the afternoon getting poked and prodded by the doctors to make sure I was well enough to come home, and I'm fine. I don't even have a concussion."

"What about that Focus? Did she really go nuts like they're saying?"

"No, Mom," Danny said. "I don't know exactly what happened because I was a bit out of it from the blast. From what my partner told me, Focus saw me go down, and decided to end the threat. Gammawave was a known killer. Focus does her best to avoid killing. If you look up her numbers, this is only her seventh kill in thirty-two years of active service. She didn't go crazy, Mom."

"Sweetheart..."

"I know, Mom. I'm sorry I scared you."

"This is why I hate your job so much."

"Not because I'm a fascist with my jackboot on the neck of the oppressed?"

"You're not," her mom said. "I know you, sweetheart. I know you're trying your best to do good. But I also know that you're in danger every day. I've been living with death threats my whole career. It comes with the sort of things I do, but I never wanted you or your sisters to have to deal with that. That's why I was so happy when Max became a social worker, and Sam got into urban farming. I kept hoping you'd do something nice and safe with your policy degree."

"I know, Mom, but I've got too much of you in me. I want to help make a difference."

"I'm proud of you," her mom said. "I know I don't say it often, but I am. And if something had happened to you..."

Danny heard a soft knock on the sliding glass door that led out to her back yard. She looked over, and saw Focus standing there.

"Mom, I've got to go," she said.

"Why? Is something wrong?"

"No, Mom. Someone from work is at the door, and I need to talk to them. I love you."

"I love you, too," her mom said.

"Bye."

"Bye."

Danny ended the call and walked over to the sliding glass door. She opened it and took in the sight of Focus out of uniform. Instead of the white, blue, and red suit with the red, black, and blue ray diagram symbol on her chest, Focus was standing there in blue jeans, work boots, and a tank top, with a lightweight jacket over top. It was a good look on her.

"Hey," Focus said.

"Hey," Danny said.

"Can, um...can I come in?"

Danny nodded and stepped back, letting Focus step inside. Danny slid the door closed, then turned around to face Focus. Before she could say anything, or even register what was happening, Focus pulled her into a hug so tight Danny was sure it was going to break a few ribs. It went on and on, until Danny was genuinely starting to struggle for air before Focus let go. She stepped back, resting her hands on Danny's shoulders, and looking her over slowly. It didn't take a genius to know Focus was using her powers, and Danny found herself feeling a little shy about that, but finally Focus looked up at her.

"You're really okay," she said.

"Yeah," Danny said. "I'm fine."

"I'm sorry to bother you at home. I just...I had to know. To see for myself. I don't think I could survive if I lost you."

Danny stared at Focus, her words turning over and over in Danny's cop brain. She knew it wasn't the time to ask, that Focus was upset, but it was too much, and she had to ask.

"Why?"

"What?"

"Why me? Why all of this? I know you care about me, but I don't understand why. It would be one thing if you were attracted to me and we'd been flirting, or even if I could explain it away because of the mental connection that first day, but it's more than that. You asked for me by name before we ever met. I've let it go until now because I like you, because I've had a crush on you since I was five years old and it's flattering and exciting to feel like you like me back, but today you killed somebody because they hurt me, and I need to know why."

Focus looked down, and Danny felt a bit like she'd kicked a puppy, but then Focus nodded. "Yeah. That's...that's..." She let out a sigh. "Can we sit down?"

"Sure," Danny said. "Come on." She led the way over to the couch and took a seat. Focus sat down a little further away than Danny had expected, but she reached out and took one of Danny's hands in hers.

"Is this okay?" she asked.

"Yeah."

Focus took a deep breath and looked up at Danny with an expression on her face like she expected the world to end at any second. "I can't tell you everything," she said.

"Why not?" Danny asked.

"Because if I do, it will change things that can't be changed," Focus said. "I want to. I want to tell you everything. I've wanted to tell you everything since that first day. You can't understand how hard it is to hold back, when all I want to do is take you in my arms and hold you and tell you everything. To protect you from...to protect you."

"To protect me from what?"

"I can't tell you."

Danny let out a frustrated sigh. "What can you tell me?"

"You asked me once why I left my home world," Focus said. "I can tell you that. I can tell you why I don't let myself get close to the other Marshals."

"Okay. Let's start there."

"My world died. 240-some odd years ago. I don't know the exact date because I lost some time along the way."

"What happened?" Danny asked.

"My people were gifted. What you would call psionic abilities. All of us had them. Some were telekinetic, some could conjure force fields, some could teleport, some could fly at incredible speeds, some could project beams of energy…some could see the future. Some species out there are just like that. We weren't the only ones, but we were unique in one way. We could loan our power to each other. It became part of how our culture and society worked. A group of telekinetics would all loan their power to the most skilled person among them so that person, called a Focus, could lift more. Teleporters would loan their power so one of them could carry more, or teleport further. People who could see into the future would loan their power to the most gifted seer, so they could see further and more clearly.

"Being a Focus carried a lot of respect, and so did being a seer. So, when the seer Focuses all started reporting that they were seeing a danger coming, my people listened. Groups of seers started working together to see further, and they all saw the same thing. Our world ending. For months, they all worked to find a solution, a way to save us, but all they did was learn more about how we were going to die.

"A monster was coming. A creature as close to pure, elemental evil as ever existed. We called it Idimoni. The seers explored every possible future and didn't find any way to save our world, but they did find a way to stop him. Not for good. They couldn't find a way to kill it, but they could find a way to imprison it for hundreds of billions of years.

"They chose a Focus. They chose me. And everyone on my world, every single person, gave me their power. Every last drop, until even their life force was drained. There were over sixteen billion people on my world, and every last one of them poured their power and their life force into me. When it was over, I was the only one left, and when Idimoni came, I fought him. I fought him for years. I fought him across lightyears. I fought him on a hundred worlds. I fought him until I finally managed to trap him inside a black hole.

"When it was over, I slept for almost a decade. Then I came here. I lived among your people for a bit, but I was still tired, so eventually, I went back to sleep. I woke up in the seventies, and I tried to forget, I tried to live a normal life until I couldn't take it anymore, and I started to help.

"That's why I reacted the way I did today," Focus said. "It's the reason I don't let myself get close to the other Marshals. I've lost so much. My world, my culture, my friends, my family. The idea of losing more is horrific. It scares me, even with the friends I do have, but I try not to get close to people who put themselves on the line every day. Sometimes, I can't help it. People like Cecile, or Ice Dragon and Airheart have wormed their way in over the years, but I try to be careful. But I couldn't, not with you. When Gammawave shot you, when I thought for a moment that I'd lost you, all I felt was rage. I'm not proud of what I did, but I couldn't bear the thought of losing you."

"But why me?" Danny asked. "What makes me so special?"

"I can't tell you. I knew this would be hard. When I asked for you to be assigned to the unit, I knew it would be hard to keep my distance, but I thought I could do it. I thought it would be like it was before." Focus froze, and Danny knew immediately that she'd said more than she meant to.

"Before?" Danny asked. "What do you mean, before?"

Focus stood up. "I should go," she said. "I'm sorry. I shouldn't have come here tonight. I just..."

"You had to make sure I was okay," Danny said as she got to her feet. She reached out and took Focus' hand in hers. "I'm not upset."

"You're not?" Focus asked.

"No," Danny said. "I'm not. I just don't understand. Every time you look at me, it's like you're looking at the most important person in the world, but I don't even know your name."

"Ayanda."

"What?"

"Ayanda. My name is Ayanda."

"Ayanda," Danny said. "It's beautiful."

Ayanda reached up and cupped Danny's face in her hands, and Danny knew what was about to happen. Her heart pounded in her chest, and her stomach fluttered as Ayanda leaned in.

"Can I?" Ayanda asked.

"Yes."

Danny had been kissed before. Of course she had. She was twenty-six years old, and she had three girlfriends under her belt, but she had never been kissed like this. Ayanda kissed her like she was the most precious, most delicate thing on Earth. She was slow and gentle and soft, and at first, their lips barely touched, but Danny leaned into it, seeking more contact. She felt Ayanda's tongue slide across her lips. She opened them, not just granting access, but begging Ayanda to take it, and when Ayanda's tongue slipped into her mouth, she wrapped her arms around Ayanda and started backing her towards the couch.

It only took two steps before they fell together, Ayanda on the couch, and Danny straddling her lap. Ayanda's hands moved away from her face, sliding down and cupping her ass, pulling her close, and Danny felt that same ghostly touch on her mind she'd felt that afternoon. She reached out for it, unsure if she was doing it deliberately or instinctively, but not caring when the connection was made. The wave of emotions that hit her were just as overwhelming as they had been that first day. Need, longing, desire, anticipation, love. So much love. Such deep and overwhelming love. It surrounded her and embraced her and flowed through her. Danny felt tears falling down her face, because how could anyone love her like that?

She pulled back and looked Ayanda in the eyes, and she felt the emotions fade as Ayanda broke the connection between them. She looked away and shook her head.

"I'm sorry," she said.

"For what?"

"You weren't ready for that," Ayanda said. She turned and looked at Danny. "I'm normally so strong, so controlled, but God, you make me weak in all the best ways." She leaned forward, resting her forehead between Danny's breasts. "I need to go."

"You could stay," Danny said.

Ayanda let out a whimper and shook her head. "I can't. God, I want to, but I can't." She sat up straight and looked Danny in the eyes. "I love you. I shouldn't say it, but you felt it, didn't you?"

"Yes."

"I love you. I know you don't understand why, but please, just trust me. I promise you'll understand soon. Just a couple of weeks, and everything will make sense."

"Okay," Danny said. "I'll trust you."

"I need to go."

"I want you to stay."

"I can't." She leaned up and pressed a quick kiss to Danny's lips. "Just trust me a little longer."

"I can do that," Danny said. She climbed off Ayanda's lap and watched as Ayanda stood up and turned to look at her.

"Whatever happens, I need you to know that I love you."

"I do," Danny said. "When will I see you again?"

"When you come back to work," Ayanda said.

Danny nodded and stood up. Ayanda took one last look at her and headed for the sliding glass door. Danny followed to lock it after she left, but she needn't have bothered. Ayanda walked right through the glass as if it were nothing but air, then she turned and gave Danny a smile before she drifted up and vanished into the night sky.

Chapter Four

DANNY'S FIRST DAY BACK went about the way she expected. Perez pulled her in for another interrogation about her relationship with Focus, and Danny told her the truth. She had no idea why Focus seemed to have fixated on her. That Focus hadn't in any way been inappropriate, nor had she made any unwanted advances. That Focus seemed interested in being friends and that she had been trying to engage with Focus on that level. That most of their discussions had been fairly casual topics. Movies, music, food, art, books, and similar things.

She didn't tell Perez about the solo meetings in the hallways, about the flirting, about any of the things Focus had told her in confidence. She didn't say a word about Focus being an alien, about her world being dead, about the fact that her powers were given to her in an act of species-wide suicide intended to protect the rest of the universe from a world-killing monster. She didn't say a word about the kisses, about the fact that Focus was in love with her. She didn't tell Perez Focus' name.

In short, she told Perez everything about Focus, and nothing about Ayanda. Ayanda had trusted her, and Danny had decided to keep that trust, so she guarded Ayanda's secrets. She also promised to return that trust. To not push Ayanda for the answers that Ayanda had promised would come.

But Danny was a cop. A Deputy US Marshal, technically, but still a cop. And no matter how much she wanted to just trust Ayanda and wait, the cop part of her couldn't let the mystery go, so she started investigating. She couldn't exactly look Ayanda up in the phonebook, or pop over to her house, or look up her home world on Google, so she did what most cops did and started with witnesses. There was one person in the unit who worked more closely with Focus than anyone else. Deputy US Marshal Stuart Archer. Focus's handler.

So, Tuesday morning, once the briefing was done and Focus had left for her morning patrol over the city, Danny knocked on Archer's door and waited. It only took a moment before the door opened and she found herself face to face with the short, curly haired man she'd seen in the situation room almost every time she was there.

"Ah," he said. "I'd been wondering when you would show up."

"You were expecting me?"

"You're surprised?"

"Not really."

"Come in and have a seat," he said, stepping out of her way. She took one of the chairs in front of his desk and waited while he closed the door and sat down.

"I'm afraid I don't have a lot of answers for you," Archer said.

"What can you tell me?" Danny asked.

"Probably less than you already know. I've been on the team for nine years. I was Alpha leader before I took over the handler job four years ago. In all that time, I've never seen Focus open up to anybody other than Cecile La Saint."

"The previous Officer in Charge?" Danny asked.

"Yes, and Focus's first handler before that. She was probably the closest thing Focus had to an actual friend among us lowly mortals."

"Do you know where she is?" Danny asked.

"Yep." He opened a drawer in his desk and pulled out a slip of paper. Danny took it and read it. It had Cecile's name on it, and an address out in the suburbs north of the city. Danny slipped the note in her pocket.

"I take it she's expecting me?" Danny asked.

"Yeah," Archer said. "When all this started, I called her and asked her what the hell was going on, and she told me that when you came asking, to give you her address, and a message."

"What's the message?"

"Don't wait," Archer said.

"Well, that's cryptic."

"Welcome to my fucking life." He leaned back and stared at her for a minute. "Just...do me a favor."

"What?"

"Focus...she's never told me any of this, but I have a degree in psychology. I started out as a hostage negotiator. Found out pretty quick that I wasn't cut out for it, so I transferred over to field ops, but I remember my training, and I know trauma when I've seen it. Focus has been through something horrific. Not just the shit you see on the streets, though that's bad enough. She has some kind of Core Trauma, something that makes her keep her distance from almost everyone. It's like she's terrified of forming attachments, which is why you are freaking everyone out.

"If it was just a matter of her looking for a tumble, I don't think she'd bring that to work. God knows, all she'd have to do is walk into any lesbian bar in the country and she'd have her pick, but there's never been any indication of her dating since her former partner Scatter disappeared almost twenty-nine years ago. There's something about you, something special. I don't know what it is, and frankly, I don't care. You're not my responsibility. Focus is. And I am asking you as her handler, and I am begging you as someone who cares about her, please, for the love of God, be careful with her heart. I don't know how much more pain that woman can take."

Danny nodded. "I promise," she said. "I will do everything I can to take care of her."

"Thank you," he said. "Now get back to work before Perez catches us goldbricking."

***

That night was the first time Danny set foot in North Beach. It was one of the larger neighborhoods north of the city, and while hardly the richest of the neighborhoods, this Cecile had to be doing pretty well for herself. Better than any retired Marshal should be. Danny tried not to think too hard about that. Maybe Cecile had a rich husband or something. All Danny really knew was that she felt out of place and wanted to go home more than she wanted to knock on the door of the house in front of her.

Except she needed to do this. For Ayanda's sake, if not for her own.

She took a deep breath and got out of her car, then took a moment to double check her appearance. Boots shined, slacks straight, shirt neat. Badge clipped to her belt. Jacket covering her gun. Once she was sure she looked okay, she headed up to the door and knocked.

It took a moment, but a short, stoutly built woman opened the door. She had bushy brown and gray hair, wore large glasses, smelled faintly of wood smoke, and put on a huge smile the moment she saw Danny.

"Hello," she said.

"Cecile La Saint?"

The woman burst out laughing and shook her head. "Child, do I look like a six-foot-tall half-Haitian, half-Cuban badass to you?"

"No, ma'am."

The woman shook her head again. "I'm Rachel. Cecile's wife. Come on inside." She backed up and let Danny step into the house. Once Danny was inside, Rachel closed the door, then turned and yelled, "Cecile, there's a Deputy Marshal here to see you."

Rachel turned back to Danny. "Come on into the living room. Cecile will take this side of forever to get down here." She led Danny into a nice, richly decorated room that Danny was sure didn't get very much use. Everything in the room was brand new, and while it was kept meticulously dusted, it lacked any sort of lived-in feel.

"Pardon the smell of smoke," Rachel said. "I spent all day running the charcoal smelter."

"Smelter?" Danny asked.

"Yes," Rachel said. "I'm a blacksmith, though mostly I'm a teacher these days. I teach classes on blacksmithing four days a week. Today's class was on making crucible steel."

"That's incredible."

Rachel waved her hand dismissively. "Can I get you anything? A bottle of water, a Coke, a beer?"

"Do you have any unsweetened tea?"

"You do know you're in Florida, right?"

"Yes, ma'am."

"Well, lucky for you, I'm a Jewish girl from New York, so yes, I do happen to have some unsweetened tea. Just don't tell any of your work friends. They're liable to arrest me for it."

Danny let out a small laugh as Rachel stepped out of the room. She took a moment to glance around and see if she could learn anything, but the room was something right out of Better Homes and Gardens. Pretty enough to look at, but plain enough that it didn't give any clues about its owner. Which was a clue in and of itself. The room was camouflage.

She turned at the sound of shoes on hardwood and saw a six-foot tall, light-skinned black woman walk into the room. She was dressed casually. Jeans, work boots, a t-shirt with a flannel over it. Hold-out pistol in an ankle holster on the outside of the right leg. Sidearm in a paddle holster on the right side, covered by the flannel, pocket knife clipped in the right front pocket.

Danny stood up.

"Cecile La Saint?" she asked.

"I am," Cecile said. "And you're Danny Martin." It wasn't a question.

"Yes, ma'am."

"Well, sit back down. If Rachel comes in and finds you standing, I won't hear the end of it for weeks."

Danny smiled and sat back down on the couch. Cecile sat down on an armchair right across from her and studied her for a minute.

"You don't look as happy as the last time I saw you," Cecile said.

"I'm sorry, have we met before?" Danny asked.

"We have, though I don't reckon you'd remember it."

"I can't say that I do. I'm sorry."

"Don't be," Cecile said. "I'm sixty years old. I'm used to it. I'm lucky if I remember my own face when I look in the mirror."

"Don't listen to her," Rachel said as she came back into the room carrying a glass of tea and a bottle of water. She set the tea in front of Danny, and the water in front of Cecile. "Her memory is just as sharp as it ever was." She leaned down, and as if on cue, Cecile turned towards her. The kiss was short and chaste. Just a peck on the lips before Rachel straightened up. "I'll be in the kitchen if you need me."

Cecile nodded and watched as Rachel disappeared out of the room.

"You have a lovely wife," Danny said.

"I do," Cecile said, fondness in her voice. She turned back to Danny. "So, I'm guessing you're here about Focus."

"I am. Archer said you know her better than anyone else."

"Maybe, though I wouldn't bet on it. She and Ice Dragon have been friends for a long time, though Rachel and I probably see more of her since Ice Dragon and Airheart got married."

"So you're still close to her."

"We are."

"What can you tell me about her?" Danny asked.

Cecile shook her head. "That's not the right question. I could sit here for years and talk about missions we ran and villains we caught, and performance metrics and power ratings, but you didn't come here for that. So, I'll ask again, why are you here?"

Danny sat back and looked at Cecile for a minute, trying to decide how much she wanted to share. "Archer said you're Focus' friend."

"I am," Cecile said. "Aside from my wife, Focus is my best friend."

"She asked for my assignment to the unit. By name. I don't know why. We've never met. Not even at an autograph signing or public appearance, but she knows me, somehow. For some reason, I matter to her, and I can't understand why."

"You're a pretty girl. She's very gay. The math isn't that hard."

"If I had been assigned to the unit by chance, I'd be able to believe it was just that, but it's not. My first day at the station, I met her, and we connected somehow. I felt her emotions, and it was like she'd been waiting for me. She knew who I was."

"Of course she did," Cecile said. She picked up her water, opened it, and took a drink.

"What does that mean?"

"It means that that useless lesbian disaster can't keep a secret to save her life," Cecile said. "You know Focus had a partner once, right? A hero named Scatter."

"I do," Danny said. "I actually have the poster in a tube in the back of my closet."

Cecile laughed so hard she almost fell out of her chair. "That is fucking hilarious."

"Why?" Danny asked.

"You'll find out," Cecile said. "But it's not important right now. You know the story about how she came out?"

"Not all the details. Just that someone took a picture of her and Scatter making out, and Focus held a press conference to say 'yes, I'm gay'."

"That's not too far off. The thing is, Scatter kind of came out of nowhere, but they worked together like a well-oiled machine. The two of them loved each other. They didn't even try to hide it. Some of the Marshals weren't happy about that, but it was the 90s. You got a free side of homophobia with breakfast most places back then, but Focus and Scatter didn't seem to give a shit. A reporter got ahold of pictures of the two of them kissing. Focus didn't get why it was a big deal, but our media liaison was a nice, cheerful little bigot, and honestly, I was just as scared of the potential consequences of Focus and Scatter getting outed. Scatter made this speech about how the world wasn't going to change unless people like Focus stood up and set the example, but we were still arguing against Focus coming out. Scatter pulled Focus aside and talked to her for a couple of minutes, and when she was done, Focus told David to arrange a press conference. Focus just walked up to the podium, and said, 'I'm gay. A reporter named Nathan Price with the Pontian Tribune took a photo of me kissing my girlfriend and tried to blackmail me with it. I refuse to be blackmailed because I am not ashamed of who I am, or who I love,' then just walked right over to Scatter and kissed her like the world was ending before the two of them flew away while a crowd of reporters screamed questions at their backs.

"A couple of months later, Scatter disappeared. Focus tried as hard as she could to be strong, but I could see it in her eyes. The pain, the loneliness. I asked her one night if she was going to be okay, and she looked at me and she said, 'Someday.' I said, 'You sound pretty sure of that,' and she said, 'I've seen my future, and I won't be alone forever.'

"I've never told anyone about that, so don't do something stupid like file a report."

"I won't," Danny said. "She told me…" Danny shook her head. "Doesn't matter. I didn't put it together. That she could see the future."

Cecile looked like she wanted to say something, but she just shook her head and took a sip of her water.

"Do you know if her visions are always right?"

"No," Cecile said. "Why? Do you not want to be with her?"

"No, it's not that. It's just…"

"If she can see the future, then why didn't she stop every horrible thing that happened in the last thirty years?"

"Something like that."

"If you could look into the future, would you? If you had the choice to see all the horrible things people were going to do to each other or to not see it, which would you choose?"

"I see your point," Danny said.

"I don't know if she's told you this, but Focus is old. Hundreds of years old. She's lived through things no one should have to live through and seen things no one should ever see. So if she chooses not to look, I don't blame her. She does more for humanity than we have any right to expect, so let her find peace how she can."

Danny nodded.

"Just, two things."

"Okay."

"First, take care of her. She'll never ask for it. She'll never show you that she needs it, but she's been alone longer than you've been alive. She lost the love of her life twenty-nine years ago, and she hasn't even looked at a woman since. Not until you came along. She's helped so many people, and she deserves to be happy. Please don't break her heart."

"I won't," Danny said.

"Good. Now, second, drink your tea. Otherwise, Rachel will be upset, and then I'll have to shoot you."

***

She wasn't quite sure if she was early, or Lori was running late, but whichever one it was, Lori was right beside her as she exited the locker room. It was Thursday morning, a week and two days after her visit to Cecile. Two and a half weeks after the night Ayanda had shown up at her house. Truth be told, Danny was starting to get a little nervous. Ayanda had said she'd understand everything in a couple of weeks. So far there had been no flash of light, no blinding revelation, but something was coming. She knew it was because she trusted Ayanda.

She knew she'd be okay. That much had been made clear, but still, knowing something was coming was terrifying in its own right. What if she did something wrong and screwed everything up? What if Ayanda ended up hating her for it?

"What is it?" Lori snapped.

"What?" Danny asked.

"You're more nervous than a long-tailed cat in a room full of rocking chairs, and it's starting to make me worry."

"Sorry," Danny said.

"Don't be sorry. Just spill."

"I—"

"Danny!"

Danny turned towards the sound of Ayanda's voice. She was more than a little surprised. Ayanda usually only called out to her in the halls if she was alone, but she couldn't keep the smile off her face as Ayanda walked up to her.

"Lori," Ayanda said, giving Lori a small nod of acknowledgement.

"Focus," Lori said.

"Could I have a moment with Danny?"

"Sure," Lori said. She turned to Danny. "We'll talk later."

Danny nodded and watched as Lori walked away.

"She doesn't seem happy," Ayanda said.

"She knows something's up." Danny turned back to Ayanda. "You said I'd know what was going on in a couple of weeks."

Ayanda nodded and held up a small manila envelope that had been folded in half. "You're going to need this today," she said.

"Today?" Danny asked, the question carrying more weight than it should. *Is today the day I find out what's going on? Is today the day whatever it is happens?* A hundred more variations on the same question.

"Today," Ayanda said.

Danny took the envelope and started to open it, but Ayanda stopped her.

"Not yet," she said. "You'll know when it's time to open it."

"How?"

"When you're out of options, what's in the envelope will give you everything you need."

Danny looked at the envelope for a moment, and then slipped it in her pocket along with her credentials. When she looked up again, Ayanda reached up and cupped her face in both hands and pulled Danny into a kiss. Danny didn't even hesitate before wrapping her arms around Ayanda and kissing her back.

Ayanda broke the kiss, and she stared at Danny for a moment, and Danny felt Ayanda touching her mind, and she felt the same love she had felt the night Ayanda had visited fill her and surround her.

"I love you, Danny. I know that might not mean a lot to you right now, I know you don't understand it, but if you believe nothing else I've said, please believe that I love you. That I will always love you."

"I do," Danny said.

Ayanda kissed her again, and then backed away with a smile. "Let's get to the briefing."

***

The alert came at a little after 10:00 AM. A call back to the briefing room. All squads, along with Focus, were pulled in. Danny and Lori got there early enough to grab seats in the front row and waited while the briefing room filled up. Perez walked in at 10:10 AM, with Archer and Focus a few steps behind. She stepped up to the podium and looked out over the crowd.

"The contents of this briefing are top secret and code word classified. I cannot emphasize enough how dangerous the information you will hear is. Repeating it is not just a violation of your security clearance and treason, but if this information leaks, it could very well lead to hundreds, if not thousands of mass casualty events. So please, for the love of God, keep your fucking mouths shut," Perez said.

"Roughly nineteen minutes ago, we detected the energy signature of one of the components stolen during the Kaiju incident two and a half months ago. We believe the Supervillain who stole those components has resurfaced and is preparing to use whatever device he built out of the technology he stole. Normally, we would consider this a low-threat response. However—and this is the part you need to carry to your grave—we have every reason to believe that the Supervillain we are about to go after is responsible for the Kaiju incident. Focus."

Perez stepped back from the podium and Focus took her place. "During the Kaiju incident, I heard a sound coming from the bay. The sound was outside of the range of human hearing, but I was certain it would be within the range of Kaiju hearing. As I followed the Kaiju around the bay, the sound shifted position constantly, and the Kaiju followed it. The sound was a lure. When the Kaiju turned back out to sea, it was following the device which was emitting the sound, and when the sound stopped, the Kaiju went deep and headed back to its deep ocean trench home."

Focus stepped back from the podium, and Perez took her place. "I do not have to tell you the kind of disasters that would follow if the technology to control a Kaiju fell into the wrong hands. Even the knowledge that this technology exists would be enough to send our enemies and Supervillains alike into a frenzy to figure out how it was done and reproduce it. We cannot, under any circumstance, allow our target to escape, or to activate whatever device he has created. Is that clear?"

"Yes, ma'am," came every voice in the room.

"Then grab your gear and get saddled up. We roll out in twenty minutes."

***

The target site turned out to be in South Shore, because of course it did. Danny wasn't quite sure when the first of the Panther's scouts spotted them, but by the time they pulled up outside the dockside warehouse, the Panthers were right behind them.

"What do we do?" Danny asked.

"We get ready," Lori said as she climbed out of the SUV. "Perez will handle the Panthers."

Danny wasn't so sure of that. Not from the way Kipengele was reading Perez the riot act. But she decided to follow Lori's lead for now.

"What do you think?" Lori asked. "Shotgun or rifle?"

"There's only supposed to be one guy," Danny said. "I'd say rifles. They have the range and the penetration."

"And if there's more than one guy?" Lori asked.

"That's what backup is for," Danny said.

"You have a point," Lori said. "Alpha Squad, we are going for rifles and flash bangs."

Danny smiled and clipped a couple of grenade pouches to her belt. She double checked that her Glock was in its holster and that her AR pistol was ready. Then she grabbed her rifle, clipped it to her sling, and waited.

A couple of minutes later, Perez jogged over.

"The Panthers have agreed to help us hold the perimeter, but Kipengele will be going in with Focus. Otherwise, none of the mission parameters have changed. Focus secures the bad guy, you secure the tech. Lethal force is authorized if it's the only way to stop this guy from turning on whatever doomsday device he's been building."

"Understood," Lori said.

Danny took a second to double check that she still had the envelope Ayanda had given her. It was still there, in the pocket with her badge and credentials.

"Ready," Perez said.

Alpha squad lined up and got ready.

"Go," Perez said.

Robbins took point as they approached the building. He was one of the three members of Alpha squad who ran with a breaching shotgun. When they reached the door, he rammed the breaching choke on the shotgun into the door and looked at Lori. She gave the nod, Robbins pulled the trigger, blowing open the lock. He kicked the door in, and Lori and Danny charged through with the rest of Alpha at their back.

"*US Marshals! Down on the ground,*" Lori yelled as she charged forward towards the man in the center of the room. He was mostly human-looking, aside from the oddly colored skin and the antenna sticking up through his hair.

"No," he yelled. "You can't be here! You have to leave."

"*Down on the ground now,*" Lori shouted.

"Stay back!" he yelled. "It's already charging. I just need five more minutes."

Danny looked over at the machine as Focus and Kipengele dropped down next to the man. He turned to run towards the machine, but Focus locked him in a force field.

"Hostile is neutralized," Focus said, but Danny barely heard her.

"No! Please! I just want to go home!" the target yelled.

The machine, whatever it was, was cycling up, and all Danny could think of was the damage it could do. A doomsday device in the middle of a city with millions of people in it. She didn't even hesitate. She just ran for the machine.

"Danny," Lori called out, but she was too far away to stop her.

"Don't," the man in the forcefield yelled. "You can't stop it mid-cycle!"

Danny reached the machine, but she couldn't make any sense of the controls. They were labeled in a language she didn't understand, but she could make sense of the power cable that ran over to a junction box on the wall and connected to a breaker box on the side of the machine. She grabbed the red, rubber coated handle, and looked over at Focus, ignoring everything else in the room. Focus gave her a small nod. Barely there. Too small for anyone who wasn't looking right at her to notice. but it was enough for Danny.

She pulled the lever. The room, for one brief moment, was filled with blinding light, then pain, and finally, darkness.

Chapter Five

"MA'AM?"

Danny winced as the word thundered in her ears. She tried to open her eyes, to see where the scream was coming from, but the light burned and she slammed them shut again.

"Ma'am, are you okay?"

She reached up, covering her ears. "Stop yelling," she said, but the words boomed in her ears like cannon fire.

She opened her eyes again, and the light was only blinding this time. She turned her head away from it, but no direction was safe. She blinked, which seemed to help, to dim the light, so she did it again and again until the light faded until it was barely enough to see by. When she could do it without feeling like the light was an icepick being driven into her brain, she looked around, and saw an old man in some sort of uniform kneeling down next to her.

"What happened?" she asked.

"I don't know, ma'am," he said. "I heard a scream, and I came running, and you were just lying there on the floor."

"How long was I out?"

"Not long," he said. "A couple of minutes. I would have called an ambulance, but the phone is on the other end of the warehouse, and I didn't want to leave you."

"You don't have a cell?" she asked.

"What?"

"A cell phone?"

The old man laughed. "Ma'am, I'm just a security guard. Not a millionaire."

Danny looked around the room. The warehouse. It looked like the warehouse they'd raided, but there were differences. Different lighting fixtures. Different paint on the walls. The security guard that was there, and the doomsday machine and her squad that weren't.

"Where am I?"

"You don't know?"

She shook her head. "I was with my squad," she said. "We were raiding a warehouse down in South Shore."

"Well, you're in South Shore, ma'am, though I don't see any squad. Your outfit says you're a Deputy US Marshal, but you're dressed more like a soldier."

Danny frowned a bit and wondered if this guy even owned a TV. "Can you help me up?"

"Are you sure you should be standing, ma'am?" he asked.

"I think I'm okay," she said. "I just...I think I took a bit of a shock."

He gave her a dubious look, but offered her his hand, and when she took it, he helped her get to her feet.

"Where am I?" she asked again.

"You're in a warehouse on the docks. Pier fourteen, building seven."

Danny looked at him for a moment, then shook her head and looked around at the building again. Same structure. Different details. It couldn't be the same building she was in just a couple of minutes ago.

"You're sure that's the right address?" she asked.

"Yes, ma'am," he said.

Danny looked around again, a sinking feeling in her gut. "Can you take me to that phone?"

"Yes ma'am," he said.

Danny shifted her rifle so it was slung over her back and followed as the security guard led her across the floor of the empty warehouse.

"You have a name?"

"Archie," he said. "How about you?"

"Danny," she said. "Deputy Marshal Danny Martin."

"Nice to meet you, Deputy Martin."

"Likewise," she said.

When they reached the office, it was clear this was where Archie spent most of his time. There was a bank of old CRT monitors that showed CCTV feeds from security cameras all around the building. A large thermos and a lunch box, an old phone that looked like it belonged in the 80s, and a swimsuit calendar on the wall.

Danny froze as she looked at the calendar, and even though she was very, very gay, the barely covered model hadn't stopped her in her tracks. The month and the year on the calendar had. Miss June was smiling at her from 1991.

"Archie, what's the date?" she asked.

"It's June seventh."

"What year?"

"Ma'am?" he asked, confusion clearly written on his face.

"What year is it?"

"1991. Ma'am, are you sure you're okay? Maybe I should call that ambulance."

"No," she said. "No. I'm fine. I just...can I sit down for a minute?"

"Of course," he said.

Danny unclipped her rifle from its sling and sat down in one of the chairs along the wall of the office. She stared at the calendar, turning over what Archie had said in her head. June 7th, 1991.

Time travel. She didn't want to believe it. It wasn't supposed to be possible. But then, neither were Kaiju and Superpowers and fire-breathing dragonkin and telepathy and people who can see the future, and she dealt with those every day. Hell, she was practically dating an alien, but time travel? It felt like a bridge too far, but the evidence was right in front of her. At least, a little bit of it.

She closed her eyes and took a deep breath, trying to calm herself. Romance might have been her preferred genre when it came to books, but it wasn't the only thing she read. Science fiction, fantasy, mystery, and spy thrillers were all on the list. Same when it came to the movies. And something she always hated about time travel stories was the part where the protagonist did something stupid because they refused to accept the reality of their situation.

So, time travel. Accept for now that she was thirty years in the past. Accept that there was no internet. Accept that her cell phone was back at base thirty years in the future, and 4G wouldn't exist for decades anyway. Accept the reality of her situation and deal with the current crisis. Get some place safe and then she could fall to pieces.

So, start with basic problem solving. What did she have? What did she need?

She had weapons. The AR pistol. She had three magazines before it would be useless. 300 Blackout didn't go on the market until 2011. When did the assault weapons ban go into effect? She wanted to say '94, which meant she could probably get the parts to convert the AR pistol to .223 if she needed to, but that would take money. Same with refilling on ammo for the AR-10, though that would be easier. 7.62 NATO was common enough, and worst comes to worst she could load .308 Winchester. Her Glock was chambered for .45 ACP, which was about as common as white on rice.

She would need money, clothes, a place to stay, and a place to hide the weapons, because she couldn't carry them around with her. Sure, she had a badge, but her Marshal's credentials were effective as of

2017. If anybody checked them, they'd assume the badge was fake, and if they ran the serial number on the badge, it would confirm it.

But where? Where was she going to get money? Where was she going to find a place to stay? She couldn't just call the Marshals. They'd think she was crazy, in which case she'd wind up in a mental institution, or they'd believe her, which would be worse. She didn't have a lot of options. In fact, she didn't have any options.

"When you're out of options, what's in the envelope will give you everything you need," she said, the words echoing in her head in Ayanda's voice.

"What was that?" Archie asked.

"Nothing," Danny said. "Just remembered something one of my co-workers said before the raid."

She reached into her pocket, and pulled out the envelope Ayanda had given her, and opened it. Inside, she found a black hardcover notebook held closed by an elastic strap. She opened it, and tucked in the front cover were five twenty-dollar bills, all printed in 1990. There was also an old, yellowed business card for a cab company, and on the first page of the notebook, there were three dates. May 20th, 2021. The day of the raid. June 7th, 1991. The day she was currently living through. December 27th, 1992. Under the third date, there was an address for Sunrise Tower, and an apartment number.

She flipped the page, and found what looked like a lot of scribbles, but the more she looked, the more she realized there was a pattern to it, and as she flipped through the rest of the book, she realized what she was seeing. Ayanda's language. Ayanda had written her younger self a letter. A long one.

Danny flipped back to the front of the notebook. She wasn't sure she liked the implication of that third date, but she'd worry about that later. For right now, Ayanda was right. The envelope gave her everything she needed.

Well, almost everything.

"Archie?"

"Yes?"

"Can you hand me the phone?"

***

A trick Danny had learned early on in her fugitive retrieval days was to carry a large nylon laundry bag with her in a pouch on her belt, or on her vest. They were cheap, they folded up to a ridiculously small size, and you could shove all of your gear in one. That last bit hadn't quite held true when she moved over to Superhero support. The bag she had with her had room for her AR pistol, her tac vest, her helmet, her thigh holster, and mag pouches, but the AR-10, her main rifle, didn't fit without being broken down. Archie, unfortunately, didn't have a bag that could fit a full-sized battle rifle in it, so she'd gotten a couple of trash bags, and wrapped the broken-down pieces of her rifle in them, then stuffed them in the laundry bag. They just barely fit.

Archie asked her why she was taking off her gear, and she said she didn't want to scare any civilians by walking around looking like a soldier. He seemed to accept that at face value and didn't pay too much attention when she made a phone call. Instead of calling the local Marshal's station, she called the cab company and asked for a pickup, then thanked Archie for his help, and headed outside to wait for the cab. As soon as she was outside, she untucked her shirt, letting it hang down over the badge clipped to her belt.

She was a little afraid that Archie would call the cops as soon as she was out of sight. A strange woman showing up in the middle of a warehouse, acting weird and packing enough firepower to invade a small country? She would have called the cops, but she had the feeling Archie was more interested in getting rid of her than anything else. It was probably the first time in her career she'd ever been grateful for sloppy security, but if it let her get to Ayanda before the Marshals or PPD were on to her, she could live with it.

The cab pulled up, and she practically fell into the back seat. She could feel the exhaustion creeping up on her, but she needed to be careful. She gave the cab driver an address a couple of blocks away from the one in the notebook and prayed that '91 was too early for traffic cams and CCTV that would let her be easily tracked.

She nearly dozed off a couple of times on the ride across town. She wasn't sure if that was a result of the time travel, or if she'd smacked her head hard enough to give herself a concussion. Honestly, she was hoping for a concussion. She was actually hoping she was delusional, and she was going to wake up tomorrow in the hospital and find out she'd taken a huge electric shock that scrambled her brain for a bit.

The billboards for Robin Hood: Prince of Thieves and Terminator 2: Judgement Day she saw along the way made the idea seem less likely, but what she didn't understand was how this happened. Something to do with the machine the hostile had built, obviously. The other part that was bugging her was that Ayanda obviously knew this was going to happen and didn't stop it.

She told herself to trust Ayanda. Ayanda obviously knew how this was going to turn out, so she just needed to trust her.

"Here you go," the cab driver said as he stopped in front of an apartment building.

"How much?" she asked.

"$63.75."

Danny handed him $80. "Keep the change," she said. She got out of the cab and waited until he pulled away to start walking the two blocks down to the address Ayanda had given her. When she got there, the doorman moved to block her way. She lifted the tail of her shirt, showing the badge clipped there. He frowned for a moment, then stepped back, letting her pass. She stepped into the elevator and looked at the buttons. The building had forty floors. She figured apartment 4004 was probably on the fortieth so she hit that button and rode up, fighting to stay awake the whole way.

When the doors parted on the fortieth floor, she shook herself a little to wake up, and stepped off, then started down the hall. It turned out there were only four apartments on the fortieth floor. Ayanda's was the second door on the right. She took a deep breath and knocked.

When the door opened a couple of minutes later, instead of the five-foot, ten-inch blonde alien with vivid cobalt blue eyes Danny had been expecting, she found herself face to face with a five-foot, four-inch brown haired, brown eyed woman. For a moment, Danny was sure she had the wrong apartment, but then she looked into the woman's eyes, and her heart leapt in recognition, and without thought, her mind reached out and she felt the same connection she had with Ayanda the day they met, except this time the emotions were very different. Danny staggered back under the weight of them. Loss, pain, grief, sorrow, and above all else, loneliness. Fathomless, crushing loneliness. Loneliness that made the whole world bleak and gray, that made existing agony.

The connection disappeared as if someone had cut it with a knife. Danny looked up at the brown-haired woman and knew exactly who she was.

"Ayanda?"

"How do you know that name?" Ayanda asked.

Danny reached into her pocket and pulled out the notebook. "This should explain everything," she said as she held the notebook out.

Ayanda took it and opened it. She flipped to the second page, and Danny could see the shock on her face. Ayanda looked up at her.

"Come inside," she said.

Danny stepped into the apartment and was a little shocked at how big and luxurious it was.

"Where did you get this?" Ayanda asked.

"You gave it to me," Danny said.

"No, I didn't."

"Yes, you did," Danny said. "On May 20th, 2021."

Ayanda looked down at the notebook for a moment, then back up at Danny, and Danny stepped back. There was none of the warmth she was used to. Just anger pointed right at her.

"Sit down on the couch," she said. "Don't touch anything."

"Ayanda—"

"Don't say that name!" she snapped.

Danny flinched. "I...what should I call you? Focus?"

Ayanda glared at her. "You can call me Kelly," she said. "Now sit down."

Danny walked over to the couch and sat down.

Ayanda took a seat across from her, opened the notebook, and started to read.

***

Danny woke up slowly, which was unusual for her. One of the things about being a cop is that you get used to rolling out of bed at a moment's notice, and you have to be awake when you do, so she'd trained herself to go from asleep to awake pretty damn close to instantly. Not this time, though. She slowly crept up towards consciousness as she felt hands running over her head. The touch was familiar, and it made her feel safe. There was warmth with the touch, and she leaned into it.

"Stop moving," someone said. The voice sounded a discordant note. That voice shouldn't sound so cold and harsh. It should be soft and gentle, filled with a smile or a laugh, or heavy with promise.

She opened her eyes and found herself staring up at the ceiling.

"Don't move," Ayanda said. Not her Ayanda, though. This person, the one who wanted to be called Kelly, who stared at her with caution, was standing above her, slowly running her hands over Danny's head.

"You have a concussion," she said. "I'm knitting the broken capillaries back together and reducing the swelling."

"Thank you," Danny said. Ayanda let out a small grunt of acknowledgement. "Did I do something wrong?" Danny asked.

"You mean aside from trying to shut off a temporal displacement engine mid-cycle and getting yourself dumped into my lap? No. Nothing at all."

"I did what?"

"You tried to turn off a time machine," Ayanda said.

"Oh," Danny said. "I thought it was some kind of weapon."

"Yeah," Ayanda said. "The notebook mentioned that."

"What else did it say?"

"That you've been saturated with anti-chroniton particles and any attempt to retrieve you would just throw you further into the past."

"What?" Danny said, trying to sit up.

"Don't move!" Ayanda snapped.

"Sorry," Danny said.

Ayanda sighed. "It's fine," she said. "I'm just...I don't do this often."

"Why not?" Danny asked. "It's one of the powers you got from your people, right?"

"It is," Ayanda said.

"Then why not use it more?"

Ayanda was quiet for a moment, and Danny thought maybe she'd asked the wrong question. She was about to apologize when Ayanda spoke.

"I wasn't trained for it."

"What?"

"I was a soldier. My natural gifts were telekinesis and flight."

"Oh. I didn't realize you could have more than one."

"Most of my people didn't. Everyone had a gift. Less than ten percent of the population had more than one. I had five."

"That's a lot," Danny said.

"It's the reason I was chosen as the Focus. There wasn't anyone else alive at the time who had as many gifts as I did. Telekinesis, flight, force fields, telepathy, and empathy. They trained me to use as many of the gifts as they could, but when they taught me healing, they only taught me how to heal myself. Not others."

"Why not?"

"Because I was a weapon. My purpose was to fight Idimoni and lock him away. Healing myself so I could stay in the fight was necessary. Healing other people...what use did a weapon have for that?"

"But what about after the fight?" Danny asked.

"There wasn't supposed to be an after."

"What?"

"I was supposed to die sealing Idimoni in his prison. Not a single one of the seers saw a future where I survived the battle."

Danny felt rage bubbling up inside her. The fact that her people had sent her out to die made her want to curse them, to scream at the injustice of it, but she held her tongue. Every one of them had made the same sacrifice they had expected of Ayanda. The only difference was, Danny didn't care about them. She cared about Ayanda, about the woman who was opening up to her, who loved her.

"You shouldn't be angry," Ayanda said.

"How did you know?"

"Empath," Ayanda said. "The rage is practically boiling over inside of you. but I was at peace with it. If I had died, I would have joined my people, my family. Instead, I'm alive and alone." Ayanda lifted her hands off Danny's head. "There. Your brain is fixed. Try not to break it again."

Danny sat up on the couch as Ayanda took the love seat.

"According to my future self, it will take about eighteen months for enough of the anti-chroniton particles to decay to the point where she can use the time machine to bring you back."

Danny closed her eyes and took a deep breath. She wasn't surprised. She'd seen the date in the notebook, and she'd known that was probably what it meant, but now that she had confirmation, a lot of things were starting to make sense. How Ayanda knew her before they met. Why Ayanda loved her when they barely knew each other. How Ayanda knew to give her the notebook, or to even make the notebook.

But eighteen months. That was a long time to be trapped in the past. A long time to go without speaking to her family, without seeing any of her friends, without a job, or money, or control of her own destiny.

"My future self didn't give a lot of detail. I don't know what your relationship is with her, but she said that she promised you that you would have everything you need, so that promise is mine now. You'll stay here with me. I'll get you set up with a driver's license and all the other papers you'll need. Money won't be an issue. You'll need to sleep on the couch tonight. It's too late in the day to get a bed delivered, but I'll get a room set up for you tomorrow."

"Great," Danny said.

"You're upset," Ayanda said.

Danny opened her eyes and looked at Ayanda. "You think?"

"I wish I could tell you something that would make this easier."

"You could tell me why you would do this to me."

Ayanda nodded. "I suppose that's a fair question. I'm not sure you'll understand the answer. It's...I don't want to use the word destiny, because it makes it sound mystical, but it's not. Not really. You're just trapped in what humans called a Predestination Paradox. Long story short, you had to travel back in time, because you already had traveled back."

"So, what? The future is set?"

"The future isn't set," Ayanda said. "Not normally. The past is set. Unchangeable. But we're in a causality loop. Effectively, the moment you appeared here, everything that happened between that instant and the instant you left the future became the past. Fixed and unchangeable."

"That doesn't make any sense."

"Neither does time travel," Ayanda said. "I wish I could explain this better, but like I said, I'm a soldier. Temporal mechanics isn't my field any more than medicine. If I used my powers, I could look and see the loop. I've done it before. But just because I know loops like this exist doesn't mean I understand them any more than you do. Just...accept that there isn't any way you could have avoided this. There isn't any timeline where you traveled back for the first time, or where you didn't travel back. This loop is how the timeline has always unfolded."

Danny reached up and started rubbing her temples, trying to quell the headache she could feel starting.

"Maybe when you get home, I'll know more. Be able to explain things more clearly. I don't know."

"What was in the letter you sent? It had to be more than that."

"Things I need to know," Ayanda said. "She did request that I pass on a message though."

"What is it?"

"She said that she knows you're upset, but to please remember what she said to you this morning before the briefing, and to trust both of us."

Danny thought back to the moment she and her Ayanda had shared in the hall, to when their minds had touched, and she'd felt so much love coming from Ayanda. She thought of the way it filled her and surrounded her with warmth and made her feel so safe. She looked at the Ayanda in front of her, who felt none of those things.

She wanted to trust the Ayanda in the future, but there were so many questions that were unanswered, and this Ayanda was so different, but this Ayanda would become the one she knew, and the one she knew, the one she wanted to trust, was telling her to trust this version of herself.

She had to decide if she trusted future Ayanda enough to trust present Ayanda, but then, that's what it was, wasn't it? A decision. A choice.

Trust was a choice. And when she looked at Ayanda and remembered what it felt like to be loved by her, it was an easy one.

"Okay," she said. "So, where do we start?"

"How about dinner?" Ayanda asked. "I could order pizza."

"Always a good choice," she said. "Just no peanut butter, okay?"

For the first time since Danny arrived, Ayanda smiled, and Danny felt that familiar flutter in her heart.

Molly J. Bragg

Chapter Six

DANNY GLANCED OVER AT the clock as she took the plate out of the oven. She wasn't sure what time Ayanda actually left for the Marshal's station in the morning, but she'd always been there by the time Danny reported in around 8:00 AM, so she'd figured 7:00 AM was a good time to have breakfast on the table and coffee ready. She'd started a little early because she wasn't familiar with the kitchen and because she wasn't familiar with Ayanda's schedule, so she kept the hot food hot by sticking it in a low oven, and just set the cold food back in the fridge. When she heard Ayanda moving around in her bedroom, it seemed like starting early had been a good idea. She put the food on the table and was just pouring the coffee when Ayanda appeared out of her bedroom.

"What's this?" Ayanda asked.

"Breakfast," Danny said. "I don't know when the last time you went shopping was, but you're out of a lot of things. I'd have run to the store, but I don't have a key to get back in, I have no idea where the store is, and I only have twenty dollars, so I had to make do. I figured you'd be okay with everything bagels with peanut butter, and there were some canned pineapple chunks. Not as good as fresh, I know, but I put them in the freezer for a bit so at least they're cold. There's apple slices and grapes and a bit of sliced cheese too."

"You made me breakfast?" Ayanda asked with a confused expression on her face.

"Yeah," Danny said. "I always see you in the cafeteria in the morning grabbing a bagel and a fruit cup, and I just thought that since I don't have anything better to do..." She shrugged. "Come on, before the coffee gets cold."

Ayanda walked over to the table and sat down. Danny set a cup of coffee next to her.

"Two packs of swiss miss," she said as she took her own seat. "Be careful. The plate is hot." She picked up her own bagel, which just had a bit of butter on it, and took a bite. Ayanda watched her for a minute before picking up her own bagel and taking a bite.

"So, are you going to be at the Marshal's all day?" she asked.

"Yes," Ayanda said. "I called and made arrangements yesterday to take care of the furniture situation. A crew will be here around 11:00 AM. They'll pack up the room at the end of the hall and deliver a bedroom suite, clothes and shoes in your size, toiletries, and other items. A man named Carson will be with them. He'll have your door key. If you don't like any of the clothes, or would prefer different toiletries, or if there's anything else you need, just let him know. I'd prefer if you didn't leave the apartment today."

"Why not?" Danny asked.

"You have no ID," Ayanda said. "If something happened to you, no one would know who to contact. I'll have ID and other papers for you when I get home today. If you need to go out, you can do it tomorrow."

"How are you going to arrange that?"

"It's probably best if you don't know. That way you won't feel obligated to arrest me when you return to your own time."

"I see," Danny said.

"I would get you documents legally if I could, but you do not want the Marshals to know you're a time traveler."

"Yeah, I already figured that one out."

"Good. So you'll stay in?" Ayanda asked.

Danny nodded. "Yeah."

The two of them ate in silence for a few minutes, but as Ayanda was finishing up her fruit, another thought occurred to Danny.

"Could you get me a student ID for University of Florida Pontian?"

"That shouldn't be a problem. Would you like ones for Saint Pontian College and Suncoast University as well?"

"How are their academic libraries?" Danny asked.

"I don't know."

"Get them," Danny said. "Better to have and not need, than to need and not have."

Ayanda nodded. "Thank you for breakfast," she said as she started to gather up her plates.

"Leave it," Danny said. "I'll take care of it."

"Are you sure?"

"Yeah. I mean, YouTube won't exist for another fifteen years, so it's not like I've got anything else to do."

"YouTube?"

"Don't worry about it."

"I'll see you this evening," Ayanda said as she headed for the door.

Danny watched her go, then turned back to the remains of her breakfast.

"Well, that wasn't painfully awkward at all," she said as she stabbed a chunk of pineapple with her fork.

***

By the time the crew showed up at 11:00 AM, Danny was firmly of the opinion that the early 90s sucked. The reasons were numerous. First, there was no Wikipedia, so she couldn't even start digging into time travel theory. On top of that there was no lesbian romance section in the eBook stores, because eBook stores didn't exist yet. There was no YouTube, no Netflix, no way to watch her favorite movies or TV shows when she wanted, which was fine, because most of them hadn't been made yet. No Xbox, no PlayStation. She spent ten minutes looking for Xena reruns before she remembered Xena didn't exist yet. She couldn't even order what she wanted off the internet, because it would be twenty-two years before she was eighteen and could apply for a credit card. Not that that mattered, because online stores didn't fucking exist. She couldn't go to the range because she didn't have money, and oh yeah, two of the three guns she had were extremely illegal. There were no board games in the house, not that she had anyone to play with, but there wasn't even a deck of cards.

Nothing to distract her from the growing panic as it slowly sank in that this was real. That she was trapped thirty years in the past at the mercy of someone who didn't like her very much, and who definitely didn't want her there.

When she couldn't find anything else to do, she found a pen and a notepad and inventoried the kitchen, then wrote a grocery list and a list of missing cooking implements. It took a lot less time than she expected, so she sat down and started making other lists of things she would need if she was going to be in the past for eighteen months. Eventually, she couldn't think of anything else she might need and couldn't think of anything else to do to stave off a panic attack, so she took the dishes out of the cabinet and just started washing them to give herself something to do.

It didn't help. Washing dishes wasn't exactly the most mentally engaging task, so her mind had plenty of time to turn over the implications of being trapped in the past. Things like what would happen to her if the government found out, or what would happen if she missed her chance to go home. What would it be like to have to live through thirty years before she could see her mother and father and sisters again? What would it be like to turn up on her parents' doorstep thirty years older than she should be?

She was halfway through the pots and pans when another thought hit her. She'd been thrown back in time. She was Focus' roommate. The roommate she didn't want but had to take in because it was her fault Danny didn't have anywhere else to stay. Did that mean she was going to become Scatter? The timing would be right, since Scatter disappeared right around the time she was supposed to go home, but how would that even work? She didn't have any superpowers. She wasn't even a carrier of the metagene. Scatter was a Tier Three asset.

Maybe she wasn't Scatter. Maybe she was destined to watch Ayanda meet and fall in love with someone else. Just the thought of that made her sick to her stomach. She wasn't in love with Ayanda yet, but that sentence always ended with 'yet' in her heart. Somewhere along the line, she'd just accepted that she and Ayanda were inevitable, and the thought that they might not be was every bit as painful as the idea that it might be three decades before she saw her family again.

There was a knock on the door and Danny rushed out to answer it, not even bothering to check who it was before she opened it. At least if it was a Supervillain there to kill her, she'd have something to do other than worry about her situation. Unfortunately for her stress level, instead of a Supervillain, she found a man who screamed 'stern, disapproving English butler.'

"Hello," she said.

"Ms. Martin?" he asked.

"Yes."

"I'm Carson Winters. I was told you would be expecting me."

"Yeah. Um...come in." She stepped back out of the way, and Carson stepped inside. Seven large muscular guys, and one large muscular woman who reminded Danny of just how gay she was followed him. All of them were carrying boxes or other packing supplies. Behind them was a small man in an outfit that might as well have had 'Move, I'm gay' written on it, along with three women, all pulling rolling racks full of clothes. Two guys wearing tool belts that made them look like cable repair men pulling a rolling cart filled with shopping bags from Toys "R" Us came in next, and two women who looked mildly bored brought up the rear.

"My moving crew will pack up Ms. Robinson's meditation studio and load the items into the moving van to take them to storage. Once her things are in the van, they will bring up the new furniture and set up your bedroom. The electronics team will handle the installation of the video game consoles that Ms. Robinson requested. While they work, you will go through the selections the personal shoppers have made and decide which items meet your needs. Ms. Robinson did inform us that your taste in clothing would likely run towards the more utilitarian and less flamboyant, so selections were made with that in mind. I also have two runners with me who can make any purchases you need while we work."

"Um, sure," Danny said. "That's great. I actually got bored enough to make a grocery list, so maybe one of them could run to the store."

"Give me the list," Carson said. Danny grabbed the list off the table and handed it to him. He looked it over, and Danny could see the surprise on his face.

"This is adequate," he said, before looking up. "Is there anything else you need?"

"Well...um..."

"Ms. Martin, Ms. Robinson said that you would very likely express some degree of discomfort about requesting items that you need. She told me to remind you of what she said. That money is no object. She also told me to remind you that since she is at least partially responsible for your current predicament, that she would take it as a personal slight if you needed something and did not ask for it. So, I will ask again. Is there anything you need?"

Danny took a breath and nodded. "I'll need a cell phone and two computers. The most powerful desktop and portable computer you can find."

"I see. Do you want Apple, IBM compatible, Unix, or OS/2?"

"Um...Microsoft," Danny said.

"She means IBM compatible," one of the guys in the tool belts said.

"Right. What he said."

"Very well," Carson said. "Software and peripherals?"

Danny thought about it for a minute and turned to the tech guy who had spoken up. "You, come here."

He looked at Carson, and when Carson nodded, he came jogging over.

"What can I do for you, ma'am?"

"I'm guessing you know computers really well."

"Yes, ma'am."

"Okay, I'm going to give you a list of requirements, and you're going to tell Carson what his shoppers need to look for."

"Yes, ma'am."

"I need a desktop and a laptop. I need to be able to move data back and forth easily. I need a Graphic User Interface. I need a word processor, a spreadsheet, a relational database package, software to read and prepare LaTeX documents, I need to send and receive faxes, and if possible electronic mail. I'll need to be able to print documents, and if possible, scan them. Internet service if it's available in the area, with the fastest connection I can get. Also, instructions on how to use all of the hardware and software."

"Okay," the tech guy said. "Some of this is going to get a mite expensive, ma'am."

"I've been told that money is no object."

Tech guy nodded and turned to Carson, then started listing off hardware and software and all sorts of things that made no sense whatsoever to Danny, but he seemed to know what he was talking about, and she didn't have a lot of choice other than to trust him. Where she came from, Danny would have been able to walk into a store and pick out exactly what she needed and would know exactly how to use it. Here, she was about as computer literate as the average jellyfish.

She intended to change that. She intended to change a lot of things.

***

Danny was exhausted by the time Carson's crew left. She had everything she'd asked for. A computer set up that Bill Gates would probably envy, a flip phone because apparently those existed in 1991, even if it was the approximate size and weight of a boat anchor while folded up, plenty of clothes, even if fashion guy had kept asking her if her goal was to make sure everyone in the country knew she was a lesbian, and a kitchen full of groceries. She also had a Nintendo, a Sega Genesis, and a Gameboy, plus what she was pretty sure was every game that had been on the shelf in Toys "R" Us when the team had gone in to purchase the consoles. Something she hadn't asked for but was happy about.

She picked up the remote for the TV, fully intending to spend some time in the Mushroom Kingdom slaughtering Koopa Troopas, but when she turned it on, the first thing she saw was Focus. Not Ayanda as she'd left that morning, but Focus in full Superhero regalia. The white and blue uniform, the Ray diagram symbol on her chest. Blonde hair, blue eyes. Bruised and bleeding.

The caption on the screen read "Focus battles Supervillain Null."

It wasn't an accurate caption, because Focus wasn't just fighting one person. She was in the middle of a group that seemed intent on kicking the shit out of her. Focus wasn't just standing there and taking it, though. She was fighting back, using one opponent to block another from being able to hit her. It would have been a successful strategy if she had only been fighting two opponents, but she wasn't fighting two, but nine.

Danny watched helplessly as Focus dodged a shot to the head only to get punched in the kidneys. Or at least where the kidneys would be on a human. She thought maybe they were in the same place because Danny could attest that a kidney punch hurt like a bitch, and Focus screamed when she got hit. Danny clawed at her hip, reaching for the sidearm she wasn't wearing, and wondering where the hell Focus' backup was.

One of the goons stepped towards her, a huge knife in his hand, and Danny screamed, *Duck!* She felt a surge of surprise go through her, but Focus ducked and rolled, coming up facing the man with the knife. He lunged towards her, but she caught his wrist in her right hand and used her momentum to drive her left hand up into his elbow. He screamed as it bent the wrong way.

"Gun!" Danny snapped as another of the goons drew a pistol. She felt a hint of gratitude as Focus caught the falling knife. She turned and flung it, embedding the blade in the shoulder of the second goon's gun hand.

"On your right," Danny said. Focus kicked out to the right, her foot breaking the knee of a goon coming at her with a machete. She came to her feet, plucking the machete out of his hand as he fell. She reversed it and swung it, bringing the spine of the blade down on another goon's shoulder, snapping his collar bone.

"Behind you," Danny said. Focus spun and swung the machete again, smacking her next attacker across the face with the flat of the blade, sending him stumbling into one of his buddies. Both of them went down, and before they could get up, Focus turned to the last two goons and to Null himself.

Null pressed a button on some kind of arm band and vanished in a flash of blue light. The instant he was gone, the pain Danny didn't even realize she'd been feeling vanished as Focus's wounds closed up and the blood on her and her uniform vanished. Focus dropped the machete as she slowly lifted into the air. She pointed her palms at the last two standing goons, and energy beams knocked them back a good ten feet.

The caption on the screen changed from "Focus battles Supervillain Null" to "Supervillain Null escapes fight with Focus." Danny sat there, watching as the Marshals finally pulled up on scene. She tried to tamp down the anger she felt at them. Where the hell had they been when Focus needed them?

A flash of pain and loss went through her as the connection she felt to Focus broke. One second it was there, and the next it was gone, like someone had just flipped a switch. The pain only lasted for an instant, but the loss, the feeling that a part of herself was missing, that stuck with her as she watched the Marshals move in. Focus, for her part, drifted over to talk to a black man with a Marshal's badge on his belt, and a woman Danny was pretty sure was a younger version of Cecile. The conversation was short, and then Focus shot into the sky.

Danny stared at the screen for a moment, aching and empty, before she reached for the remote.

***

Danny was sitting on the couch playing Gameboy when she heard the key in the lock. Her first instinct was to jump up and rush to the door to make sure Ayanda was okay, but she stepped on it because she was mad. No, not mad. Mad was insufficient. Mad was 'I used the handwritten report you'd spent hours on as a coaster.' Danny was furious. She was furious because she'd watched someone she cared about nearly get eviscerated on live TV, and that person hadn't called, she hadn't come home, and she'd basically just slammed the door in Danny's face, even after Danny had probably saved her fucking life. So, no, she wasn't going to jump up and rush to the door like an overeager puppy.

The Gameboy hit the couch cushion when the sound of the deadbolt clicking open reached Danny's ears, and she raced across the apartment, anger be damned. She was a couple of steps away from the door when it opened, and she reached out and grabbed Ayanda, pulling her into a hug.

"Thank God," she said. She stepped back, holding Ayanda by the shoulders and looking her up and down. "Are you okay? Have all the wounds closed up? Did you go back to the station and let a doctor look at them?"

Ayanda pulled away from her with an annoyed expression and shut the door. "I'm fine," she said.

"You're fine?" Danny asked.

"Yes," she said as she locked the door. "I told you last night, I have the ability to heal myself. The wounds are gone. No doctor needed."

"Well, excuse me for being concerned when I saw you bleeding all over the fucking news."

Ayanda turned towards her. "That's how you saw what was happening?"

"Well, it wasn't because I was with the backup team that wasn't where the fuck they were supposed to be."

"They had to get through traffic. I got there faster because I flew."

"And it didn't occur to you to wait for backup?"

"I am backup," Ayanda said. "There were people in that building. They needed my help."

"So, you just walked into a situation where you didn't have your powers without backup?"

"Why do you think I didn't have my powers?"

"I don't know. Maybe the part where you were bleeding? Or the part where a bunch of guys you would normally be able to handle in your sleep nearly killed you?"

"I had the situation under control," Ayanda said.

"Under control? Bullshit. You were about two seconds from being gutted. If I hadn't warned you—"

"I didn't need your fucking warning!" Ayanda snapped.

"You could have fooled me."

Ayanda took a step towards her. "I didn't ask for you to be here, and I didn't ask for your help."

"Yes, you did," Danny said.

"What?"

"You set all of this up," Danny said. "You practically walked me over to that lever and told me to pull it. You gave me instructions on how to find you, and you told yourself to take me in and take care of me. You wanted me here and you wanted me to care about you. Maybe not right now, but you sure as hell wanted it thirty years from now, so yeah, you did. You asked for me to be here, and you asked for my help."

Ayanda shook her head. "Fine, believe what you want," she said. She stepped around Danny and headed towards the kitchen. Danny followed her.

"So, tell me about this Null," Danny said.

"You didn't read about him in some report or something?" Ayanda asked.

"No," she said. "I've never heard of him."

"He's some new Supervillain," Ayanda said. "Thinks he's hot shit because he's got a bunch of tech that helps him escape when he's cornered."

"He nullified your powers."

"You noticed that, huh?"

"I could feel it," Danny said.

Ayanda spun around and glared at Danny. "How?" she asked. "How did you get into my head?"

"How the fuck should I know?" Danny said. "You're the one who told me I'm an empath, but the only one I've ever been able to mind read is you."

"Empaths don't read minds. They sense emotions," Ayanda said.

"Thoughts, emotions. Whatever. The day we met your emotions hit me like a tidal wave."

"That was yesterday, and I was there," Ayanda said. "You're exaggerating."

"I'm not talking about yesterday. I'm talking about two months ago. Or, I guess, thirty years from now," Danny said. "Our eyes met, and I could feel everything you felt, and when you broke the connection, it was like having a piece of me ripped out. I would have fallen over if you hadn't caught me."

Ayanda stared at her for a moment, then shook her head. "You're still exaggerating," she said.

"No, I'm not," Danny said.

"You have to be," Ayanda said.

"Why do I have to be?"

"Because that kind of connection isn't something that happens between two people who just met. It's not possible."

"Well, it happened."

Ayanda stared at her for a minute, then turned away. "Just stay out of my head."

"I didn't mean to get into your head," Danny said. "When I saw you on the news and I saw the guy with the knife, I just...I panicked. I called out to you, but it was just instinct. I'm so used to being out in the field with you, I didn't even think about it. Not until I felt you react."

Ayanda went still for a moment, before asking, "You formed the connection accidently?"

"Yeah," Danny said.

Ayanda sighed and turned around to face Danny. "I'm sorry."

"For what?"

"I thought you'd made the connection on purpose," she said.

"I'm not even sure I can do it on purpose," she said. "I think I know how, but half the time when I tried, you didn't respond."

"Just don't try again," Ayanda said. "You can't keep connecting to my mind like that."

"Why not?"

"Because what you're doing isn't an empathic connection. It's something else, and the longer a connection like that is open, the harder it is to close."

"So, if it stays open too long..."

"You won't be able to close it at all," she said. "Neither of us will."

"Oh," Danny said. "But you said I was an empath."

"You are. You wouldn't be able to open a connection like that if you weren't, but empathy is a skill that can be used in a lot of different ways. It's like sewing. You can sew a pair of pants, or you can stitch a wound back together. The stitches are the same, but the difference is the material you're putting the stitches in. If you trained with your ability, you could reach out to another human and feel their emotions, and that would be an empathic connection, but I'm not human, the same way skin isn't cloth. If you sew up cloth, it will only hold together as long as the stitches are in place. If you sew up skin, the edges will grow together. Leave the stitches in long enough, and even when you take them out, the two pieces of skin have grown together, and you can't separate them without inflicting harm. You understand?"

"I think so," Danny said.

"Good," Ayanda said. She turned around and opened the refrigerator, and Danny saw her freeze again. "What is all of this?" she asked.

"I had Carson get groceries," Danny said. "And there's lasagna in the oven."

She turned around and looked at Danny. "You made me dinner?"

"Yes."

"But you were angry with me."

"I was upset because I care about you. I saw you get hurt, and you didn't let me know you were okay. And because I didn't understand why you broke the connection the way you did. I got angry because anger is easier for me to deal with than fear, but Aya...Kelly, I only wanted you to be safe. I care about you."

Ayanda was quiet for a minute. Danny could feel the weight of the moment, but she wasn't sure if she'd said the right thing or the wrong thing until Ayanda spoke.

"Eat with me?" Ayanda asked. Danny smiled so wide she was a little afraid she'd pulled a muscle in her face, but if she did, it was worth it.

"I'd love to."

Chapter Seven

DANNY WASN'T SURE EXACTLY when she started to differentiate between Ayanda, Focus, and Kelly in her head, but in the six weeks since she had arrived in the past, the differences had begun to define her life in unexpected ways. She had never thought of herself as the housewife type, but it had been surprisingly easy to fall into that sort of rhythm. She got up in the morning and made breakfast and ate it with Kelly Robinson, her unwilling roommate who ran hot and cold in unpredictable ways.

After Kelly left, Danny would wash the breakfast dishes, and Kelly was replaced with Focus. Focus was the Superhero who protected Pontian, and sometimes the world at large. Danny would sit down on the couch and crack open the computer manuals or the physics textbooks she was working her way through, or she would set up the stone slab that passed for a portable computer and read academic papers that mostly went over her head. But the whole time, she kept the TV on one of the local channels, praying that the news wouldn't cut in, or when it did, praying that it wouldn't be about Focus. It always was, because in 1991, Pontian didn't have the Ironclads or the Myrmidons or the Black Panthers, and the Champions, who maintained Tier One teams in almost every major city in the US, wouldn't be founded until 2005. Some days, when she'd gone through whatever physics book she was reading, or when she just needed a break from worrying about Focus, she'd make a run to one of the libraries, or to the campus bookstore, or the corner store, or the park a few blocks away, or sometimes just out to explore the neighborhood.

Around 4:00 or 5:00 PM, depending on what she was making, Danny would get up and start dinner, and sometime around 6:00 PM, she would hear the key in the lock, and she would fight back the urge to rush over to the door. Kelly would come in and they would eat. Sometimes they would talk, sometimes they wouldn't. Kelly would help her with the dishes, and then Danny would drop down on the couch and spend some time playing The Legend of Zelda, or Castlevania, or one of the Mario games. Sometimes Kelly would join her. Other times she would disappear into her bedroom.

Eventually, Danny would get tired and go to bed, where Ayanda was waiting for her. Ayanda was the woman she'd known in the future. The woman who ate lunch with her most days, who brought her gifts, who came to her apartment and made out with her on the couch and who held her and kissed her and loved her. Ayanda was who Focus was and who Kelly would become. She was the woman who haunted her dreams. She was the woman Danny wanted back.

The problem was, no matter how Danny might split them up in her mind, they were the same woman, just separated by time and experience, and her newfound empathic abilities seemed to know that. The longer she went without feeling the connection to Ayanda, the more she craved it. The more she craved it, the more she had to fight not to reach out when Kelly was close by, or when Focus was in danger. The more she had to fight it, the more frequent the trips to the library, the bookstore, the corner store, and the park became. They gave her a way to practice her empathy, to learn how to open up to people other than Ayanda, and to learn how to close off.

She was getting quite good at it, too. She knew the two girls who worked the reference desk at the main branch of the Pontian County Public Library were both pining for each other. The clerk at the corner store hated his job. The girl who worked the counter at the UFP Campus bookstore thought Danny was hot, and the woman who brought her kids to the park on Saturdays hated her husband.

It wasn't always pleasant, but the control she was learning was probably doing more to make her stay in the past tolerable than her attempts to teach herself temporal mechanics when the field barely existed as an academic discipline. At least, it was until she decided she wanted tacos from the little hole in the wall Mexican joint at the corner of Orange and Magnolia and walked right into the middle of a Supervillain fight.

The funny thing about it was, Danny was doing everything right. She was watching where she was going, she was checking for a tail, she was maintaining good situational awareness, and most of all, she was minding her own damn business when the van pulled up. She was right in front of the entrance to a little jewelry store that was on Orange between Cottonwood and Willow, and suddenly there were four guys with MAC-10s spilling out of a black panel van, along with some clown in a red three-piece suit with matching shoes, cane, domino mask, and porkpie.

"Who the fuck wears a fucking porkpie?" Danny asked as she reached into her pocket. She only realized she had said it out loud when the muzzles of the MAC-10s swung her way. She was a little torn between being worried about the amount of lead that was about to come her way, and being insulted that the pack of village idiots were actually going to try and kill her with MAC-10s. Between that and their boss' shitty costume, she was pretty sure it was amateur hour.

She pulled out her snap baton and extended it with a flick of her wrist as she stepped into the group. Normally, closing with a bunch of goons with guns would have been a spectacularly bad idea, but in this case, she was so close that getting closer actually made it harder for them to shoot her because it put the other members of their gang in the line of fire. Well, at least in theory. A theory which did kind of assume they cared about not shooting each other. Not necessarily a good theory, but it was what she had to work with.

Operating on the theory that Captain Porkpie was the biggest threat, and also on the theory that it was harder to use Superpowers when you were choking, Danny swung the snap baton into Captain Porkpie's throat. He staggered into the guy she'd designated Village Idiot number Two, sending them both to the ground. Danny smiled at her luck at getting a twofer, and spun, driving the end of her baton into Village Idiot number One's temple. He dropped like a sack of potatoes and Danny turned back to Idiots Three and Four, who were staring at her in shock. She drove a snap kick into Three's balls and grabbed his head as he fell, slamming it into her knee before throwing him aside to writhe on the ground, clutching a broken, bloody nose as his eyes swelled shut. Then she swung her baton again, slamming the round ball at the tip into Four's temple. He staggered, the MAC-10 falling from his hand as he reached up to clutch his head, but Danny wasn't done. She grabbed him by the collar and pulled him forward, slamming his head into the side of the panel van. This time, he collapsed, falling on top of a still gagging Captain Porkpie. By this time, Idiot Two was trying to get out from under Captain Porkpie, and now Idiot Four, so Danny stomped on his gun hand, the sound of breaking bones reassuring her that he wouldn't be a threat for at least a couple of minutes.

She turned and jumped into the van, using her momentum to slam the driver's head into the far side of the van, then she reached down and hit the buckle on his seatbelt. She grabbed him by the collar, and dragged him back out of the van, throwing him into the pile with the rest.

With Captain Porkpie and the village idiots out of commission for the moment, she leaned down and started picking up weapons. Four MAC-10s got tossed into the van, along with Porkpie's cane. That done, she looked down at the pile of bad guys at her feet after what couldn't have been more than ninety seconds and smiled.

"And that, assholes, is why you do not come into my town and try and start some shit."

"That was most efficient," someone said in a thick Welsh accent, and Danny felt a chill go down her spine. She turned towards the sound of the voice and saw an old man in wire-rimmed glasses and a suit that was probably fashionable around the time the Titanic sank. She could feel the rage pouring off of him, and if it had just been that she wouldn't have worried. After all, the guys had obviously arrived with the intent of either robbing him or doing him harm, but there was something distinctly inhuman about the way he felt through her empathic sense. He felt enormous and old and powerful.

"I suppose I should thank you. You probably saved me from having to repair quite a bit of damage to my shop."

Danny tried to smile, but she was sure it came across as pained and weak.

"So, I'm guessing Captain Porkpie here was the idiot trying to rub out a bigger, badder Supervillain?" Danny asked.

"Captain Porkpie?" the old man asked. He looked down at the man in question and Danny felt genuine amusement coming from him. "Oh, I see. Yes, very clever. Both descriptive, and at the same time, belittling." He looked up at her again. "I don't suppose you're in the market for a job?"

"Afraid not," Danny said. "I know the life expectancy of the average minion."

"Oh, I'm not a Supervillain, dear. I'm normally quite content to stick to legitimate business and tend to my own affairs. This isn't about Supervillain rivalry, as exciting as that would be. Rather, it's a simple case of extortion. The local mob looking for protection money."

"The mob doesn't usually send Supervillains and goons armed with submachine guns to squeeze senior citizens for protection money," Danny said.

"No," the old man said. "But then, we both know I'm not your average senior citizen, don't we?"

"I suppose we do."

"Now, are you sure I can't interest you in that job?"

"I'm afraid not."

"Ah well. A pity, truly. Good help is so hard to find."

"I don't suppose there's any chance you could go back into your store, and I could call the Marshals to haul away Captain Porkpie and the Village Idiots here?"

"I wish, my dear. Unfortunately, it was already far too late for that by the time you became involved. Captain Porkpie, as you call him, has challenged my authority, and I'm afraid I simply cannot allow that to go unanswered. However, as I said, I do owe you for keeping them from damaging my shop, so I will make you a counteroffer. Walk away and forget what you saw here, and I'll spare your life."

Danny sighed and shook her head. "This shit just had to happen on a Tuesday, didn't it?"

The old man tilted his head slightly, and she could feel his curiosity. "Why is that significant?"

"I was on my way to get tacos."

"Oh. Taco Tuesdays. Yes. That does seem to be a rather unfortunate happenstance. Last chance, my dear. Walk away."

"I appreciate the offer, but you and I both know that isn't happening."

"I had gathered as much, and I am sorry my dear. You seem like a lovely person." Danny believed he meant that, because she could feel both admiration and genuine regret coming from him.

"I like to think so," Danny said. "But not very smart, apparently."

"Sadly, no," he said. "But I will endeavor to make it both quick and painless."

"I should warn you I plan to go down kicking and screaming."

"I would expect nothing less. Shall we begin?"

Danny held up her baton. "Will this do me any good?"

"Not even a little bit, I'm afraid."

Danny knelt down and drove the tip of the baton against the ground, collapsing it. She slipped it into her pocket as she stood up and looked at the sky, hoping like hell she'd see Focus coming, but sadly, the sky was empty. She looked back down at the old man. "Day isn't getting any younger."

"Very true," he said. Then he took a deep breath and exhaled slowly, smoke pouring out of his mouth and his nose. Danny tried not to panic when she realized what she was seeing. She hoped she was mistaken, but as the smoke began to surround the old man, she looked up at the sign above the jewelry shop, and sure enough, there was a Welsh dragon right in front of the name of the place.

"Fuck. My. Life," Danny said as she turned and dove into the van. Once she was inside, she snatched up the object she'd mistaken for a cane and started looking for the button that had to be there. She hadn't found it when the screaming started. She turned and looked and saw the form in the smoke beginning to grow and change shape, and scrambled towards the back of the van, opening the rear door and stumbling out onto the street just as the dark shape in the smoke swung a claw at the van, sending it flying across the four-lane street to smash into a shop. Wings emerged, and gave a powerful down beat, the gust they created blowing Danny off her feet. She looked up into cat-like golden eyes and stared her death in the face as the dragon loomed over her.

"Today is not the day I die," she said, trying to convince herself more than the monster that was about to kill her.

"I'm afraid it is, my dear," the dragon said. He reared back, taking a breath, getting ready to breathe fire, and Danny rolled to the side, scrambling to her feet and running towards him. He was enormous, and if she could get under him, she might have time to figure out the weapon in her hand. She dove at the last second, hitting the ground and rolling as the dragon breathed a stream of fire right at the spot where she had been.

She came to her feet and took another look at the cane that she hoped wasn't just a cane. Surely Captain Porkpie wouldn't go after a dragon without a weapon that could kill a dragon, would he?

Okay, yes, he probably was that kind of dumbass, but God, she did not want to die before she got a chance to kiss Ayanda again. To feel Ayanda's hands tangling in her hair, and Ayanda's mind caressing hers.

The dragon moved, turning to look for her, and she ran, trying to stay with it, to keep under it, and wondering where the hell Ayanda was. Someone had to have called the Marshals about a fucking dragon in the middle of downtown.

He flapped its wings, lifting into the air, and Danny looked up, wondering how the fuck something that big could fly, much less hover like a hummingbird.

"A clever strategy," he said, and Danny could feel his admiration again. "Staying under me so I couldn't aim properly. You would have made an excellent servant, my dear. I am sorry."

"You're going to be sorry," Danny said.

"Goodbye," he said, and his regret washed over her. He took another deep breath and Danny did the same, and all at once, she felt someone there with her. A presence that was familiar, calming, and soothing. One that knew with absolute certainty what to do.

Danny raised her left arm, moving it as if it were being guided by a hand on her wrist, until it was in just the right place. She pushed with her mind, and felt power flow through the connection, up her arm, and out through her palm. When the fire came, it was caught in a perfect parabola and reflected back, washing over the dragon who breathed it out.

She threw aside the cane she'd been holding. Even if it was the dragon blade she suspected it was, she didn't need it anymore. Not as she lifted up off the ground. She flew forward so fast that the city around her blurred, and at just the right moment, she swung, power flowing up her right arm, making her right fist unbreakable and unstoppable as she punched the dragon right between the eyes. He was knocked back, right into the path of another figure, one in white, blue, and red who fell from the heavens like the hammer of God.

Focus slammed down on top of him, driving him to the ground. Before he could recover, Focus wrapped her arms around his neck, and shot up into the sky. Danny watched as the two fought. Focus dodged fire and claws and fangs and tail with ease. She struck the dragon again and again as the beast howled in rage.

There was more going on than physical combat. A battle of wills as much as a battle of blows. She couldn't hear what Focus was saying, but she could feel the moment victory came. The blows stopped and Focus and the dragon both turned and descended to the city street. He touched down, and the moment all four claws were on the ground, he turned into a cloud of smoke that vanished far faster than it should, leaving only the old man. Focus touched down beside him, and the two of them walked up to her.

Focus held out her hand, and the cane jumped up off the ground. Focus caught it in two hands, and brought it down across her knee, snapping it in two. The old man nodded and looked over at his shop.

"I will miss this place," he said.

"I am sorry, old father," Focus said.

"It's my own fault. She offered to let me walk away. I was too proud." He turned towards Danny. "I am glad I did not manage to kill you."

Danny was a little surprised to feel relief coming from him.

"That would make two of us," Danny said.

"I admit I underestimated you. Offering you a place as a servant was an insult. You would make a fine bride."

Danny did her best not to cringe at the thought, and at the desire she felt coming from him. She very deliberately shook her head. "I am honored, but I am also already spoken for," she said.

"Not yet," he said. "But I can see it in the works. Ah, well." He turned to Focus. "How long do I have to wait for these Marshals of yours?"

"Not long," Focus said. "I have your word. No mischief if I turn my back?"

"My word," he said.

Focus nodded, and took Danny by the arm, leading her halfway down the block.

"*What the hell*?" Focus asked. "You're fighting dragons?"

"Hey, I was just trying to get some tacos."

Focus glared at her for a moment, then shook her head. "You know what? I can't do this right now. Go home."

"Go home?" Danny asked. "That's it? Go home, like I'm some misbehaving child."

"No, go home like the Marshals will be here in less than five minutes, and if you're still here, after the shit you pulled, they will decide you're an unregistered metahuman, and register you right into a jail cell next to Eurion."

"Who?"

"The dragon," Focus said. She lifted her right hand and waved it, and Danny felt all the scrapes and bruises she'd gotten during her brief fight with the dragon vanish, and when she looked down, her outfit was clean and neat. "Now go home, before I send you."

Danny huffed and started walking in exactly the opposite direction from home.

"Where are you going?" Focus asked.

"Like I said. I want tacos."

***

The thing Danny always hated about acting like an ass to someone she cared about was the part where she felt guilty afterwards. She knew Ayanda had every right to be angry with her. She'd been dropped in her lap by her future self without so much as a please and thank you. Then she'd done exactly what Ayanda had told her not to do. She'd connected their minds. Yes, it had saved her life, but that wasn't the point. She didn't want a connection with her, and Danny had risked forging a permanent one after Ayanda had not only specifically told her not to do it, but made her fully aware of the consequences.

What's worse was that Danny had put herself in a position where she had to do it to save her life. She could have just let Captain Porkpie and the Village Idiots go into the store, and then taken out the very expensive cell phone she carried everywhere and called the fucking police, but no, she had to get involved. She had to play the fucking hero and wade into the middle of a fight she had no business getting involved with.

It was one thing to step into a fight like that when she was a Marshal. When she was wearing her badge, not only did she have the legal authority to do it, but she had a moral obligation to protect people. That was what it meant to wear the badge. That you protected people who couldn't protect themselves. You upheld the law and you brought criminals to justice.

But she wasn't a Marshal. Not here. Not now. She was a civilian, and she had every reason to stay off the Marshals' radar. If she got found out, if people discovered she was from the future, they might decide that since Ayanda was hiding her, she couldn't be trusted, and that would be disastrous. Focus was going to save the world more than once over the course of the next thirty years. Not to mention the fact that if people found out Danny was from the future, there was a good chance she'd never get to go home.

So, yeah, she shouldn't have gotten involved. She knew that. She'd still do it again, though. She hadn't known the owner of the store was a dragon. Hadn't had any idea that the people inside the store could protect themselves. And then, after she disabled Captain Porkpie and the Village Idiots, she couldn't just let them be slaughtered. Not when she'd been the one who rendered them unable to defend themselves.

Badge or no badge, she couldn't walk away from people who needed her help, but that didn't mean she couldn't have apologized and explained what happened. That didn't mean she had to be a smart ass. That didn't mean she couldn't have taken Ayanda's feelings into account.

She needed to apologize, something she'd never been particularly good at, but she was determined to at least try, so after she finished eating, she took a cab to Barnes & Noble, figuring there was less chance she could get into more trouble that way. Once she was there, she made her way to the cooking section. It took about half an hour for her to find what she needed, and once she had it, she called a cab, and called Carson, asking him to have a shopper pick some things up for her.

Then she spent the afternoon with two cookbooks spread out on the counter learning how to bake a peanut butter cheesecake with chocolate ganache icing to go with the satay curry chicken, raita, tzatziki, and naan she was making for dinner. She was mixing her cuisines, but she figured the satay would score more points than a butter chicken, and she wasn't a fan of mint, so the tzatziki was more for her than Ayanda. She just hoped that Ayanda wouldn't throw it all in her face.

She spent most of the afternoon thanking her mother for making her learn to cook. She'd hated it at the time, the same way she'd hated learning to sew, knit and crochet, and all the other girly things her mom had insisted she learn how to do. She'd learned to appreciate it, alongside the plumbing, carpentry, car repair, and other skills her mother had also insisted she learn. If she was honest, cooking was a lot more useful than any of those other skills, and she'd gotten to enjoy it over the years. Especially the way it always seemed to impress her girlfriends.

She'd never been more grateful that she could cook than she'd been the last few weeks. It was just about the only way she could figure out how to show Ayanda that she cared that didn't seem to make her uncomfortable. Although sometimes, she thought maybe even the cooking was a bit much for her, but Ayanda never said anything about it other than to thank her.

It came back to the division she'd made in her head, between Ayanda, Focus, and Kelly. She didn't know why Ayanda, the woman she'd known and cared for in the future, had been so open with her affection and emotions, and why Kelly, the woman she lived with in the past, ran so hot and cold. It was almost like Kelly was afraid of her, which didn't make any sense at all.

She gave up trying to figure it out when she heard the key in the lock, took off the apron she'd been wearing, and went out to greet her. She was a little surprised when the door opened slowly and Ayanda stepped inside, looking like she was braced for a fight. Something that made Danny feel sick to her stomach.

"Hey," she said.

"Hey," Ayanda said, and Danny could still feel the hesitancy in her voice, and knew she had to do something about it.

"Come on in and shut the door," she said. Ayanda looked like she'd rather go back out and fight another dragon, but she pushed the door closed and locked it, then turned back to Danny.

"I'm sorry," Danny said.

"What?"

"I'm sorry. I acted like an asshole today."

Ayanda shook her head. "You didn't," she said. "Eurion explained what happened, which he wouldn't have had to do if I had just listened to you."

"You were upset, and I had to be a jackass," Danny said. "If I had actually tried to explain instead of mouthing off like a fucking child—"

"I wouldn't have listened," Ayanda said. "I just...when you connected with me, and I felt how scared you were—"

"Hey, I wasn't scared," Danny said.

Ayanda's expression went from contrite to 'Are you fucking kidding me?' so fast Danny wondered if there was a bit of super speed involved. "You were fucking terrified!"

"I...yeah, okay. I mean, I guess I can admit that the dragon trying to roast me alive was a little scary."

Ayanda snorted, then promptly broke down laughing. "God, you're a fucking idiot."

"I would argue the point, but considering a couple of hours ago I got into a fist fight with a dragon, I'm pretty sure I'd lose."

"Yes, you would," Ayanda said. She took a step forward, and before Danny realized what was happening, she was pulled into a bone-crushing hug. "You scared the life out of me."

"I'm sorry," Danny said.

"When you connected with me and I felt how afraid you were, I was scared I would get there too late."

"I'm sorry. I didn't mean to do that. I know you said not to."

Ayanda pulled back and looked at her. "You didn't mean to?" she asked, and Danny could feel the anger in her voice. "What the hell were you going to do? Just wait and hope someone called it in?"

"Um...it sounds kind of stupid when you put it that way."

"That's because it's fucking idiotic!"

"I didn't want to connect again," Danny said. "I knew you'd be upset if I did."

Ayanda reached up and took a fist full of her hair in each hand. She closed her eyes and let out an incoherent scream that made Danny take a step back. When the scream was over, she let go of her hair and looked at Danny.

"You...Fucking...Idiot!" she growled, like it was physically painful for her to get the words out. "I told you not to connect because I don't want to form a permanent bond, not because I don't care if you live or fucking die. So, to be clear, in the future, if your life is in danger, you reach out and connect and you scream for me. Do you understand?"

"Yes," Danny said.

Ayanda shook her head.

"So...would now be a bad time to ask how you managed to do that thing where you took over my body?"

"I didn't," Ayanda said.

"What?"

"I didn't take over," she said. "I...your language doesn't have a word for it. The closest thing I can think of is 'mind meld.' I linked our consciousnesses so that you had access to all my power and skills."

"Is that what it's like to be a Focus?" Danny asked.

"It's more like the first step," Ayanda said. "You were still drawing power through the link. If you were a true Focus, I would have transferred the core of my power over to you. The skills don't transfer over the same way. Normally, in order for you to have access to them, we would have to stay linked."

"But if you didn't take over..."

"I didn't need to. Once you had access to my powers and skills, you knew what to do."

"Wait. Let me make sure I understand this. Our minds linked, you gave me access to your powers and skills, but I'm the one who decided to punch a dragon in the face."

Ayanda nodded. "Yep. That was all you."

"Good to know."

"Eurion was impressed."

"Great. That's...great. You seem to know him pretty well."

"He's a friend. I actually have a few friends among the dragons. They were still in hiding when I first arrived, but when I woke up back in the 70s, Ice Dragon had already had her big fight with The Imperial, so I sought a few of them out. I met Eurion when I went to get permission for one of my other friends to come into his territory to visit me."

"Oh," Danny said. "He did mention something about extortion and his authority being challenged."

"That sounds about right. A mob boss trying to squeeze a dragon would go down like a lead balloon."

"Is he going to come after me for not letting him roast Captain Porkpie and the Village Idiots?"

"No. In fact, he offered me your weight in gold to relinquish my claim."

"He what?"

"He wanted to buy you as his next bride," Ayanda said.

"He wanted to buy me as a wife?"

"He's old."

"How old?"

"I'm not sure. I know he was born in Wales before the Romans invaded Britain, so he's at least two thousand years old."

"What's he doing in Florida?"

"He migrated over in 1911. I think he knew a war was coming, and dragons hate wars. They tend to destroy too many shiny things."

"So, the hoarding thing...is that real?"

"Oh, yeah. That's what all of this was about."

"What do you mean?"

"Well, the guy in the red suit was Tony Ragusa. Son of—"

"Partinaci Ragusa," Danny said. "You're telling me I smacked Tony fucking Ragusa in the throat?"

"Yeah."

"Oh, God. I should have just let the dragon eat me."

"What? You're afraid of Tony?"

"He's only the biggest, meanest metahuman mob boss in the southeast."

"Not yet," Ayanda said.

"I need a drink," Danny said.

"Yeah, I could probably use one, too."

"I have some Cabernet Sauvignon breathing in the kitchen."

Ayanda gave her an odd look. "You made dinner, didn't you?"

"Yeah. Satay curry chicken."

Ayanda smiled. "What am I going to do when I send you home?"

Danny shrugged. "Buy stock in peanut butter?"

Molly J. Bragg

Chapter Eight

FOCUS WAS TECHNICALLY ON duty with the Marshals 24/7, but in practice, she was mostly on call. She flew a few laps around the city every day, but the reality was, Supervillain attacks were more likely on certain days of the week. Friday and Monday were the worst, statistically speaking. Lots of robberies. So, Focus was always at the Marshals' office those days. Saturday was bad in the mornings, though less so in 1991 than in 2021, because fewer banks were open on the weekends in '91. Supervillains loved robbing banks. Saturday evenings were bad for tech robberies because the labs the Supervillains wanted to hit were usually empty on weekends, but a lot of time Focus didn't get called for those because they were discovered Monday morning. Mondays and Wednesdays tended to be bad days for revenge rampages, too. Supervillains going after bosses who fired them, or regular people snapping from stress, developing psychokinetic powers, and deciding to level Tokyo. Or Pontian. Whichever was closer.

Sunday, Tuesday, and Thursday were usually pretty quiet, and much to Danny's surprise, after the dragon incident, Focus had started spending those days at home. She still kept her pager with her, and a Marshal-issued radio sat on the counter in a recharging cradle plugged into the wall. More than once, Focus had rushed off early Sunday to deal with some hung over meta busting up a diner or something similar. It was the same with Tuesdays and Thursdays, but unlike the other days of the week, she'd finish whatever it was and come back home.

Danny loved it, because they got to spend more time together. They talked about a lot of things. Dragons were one of the first topics of conversation. How they and the rest of the so called 'magical races' had gone into hiding after the Catholic Church had established the first Inquisition in 1184, and how Ice Dragon had revealed their existence to the world when a supervillain called "The Imperial" had tried to destroy Boston. After they'd exhausted that topic, they moved on to other Superheroes Ayanda had worked with over the last couple of years. They'd even talked about some of the other aliens living on Earth and working as Superheroes.

As much as she enjoyed it, there was a part of it that was incredibly frustrating. She still hadn't cracked the 'ice queen' shell that Ayanda wore most of the time. Ayanda always stayed firmly in her Kelly persona. She was always polite and friendly, but she never offered anything really personal. There weren't any more moments where their minds touched, and while Kelly was more than willing to help Danny learn how to use her empathic abilities, she skillfully redirected the conversation any time Danny asked about Ayanda's powers. It was the same any time Danny asked about Ayanda's planet or people or her past.

Danny didn't want to give up on her, though, so she filled the time by talking about her family. She talked about her mom and the cases she'd argued before the Supreme Court. She talked about her dad and all the time and energy he put into helping people as a public defender. She talked about Max's time volunteering with local community centers, and how Sam had gone from helping her high school buddies grow hydroponic pot in their basements to converting condemned warehouses into high tech urban farms to help eliminate food deserts in poor urban areas. When she ran out of things to say about her family, she talked about whatever came to mind. Books she'd read, movies and music she liked.

She mostly avoided talking about herself, the same way Ayanda did. It wasn't that she minded sharing anything about her past, but there was a small part of her that wanted Ayanda to ask her about it. It was a small thing, and she wondered if it was doing more harm than good. If part of the reason Ayanda wouldn't share anything about herself was because Danny wasn't either. Some days, she thought maybe she should just try sharing something from her own past, and seeing if it made a difference, but she didn't want to always be the one to give in and compromise what she wanted. She'd been down that route before, and it hadn't ended well at all. It was the reason she still got vaguely nauseated every time she saw an FBI badge.

Despite that determination to wait Ayanda out, when she climbed into the shower on a Tuesday morning about two months after what she'd come to think of as the 'dragon incident,' it was on her mind again. She'd arrived in the past in early June, and it was late September. Halloween decorations were filling the seasonal aisles in the grocery store, and she couldn't go into the drug store to buy a box of tampons without getting seduced by the siren call of mini-Snickers bars, which had meant more hours than she cared to think about in the apartment building's fitness center.

She wasn't sure which she was making less progress on, some days. Figuring out temporal mechanics or figuring out why Ayanda was keeping her at arm's length. She wasn't any closer to an answer on either front by the time she got out of the shower, but she did have other things to think about, at least for a few minutes. She ran through what was in the fridge, trying to decide what to make for breakfast as she got dressed, opting for a pair of shorts and a sports bra because Ayanda might be keeping her at arm's length, but she wasn't particularly good at hiding her appreciation of the extra time Danny had been putting in on the weight machines lately. It wasn't exactly what Danny wanted, but at least it reminded her that somewhere out there, in a future she was going to get back to, there was an Ayanda who definitely didn't want to keep her at arm's length.

She padded to the kitchen, humming a song that wouldn't be written for a quarter of a century by an artist who may or may not have been born yet. She'd just about decided on omelets and pancakes for breakfast when she heard music coming from the kitchen. She turned the corner and found Ayanda listening to The Unforgiven by Metallica as she dumped a huge spoon full of peanut butter into a bowl. Danny smiled and leaned against the door as she watched Ayanda pick up a whisk and stir the contents of the bowl for a couple of minutes. When she was done, she tossed the whisk and the peanut butter-covered spoon in the sink. Her timing seemed to be perfect, because the timer on the microwave went off, and Ayanda picked up a pair of tongs. She walked over to the stove, turned off the burner that was heating a small pot, and used the tongs to scoop noodles out of the pot and drop them into the bowl.

"Are you eating peanut butter and spaghetti?" Danny asked.

Ayanda jumped slightly, clearly unaware that Danny had been standing there watching her. She looked down at the bowl in her hand for a moment, then back up at Danny. "It's peanut sesame noodles," she said.

Danny straightened up and walked over to Ayanda. She looked down into the bowl. "I don't know. Looks like peanut butter and spaghetti to me."

Ayanda held up a finger. "Wait right there." She turned and opened the drawer where they kept the flatware, pulled out a pair of chopsticks, and used them to stir the noodles, getting them coated with the sauce, before she picked up some noodles and held them out to Danny.

"Go on," she said.

Danny didn't even think about it before she leaned forward and took a bite of the noodles. She slurped them up, a little shocked at how good they tasted. Nutty, a little sweet, nice and salty, with a hint of garlic, a bit tart, and finishing with a nice punch of ginger. She moaned a little at the taste as she swallowed. She looked up at Ayanda as she licked the sauce off her lips, and almost choked when she saw the way Ayanda was looking at her.

At her lips, specifically.

Danny couldn't stop herself from smiling, which made Ayanda swallow and look up at her. Their eyes locked, and Danny felt the connection snap into place. She also felt the tidal wave of raw, physical want that came with it. She took her lower lip between her teeth, biting down just a bit to try and ease the sudden ache she felt in places that hadn't been touched by anyone else's hands in far longer than she would have liked.

She didn't try too hard, though. She just needed to control herself for a moment. Just long enough to take the chopsticks out of Ayanda's hand and stick them into the bowl of noodles, then take the bowl and set it on the counter. She did it without looking away, more than a little afraid that breaking eye contact would break the spell that seemed to have filled the kitchen.

Once the bowl was on the counter, she moved her hands to Ayanda's hips, pulling her forward until their bodies were pressed together, then wrapping her arms around Ayanda's currently smaller frame. Ayanda tilted her head up, and Danny leaned down, covering Ayanda's lips with her own.

Danny had been kissed before. She'd even been kissed by Ayanda before, but this was different. The first two kisses they'd shared had been slow and gentle and soft, like she was the most precious thing in the world. They'd felt like coming home after a lifetime away. This kiss was desperate and needy, like what was happening could be ripped away at any second. There was fear in the kiss that made the need to sate the hunger that much stronger. Ayanda grabbed at her, pulling her close as she slipped her tongue into Danny's mouth. She clung to Danny as she slid her tongue over Danny's teeth and tongue. She dug her fingers into muscle and wrapped a leg around Danny's as she pulled them back against the counter.

Danny reached down, tugging Ayanda's shirt free of her pants, then slid her hands under it, running up soft skin that was stretched over hard muscle. She whimpered as Ayanda pressed a thigh between her legs. She wondered if she should stop it, because they were both lost in the emotions that were pouring back and forth through the link. Desire, need, lust, loneliness, and something else that Danny recognized but wasn't quite ready to name.

Ayanda rolled her hips and any thought of stopping what was happening went out the window as something base and animal took over. Something that said this was right, that this was how it was supposed to be. Ayanda nipped at her bottom lip and Danny could have sworn she felt fangs raking along her skin. She heard something that sounded like rustling leather, but she didn't care. Ayanda was all she wanted, all she needed. Ayanda was the only thing that mattered.

Ayanda was hers. Only hers. And she was Ayanda's. They belonged to each other. They belonged together. The rightness of it overwhelmed her as she lifted her up onto the counter. She couldn't understand why they had waited to do this, why they hadn't done this that first day. They were made for each other.

She whimpered when Ayanda broke the kiss and chased her lips, but a strong hand was there, turning her head to the side, and then Ayanda was kissing her jawline. She heard the rustle of leather again and felt needle sharp teeth scraping over her skin, and all she could do was turn her head to give Ayanda better access.

"Yes," she moaned, not knowing or caring what she was saying yes to.

"You're mine!" The words tore through her like a crack of thunder, shaking her bones and rattling her teeth.

"Yes," she said.

The noise tore through both of them, a rhythm beating against the connection and breaking whatever spell they were under. Over and over again, it drove into Danny's brain like an ice pick. She tried to cling to Ayanda, but want and need were replaced with shame and horror. She was shoved away from what she wanted as half of her was violently ripped away.

She fell, like she had that first day, but this time, there were no strong arms to catch her, no blue eyes peering into her soul, no pillow soft lips smiling down at her, making promises she wanted to beg them to keep. She hit the hard, cold tile of the kitchen floor, and looked up to see Ayanda staring down at her in pure, unadulterated terror.

The sound came again, and they both recognized it. The pager. Kelly disappeared, replaced by Focus, and Danny wanted to beg her to stop, to wait, but she couldn't. Not when it might mean lives. Focus reached over and grabbed the radio out of its charging cradle. Danny heard her talk and heard the response, but she didn't understand them. It was all so much gibberish, but whatever the gibberish was, it must have made sense to Focus, because she clipped the radio to her belt and walked right through the sink and the wall behind it like neither one existed.

Danny lay back on the kitchen floor, trying desperately to staunch the bleeding in her soul.

***

Apparently, the collapse of the Soviet Union started on a Saturday. Who knew? Oh, Danny was sure some historians knew, and it was probably on Wikipedia once Earth actually developed civilization and things like the fucking internet, but poor Deputy US Marshals who got their asses tossed into the past, not so much. Honestly, she only cared because four days after the Armenians decided to up and declare independence from the Soviet Union, some dumb son of a bitch decided it would be a great idea to cut the power feed to the Armenian Supermax prison. The results were about what you would expect if someone suddenly freed a few hundred Supervillains in southwest Asia.

A complete clusterfuck for the whole fucking world.

Superheroes from all over the world were called in to respond, and the ones who did respond were the ones who could move fast and handle just about anything a Supervillain could throw at them. In other words, Tier Three assets. Heroes like Focus, The Gentleman, Clockwork, The Alchemist, Weatherman, Dark Fire, Cú Chulainn, Silver Knight, Nightbird, Avatar, and Tomoe. With so many of the heavy hitters out of place, the local Supervillains had a field day. No one wanted to pull back their heroes until the crisis was over. Not once it became clear that the Soviet Union would not release any of its metahumans to deal with the crisis they had created. And especially once people realized Chernobog had been imprisoned in the Armenian facility and was one of the Supervillains who got loose.

So for two weeks, Danny didn't see Ayanda except on the news. She slept poorly. She barely ate, and when she did, she didn't always keep it down. She did everything in her power to keep her own empathic abilities locked down tight to keep from distracting Ayanda, but the feeling that she'd been torn in half and the pain and nausea that went with it faded slowly.

Focus, The Gentleman, Tomoe, and Dark Fire cornered Chernobog. By the time the fight was over, The Gentleman had lost an eye, earning the eyepatch that would become something of a trademark of his by the time Danny was old enough to give a crap about Superheroes, Dark Fire had to be medivacked to a hospital in Germany for emergency surgery, a small town, which had thankfully been evacuated, had been wiped off the map, and Danny was a nervous wreck.

The good news was that Chernobog was the last of the escapees, so once he was back in containment, the heroes were free to go home. Danny hoped—hell, she practically prayed—that Ayanda would come home quickly, but she didn't. Chernobog was captured at around 4:30 PM Eastern time on Wednesday, October 9th. It was 11:00 AM on Friday, October 11th before Danny heard the key in the lock.

She was up off the couch and on her way to the door before the sound even fully registered in her conscious mind. The relief that flooded through her when she saw Ayanda come through the door felt like a massive weight lifted off her chest. She just barely caught herself before she reopened the empathic connection.

"Thank God," she said as she reached out to pull Ayanda into a hug, but Ayanda stepped back.

"Please don't," Ayanda said.

Danny stopped and lowered her arms. "Is something wrong?"

"Yes," Ayanda said.

"Is this about what happened before you left?"

"It is," Ayanda said. "I owe you an apology."

"I'm honestly not even sure what happened," Danny said. "What I felt was—"

"Was something you should never have felt," Ayanda said. "And I apologize. It's my fault."

"Your fault?" Danny asked. "I'm pretty sure I kissed you."

"Only because I let myself become confused about what our arrangement is," Ayanda said. "Again, I apologize. I'm your guardian while you are trapped in this time. All I can say for myself is that I've been alone for a very long time. That's not intended to be an excuse, only an explanation. My people are not meant to live solitary lives. It's not in our nature.

"I told you that when my people made their sacrifice to turn me into what I am, it was not intended that I would survive the battle I was created to fight. I was at peace with that because it meant I wouldn't have to be alone, but I survived the battle, and while I am glad that it has afforded me the opportunity to aid your people, I do pay a price for my survival.

"I told you that a prolonged mental connection could lead to a permanent one, and that's what almost happened that day. When my people take a mate, it's not just a physical or social act. Our psionic abilities are as much a part of us as our eyes, ears, and fingers. We connect with our mates. We form permanent mental links. It tethers us, stabilizes us, sustains us. My people don't survive much past thirty or so of your years unless they take a mate. Loneliness quite literally kills us. I am two hundred and thirty of your years old, and I've never taken a mate.

"You have a number of qualities that make you attractive to me. You're smart, you're kind, you're brave, you're beautiful. I admit that I find you incredibly desirable for all of those reasons and more. I've tried my best to check that, and be what I should be to you, but when you offered yourself so willingly, my attraction to you and my desire to ease the loneliness I feel broke my resolve. I let myself reach out to you, and I got caught up in the moment. I connected to you.

"I never intended for it to be a full mating bond, but my control has been wearing thin since you arrived. Each time you've touched my mind, it's made it harder to resist my baser impulses, and when I felt my own desire reflected in you, I very nearly did something irreparable. Something you didn't know about or want. If we hadn't been interrupted, I would have created a permanent connection with you without your consent. I'm sorry."

"Don't be," Danny said.

"What?"

"Ayanda, I might not have understood exactly what was happening, but even if I had, it wouldn't change anything."

"Then you still don't understand what I'm telling you," Ayanda said.

"Yes, I do," Danny said. "You're talking about forever, or at least as close to it as I can manage. I know that I won't live as long as you, but spending my life with you...that's what I want. I think that's what I wanted since the day I met you, since our minds touched for the first time. All I've been able to think of while you were gone is how much I wanted what was happening, and how much I wanted you to come back so we could finish what we started, and how afraid I was that I had pushed you into something you didn't want. But if you want it too, then I am telling you that I am more than willing."

Ayanda shook her head. "What you felt in that moment was what I wanted. My needs, my desires. I pushed them on you. You still feel them because the link wasn't severed cleanly. When I realized what I was doing to you, I broke it too quickly."

"No," Danny said, shaking her head.

"You've been having trouble sleeping and eating, having trouble keeping food down when you can eat. Tremors, cold sweats, cramps, and headaches, haven't you?"

"Yes," Danny said. "It's the stress."

"No. It's the broken link. The symptoms will fade soon."

"I'll still want this."

Ayanda looked at her, and Danny could see the pity in her eyes. "You think you want this, but you have no idea what it is you're asking for. You look at me and you see a human. You see Kelly, or you see Focus, but you don't see me. You know I'm an alien, but you don't understand it. I am not what you see when you look at me."

"Then show me. Please. Let me in. Let me see the real you, so I can show you that I do want you. All of you."

Ayanda shook her head. "I think it would be best if we limited our contact," she said. "I will still act as your guardian while you are here in the past. You are still welcome in my home. If you need anything, feel free to ask, but no more physical contact, and we should minimize social contact. The kitchen is yours. I'll take my meals elsewhere, and otherwise, I will try to stay out of your way until it is time to send you home. Now, it has been a long two weeks and I need to rest. If you will excuse me, Deputy Marshal Martin."

Danny felt the use of her title like a physical blow, and she recoiled from it. Ayanda started to step around her, but as much as she hurt in that moment, she couldn't let this happen.

"Ayanda…" she said.

Ayanda stopped and looked at her. "Please, don't use that name," she said. "Call me Kelly, or Ms. Robinson, or Focus. That name is not yours to use."

Danny stared at Ayanda as she started towards her bedroom, unable to find any answer to what Ayanda had just said. She could only watch helplessly as Ayanda…as Kelly disappeared into her bedroom, leaving nothing but pain in her wake.

Molly J. Bragg

Chapter Nine

DANNY HAD NEVER been into the lesbian bar scene. It had been more Claire's thing when they were dating. Amber had been into it as well, though she tended to prefer bars that were a bit more subdued than the ones Claire picked. Danny, on the other hand, had always found them to be a bit of an awkward experience. Between her tendency to turn into a gibbering idiot around women she found attractive, and the meat market atmosphere of a lot of the bars, it was usually a painful experience.

It took about three weeks of "limiting their contact" before Danny had been driven out of the apartment, and The Wild Orchid had seemed like the best option. There was no chance of a man bothering her, and the place was divided into an old-fashioned pub on one side, and a nightclub on the other. The meat market atmosphere tended to stay on the nightclub side, and in the month and half that she'd been going there, she had only seen one or two hookups on the pub side. By and large, people left her alone.

Of course, some of that may have been her demeanor. She had to admit she was radiating a good amount of 'fuck off and die' vibes. She barely needed her empathic abilities to feel the concern radiating off the bartender, but thankfully, the woman never said anything. Danny suspected that was because she only ever ordered a single shot when she first got there and spent most of the night drowning her sorrows in three-dollar glasses of coke.

She honestly wasn't sure if she was glad her mood was keeping people away or not. Most days, she did genuinely just want to be left alone, but there were days when she wondered if slipping over to the meat market side of the bar and making a bad life choice or three would make what was happening hurt less. 'Trust her,' future Ayanda had said, but present Kelly didn't seem to get the memo, and now Danny was alone. She couldn't even call and cry to her mom or bitch to her sisters.

She could never quite talk herself into going home with someone, though. She wasn't sure why. She'd never made any kind of commitment to Ayanda in the future, and Kelly had made it perfectly clear she wouldn't accept the commitment Danny had offered in the present, but when she did think about it, it felt too much like cheating. So instead, every night she came here and took a shot of whiskey, then spent hours drinking overpriced coke. Some nights, she spent her time scribbling equations in notebooks. Others, she just stared into her drink, wondering if she was going to be able to last the year she had left before she could go home.

This was a 'staring into the drink' night. Focus had been in a fight that afternoon, and while normally that wouldn't have been a big deal, the fight had been her, Weatherman, and Clockwork against Deathscream and Bloodfeud. Deathscream and Bloodfeud were legends. Danny had read their files because they were required reading.

Bloodfeud was a hydrokinetic who had taught herself to manipulate the blood of living beings. She loved ripping blood out of civvies and turning it into weapons to use against the police and responding Supers, and she had wiped out entire teams before. Deathscream had sonic powers. He could use them to do everything from shattering glass to pulverizing concrete to liquifying his enemies.

Clockwork was a good choice to fight Bloodfeud since he was a human consciousness housed in an android body. There wasn't any blood for Bloodfeud to manipulate. Weatherman's ability to control the wind allowed him to deflect Deathscream's sonic attacks easily enough. And Focus was Focus. The nearly untouchable embodiment of heroism and justice.

None of that stopped Danny from being afraid. Knowing Ayanda would survive the fight, knowing she would be perfectly fine in the future where they met didn't keep Danny from sitting there, clutching a cushion in a white knuckled grip as she watched the fight play out on CNN. It hadn't kept her heart from stopping when Deathscream had gotten in a lucky shot and blown her through a building.

When Ayanda…when Kelly had walked through the door that night like nothing had happened and ignored the look Danny had given her, it had been too much. She hadn't even had dinner before she'd grabbed her jacket and cell phone and walked out the door.

She was about to order another coke when she heard the sound of something being set on the table. She glanced over and saw another coke sitting there.

"You look like you're almost empty," someone said. Danny looked up from the drink and froze. The woman in front of her obviously misinterpreted Danny's reaction, because the smile on her face was replaced with a smug grin.

"I'm Cecile, by the way."

"Cecile La Saint," Danny said. "I know."

The smug grin faded a little. "Have we met before?"

Danny laughed, because it was either that or cry, because of course she would run into Cecile in a lesbian bar.

"Did I say something funny?"

Danny shook her head. "We have met before, though I don't reckon you'd remember it."

"Are you sure? Because I don't usually forget a woman who looks as good as you."

"I'm sure. It's Danny, by the way." She gestured to the seat on the other side of the booth. "Please, sit."

Cecile slid into the booth. "Where did we meet?"

"Doesn't matter," Danny said. She pushed her empty glass aside and reached for the one Cecile brought her. "I wouldn't normally touch a drink brought to me by someone other than a waitress or a bartender, but if I can't trust a Deputy US Marshal, who can I trust?"

"You seem to remember a lot about me," Cecile said.

"A lifetime ago and way too many years from now, you were a lead in an investigation I was working. Not much help, though."

"You're on the job?"

"Used to be," Danny said. "Fugitive retrieval for most of my career."

"How long?"

"Four years," Danny said.

"What happened?" Cecile asked.

"Ran into a Supervillain on the job. Grabbed the wrong end of some machine," Danny said. "When I woke up, I found out I'd been pretty effectively benched."

"Shit. That sucks."

"You have no idea," Danny said. "I'm told the effects will wear off in another year or so."

"Well, that's good news."

"To good news," Danny said. She held up her glass, and Cecile tapped it with her bottle of beer.

"To good news."

Danny took a sip of her drink and waited while Cecile did the same. "How's babysitting a Superhero treating you?"

Cecile frowned. "You know about that?"

"You were on the news about six months back. The day Focus fought Null. I recognized you."

"After one meeting?"

"I said you weren't much help. I didn't say you didn't make an impression."

"Damn. Now I wish I could remember meeting you."

"I wouldn't worry too much about it," Danny said. She leaned forward, whispering conspiratorially. "I'm already taken."

Cecile's face fell. "Oh," she said. "I'm sorry. Lisa...the bartender said you always come in alone."

"Lisa would be correct," Danny said.

"Oh, dear. I'm sensing Lesbian Drama," Cecile said.

"You are, indeed," Danny said.

Cecile leaned forward. "Is it juicy?"

Danny frowned as she thought about it. "You know, I'm so deep in it, I can't even tell anymore."

"Well, tell Auntie Cecile about it and I'll judge."

Danny leaned back and thought about it for a minute, trying to figure out how to frame it without mentioning the time travel shenanigans. It didn't actually take as long as it should have, which was kind of sad.

"So, I met this girl. The kind of girl you dream of. Smart, funny, beautiful, kind. She seemed to have a thing for me. We had lunch together all the time. She was flirty. There were even a couple of kisses."

"Good ones?"

"Oh, yeah. The kind of kisses that make the Earth move."

"Sounds good so far."

"Yeah. I was into it. Really into it."

"So, when did the drama start?"

"When I ran into the Supervillain," Danny said. "She offered to let me stay with her while I recovered."

"I'm guessing you two don't make good roommates?"

"No, that's not it. I mean, when I moved in, things were a bit weird. She kind of runs hot and cold. One minute I think I'm making progress, and the next it's like talking to a wall, but then, a few months ago, I get out of the shower and I walk in on her making breakfast. She offers me a bit of her food, and the next thing I know, I've got her up on the counter and we're tearing each other's clothes off, and I'm thinking maybe I've finally gotten past whatever was holding her back."

"But?"

"But then her fucking pager goes off. It's like someone dumped ice water over both of us. She has to rush off on an emergency business trip, and when she gets back, she's got it in her head that she was taking advantage of me, and she's gone all stiff and formal. She won't eat with me, won't even talk to me, and I'm just...I don't know what to do."

"Fuck," Cecile said. "Man, that is some fucked up bullshit."

"Tell me about it."

"How the hell did she go from 'Let's tear each other's clothes off and fuck on the kitchen counter' to 'I'm taking advantage of you'?"

"I don't know," Danny said. "I mean, she's older, but it's not like I'm a teenager or something."

"Nope," Cecile said. "Definitely not a teenager."

Danny smiled. "Well, if nothing else, you're good for my ego."

"I could be good for a lot of things," Cecile said.

For a second, Danny expected to have a bit of a gay meltdown, the way she usually did whenever someone started flirting with her, but oddly, the meltdown never came. Instead, she just shrugged and said, "You probably could be."

"Damn," Cecile said. "That stung."

"Sorry."

"Nah. I get it. It sounds like this girl had you twisted in knots."

"If she was a girl scout, she'd have definitely earned the knot tying merit badge."

"Sounds like she'd also pick up her 'Lesbian Overprocessing' merit badge."

"I forget. Is there one for surviving the Lesbian Drama?"

"I think they were talking about adding it, but it got held up in committee when the chairwoman broke up with the vice president of cookie sales."

Danny laughed. "God, I didn't expect you to be funny."

"Why not?"

"You just seemed like the serious type when we talked before," Danny said.

"Well, if it was work related, I try to be professional. Even if the people I work with act like pouty five-year-old's."

Danny caught the frustration in Cecile's voice, and did her best to hide the spike of worry she felt. "Trouble with your Superhero?" she asked, doing her best to make it sound like idle curiosity. She took a sip of her drink, using it to cover doing something she hadn't dared do since

Ayanda had given her the 'limit our contact' speech. She opened up her empathic senses and reached out across the table, carefully taking measure of Cecile's feelings. She felt a bit of panic as Cecile realized what she'd let slip, mixed in with a whole lot of worry and frustration.

"No," Cecile lied. Danny could feel the lie. "Just one of my other co-workers."

"What are they doing?" Danny asked.

Cecile looked down into her beer for a minute, and Danny could feel the swirl of emotions. Protectiveness, worry, fear. She could also feel the desire to talk about it.

"There's this Marshal I work with," Cecile said. "She's really private. Never talks about her life outside of work, you know."

"I've known a few like that," Danny said.

"The thing is, normally, nothing fazes her. She's rock solid. I've seen her deal with things that had Marshals who'd been on the job twenty years puking their guts out without so much as a flinch, but the last few weeks, something has been off."

"How so?"

"She's been distracted. When we're out in the field or at a briefing, she's fine. Solid as ever. But when there's downtime, it's like she's a million miles away. There's been other behavioral changes too. We've worked together for two years, and for most of it, she was at the station every day. Not always all day, but she at least put in an appearance. Then, a few months back, she stopped coming in on her days off unless she got called in. For the first time since I met her, she actually seemed happy. She'd come in smiling in the morning, and when she was on her way out in the evening there was a spring in her step and a big smile on her face. I thought maybe she was seeing someone or something, but then everything just fell apart. It was like one day, she was happy, and the next all the life had gone out of her."

"Maybe she got dumped," Danny suggested, knowing damn well what had actually happened.

"That's what I thought, too," Cecile said. "I mean, I couldn't see anyone in their right mind dumping this woman, but stranger things have happened."

"Did you ask her about it?"

"Yeah," Cecile said. "She said that nothing was wrong. I tried to push, but when I did, she just apologized and said that she was sorry if her private life had been affecting her work performance, and it wouldn't happen again."

"Jesus," Danny said.

"Yeah. I mean, I try not to pry. Like I said, she's a private person, but I worry."

"Sounds like you're a good friend," Danny said.

"I don't know about that. I don't think she's let me close enough to be a friend."

Danny frowned, because this wasn't right. Cecile was Ayanda's friend. They were close. At least in the future they were. If they weren't now, that needed to change, because even if Ayanda didn't want to be with her, Danny didn't want Ayanda to be alone.

"Doesn't mean you should stop trying," she said.

"I don't know. Maybe it does. Maybe she doesn't want any friends."

"Or maybe she's just afraid," Danny said.

"Of what?"

"Sometimes, when people have really horrible things in their past, they're afraid to let anyone in. They're more afraid of the damage other people can do to them than they are of loneliness, even if the loneliness is killing them."

"How do you get past something like that?" Cecile asked.

"I'll let you know if I figure it out," Danny said.

***

"I don't know what to do," Ayanda said.

Danny froze when she heard the words. She'd come home from the bar earlier than expected. She and Cecile had been hanging out together pretty regularly since their initial run in a couple of weeks earlier, but Christmas was in two days and Cecile, unlike Danny, did have other friends and people she wanted to spend time with. Danny had wished her well and headed home, expecting to spend the next few days alone and miserable, wishing more than anything that she could go home and see her mom. She hadn't expected to come home and find Ayanda talking to someone.

"You could stop being an idiot," a lightly accented woman's voice said. It wasn't a voice Danny recognized.

"I'm trying to protect her," Ayanda said.

"Like I said, you're being an idiot," the other voice said. "She may be younger than you, but she's not a child."

"I never said she's a child. I said—"

"You said you don't respect her enough to honor her decisions."

"Jia Li—" Ayanda said, and Danny clamped down on her empathic senses to make sure Ayanda couldn't feel her shock. Ayanda was talking to Ice Dragon! Danny had to swallow the urge to run into the room just to see her.

"Am I wrong?" Jia Li asked.

"It's not that simple."

"It is," Jia Li said. "Or do you think I took my brides without making them aware of the consequences of their choice?"

"No! Of course not!"

"Or perhaps you think that because of what I am, I loved them less than you would love your human."

"No," Ayanda said.

"I have faced the same choice you have many times," Jia Li said. "Each time, I loved them, and each time, I knew what loving me would cost them. I respected them enough to give them the choice. I have made the offer thirteen times, and eleven of those times, the woman accepted. Eleven of those times they bound themselves to me as my bride. Eleven times, I asked them, at the end, if they had any regrets, and not one of them said yes. Not one of them would take it back."

"This is different," Ayanda said.

"How?" Jia Li asked.

"Because she doesn't know what I am."

"Then show her."

There was silence, and Danny wondered for a moment if they'd realized she was there, but then she heard Ayanda speak in a very small voice.

"I can't," Ayanda said.

"Why not?"

"Because I don't think I could stand it if she looked at me with fear in her eyes."

"Oh, child," Jia Li said. "This is worse than I thought."

"How could it be worse?"

"Because you already love her."

"No!" Ayanda said. "No, I—"

Jia Li snorted derisively. "Stupid child. Lie to her. Lie to yourself. Do not lie to Bīng lóng."

Ayanda chuckled. "Oh, God. Now I've done it. You're talking about yourself in the third person."

"If it makes you realize how stupid you are being."

"What if I show her, and she hates me?"

"Then she is not the person you believe her to be, but I do not think that will happen."

"Why not?"

"Because if she was, you would have warned yourself."

"Not if it would break the timeline."

"There is no timeline to break," Jia Li said. "Time is not set because of some law of the universe. Time is set because character is set. The loop will unfold the way it always has because you will always be Ayanda, and she will always be Danny Martin. That is why I am not worried. The loop will end with the two of you together, because the loop began with the two of you together. You can fight it all you wish, but she is your destiny."

"Then why didn't I tell myself that in the letter?"

"Because even thirty years is not enough time for you to stop being a stubborn fool," Jia Li said. "What time is it?"

"It's about ten to seven," Ayanda said.

"Then it's time I go. If I'm not at the Council, the other dragons might do something stupid."

"Why do you say that?"

"They are upset that the Marshals are making Eurion move his den."

"The Marshals wouldn't have to make him move his den if he hadn't decided to reveal his true form in broad daylight and tried to kill six people. He's lucky they didn't chain him up in his den."

"A fact I mean to remind them of," Jia Li said. "Even if it will make them sulk. They hate being reminded that they are no longer the masters of this world."

"Good luck," Ayanda said.

"Walk me out," Jia Li said.

Danny realized she was about to get caught eavesdropping, quickly backed out of the door, locked it as quietly as she could, and jogged halfway back to the elevator, then turned around and walked back to the door at a normal pace. Just as she was about to reach the door again, it opened and Ayanda and a middle-aged Chinese woman stepped out into the hall, and Danny realized she was right. It was definitely Ice Dragon, who would be every bit the gay icon that Ayanda was in the future.

Danny's excitement at seeing Ice Dragon was short-lived though, because the moment Ayanda spotted Danny, she stiffened.

"Is this her?" Jia Li asked.

"Yes," Ayanda said.

Danny looked back and forth between them.

"Danny, this is my friend, Jia Li. She's from Boston. She was just in town for the day and dropped by for a few minutes to visit. Jia Li, this is my roommate, Danny Martin."

Jia Li bowed slightly. "A pleasure. I am sorry we must cut our meeting short."

"Me too," Danny said. "Kelly never introduces me to any of her friends."

Jia Li smiled, and Danny could swear she could see the mischief in her eyes. "Perhaps she's afraid one of her friends will steal you away. I'm told Eurion made quite the offer."

"He did," Danny said.

Jia Li slowly looked her over, head to toe. Danny wasn't sure what it was about the way Jia Li looked at her, but she had to fight the urge to look down and make sure she was still dressed.

"I would double it, if I thought our friend would accept."

"Why do you dragons keep offering her the gold?"

"Because, contrary to legend, we are not thieves. We pay for the precious things we add to our horde."

Danny felt heat rising in her cheeks, and she could feel jealousy pouring off of Ayanda in waves.

"Well, maybe you should make your offer," Danny said. "I think she's gotten tired of me."

Jia Li laughed. "Oh, I can definitely see why Eurion liked you, but alas, I don't think our friend is quite ready to be rid of you yet."

"That's a relief," Danny said. "Because I'm not ready to be rid of her, either." She bowed to Jia Li. "It's been a pleasure to meet you. I'll let you two say goodbye."

Jia Li bowed again and stepped out of the way so Danny could get into the apartment.

***

"How did you know she was a dragon?" Ayanda asked when she came back into the apartment.

Danny looked up from the physics textbook she was reading. "She was talking about buying me for twice my weight in gold. It wasn't that hard to figure out. I mean, who, other than a dragon, would have 240 pounds worth of gold laying around?"

"You weigh a bit more than 120 pounds," Ayanda said.

"Hey! How dare you!" Danny said, a grin spreading across her face.

"She lives in Boston," Ayanda said.

"I hate Boston," Danny said. "Everyone there drives like they're in a contest to be the biggest asshole on the road."

"I asked her if she would take on your Guardianship until it was time for you to return home."

"What?" Danny asked.

"I thought it would be better for both of us. Less confusing."

Danny snapped the textbook closed and slapped it down on the coffee table so hard it cracked the glass, but she was beyond caring at that point. She stood up and walked over to the door and grabbed her jacket and her cell phone out of the charging cradle.

"Where are you going?" Ayanda asked.

"I don't know," Danny said. "Anywhere but here."

"Danny—"

"No," Danny said. "I have been putting up with this bullshit for months, and I'm tired of it. You're the one who asked for me to be assigned to your support team. You're the one who sought me out every day. You're the one who was kind to me, who opened up to me, who flirted with me, who came to my apartment, who kissed me, who told me you loved me, and who begged me to trust you. And I did.

"I trusted you when you gave me that envelope. I trusted you when you told me to pull that lever. I trusted you when I woke up thirty years in the past. I trusted you when I found the instructions telling me to come here. I trusted you even when it felt like taking me in was the last thing you wanted. I trusted you when you yelled at me for saving your life when you fought Null. I trusted you when we fought about that damn dragon. I even trusted you when you said we should keep our distance.

"I trusted you because I know you love me. I've felt it. I've touched your mind, and I've been surrounded by it and filled with it. Maybe not now, maybe not yet, but some day, you love me. I know that as sure as I know the sun rises in the East, but that doesn't mean I have to sit here and let you treat me like garbage."

"That's not what I'm doing."

"Yes, it is. Do you know how much it hurts me when I hear you leave in the morning without saying goodbye? Do you have any idea how painful it is when you come home and don't speak a word to me? Do you know how hard it is that I hear more about your day from CNN than I do from you? Do you know what it feels like to offer someone what I offered you, and to have them tell you that you don't understand what you are offering? To treat you like some child with a crush?"

Danny shook her head and pulled on her coat.

"I'm leaving," she said.

"Where will you stay?"

"I don't know," Danny said. "I don't care. Anywhere but here."

She opened the door and stepped out, then turned and looked back at Ayanda.

"I'll be back tomorrow. Sort your shit out while I'm gone."

She closed the door, walked to the end of the hall, and hit the call button for the elevator. Part of her had hoped that Ayanda would come after her, but when the elevator arrived, she stepped in and hit the button for the ground floor.

Once she was out of the building, she pulled out her cell phone and flipped it open, then pulled up her contacts. It was a short list. There were only six numbers. She selected Cecile's pager and hit send. When it answered, she punched in her phone number, and added 911 as the message. It was about four minutes before her cell phone rang.

"This is Cecile La Saint. I'm returning an emergency page."

"Hey, Cecile. This is Danny."

"Hey, Danny. Is something wrong?"

"I need a place to stay for the night."

"Shit. Are you okay?"

"Not even a little bit."

"Where are you?"

"Standing in front of my apartment building, trying not to break down crying."

"Give me the address."

"Do you know Sunrise Tower downtown?"

"Yeah."

"That's where I am."

"Okay. Give me twenty minutes."

"Thanks."

"Don't thank me. Just tell me that bitch's apartment number so I can punch her when I get there."

"Much as I appreciate the thought, that would just make things worse."

"If she kicked you out—"

"She didn't. Can you just come get me? I'll explain once I'm in the car."

"Okay. Sit tight. I'm on the way."

Molly J. Bragg

Chapter Ten

"I'M ASSUMING YOU LIKE bacon and eggs since you had both in your fridge," Danny said.

"Are you making me breakfast?" Cecile asked.

"Yes," Danny said.

"Damn. And I didn't even have to put out."

Danny rolled her eyes. "Is scrambled okay?"

"That's fine."

"I figured you left a party and drove halfway across town to let me crash on your couch. Breakfast is the least I can do."

"It wasn't a problem."

"Thanks. I'll be out of your hair as soon as I finish the dishes."

"If you need a place to stay for a while…"

Danny picked up the pan and dumped half the eggs out onto each of the two plates she had on the counter. Each one already had a few strips of bacon and a couple of slices of toast. "I appreciate the offer, but I told Kelly I'd be back today."

Cecile picked up one of the plates and took them over to the table while Danny washed out the skillet. "What are you going to do if nothing's changed?"

"I don't know," Danny said. "If I had a job, I'd just find an apartment and move out, but that's not an option."

"Do you have any family?"

"I do, but they're not an option either," Danny said.

"Oh," Cecile said. "I'm sorry. My family didn't take the whole gay thing well either."

Danny shook her head. "It's not that," she said as she sat down across from Cecile. "My parents were great about me being gay. They took me to my first pride parade when I was thirteen."

"Oh, wow," Cecile said. "That was about the age when my dad punched me in the face and told me I wasn't his daughter."

"Shit. I'm sorry."

Cecile shrugged. "It is what it is, but if your parents are good with the gay thing, why can't you call them?"

"The Supervillain thing. Until the effects wear off, I can't go near anyone who knew me before except my roommate."

"That is a weird side effect," Cecile said.

"Says the woman who arrested a dragon a few months ago."

"Point taken, but can I ask what exactly the machine did to you?"

"You can ask," Danny said. "But I can't tell you, and even if I could, you wouldn't believe me."

"I probably would believe you," Cecile said. "Remember, I arrested a dragon a few months ago."

"Touché," Danny said. "Would you report it, if I told you?"

"Don't the Marshals already know?" Cecile asked.

"They'll know when it wears off," Danny said.

"Okay, now you're just being cryptic."

"Because I'm not sure I can trust you with this," Danny said. "If I tell you what happened, and you report it, things could get bad for me."

"How bad?"

"The kind of bad where the CIA shows up and I'm never seen or heard from again," Danny said. "The kind of bad where I shouldn't even be talking to you about any of this, but you're literally the only person that I might be able to trust aside from my roommate, and I need to talk about this to someone that isn't her."

Cecile sat back and stared at Danny. Danny opened her mind, letting herself feel the emotions coming off Cecile. Curiosity, worry, a little fear, and a bit of suspicion.

"Are you a criminal?"

"Technically, yes, but only because of what the machine did to me," Danny said.

"Did you hurt anyone?

"No."

"Did you steal anything?"

"Sort of."

"You sort of stole something?"

"I didn't steal it, but I do have it, and technically it's not legal for me to have it right now, but I can't give it back."

"And now we're back to cryptic."

"Sorry," Danny said. "But if it makes you feel better, I didn't take anything that is of value to anyone without their permission."

"Okay, so, let's do this. Tell me what crimes you've actually committed."

"And you won't arrest me?"

"I won't arrest you," Cecile said.

"All my ID is fake. It has my real name, but the rest of the details are falsified. I'm in possession of two unlicensed fully automatic weapons, two Deputy US Marshal badges, and one set of Deputy US Marshal's credentials."

"Where did you get the weapons?" Cecile asked.

"From the armory at the Marshal's office I was assigned to."

"So they belong to the Marshals?"

"Yes," Danny said.

"Why can't you give them back?"

"Because of what the machine did to me."

"What did the machine do?"

"If I tell you, do you promise not to report me?"

"Yes," Cecile said, and Danny could feel the truth behind her words through the empathic link.

"It threw me back in time thirty years," she said. "I grabbed the lever to turn off the breaker box on a time machine on May 20th, 2021. It threw me across the room and knocked me out, and when I woke up, it was June 7th, 1991."

"Fuck," Cecile said.

"You believe me," Danny said. She was a little surprised, but she didn't feel any doubt coming from Cecile at all.

"Yeah," Cecile said. "And your roommate. It's Focus, isn't it?"

"How did you know?" Danny asked.

"She's the only Superhero in town, so I'm guessing you were assigned to her unit in the future. You showed up, and she's all over you. Friendly, flirty, giving you earth-shaking kisses. Just like you said. But then you get your ass tossed thirty years in the past, and your first thought is, 'hey, I'll look up the girlfriend', because she's the only one you know who might actually believe your story. She realizes it's true and she offers to take you in while, what, you wait for future Focus to come back and get you?"

"The time machine malfunctioned. It covered me with something called 'anti-chroniton particles.' They have to wait for eighteen months to pass for me before they can retrieve me."

"Okay. So, you have to wait until these particles wear off, and in the meantime, you're stuck in the past, living with your girlfriend, who is having some sort of half-assed moral crisis about banging her girlfriend from the future."

"It's a little more complicated than that, but yeah, that's close enough for government work."

"Jesus fucking Christ. So, you're telling me the reason my Superhero has been acting like a fifteen-year-old with a crush is because she's fucking jealous of her future self?"

"No," Danny said. "Look, there are still some parts of this I can't talk about, because they aren't my secret to tell, but I'm...I'm an empath."

"You're a meta?"

"No," Danny said. "I don't have the meta gene. Empathy, the kind I have, is a fairly common baseline ability. Most people just never learn how to use it on a conscious level, but when I met Focus in the future, my empathic ability reacted to her powers, and it formed a kind of link and basically turned my natural abilities up to eleven. I had to learn how to control my abilities to keep from accidentally linking to her any time I was feeling worried, or lonely, or just wanted her around."

"Okay. I think I follow."

"Issue is, if we go there, my abilities will connect to hers permanently."

"So, what, Superheroes mate for life?"

"This one does," Danny said.

The flip expression on Cecile's face vanished as the seriousness of the situation slowly sank in. "Shit, you're serious."

"Yeah," Danny said. "I wouldn't be telling you any of this if I wasn't."

"So, what you were talking about when you two were pulling each other's clothes off..."

"I just meant to kiss her, but when our minds connected, I could feel everything she was feeling, and she could feel everything I was feeling. We got caught in a feedback loop. I could feel how much she wanted me, which made me want her more, and she could feel how much I wanted her, which made her want me more. I got turned on and she could feel it which got her turned on. Back and forth and back and forth. The only thing either of us cared about was each other, but then that stupid fucking pager went off and by the time she got done putting Chernobog back in his cage, she'd convinced herself that I had no idea what I was getting into."

"And now she'll barely talk to you."

"You know how I said we got into a fight last night?"

"Yeah."

"I came home and she was trying to give me away," Danny said.

"What?"

"She had a friend there, and she was trying to get her to take me in until it's time for me to go home. I just lost it. I walked out and I called you."

"Are you sure you want to go back?"

"I don't know. I promised I would, but it's hard."

"Do you love her?"

"I don't know," Danny said. "I know that in the future, she loves me, and it's not unrequited, so at some point, I know I will love her. I know that right now I care for her. I know that I care for the woman I've been living with for the past six months, but I keep reaching out and she keeps rejecting me, and I don't know how much more of it I can take. It hurts."

"I know it might not mean much to you right now, but she's hurting, too."

"I know she is," Danny said. "That's what makes it so frustrating. She's hurting both of us for no reason."

"It's not for no reason," Cecile said. "She genuinely believes she's protecting you, which is going to make it that much harder to talk any sense into her, but you do have an advantage."

"What's that?" Danny asked.

"You know how this ends," Cecile said. "You said it yourself. She loves you. In the future, she loves you and you love her. Which means you just have to hold out a little bit longer, and she will come to her senses."

Danny closed her eyes and took a deep breath, letting it out slowly. "Thank you."

"For what?"

"For reminding me of that. For letting me vent. For giving me someone I could talk to about this."

"You're welcome," Cecile said. "And, um...if you could not tell the woman who can punch a dragon in the face that I hit on her girlfriend, we'll call it even."

***

Danny stopped by the grocery store on her way home. She hadn't been keeping the refrigerator stocked the last few weeks and she needed supplies. After her conversation with Cecile, she'd decided that the only way to sort things out was to just sit down with Ayanda and talk. Not yell, not fight, but talk. To let Ayanda lay out her concerns, and then to address them one by one. The beauty of it was, Cecile had given her the perfect counter argument to any of Ayanda's objections. One she didn't understand why she hadn't thought of herself. She suspected it was a case of not being able to see the forest for the trees.

When she got home, Ayanda was already gone for the day, but she'd expected that. She put away most of the groceries, then set up the crock pot and started a batch of collard greens. She wasn't sure if they'd turn out since she was using a recipe that they'd been giving away in the produce section at the grocery store, but the recipe had sounded good and when she'd seen them, she'd remembered the first time she and Ayanda had eaten lunch together. Ayanda had told her that the first time she had ever had collard greens was the day she and her girlfriend had gotten together, and Danny hoped that was a good sign for how tonight was going to go.

Once the greens were on to cook, she grabbed a quick shower, washing away the smell of the bar and the night spent on Cecile's couch before heading out to the living room. She had planned to skip the books for the day. No trying to figure out temporal mechanics and whether Ayanda was right about the time loop being fixed. She'd just break out the Nintendo, and spend a few hours working on saving Hyrule, then she'd make dinner. It was Christmas Eve, after all. As good a day as any to rest, and to make things right between her and Ayanda.

At least that was the plan, right up until she found the note lying on the coffee table. She picked it up and read it.

Dear Danny,

I had planned to stay home today so I could be there when you got back, but I got a page from the Marshals. I will be home as soon as I can. I know I don't deserve it, but please trust me one more time, and wait for me.

Yours, Ayanda

Danny did her best to stay calm. Focus was the city's only Superhero, so she could have been called in for anything from a wreck blocking traffic on the freeway up to the apocalypse. She tried to reassure herself that Ayanda would be fine. That nothing could happen to her, because she was alive and well in the future. She lasted about a minute before she picked up the remote and turned on the news.

"Again, we are coming to you live from Jacksonville, Florida, where the Superhero Focus along with the local Jacksonville Superhero team, The Red Rangers, are in the midst of a battle involving a number of dragons above the city. It appears that two of the dragons, a red western type dragon and a blue Asian dragon believed to be the same one that fought The Imperial in the skies over Boston in 1959, are fighting alongside Focus and the Red Rangers, while two massive western type black dragons are attacking the city. At this time, it's unclear what caused the black dragons to begin their rampage, but the battle started with the black dragons attacking a US Marshals prison transport van early this morning."

Danny watched the footage as the reporter talked. She didn't know the black dragons at all. Had no idea who they could be. The red dragon she recognized as Eurion. It's hard to forget someone who tried to roast you alive and then tried to buy you to be his wife a few minutes later. The blue Asian dragon she would recognize anywhere. It was Jia Li's dragon form. And of course, there in the middle of it all was Focus.

Danny had thought the fight between Eurion and Focus had been bad, but it was nothing compared to what she was seeing now. Danny had probably spent a bit more time going over the training material about dragons during her Superhero support training than she had anything else, because dragons were freaking cool. Different types had different abilities, but black dragons, whether they were Asian or western, were masters of the storm. They controlled the weather, and in addition to fire, they could breathe lightning.

The black dragons weren't pulling any punches, either. The city looked like it was in the middle of a hurricane. Rain filled the sky, but the wind was so strong the droplets were moving nearly horizontally. Signs were being ripped from their mounting and flying through the air. Tornadoes could be seen in the background rolling through the city.

Danny cursed, wondering where the hell Weatherman or any of the other weather manipulators were. She tried her best to remember if the Red Rangers had anyone who could help, but her knowledge of team rosters came from thirty years in the future. She had no fucking clue what the current makeup of the team was, and Google didn't exist yet so she couldn't exactly look it up.

From what she could see of the fight, it looked like Focus was leading the defense. She was floating above the city, conjuring force fields to protect buildings against lightning strikes. There were a couple of flyers in red uniforms attacking the black dragons, but without weapons specifically forged to fight dragons, there wasn't a lot they could do. Dragons and dragonkin were more magic than they were flesh and blood. That was why it had been so surprising when Genetwist had been able to clone dragonkin in the future, and why it had been so hard to fight them. It almost always took magic to really hurt dragons. Dragon blades were the go-to. Weapons with magic worked into them right from the start. They took a lot of different forms, but they were rare. Not the kind of thing a Tier One Superhero team like the Red Rangers would have in their armory.

Eurion and Jia Li were putting up a better fight than the Red Rangers. Eurion was harrowing the black dragons with fire, and Jia Li with ice. Danny thought they were trying to drive them out over the ocean, probably so they could free up Focus to join the actual fight. The problem was the black dragons were massive. The smaller of the two was easily half again Eurion's size, and the larger one was at least twice as big, which meant they were both ancient.

Danny would bet money they were a mated pair, too. That part wasn't in the training, but Danny had asked Ayanda about why Eurion had tried to buy her as a wife, and Ayanda had explained it. Dragons were jealous creatures. They didn't like to share their territory with other dragons, even mates. Most dragons preferred to simply breed with other dragons when they went into heat once a century, and took human mates for companionship. It's how the legends of virgin sacrifices to dragons got started. Since dragons were physically both male and female in their natural forms, and could assume any shape they wished, most dragons didn't have a particular preference as to the gender of their mates. Human females were more commonly taken simply because humans were far more willing to part with a spare daughter than they were a son, and dragons were often a better choice for the woman, as well. Dragons, even those who weren't especially fond of humans in general, treated their mates well. They doted on them, showered them with affection and gifts, and offered them a life of wealth, comfort, and luxury.

A pair of dragons who chose each other as mates, rather than just breeding partners, was exceedingly rare, but it did happen, and when it did, they became far, far more dangerous. A single dragon defending its den had been known to devastate entire armies. Mated pairs had toppled empires, at least according to legend.

Danny had to fight the urge to do something. To pick up the phone and call Cecile and demand to know why they weren't bringing in more backup. To call a cab and have them take her to Jacksonville. She hated sitting there and not being able to do anything. She hated watching while Focus was in danger and not being able to help.

More than anything, she had to fight the need to reach out to her, to feel her and make sure she was okay.

She picked up the remote and turned off the TV. She lasted about a minute and a half before she turned it back on, just in time to see Focus dodge lightning breath. She took a deep breath and picked up her Gameboy, hoping Tetris would help. It didn't. Neither did the math books, or the physics books, or changing the channel and trying to watch a rerun of Gunsmoke.

She finally gave up and just sat there, watching for almost an hour with both sides locked into what seemed like a stalemate. She hated it. She hated every second of it. She was supposed to be out there with Focus, backing her up, and it was killing her that she couldn't be.

The stalemate finally broke when one of the black dragons let Jia Li get a little too close. She took a chunk off its face with her claws, and both of them screamed and tried to pounce on her. Jia Li dodged and led them towards the coast, and they followed, making the catastrophic mistake of taking the pressure off Focus. The moment they were clear of the city, Focus was on them, dragging them further out to sea until the cameras lost sight of them.

With the black dragons gone, the storm above the city dissipated in moments, and Danny got a look at the city itself. It looked like a hurricane had hit it, and Danny wondered how long the cleanup would take.

She'd spent a good half hour listening to the news anchors on CNN speculate about exactly that when her cell phone rang. She jumped slightly, the sound shocking her. She rushed over and grabbed it out of its charging cradle and flipped it open.

"Hello?"

"It's Cecile. I wanted to let you know she's okay."

Danny breathed a sigh of relief. "Thank you."

"No problem."

"Can you tell me what caused the fight?"

"The black dragons weren't in our database. As far as we knew, no dragons had claimed Jacksonville, so we were relocating Eurion there after his fight with Focus in the middle of downtown. The Asian Blue is a friend of Focus, and Eurion and was along for extra security, thank God."

"So, when you brought two dragons into their territory without their permission, the two black dragons went ballistic," Danny said.

"Yeah. Clean up is going to be a stone bitch, but we're calling in people from Atlanta, Orlando, and Miami to handle it. I'm going to send Focus home as soon as I can, but I wouldn't expect her before about 7:00 PM."

"Any idea what will happen to the black dragons?"

"I don't know. It's way above my pay grade. The fact that they claimed a territory and didn't inform the Dragon Council won't sit well with some of the other dragons, but a lot of the dragons are already angry at us for forcing Eurion to relocate over what they consider a territorial dispute with a human."

"Wonderful," Danny said.

"Yeah," Cecile said. "Get some rest. I'll send your girl home to you as soon as I can."

"Thank you."

***

Danny looked over the meal she'd fixed. Cornbread, collard greens, pan fried chicken, southern style macaroni and cheese, and a chocolate cake. All things she knew Ayanda loved. She hoped, after what had to have been a rough day, it would put her at ease. Cecile called her right before she told Focus to go home, and Danny was glad of it, because it had given her a chance to get everything on the table.

Danny didn't want this to turn into a confrontation. More than anything, she wanted Ayanda to understand that yes, she was hurt, but that the hurt came because she cared about her, and Ayanda didn't believe it. That she'd gone out of her way to trust Ayanda and have faith in her, and all she wanted was for Ayanda to do the same. To trust that Danny cared for her.

The food was a tangible sign of that. At least, it was to Danny. She knew it was something she'd picked up from her father. Even though her mother was the one who insisted she learn to cook, her father had been the one who made most of the food at home. Food was his way of showing love. Every accomplishment was rewarded with food. Any time you were in trouble, he would always fix you a snack or give you ice cream to remind you that even though you'd messed up, he still loved you. It was maybe not the healthiest way to show love, but it was something familiar and comfortable to Danny, and she hoped, over the last few months, it was a language Ayanda had come to understand.

She heard the key in the door, and she opened herself up just a little as she stepped out into the entryway, letting her empathic sense reach out enough that she could feel Ayanda. She felt the tug inside, the desire to connect and open the channel all the way the moment she felt Ayanda, but she worked to hold it back. She felt exhaustion and grief, but they were surface emotions, covering deeper veins of dread, regret, self-loathing, and loneliness. The loneliness ran deepest of all, and it made it harder not to complete the connection, but she drew back, closing off her empathic sense now that she had an idea what she was dealing with.

She took a deep breath and let it out slowly, putting on the best smile she could as the door opened. Even with her empathic sense drawn all the way in, she still felt the moment Ayanda saw her. There was a split second of disbelief, followed by a tidal wave of relief and joy.

"You're here," Ayanda whispered.

"I said I would be."

"I didn't know if you would wait."

"I made a promise," Danny said. "Close the door."

Ayanda let go of the door and it swung closed on its own and locked itself. Danny laughed and shook her head as she stepped forward.

"Show off," she said. She wrapped her arms around Ayanda and pulled her into a hug. Ayanda hugged her back, squeezing so tightly Danny had trouble breathing. She considered it a worthwhile trade, just for the chance to hold Ayanda. She wanted to stay in that moment forever, but she knew she couldn't. It was a good start, but they still had too much to work out.

She pulled back from the hug, and Ayanda let her go. She took one of Ayanda's hands in hers and gave her a small smile. "Come on," she said, giving a small tug. She led them through to the dining room. She heard a small gasp and felt Ayanda stop. She looked back to see what was wrong and found Ayanda with tears welling up in her eyes.

"You did this?" Ayanda asked in a small voice as she stared at the table.

"You always sound so surprised."

She looked at Danny. "You did this after the way I treated you?"

Danny took a deep breath, trying to steady herself, because apparently, they were doing this now instead of after dinner like she'd planned. She turned around so she was facing Ayanda and took her other hand as well.

"You were trying to protect me," Danny said. "I'm not going to pretend that you didn't hurt me, because you did, and pretending otherwise wouldn't do either of us any favors, but I forgive you. I forgive you because I know that you did what you did because you believed you were putting my best interests before your own. You did what you did out of love, not out of malice. Believe me, I know the difference. But you also did it out of fear. You're afraid that I don't understand what being with you means, and you're right. I don't understand, not completely, because you don't trust me enough to tell me.

"That's what hurt me. I trusted you. Again and again, I trusted you, and more than anything, I want you to trust me the way I've trusted you. When you told me you were trying to pass me off to Jia Li, it was just another reminder that you didn't trust me. That's why I left. It just hurt too much."

Ayanda pulled her hands out of Danny's and pulled her into another hug. "I'm sorry," she said. "I'm so sorry."

"I am, too," Danny said. "I'm sorry I left."

"Don't do it again," Ayanda pleaded. "Please. Please don't leave me."

Danny squeezed Ayanda tightly. "I won't," she said. "But you have to trust me. You have to let me in. Whatever it is you're afraid of, I need you to share it with me."

Ayanda was silent for a long time while they just stood there and held each other. Without even trying, Danny could feel the turmoil inside Ayanda. The loneliness and fear tearing at her. She also felt the moment Ayanda came to a decision.

"Okay," she said. "Okay. I'll show you."

"Good," Danny said. "But after dinner."

Danny felt Ayanda's arms loosen, and she let go of her, expecting her to step away and go to the table. Instead, Ayanda pulled back just enough that she could lean in again and cover Danny's lips with her own.

It was a soft, slow kiss. Nothing like their last one. There was no ravenous pawing at each other, no frantic need surging back and forth.

For all that it wasn't, it was still amazing. Ayanda's lips just brushing hers, the light sweep of Ayanda's tongue over her lips. Soft, slow, gentle, heavy with longing and feeling. Danny leaned into her, her toes curling inside her boots, chasing Ayanda's lips as she pulled away.

"Dinner," Ayanda whispered. "Then the truth."

Chapter Eleven

DINNER WAS A MOSTLY silent affair, but it was an oddly comfortable silence. Ayanda complimented the food a few times, and Danny thanked her, but other than that, they just took their time and enjoyed the meal, both knowing that they would talk afterwards. The talk itself was no longer a scary prospect for Danny. She had worried throughout the day that it would be like pulling teeth to get Ayanda to open up to her, but now that she had a promise that Ayanda would share the truth, it was more a matter of curiosity than anything else.

She could feel the worry radiating off of Ayanda, though, and she opened up her empathic abilities just enough to push affection, reassurance, and calm out to Ayanda without actually opening a full-blown connection. She felt the surprise coming from Ayanda, and the gratitude, and she felt Ayanda's feelings toward her being sent back. It wasn't the fathomless love she had felt from Ayanda's future self, but that was okay. Danny knew that would come in time, just like she knew she would return those feelings.

There was a moment of laughter when it came time for dessert. Danny cut the cake and plated up a slice for each of them, then disappeared into the kitchen for a moment, and came back with some peanut butter ice cream. Ayanda laughed and blushed at the same time, and Danny couldn't resist the urge to lean down and kiss her on the cheek, which just made Ayanda blush even harder.

When dinner was finished and the leftovers packed away, they did the dishes together. Ayanda washed while Danny dried. She could feel the nerves coming from Ayanda, knew she was stalling because the dishes could wait until morning, but she didn't fight it. She gave her the time she needed, while at the same time sending back all the reassurance she could, but eventually everything was done. The dishes were washed and dried and put away, the table and the countertops were wiped down, and there was no more stalling.

Ayanda looked at her, and Danny didn't need her empathic abilities to feel the fear coming from Ayanda. She took Ayanda's hand and lifted it up, pressing a kiss to the palm.

"I'm here," she said.

"Promise you won't leave me?" Ayanda begged.

"I promise," she said.

Ayanda led them out to the living room, and they sat on the couch, both turned slightly so they were facing each other. Danny took both of Ayanda's hands in hers, holding them and stroking the backs of Ayanda's hands with her thumbs.

Ayanda took a deep breath and let it out slowly. "I'm sorry," she said. "This is just hard."

"Take your time," Danny said. "Just know that I'm here, and I'm not going anywhere."

Ayanda nodded and closed her eyes. "You know I'm an alien," she said.

"Yes," Danny said.

"You also know I'm a shape shifter," Ayanda said.

"I figured that one out, yeah."

"Shape shifting isn't a natural ability of my people," Ayanda said. "It wasn't even something that was a psionic gift. At least, it wasn't in any of the records or memories I saw. The thing is, one of the strictest tenets of the practice of Focusing was that no one was ever to give their power to someone with a different gift. It was considered...I think the closest word your people have would be sacrilegious. When the seers proposed giving all the powers of my people to a single person, there was a great deal of shock and dismay because of that. At least until the telepaths shared the vision of what the seers had seen with the people.

"The reason that it was forbidden to Focus across gift lines is because the powers could interact in strange ways, and the person chosen as the Focus could end up with new abilities. You would think that would be a good thing, but without training in those abilities, they could be a danger to themselves and to others.

"When I became the Focus, I gained all sorts of abilities that were not normal among my people. Some of them, the seers foresaw. The ability to fly through space faster than the speed of light. The ability to phase through solid matter. The ability to conjure matter out of thin air, or banish matter into nothingness. Others, they never dreamed of. The ability to pluck languages out of the mind of any being I encounter and speak, read, write, and understand it in an instant. The ability to loan a portion of my power to people of a different species. The ability to choose any form I wished. Nothing could have prepared me for that."

Ayanda closed her eyes.

"You know that there are a number of aliens living on Earth."

"Yes."

"You know some species look enough like humans to pass for one."

"Yes."

"My species was not one of them. If I hadn't gained the ability to shape shift, I would never have been able to pass for human."

"Show me?" Danny asked.

"Not yet," Ayanda said. "I will, I promise, but not just yet. You said you wanted to understand what you're offering, and I want to make sure you understand all of it."

"Okay," Danny said.

"I told you before that I wasn't supposed to survive the battle I was created for. That I was meant to die locking Idimoni in his prison."

"I remember."

"I also told you that my people didn't just transfer their powers to me, but also their life force. There was a side effect."

"What do you mean?"

"It was something they knew would happen, but no one thought it mattered, because Idimoni was supposed to kill me, but somehow, I got lucky. I escaped before I could be locked in the cage with him, but Danny, there were sixteen billion people on my planet when they transferred their power and life force into me. And it wasn't just the healthy adults. The telepaths linked everyone on the planet, from the youngest child to the oldest of our people. I absorbed the life force of sixteen billion people, and the average life span on my world was 150 years. My guess is that I received seventy-five years for every one of my people. I've done the math over and over in my head and it gets more horrible every time. My best guess is that, unless something comes along and kills me, I'll live for 1.2 trillion years, give or take."

"My God."

"I'm not even sure something could kill me. There's so much life inside me that I'm not sure if it's possible for me to die. Maybe that's why Idimoni couldn't kill me when we fought. It means I can't grow old with you, but you've felt the power I have flow through the connection before. If we do this, if we make the connection, the life force within me will flow through it as well. You won't grow old. You might not even be able to die. You'll watch your entire world grow old around you, maybe watch your species die out the way I did.

"If you choose this, it would just be us, going on and on while everything around us withers and dies and passes out of time until we're the only ones that remember it. That's why I got so scared when I realized what I had almost done. I'm barely two and a half centuries old. I've spent most of that sleeping, but I already feel the weight of it. A near endless future stretching out in front of me. That's all I have to offer. The curse of an unnaturally long life and the near impossibility of death."

"That's not all you have to offer," Danny said.

"Maybe not, but I'm not sure my love is worth the price that comes with it."

Danny wanted to argue, but she wasn't sure Ayanda would believe her, so she sat there, holding Ayanda's hands while she turned over what she'd just heard in her head. It should have been a hard decision. It should have been something she weighed carefully in her heart and mind for hours, maybe days, or even weeks, but the thing was, she had known what her answer would be before Ayanda had even started speaking, because she knew the choice she would make. She would choose to be with Ayanda, and she would be happy with that decision. She knew because she had felt the way Ayanda loved her in the future, and that wasn't an unrequited love, or a love filled with regret. Knowing that it was the right answer made the choice easy, but there was still one barrier left.

"Ayanda, look at me," Danny said.

Ayanda opened her eyes and looked at Danny.

"If I said yes right now, would you accept it? Would you believe I meant it?" Danny asked.

Ayanda looked down. "I don't think so," she said. "I know you believe it, but I want you to think about it. Think about the consequences. Once this is done, it can't be undone."

"Okay," Danny said. "Then that's what I'll do. We'll go to bed because it's been a long, hard couple of days for both of us, and because it's Christmas eve, and I'll think it over, and then tomorrow, I'll give you my answer. Okay?"

"Okay," Ayanda said.

Danny stood up and tugged on Ayanda's hand. "Come on."

Ayanda stood up, and Danny had to fight not to laugh at the confused look on her face. "Where are we going?"

"To bed," Danny said. "Weren't you listening?"

"Together?" Ayanda squeaked.

"I want you to hold me tonight," Danny said. "Please?"

Ayanda nodded. "I can do that."

Danny smiled, and led Ayanda down the hall to Ayanda's bedroom. She'd never been inside before, but she loved it the moment she saw it. The walls were done in a warm, earthy tone. Something close to terracotta but decidedly redder, and there was a texture to it, almost as if the walls were rough stone. The furniture was old and worn, all heavy wooden pieces that looked like they were designed to stand up to daily use by an enraged elephant. The bed was obviously custom. It was square, and at least ten feet on a side, and covered with what looked like a bearskin, though thankfully there was no head or claws. There were big, fluffy pillows, and a huge teddy bear that was a good four feet tall lying near the head. She glanced over at Ayanda, who was blushing a little, but just shrugged.

"Do you want the bathroom first?" Danny asked.

"You go ahead," she said.

Danny nodded and slipped into the bathroom. She got ready for bed quickly, and after giving herself one last look in the mirror, she headed back out to the bedroom.

"I'll be quick," Ayanda said. "Why don't you grab your pajamas and get changed while I'm in there? There's one more thing I have to show you before you make your decision."

"Okay," Danny said. She waited until Ayanda closed the door, then ran across the hall and stripped down. She pulled on a pair of panties and the thinnest tank top she could find, then rushed back and sat on the bed. She was a little surprised to find that what she had thought was a fluffy comforter was actually another fur, though she had no idea what kind of animal was large enough to cover a ten-foot square bed.

Before she could think too much about it, Ayanda opened the door and stepped out, and Danny's breath caught in her throat, because Ayanda wasn't wearing so much as a stitch. Ayanda swallowed and stood up almost painfully straight.

"I thought this would be best. To let you see everything. Are you ready?"

"Yes," Danny said, sounding more confident than she felt.

Danny had seen Ayanda shape shift before, but it never failed to surprise her how fast it was. It wasn't like any of the movies she'd seen, where there was some slow stretching of the features or weird CGI effects. It was just one moment Ayanda was standing before her in her Kelly form, and the next moment, there was an alien there.

And what an alien it was. Ayanda had a basically humanoid female frame. She was curvier like this than even in her Focus form, though her breasts weren't as big, but there were so many differences. The legs were digitigrade, like a dog or a cat's hind legs. There was a long thin tail hanging down, easily longer than the legs themselves, with the end resting on the floor. The arms were close to human, but the hands had three fingers and two opposable thumbs, one on each side. Ayanda's real face was closer to Kelly's than Focus', but the nose and mouth were pulled forward into an almost catlike snout. She didn't have any hair or fur anywhere on her body, but she did have long, almost rabbit-like ears that were nearly transparent, but shot through with a spiderweb of blood vessels. Then there were the wings. She couldn't see where they attached, but thought it must have been near the spine and below the shoulders. They were batlike in the way they were built, closer in structure to an arm than a bird wing. There was a bicep and a forearm that ended in something like a tiny hand with a thumb and two fingers, but with a massively oversized ring finger forming the leading edge of the outer portion of the wing, while the pinky, equally oversized, formed a sort of support rib. The membrane of the wing, like Ayanda's ears, was nearly transparent, the wing defined more by the web of veins, arteries, and capillaries than anything else. Her skin, where it didn't fade into transparency, was a light blue. The irises of her eyes were the rich cobalt blue she'd come to associate with Focus, only they glowed, but by far, the most alien feature had to be her blood. It was a vivid blue, and bioluminescent. The spider web pattern of blood vessels in her ears and wings glowed brightly, while the vessels under her blue skin left a much fainter but still visible pattern across her body.

"You're beautiful," Danny said. She wasn't sure if she was more surprised by the words, or by their breathless quality, but it was true. She'd never seen anything so beautiful in her life.

"Really?" Ayanda asked, and Danny could feel the insecurity in her voice. She stood up and walked forward, wrapping her arms around Ayanda. She stood up on her toes and kissed her. It was a little strange, getting used to the muzzle, but when Ayanda kissed her back, it was easy enough to figure out.

When the kiss was over, she stepped back, taking a moment to look Ayanda over again. Ayanda blushed, and Danny couldn't stop herself from laughing, because Ayanda's face literally glowed from the rush of bioluminescent blood.

"I'll um...I'll shift back."

"No!" Danny said. "This is how you usually sleep, isn't it?"

"Yes."

"Then stay like this."

"I...I don't have anything to wear," Ayanda said.

Danny smiled and reached for the hem of her shirt. Several places on Ayanda's body glowed brighter as Danny pulled it off, but she didn't stop there. She slipped the panties off, leaving herself naked in front of Ayanda.

"Fair's fair," she said. "Now, take me to bed."

Ayanda didn't argue.

***

Danny woke up to the feel of hot air on the back of her neck. She tried to turn to see where it was coming from, but quickly found she couldn't move. There was something thick and warm wrapped around her waist, squeezing gently, a leg thrown over both of hers, an arm wrapped around her, the hand cupping her left breast, two heavy furs pulled over top of her, and on top of that, a leathery, glowing wing covering her almost completely.

A smile spread across her face as the night before came back to her. Seeing Ayanda's true form for the first time, curling up against her, the way Ayanda had wrapped her tail around Danny's waist and covered them both with her wing after pulling the furs over them.

She relaxed and settled back against Ayanda, sighing when she felt Ayanda nuzzle against the back of her neck. Ayanda shifted slightly, clutching Danny closer. Danny loved it, the way the leg thrown over hers pulled her legs back, the way the hand on her breast squeezed gently, the way the tail wrapped around her tightened as Ayanda blew another puff of hot air across the back of her neck.

She felt Ayanda's nose press against her and heard Ayanda inhale deeply. She couldn't stop herself from moaning as she felt Ayanda's hips rock against her. Ayanda's muzzle shifted, and she felt Ayanda pressing kisses along the back of her neck. She squeezed her legs together, trying to ease the building ache between them, but it didn't help. Not when she could feel the growing arousal pouring off of Ayanda.

She gasped as she felt Ayanda run her tongue up the length of her neck. It wasn't a one-time thing, either. Ayanda shifted a little to the side and did it again and again, moving slightly each time, like she was determined to taste every inch of Danny's neck. Danny got more and more turned on with each stroke. She could feel Ayanda's mind reaching out for hers, feel the want coming from her.

"Are you awake?" Danny asked.

"Yes," Ayanda said. "Do you want me to stop?"

"God no," Danny said. "Never."

Ayanda slid her other arm under Danny and clutched her even more tightly. "I want you," Ayanda whispered, and Danny whimpered. "God, I want you so much."

"Then take me," Danny said.

The connection snapped into place, and she could feel the same raw need flowing through the link she'd had the morning they'd kissed in the kitchen, but this time, it was more controlled. This time, Ayanda knew what she was doing.

"I want you," Ayanda said. "I want to claim you, to mark you as mine."

"Do it," Danny said.

"Your body isn't made for it," Ayanda said. Danny felt needle sharp teeth scrape over her neck. "It will hurt."

"Do it anyway," Danny said.

"It will bleed," Ayanda said. "And scar. Everyone will see it. Everyone will know you're mine."

"Do it," Danny said.

Ayanda licked her neck again. "You're sure this is what you want?"

"Yes."

"A life with me. Forever. Countless years together. Never growing old."

"Yes."

"Feeling me in your mind. Bonded to me."

"Yes."

"You'll see things in my mind. Horrible things."

"We'll be together," Danny said. "That's what I want."

"You're sure? It can't be undone."

"I'm sure," Danny said. "Take me. Mark me. Make me yours and be mine."

The link opened wider, and any control either of them had vanished under a flood of emotions from both of them. Need, want, love, desire, loneliness, sorrow, comfort, and joy.

Ayanda rolled onto Danny, and Danny expected to be pinned to the mattress, but what she hadn't counted on were Ayanda's wings. Ayanda planted them on the bed the way someone would plant their hands and pushed up so she was balanced on wingtips and knees. Danny's knees were pressed into the bed and she scrambled to get her hands under her, even though she knew Ayanda wouldn't let her fall. Ayanda's right hand, which had been cupping Danny's left breast, moved down, sliding over her chest, and over the tail still wrapped tightly around her waist, then over her stomach. Danny bucked slightly as the fingers slid through the damp mass of curls between her legs. She moaned as those same fingers parted her folds and began to stroke the wet pink flesh inside.

Danny felt the teeth on her neck again, and it felt like a line of pure, molten desire ran down her spine right to her clit.

"Don't tease," she said.

Ayanda kissed her neck again. "I...I've never done this before," Ayanda said.

"You haven't?"

"No," Ayanda said. "I was young. I'd thought of it, fantasized about it, dreamed of it, but you're my first."

For a moment, Danny didn't know what to say. It was overwhelming, and a little frightening, but then the moment passed because she realized she knew exactly what to say.

"I trust you. I want you." She paused for a minute, considering her next words, making sure they were true, because Ayanda would be able to feel if they weren't. She was a little surprised by how much she meant them. "I love you."

Danny felt Ayanda bury her muzzle in the back of her neck.

"Say it again," Ayanda begged.

"I love you," Danny said.

Ayanda kissed Danny's neck again, and Danny moaned as Ayanda slid a finger inside her.

"Is that good?"

"Yes," Danny said as she started to rock her hips.

She felt Ayanda's teeth scrape lightly over her skin again. "I love you," Ayanda said.

"You do?" Danny asked.

"Ever since you punched a dragon," Ayanda said.

Danny laughed, but the laugh turned into a low moan as Ayanda curled her finger inside Danny, finding the sensitive spot in her front wall.

"Oh, God," she whimpered as she fisted her hands in the sheets.

"Is this good?" Ayanda said.

"More," Danny said.

"You sure?" Ayanda asked.

"Yes."

Ayanda pulled out of her, drawing a whimper of protest from Danny, but before she could say anything, she felt two of Ayanda's fingers push inside her. Danny rocked her hips, riding Ayanda's fingers, but Ayanda wasn't nearly as passive as she was before. She worked her hand, pumping in and out of Danny, meeting each roll of Danny's hips, grinding her fingers over the sensitive spot inside.

"Oh, God damn," Danny said.

She felt Ayanda's teeth again, this time biting lightly into her skin for a moment before Ayanda soothed the marks with her tongue.

"You're mine," Ayanda said.

"Yes," Danny answered. "God, fuck me."

Ayanda didn't disappoint. She picked up the pace, driving into Danny harder and faster. There was no hesitation or doubt, because Ayanda could feel what Danny was feeling through the link. She could feel what Danny wanted.

"More," Danny begged, only to hear a laugh. Ayanda pulled out of her again, and drove back in with three fingers, stretching Danny to the edge of pain. Danny hung her head down and whimpered, because being filled and stretched like this was incredible and overwhelming. It was further than she'd ever been pushed before, and every ache, every burn just made her wetter and needier, but there was frustration too. She'd been begging for Ayanda to touch her clit, and Ayanda knew it.

"Please," she said, tears welling in her eyes, because she needed release. Her own desire was mixing with Ayanda's through the link, driving her mad with need. She knew Ayanda could feel it too, but she could also feel the other need building between them. Ayanda's need to mark her. She didn't understand it entirely, but it was there, and it was real, and she wanted it every bit as much as Ayanda did.

She didn't feel it at first. She was too lost in the feel of driving herself back onto Ayanda's fingers, of stretching herself open to take them, but the tail wrapped around her waist shifted. She realized it when she felt the tip sliding through the damp curls between her legs, which only gave her a couple of seconds warning before it found her clit. She let out a scream as Ayanda began rubbing her clit with the tip of her tail. It felt like an oversized thumb pressed firmly against her. It was almost enough, and when Ayanda curled her fingers again, driving all three of them into that sensitive spot inside Danny, she felt herself about to fall over the edge.

Ayanda felt it too, and Danny felt something inside her snap. Sharp teeth dug into the back of her neck, sending spikes of pain through her, but she was so close to the edge, all they did was shove her over. She screamed as she came, Ayanda's fingers buried inside her, Ayanda's tail rubbing her clit, and Ayanda's teeth sunk into the back of her neck.

She wasn't sure if she passed out or not, but she definitely lost the thread for a few minutes. When she came back to herself, she was lying on her side in mostly the same position she'd woken up in. The only difference was, instead of Ayanda's right arm being wrapped around her, and her right hand cupping Danny's breast, this time Ayanda was stroking the back of Danny's neck with her right hand.

"It closed up," Ayanda said in wonder.

"What?" Danny asked.

"My mark," she said. "It closed up. The scars are there, but it closed up the way it would if you were one of my people."

Danny shifted a little, before realizing she was still trapped in position.

"Let me roll over."

Ayanda moved her leg and uncoiled her tail from Danny's waist, letting Danny roll over to face her.

"The link?" Danny asked.

"I think so," Ayanda said. "Can you feel it?"

Danny thought about it for a moment, and realized yes, she could. It wasn't as all-encompassing as she had half expected, but it was there. She could feel Ayanda, could feel her emotions, and if she tried, could hear her thoughts, and she had to take a deep breath, because even though it wasn't drowning out her own thoughts, even though it wasn't as all-encompassing as the link they'd shared during the fight with Eurion, it was overwhelming in its beauty. She could feel Ayanda, because Ayanda was a part of her, now and forever.

"I feel it," Danny said, even though the words were inadequate to what she was actually experiencing.

She watched as Ayanda licked her lips, cleaning away a spot of red blood, and she couldn't stop herself from leaning in and kissing her.

"I love you," she said.

Ayanda smiled. "I love you, too," she said.

Danny reached up, doing something she'd wanted to do the night before. She carefully traced the glowing lines created by the blood vessels in Ayanda's face.

"You are so beautiful," she said.

"You think so?" Ayanda asked.

Danny smiled, and instead of words, she let Ayanda feel what she did when she looked at her. Ayanda's face lit up with wonder, and she leaned in and captured Danny's lips with her own. It was a very long time before either of them got out of bed.

Chapter Twelve

THERE WAS SOMETHING ABSOLUTELY decadent about living with your girlfriend, Danny decided. It wasn't an experience she'd had before. When she had dated Helen, they'd both been in high school. When she had dated Claire in college, they'd lived in the same dorm, but had never been roommates. When she had dated Amber after college, they'd just never gotten to the point where they even considered moving in with each other. Living with Ayanda, though, was amazing. Being able to reach out and touch the woman she loved any time she wanted, being able to curl up in her arms every night and wake up with Ayanda spooned against her back every morning made Danny's heart soar.

The sex didn't hurt either. They were very much in a honeymoon phase and were making love every chance they got. In the two weeks since Christmas, they'd managed to christen every room in the house, and damn near every piece of furniture. Focus had gone back to being on call instead of going into the Marshal's station on Tuesdays, Thursdays, and Sundays. They tried to be responsible, and not get too carried away during the hours where Ayanda was most likely to get called in, but sometimes it was hard to hold themselves back.

The mating mark made it harder. Even Ayanda was surprised by that. She hadn't expected it to work the same way on Danny that it did on her own people, but whatever made the mark work seemed to have the same effect on humans. Danny, for her part, loved it. She loved touching it and feeling the ragged edges. Every time she was in the bathroom, she found herself turning her head this way and that, trying to get a good look at it. It looked like a large animal had tried to bite through her spine. It should have been ugly, but it wasn't. Danny loved the way it looked and felt, though she learned very quickly not to touch it. Touching it herself had an immediate and profound effect on both her and Ayanda, though it was nothing compared to Ayanda touching it. Any time Ayanda ran her fingers over it, or kissed it, or licked it, or even breathed on it, Danny wasn't just ready to go, she was baring her neck and begging, already halfway to the finish line. Something Ayanda took ruthless advantage of, much to Danny's delight. For an inexperienced lover, Ayanda was surprisingly inventive and enthusiastic.

For all that, though, Danny's favorite moments were when they were just curled up together, which is how they found themselves on a Thursday morning two weeks after Christmas. Ayanda had checked in with Cecile after breakfast and had been assured that the schedule was clear for the day, and Cecile would call over the radio if there were any emergencies. Once they were sure Ayanda was free, they'd crawled back into bed. Ayanda was on her back, with Danny pressed up against her side. Danny had her head resting on Ayanda's right shoulder, and her left leg thrown over Ayanda's right. Ayanda had her right arm wrapped around Danny, her tail wrapped around Danny's waist, and they were both tucked in under the beaver pelt blanket on Ayanda's bed, with Ayanda's wings folded around them like a cocoon.

Danny let out a soft sigh as she felt the fingers Ayanda had threaded through her hair slip down towards the mating mark.

"Don't start something you can't finish," she warned.

"I hadn't planned on it," Ayanda said. "You already wore me out this morning."

Danny laughed. "I wore you out, huh?"

"That's my story, and I'm sticking to it," Ayanda said. She leaned forward and pressed a kiss to Danny's forehead.

"Well, I suppose I can live with that," Danny said.

"That's good," Ayanda said. "Because I don't know what I'd do without you."

"You'd get along just fine," Danny said. "You did before I showed up."

"Not really," Ayanda said. "I was miserable before you showed up."

Danny tightened her hold on Ayanda and pressed a kiss to her collar bone. "I'm sorry."

"Don't be," Ayanda said. "You're here."

"I am," Danny said. "I just wish I could be with you out there."

"You could be, if you wanted," Ayanda said.

"What do you mean?"

"I mean I could give you some of my power, the way I did the day you fought Eurion."

"Wouldn't that make you weaker?"

"Not enough to matter," Ayanda said. "If I gave you part of the power I use to fly, it wouldn't make any practical difference. I don't have a lot of use for traveling five hundred times the speed of light on a day-to-day basis."

"Point taken," Danny said.

"I could give you half of the power I have, and it wouldn't make much difference. It might even help. I spend more time holding back my power to avoid collateral damage than I do letting loose."

"You know, I don't even know all the powers you have," Danny said.

"Honestly, I'm not sure I do either," Ayanda said. "I know the ones that were common gifts among my people. Flight, telepathy, telekinesis, teleportation, empathy, astral projection, healing, precognition, postcognition, clairvoyance, psionic force fields, knowledge transference, elemental kinesis, and dream walking. I was trained in how to use all of those, but the combination of powers also gave me the ability to shape shift, to phase through matter, to pluck languages out of others' minds, conjuring and banishing matter, matter transmutation, loaning my power to others, the ability to pull energy out of the very fabric of the universe and turn it on an enemy. I had to discover and learn most of those on my own, after my people were dead. There may be other abilities in there I haven't discovered yet, and honestly, some of those abilities I chose not to use. I never look into the future. I avoid looking into other people's minds, leaving my own body, or entering other people's dreams, but I could give you all of those abilities, and I could teach you how to use them."

"Would it distract you?" Danny asked. "Having me out there fighting with you?"

"No," Ayanda said. "No more than fighting alongside Jia Li does." Ayanda leaned down so their foreheads were pressed together. "I don't want to minimize what you mean to me, but I know the fear that comes with going into battle alongside people I love. I've gotten used to it."

"Then yes," Danny said. "Teach me, so I can go out there with you."

"Okay," Ayanda said. "When do you want to start?"

Danny thought about it for a second, then snuggled a bit closer to Ayanda. "Later," she said.

Ayanda laughed.

"What? Cuddles are important!"

Ayanda pressed a kiss to Danny's forehead. "I couldn't agree more."

***

"Are you sure you're ready for this?" Ayanda asked.

"No time like the present," Danny said. She knew Ayanda could feel how nervous she was, so there was no point in denying it. She also knew there wouldn't be a time when they could do this that she wouldn't be nervous about it, so there was no point in putting it off. She wanted to help, to go out there with Ayanda. It was where she belonged.

Ayanda's eyes softened as she watched Danny, and Danny could feel Ayanda's love through the link. It made her feel warm and safe, and she let herself lean into the feeling. The two of them were sitting on Ayanda's bed, legs crossed, facing each other. The lights were turned off, and a heavy blackout curtain covered the window. The only light in the room came from a couple of candles and the soft glow of Ayanda's blood. It made the moment feel personal and intimate, which it was, and what they were doing made it feel important, which it also was.

Ayanda reached up, placing the three fingers of each of her hands on Danny's temples.

"Will it hurt?"

"No," Ayanda said. "But…it will be overwhelming."

"Okay," Danny said. "Do it."

Ayanda nodded, and the tidal wave hit before Danny could even try to brace herself. Overwhelming was an understatement. She could feel the power flowing through their bond, hitting her like water from a firehose. It filled her, but it kept coming, and she could feel a pressure build inside her, trying to stretch her, trying to tear its way out, trying to fight its way back the way it came, only to be forced back by the power still flowing in. It took forever and no time at all for the rush to stop and for equilibrium to come. The rush stopped, but the pressure was still there. The crushing weight of what she had been given.

She felt Ayanda reach out to her through the link, the touch of her mind heavier, more solid than it normally was. It felt like Ayanda taking her hand and guiding her. Showing her how to let the power flow through her, to control it. How to let it become a part of her, instead of something that was crushing down on her.

She felt the pressure fade and slowly vanish as she learned how to fly, how to read minds, how to heal, how to transform matter or conjure it out of thin air, how to forge force fields of pure psionic energy, how to manipulate the elements, how to pluck languages out of other people's minds, how to give and take knowledge with a touch, and even how to look into the future. Ayanda taught Danny everything she knew about how to use the powers they now shared, and Danny soaked up the knowledge, desperate for anything that would let her help Ayanda in the field.

When Ayanda finally pulled away, Danny opened her eyes, not entirely sure how much time had passed. She felt lighter somehow, and when she looked at Ayanda, she saw a smile that made her think she was missing the joke. Ayanda glanced down slightly, her smile getting even bigger, and Danny looked down to find them both floating a good three feet off the bed.

She looked back up at Ayanda.

"I'm flying," she said.

"Yes, you are," Ayanda said. She reached forward and took Danny's hand. "You ready to be a Superhero?"

***

Danny followed Ayanda into an alley a couple of blocks down from their building and watched as she shifted from her Kelly form into Focus. She took a deep breath and reached out with her own powers, transforming the boots, t-shirt, and jeans she was wearing into her new Superhero uniform.

The design of the uniform was fairly simple. A dark navy-blue jumpsuit with red gloves and boots, and her emblem in the center of her chest. The name had never been in doubt. Scatter. And the emblem Ayanda had come up with reflected that. It was a white Feynman diagram over a big red S. A little nerdy, something Danny didn't plan to let Ayanda forget, but she liked it. She'd also opted for a mask rather than a completely different appearance.

"Ready?" Focus asked.

"As long as the Marshals know not to shoot me down," Danny said.

"Oh, good point," Ayanda said with a twinkle in her eye. She reached up and tapped her earpiece. "Focus to La Saint, do you copy?"

Danny waited a second while Focus listened to the response.

"I'm taking a couple of laps around town. I have company, so don't break out the SAMs when you see her on radar."

Ayanda rolled her eyes in response to whatever Cecile said over the radio.

"Call sign will be Scatter. You can meet her tomorrow." Ayanda gave her a thumbs up. "Focus out."

Ayanda gave her one last look before she lifted off. Danny took a deep breath and followed, shooting into the sky alongside Ayanda until they were high enough to see the whole city. The first thing that struck her was how much detail she could see. It was like she was looking through a telescope. She could zoom in close enough to read the label on a woman's purse clear on the other side of the city and hear her heartbeat at the same time.

"You didn't tell me we had enhanced senses," Danny said.

"We don't," Ayanda said. "Not the way you're thinking. What you're seeing and hearing is your clairvoyance. You're sensing things psionically, rather than through optical magnification."

"Huh," Danny said. "What's the limit?"

"I don't know, honestly," Ayanda said. "But I love the view from Titan."

"Saturn's moon?"

"Yep," Ayanda said. "Come on. Let's do some laps."

Ayanda shifted from hovering in an upright position to flying in a horizontal one, and Danny followed, coming up beside her as they took slow circles around the city.

"Open up your empathic sense a bit as you look out over the city," Ayanda said.

Danny nodded and slowly opened her empathic senses as she scanned the city. She could feel a bit of what was going on. People who were happy, people who were sad, people who were bored or lonely or didn't feel much at all. It was interesting, right up until she felt the panic call to her. All her senses snapped into focus inside a convenience store, where a guy in a mask had a huge gun pointed at a little Indian woman.

Danny was moving before she even considered it, shooting across the city towards the store. She swung upright and phased through the door, slowing herself down to a run as she pulled the gun out of the robber's hand telekinetically, careful not to set the gun off. She gave a small squeeze, crumpling it into useless, twisted metal before dropping it. The next moment, she grabbed the guy's arm and slammed him down on the counter. The woman behind the counter screamed in shock, and Danny looked up at her.

"It's okay, ma'am. I'm here to help," she said.

The woman nodded, then turned at the sound of the bell on the door ringing. Focus stepped inside. Danny turned back to the robber she had pinned down.

"Let me go," he yelled.

"No," Danny said. "I don't think I will." She held up her hand, and a roll of duct tape shot off one of the pegs and into her hand. She held it up for Focus to see, and Focus nodded, so she started taping his hands together.

"You know, it's not nice to point guns at people," Danny said. "Especially not little old ladies who are just minding their own business."

"Fuck you," the guy yelled. Danny had to fight down the urge to bounce his face off the counter.

"Got a mouth on you, don't you?" she said.

"Shut up and let me go, bitch," he yelled.

Danny looked up at the shop keeper. "Call the police, please."

"I already stepped on the silent alarm," she said.

"Thank you," Danny said. She looked over at Ayanda. "How'd I do?"

"You forgot one thing," Ayanda said.

"What's that?"

Focus picked up the roll of duct tape and tore off a strip, then slapped it over the robber's mouth. She patted the robber on the shoulder a couple of times as he screamed into the duct tape.

"Perfect," Ayanda said. "Now we just wait for the cops to take him off our hands."

"How long does that usually take?"

"Not long," Ayanda said. She turned to the woman behind the counter. "You have Nutter Butters?"

"Aisle three," the woman said.

Ayanda turned back to Danny. "Cookies?"

***

"Did you see the look on that guy's face when I just yanked him right through the roof of the car?" Danny asked.

"I did," Ayanda said through barely contained laughter.

"I can't decide which is more fun. Flying, or phasing," Danny said.

"Flying," Ayanda said. "Phasing is cool, don't get me wrong, but the shiny wears off a lot faster than with flying."

"You know, that does bring up a question," Danny said.

"What's that?"

"Well, your people have wings, right?"

"Yes," Ayanda said.

"So why was psionic flight a big deal if everyone could already fly?"

"Ah," Ayanda said. "I was wondering how long it would take you to ask. The answer is simple, though. Speed. On wing, I can make about a hundred knots, which isn't too bad, but even before I became Focus, with my psionic flight powers, I could break the sound barrier. That was rare, but then, all my abilities were stronger than normal. That was something we figured out a long time ago. The more abilities a person had, the stronger each individual ability would be. Since I had more than anyone else, all of mine were stronger than anyone else with those powers."

"Which is part of why they picked you."

"Exactly," Ayanda said.

Danny gave Ayanda a smile as she took her hand and squeezed it. "I'm glad they did," she said. "I'm glad I got to meet you."

"I'm glad too," Ayanda said.

Danny turned away from her to look out over the city towards the bay. The sun was setting behind them, and the bay was already shrouded in darkness, but Danny could make out every detail. The boats in their marinas, the ships tied up in port, the mix of boats and ships out on the horizon. If she looked down on the city, she could see the cars and the people moving through the streets. It was amazing, just sitting there on top of the radio tower on the Marshals' station, watching life go by below them.

She felt a small tug at her empathic sense and let out a sigh.

"Today has been amazing," Danny said.

"I'm glad," Ayanda said. "It's been a long time since I had a partner."

"I'd kiss you, but we have company."

"I know," Ayanda said. "We should probably go say hi."

"Probably," Danny said.

Ayanda tipped forward, pulling Danny off the tower with her, and the two of them drifted down towards the figure standing on the roof of the Marshal's station. He was a tall, well-built black man. Covered in muscle and holding himself like he owned the whole city. Danny had seen him once before on the news and knew he must be Ayanda's Officer in Charge.

"Hello, David," Ayanda said.

"Focus," David said. He turned to look at Danny. "And I'm told you're called Scatter."

"Yes, sir," Danny said.

"I don't suppose you'll be any more willing to tell me your name than she will," he said.

"I'm afraid not," she said. "But if it makes you feel any better, I was law enforcement where I came from."

"It might, if I knew where you came from," David said.

"Close by," Danny said. "But that's all I can tell you."

"Powers?" David asked.

"Same as mine," Ayanda said.

David sighed. "That doesn't help, since you won't give us a complete list of your powers."

"I've told you before, David, I don't have a complete list of my powers."

"Fine. Is she sticking around, or is this just training day before she goes and finds her own Marshals to drive crazy?"

"I'm sticking around," Danny said.

"She'll be here for about a year," Ayanda said.

"A year?" David asked. "That's pretty specific for you lot."

"She has to go back where she came from," Ayanda said.

Danny frowned slightly, but she gave David a small nod.

"Well, if she's going to be here for a year, bring her by so we can get some paper on her. It will make the arrests and prosecutions go easier."

"First thing in the morning," Ayanda said.

"I'll hold you to that," David said. "Now, get out of here. It's bad enough I've got pigeons and seagulls fouling up my radio signals. I don't need to add love birds to the list."

Ayanda laughed. "Goodnight, David," she said.

"Goodnight," David said, not quite able to keep the affection out of his voice.

"Come on," Ayanda said as she lifted into the air. "Let's go home. I'll fix your dinner for a change."

"All right," Danny said. "As long as it's not peanut butter and spaghetti."

***

Danny ended the day the way she started it, wrapped in Ayanda's arms, wings, and tail, with her head resting on Ayanda's shoulder. She felt safe and happy and at peace, save for one little thing that niggled at the back of her mind. She kept trying to push it away, wanting to hold on to the memory of a perfect day. A day spent with Ayanda, the day she became a Superhero, the day she truly started fighting by the side of the woman she loved. Try as she might, it wouldn't go away, and she knew Ayanda could feel it, too.

"What's wrong?" Ayanda finally asked.

"I was just thinking about something," Danny said.

"You're thinking pretty loud," Ayanda said. "And not happy thoughts."

"I know," she said. "I'm sorry. I didn't want to spoil the day."

"Love, you can always tell me what you're thinking," Ayanda said.

"You told David I'd be here for a year," Danny said.

"Yeah," Ayanda said. "I thought it was best to let him know up front."

"That's not what bothered me," Danny said.

Ayanda frowned slightly. "Then what was it?"

"If I go back, I'll be leaving you alone," Danny said.

"Not forever," Ayanda said. "You know that. I'll be waiting for you on the other end of the time portal."

"But that's twenty-nine years," Danny said. "That's a lifetime for some people."

Ayanda leaned forward and kissed Danny's forehead. "A day is a lifetime for some people, but not for us, love."

"You begged me not to leave you," Danny said.

"When I thought you leaving would mean forever," Ayanda said. "When I thought I would be alone again. That's not what this is. I can wait for you."

"But why?" Danny asked. "If you've shared your life force with me, if I am going to live for as long as you say, why go back through the portal? Why not just stay here until I catch up with myself?"

"You'd do that for me?"

"You have to ask?"

Ayanda laughed again and squeezed Danny tightly. "No. No, I should know better by now. You're my stubborn little miracle. But love, you have to go back."

"Why?" Danny asked.

"Because you already went back," Ayanda said.

"That doesn't make any sense," Danny said.

"The loop is fixed," Ayanda said. "You have to go back this time, because you went back last time. And you'll have to go back next time, because you went back this time."

"That still doesn't make any sense," Danny said. "I'm here, with you. What does it matter if I stay and take the long way round?"

"I don't know what difference it would make, but your Focus, the one from the future, told me I had to send you back. That I couldn't let you stay. I'm not sure why, but as much as I love you, and as much as I wish you could stay, you belong to her more than you belong to me."

"You're both the same person," Danny said. "How can I belong to one of you more than the other?"

"Because I only get to keep you for a year. She gets to keep you for eternity. And because she knows better than either of us what the next thirty years will bring. She's lived it. Every day of it. She's more fit to judge than either of us."

"What if she's wrong?"

"You said you trusted her."

"Not if it means leaving you alone in pain."

Ayanda tilted Danny's head back and kissed her, slow and soft, letting it drag on until Danny shifted a bit and climbed on top of Ayanda, straddling her. She moaned in disappointment when Ayanda broke the kiss but looked down into glowing cobalt eyes.

"I love you, and I would do anything to be able to keep you here with me, but you have to go back, and I have to send you."

"But why?" Danny asked.

"I don't know," she said. "But I trust her enough to do what she says."

Danny leaned down, pressing her forehead to Ayanda's. "I don't want to leave you."

"I know, but I don't want to spend what time we have fighting over this. We have a year, and then I will give you back to her. For you, it will be a few seconds. You won't even have time to miss me."

"But you'll have twenty-nine years," Danny said.

"Twenty-nine years to remember how happy you make me, and to look forward to the day I see you again, and the day you truly come back to me."

"Twenty-nine years to be alone," Danny said.

"Yes," Ayanda said. "So why don't you spend the next year helping me make memories that will keep me going until I get you back?"

"I can do that," Danny said.

"Good," Ayanda said as she slipped her hand up and found the mating mark. It was the last coherent word either of them spoke before morning.

Molly J. Bragg

Chapter Thirteen

"GOD, YOU'VE GOT IT bad," Cecile said.

"What?" Danny asked, turning away from Focus, who was across the situation room talking to David.

"Seriously, most people are just taking it as a case of hero worship, but then, most people don't know you're a huge lesbian," Cecile said. "Every time I look at you, you're standing there looking at Focus like she hung the fucking moon."

Danny shrugged. "I can't help it. She's amazing."

"That's not what you were saying a few weeks ago."

"That's because a few weeks ago, she was being an idiot. I said she's amazing. Not flawless."

"Well, amazing, flawless, whatever. You need to knock it off or someone is going to figure out it isn't just hero worship," Cecile said.

Danny shrugged. "So?"

"So? Look, I get that you're going back to where you came from, but Focus has to actually live through the next three decades."

"You say that like being out is some terrible thing."

"Maybe not where you come from, but in the here and now, it can be pretty devastating to someone's career."

"You seriously think they'll put someone as powerful as Focus on the bench if word gets out that she's gay?"

"They might," Cecile said.

Danny shook her head. "They won't," she said. "I'll let you in on a little secret. Where I come from, there are a lot of out Superheroes. Some of the really big names, too. There's a team over in Sun City that's four lesbians, a non-binary bisexual, a gay guy, an ace guy, and one straight guy."

"Ace?"

"Asexual. Aromantic too, I think. Left his original team and sued the shit out of them for sexual harassment because the team leader wouldn't leave him alone. Not really the point though. Heroes coming out is one of the things that helps change the world for the better. I'm not saying the world's perfect in my day. There are still bigots, and places you have to be careful, but it's a lot better than it is now."

"If you say so."

"If you don't believe me, wait twenty-nine years and ask your wife."

"My what?" Cecile sputtered.

"Your wife," Danny said as she patted Cecile on the shoulder. "She's adorable, by the way."

***

Danny dropped into the chair to Ayanda's left at the corner table in the cafeteria. They both had their back to the wall, looking out over the small crowd. Danny was still a little surprised at how small the complement at the Marshals' station was, but then, Ayanda was the only Superhero active in Pontian in 1991. She was used to a station that not only ran Focus as a solo hero, but also ran six fully-sanctioned Metahuman Emergency Response Teams, in addition to working with the local Black Panthers. Even in 2021, it wasn't quite as big as some place like Sun City, Boston, or LA, but in '91, the Marshals rattled around the place like a handful of peas in a coffee can.

She picked up her fork and started attacking the macaroni and cheese on her plate a little more viciously than she'd intended, but she understood now why she always saw Ayanda eating. Using her powers always left her starving, and it had to be worse for Ayanda, who spent all her time holding a human form.

"That was some conversation you were having with Cecile this morning," Ayanda said between spoonfuls of apple crumble.

"Yeah," Danny said. "She told me I needed to tone down the heart eyes when I look at you."

"What?"

"She's worried I might sully your reputation."

"As I recall, I did all of the sullying this morning."

"Only because you...you know. And you know I'm always useless for at least a half an hour after you..." Danny waved her hand in Ayanda's direction. She could feel her cheeks burning. Especially with the smug look Ayanda wore.

"I have noticed that you like it when I 'you know'," she said.

"Shut up," Danny said.

Ayanda laughed. "You're cute when you blush."

"Now you're doing it on purpose," Danny grumbled.

"I am," Ayanda said. "But how was she worried about you 'sullying' my reputation?"

"She was worried people would figure out we're lovers," Danny said.

"So?"

"So, she was worried about the public reaction if people found out you're…you know, I never asked how you identify. Gay, bi, pan?"

"None of the above," Ayanda said. "Those are all human concepts of identity. We didn't do categories back on my world. The mating mark worked regardless of your partner's anatomy, so we never much cared. Actual breeding was a bit different than mating marks. When the women went into season, things were a bit of a free for all. And if a woman didn't care for male company, we'd developed artificial means of impregnation centuries ago."

"Okay," Danny said. "But Cecile was worried about the damage getting labeled as gay could do to your reputation."

"Is that something you're worried about?" Ayanda asked.

"No," Danny said. "I've been out since I was in middle school. I don't give a damn who knows it."

"Well, there's your answer," Ayanda said. "I don't care, so if you don't, it's not an issue."

"Good to know," Danny said. "For the record, I haven't got any problems with public displays of affection, but let's save any actual sullying for when we're alone. Exhibitionism isn't my thing."

"Pity," Ayanda said. "Jia Li will be disappointed."

"What?"

"She's been asking when she can come over and watch."

***

"You forgive me yet?" Ayanda asked as the two of them touched down at the site of a jack-knifed truck that was blocking all four lanes of the interstate.

"No," Danny grumped, which just made Ayanda laugh. "Can I take this one?"

"By all means," Ayanda said.

Danny walked over to the officer who was directing the scene. "Officer," she said.

"Ma'am," he said. "What can I do for you?"

"I was actually going to ask you that question. I'm Scatter, Focus's partner. What's the situation, and how can we help?"

"Pleased to meet you, ma'am," he said. "It's just a jack-knife. No injuries, luckily, but the truck is wedged up under the trailer and it ain't moving again without some shop time. We got a tow truck and another truck on the way to handle the cargo, but if y'all could clear the rig off the road so we could get traffic flowing again, that would be a huge help."

"Not a problem. You want it on the median, or off to the side?"

"Best put it off to the side."

"Want me to face it backwards so it will be easier to cross load?"

"If you could ma'am."

"Clear your men out of the way."

The officer started pulling his men back, and Danny took a moment to let her senses wander over the truck, checking for unseen damage. She didn't want to spark a fire with an unnoticed fuel leak or accidently shear the trailer in half. Once she was sure she had a good sense of everything, she looked over at the officer, who gave her a thumbs up. She reached out and lifted the truck telekinetically, using a bit of force to straighten out the rig, then turning it so it faced into traffic before floating it over to the side of the road. As she did so, she lowered the support legs on the trailer, and decoupled it from the truck, setting them down separately with enough room between them that the tow truck shouldn't have any problem hooking up. She let off her telekinetic grip slowly, watching as the truck and the trailer settled into the grass, making sure they were both stable before she released them completely. Once she was done, she turned to the officer.

"Anything else we can help with?" she asked.

"No, ma'am," the officer said. "That will do nicely."

"You have a good day, then," Danny said. She turned and walked back over to where Ayanda had waited, watching the whole thing.

"How'd I do?" she asked.

"That was perfect," Ayanda said. "Come on. We'll do a couple of laps, and if nothing turns up, we'll head home for the night."

"Sounds like a plan," Danny said.

They lifted up into the air and headed out towards the bay, doing a low pass, checking for any ships in trouble before heading back into the city.

"You know, if you're really upset, I could always ask Jia Li if she would like to come watch sometime," Ayanda said.

"Keep pushing it," Danny said.

Ayanda chuckled and drifted a little closer. "You know I love you, right?"

Danny looked over at her. "Yeah," she said. "I do. I love you, too."

Ayanda turned back to the city, and Danny did a slow sweep as they circled it. They were just coming up in the industrial parks when Danny swept over an area where her senses suddenly cut off. She pulled up short, stopping in midair to stare at the area.

"What is it?" Ayanda asked as she came to a stop.

"There," Danny said. "In the industrial parks. You see it?"

Ayanda frowned as she scanned the area. Danny felt the moment she spotted it. A huge black hole where their psionic senses couldn't reach.

"What is it?" Danny asked.

"It's Null," Ayanda said.

Danny felt a chill run down her spine. Null. The Supervillain Ayanda had fought the day after Danny had arrived in the past. The one who had almost killed her.

"We're not going in without backup this time," Danny said.

"Agreed," Ayanda said as she reached for her earpiece.

***

"I don't like this," Danny said. She and Ayanda were standing on top of a building just outside the edge of the blackout zone created by Null's powers.

"I'm not crazy about it either," Ayanda said.

"Any idea what he's doing in there?"

"Null's a high-end thief, so I'm guessing he's stealing something."

"What was he after the last time you fought him?"

"A shipment of microprocessors."

Danny reached up and touched her earpiece. "Scatter to control. Do we know what companies have offices in the Griffin Industrial Park?"

"There are eighteen tenants," David said over the coms. "You want the full list?"

"No. Just the ones that are doing high tech research," Danny said.

"You think that's what Null is after?" David asked.

"Last time he was in town, he went after a bunch of microprocessors. It would make sense," Ayanda said

"There are two companies in the park that fit the bill," David said. "Parker Imaging makes MRI machines. The second one is called Luminous Technology. They do fiber optics research."

"That's the one," Danny said.

"You're sure?" David asked.

Danny looked over at Focus, who nodded.

"We're sure. MRIs are as big as a car, take a hell of a lot of power, and are pretty much worthless outside of a research lab or hospital, but fiber optic tech is generally small, lightweight, portable, and extremely valuable to the right people."

"That's a pretty good argument," David said. "You sure you're not a detective?"

"In another life," Danny said.

"Where's our backup?" Ayanda asked.

"Cecile and the teams are two minutes out," David said. "Just hold tight and do not engage. I don't want a repeat of last time."

Danny glanced over at Ayanda. She could feel the anger and frustration rolling off of her and she understood it. Null had gotten away from her the last time they went up against each other, and it was something that stuck in Ayanda's craw. Danny wanted a piece of the bastard for an entirely different reason. He was one of the few villains out there who actually posed a significant risk to Ayanda. For that reason alone, she wanted to end him.

She reached down and checked to make sure the two snap batons she had conjured were clipped to her belt. They were there, just like she expected, but they weren't much of a comfort. She really wanted her gun.

"It will be okay," Ayanda said.

"He hurt you," Danny said.

"I wasn't ready for him last time. I didn't have backup, and you weren't with me. It will be different this time."

"I hope so," Danny said.

"Backup is here," Ayanda said, nodding towards a small convoy of black SUVs pulling onto the industrial park.

"Let's go."

"Wait," Ayanda said.

Danny turned to her. "What is it?"

"When you get down there, you're going to realize that your powers aren't completely gone," she said. "He can't take them away completely. Even with my power split between us, he's not strong enough for that, but he doesn't know that. Save your power for the right moment."

Danny nodded. "Got it."

They lifted up into the air and flew down to meet the support teams.

***

Danny knelt behind one of the SUVs next to Ayanda and Cecile, waiting for Null and his gang to come out. She wanted to storm the place. Kick down the door, find Null, and kick in the bastard's teeth. The problem was, they didn't have probable cause for a raid. The fact that two Superheroes couldn't use their powers to peek into an area wasn't enough for a warrant, and there hadn't been any alarms sounded. That worried Danny more than she wanted to admit. It was a weekday, which meant there should be people inside the building. People who could be in danger. People could be dead, and they would have no way of knowing it.

"I hate this part," Cecile said.

Ayanda turned to Danny. "Last time, Null's power didn't stop you from reaching me with an empathic connection."

Danny glanced over at Ayanda for a second, before turning back to the building. "I'll give it a try," she said.

Null's ability had pushed the powers she'd gotten from Ayanda down, crushing them under an oppressive weight until Danny could just barely reach them. It felt like someone standing on her chest, and the only thing that Null's powers didn't seem to be smothering was the link she had with Ayanda. She could still feel her just as surely as if they were at home in bed, though Danny did feel a slight burning sensation in the mating mark. She hadn't thought to reach for her empathic senses, but now she did, and was surprised at how easily they came to her. She could feel Ayanda next to her, like an echo of what she felt through their link. Beyond that was Cecile, and then the other Marshals, right where they should be. She reached out further, focusing on the building, trying to get a feel for what was inside.

She almost recoiled when she did. Fear. So much fear from so many people. Anger. Fury. Frustration. Something darker. Murderous intent.

"There are hostages," Danny said.

"You're sure?" Cecile asked.

"Yes," she said. "We have to move. He's going to kill them."

"Control, did you hear that?" Cecile asked.

"I did. Go for breach on my authority."

"Breaching team, move up," Cecile ordered.

Danny felt a spike in the rage coming from inside and turned to Ayanda. "We're out of time."

Ayanda grabbed her hand and the link swung open wide, the way it had the day Danny had fought Eurion. Their minds merged into one as they reached for their power, finding it deep down, buried under the weight of Null's ability. They would only get one chance to pull this off, so they let Danny's empathic sense home in on the people inside who didn't feel fear. The ones who felt powerful. Then they reached out through spacetime, finding a point in the middle, a point where they could do the most damage. They grabbed hold of that spot, and they pulled.

It was agony. Teleporting usually felt a bit like falling. For a brief moment, the world was moving the wrong way before you settled into your new location. Teleporting didn't usually hurt; this time, it was like running naked through a briar patch. Pain ripped at them the whole way, and instead of a slight wobble when they landed, both of them staggered into a room filled with eight gunmen and thirty or so hostages.

Surprise saved their lives. It bought them time to recover. Time they used to good effect. They picked targets and attacked. Danny drove a snap kick into a gunman's throat and snatched his submachine gun out of his hands. She turned and slammed the gun into the face of a second gunman as Ayanda slammed the head of another one into the wall.

Danny dropped the submachine gun and reached for her batons, deploying them with a flick of her wrist and the characteristic snap as they locked open. A fourth gunman caught cold steel to the temple as Ayanda kicked two others in the head in rapid succession. Six gunmen down in a matter of seconds and they were moving, headed towards the last two, who were over by the door. Their backs had been turned when Danny and Ayanda had appeared, and only the pained cries of their comrades had alerted them to the danger, but the warning came too late. Danny's and Ayanda's minds were still merged. They moved and attacked as one. Both leapt at the same time, both drove their feet into the face of their chosen target, slamming their heads back against the wall with enough force to put them down.

Danny picked up one of the submachine guns and stationed herself at the door, ready in case the other hostiles she could still feel in the building came their way. Ayanda pulled zip cuffs off her belt and restrained the two hostiles by the door, then went back for the others. They felt Null's rage building through Danny's empathic sense. They knew they didn't have much time, but without access to their powers, they could only move so fast.

Once the last of the gunmen was zip tied, Danny put down the gun and grabbed her batons again. They could feel the breach team inside, heading their way, but they didn't have time to wait. They charged ahead, moving down the hall at a dead run until they came to the right room. They didn't wait. Danny kicked in the door and Ayanda went through. Danny followed.

Three more hostiles. Two gunmen and Null. A man on his knees. Null had a gun to the back of his head.

"Where are the schematics?" Null yelled, not realizing what was coming for him. The gunmen, less enraged, less focused on the hostage, turned and fired. Danny dove left. Ayanda dove right. The first blast of gunfire missed.

If they'd had their powers, it would have been over, but they didn't, and the gunmen were already tracking on them. They reached for their power, but the teleport had taken too much. They couldn't pull another miracle through the strength of Null's ability, but their minds were still linked. They still had Danny's empathic abilities. Danny reached out and touched the minds of the gunmen and Ayanda reached deep inside herself, into the bottomless wellspring of pain that had been with her since the day she became Focus. The pain of watching her species die. The pain of surviving when she wasn't meant to. The pain of centuries of being alone. She pulled that pain up and pushed it down Danny's empathic link with the gunmen, and they fell to their knees, screaming in psychic agony.

Null turned, attention drawn by the gunfire and the screams, a huge pistol in his hand.

"You!" he screamed, aiming for Ayanda.

It broke the connection between Ayanda and Danny. Not because of shock or fear, but because for the first time since they had teleported, they didn't agree on a course of action. Ayanda told Danny to take Null out while he was distracted. Danny only saw the gun pointed towards Ayanda, and she reacted.

***

Getting shot was an entirely new experience for Danny. Oh, she'd been shot at before. She'd been punched, kicked, spit on, bitten, had her foot stomped on, been kneed in the crotch. Once she'd had someone try to stab her, and of course, she'd gotten zapped by Gammawave. The hazards that came with hunting fugitives and fighting Supervillains. But an actual bullet to the chest was a new one.

She hit the ground, clutching the impact site as agony blossomed through her chest. There was no blood. When she'd created her uniform, one of the things she'd made sure of was that it was bulletproof, but wearing a bulletproof costume didn't stop getting shot in the tit from hurting like a bitch.

She heard a scream, and she felt the terror and rage that came with it. Felt them drive Ayanda to reach down and connect with the power Null was still suppressing. She felt the force of Ayanda's rage shatter Null's power suppression field and felt her powers snap back to her, washing away the pain as her healing kicked in.

Ayanda raised her hands, energy surrounding them. She hurled a blast towards Null, but she was a second too late. Before she let go of the blast, he touched a button on his gauntlet and vanished, just like he had the last time they fought. The energy blast blew out the wall behind where Null had been standing, but Ayanda barely noticed.

She dropped down by Danny's side, looking her over.

"Are you okay?" Ayanda asked.

"Fine," Danny said.

"Are you fucking crazy?" Ayanda asked. "What the fuck was that? Why did you dive in front of a bullet?"

"Reflex?"

Ayanda screamed. "You fucking idiot!" she said as she pulled Danny into her arms. "You scared the shit out of me."

"I'm wearing a bulletproof costume," Danny said.

"And what if he'd shot you in the head?" Ayanda asked. "You fucking idiot," she growled before she pulled Danny into a kiss.

"Less yelling. More of that," Danny said when the kiss was over.

"Um...help," someone said, and both of them turned to see the hostage still on his knees.

"Oh," Ayanda said. "I'm sorry."

"It's okay," he said. "But can you cut me loose?"

"Yeah," Ayanda said. "I think I can manage that."

***

Danny was sitting on the back bumper of one of the ambulances while an EMT checked her over and Ayanda hovered and looked worried. Neither one of them were ready for it when Cecile appeared out of nowhere, looking ready to spit nails.

"You mind telling me what the hell that was?" Cecile asked. "We had a plan. We were going to send in a breaching team. You were going to follow."

"They were going to kill one of the hostages," Danny said.

"They were going to kill one of the hostages," Cecile said. "You couldn't share that information?"

"There wasn't time," Ayanda said.

"How did you even do that, anyway?" Cecile asked. "I thought Null's ability neutralized all your powers."

"Not entirely," Ayanda said. "He's not strong enough to shut us down completely. It takes a lot more effort to use our powers inside his field, and we usually only get one shot before we have to…recharge."

"But if you used that one shot to determine if there were hostages, then how did you teleport inside?" Cecile asked.

"Scatter is an empath," Ayanda said. "She was before she got her powers."

"And Null's field doesn't work on empaths?"

"No," Ayanda said. "Empathy isn't a metahuman ability or even a superpower. It's just a normal part of being human. Something like ninety-six percent of all humans are empaths to one degree or another. When I say Scatter is an empath, I mean that she's an exceptionally strong empath. Maybe one in a thousand humans has her potential, but most of them never learn to use it. I helped her learn how to use her abilities. And since it's not a metahuman power, Null's abilities don't seem to affect it."

"Good to know," Cecile said. "Any idea where Null escaped to?"

"None," Ayanda said. "I was a little busy at the time, because this idiot got herself shot."

"This idiot took a bullet meant for you," Danny said. "And my uniform is bulletproof."

Ayanda stared at her for a minute, then turned to Cecile. "You see what I have to put up with?"

"Yeah," Cecile said. "Someone who loves you enough to take a bullet for you. Woe is you. And why the hell isn't your costume bullet proof?"

"I've never needed it to be before now," Ayanda said.

"Well, get an upgrade," Cecile said. "Because we both know this bastard will be back."

"Will do," Ayanda said. She turned to the EMT. "Is she okay?"

The EMT nodded his head. "Yes, ma'am."

"Thank you," Ayanda said. She turned back to Cecile. "I'm going to take this idiot home and yell at her some more. We'll fill out our reports in the morning."

"Okay," Cecile said. "And thanks. You guys saved a lot of lives. I might be mad about you breaking protocol, but I appreciate the results."

"It's why we're here," Ayanda said. She reached down and took Danny's hand. "Come on. Let's go home."

Chapter Fourteen

"HEY," AYANDA CALLED OUT. Danny looked up from the report she was finishing up and smiled as Ayanda walked into the office they shared.

"Hey. What's up?"

"Nothing big," Ayanda said. Danny frowned, because she could feel something was off through their connection. "There's been another breakout in one of the former Soviet bloc countries. Just a couple of prisoners. They asked if I could come over and help out."

"When do we leave?" Danny asked.

Ayanda winced slightly, and Danny could feel tension pouring through their link. "I was going to ask if you could stay and cover the city. Last time I was over there, the locals got restless."

"I can do that," Danny said. She immediately felt the tension coming from Ayanda ease off. She leaned back in her chair and smiled. "You were worried I'd make a stink about you going without me, weren't you?"

"Kind of," Ayanda said. "We haven't done any separate missions since you became Scatter."

Danny shook her head. "Love, we're both heavy-hitters. The idea that they would need us to handle more than one emergency at a time isn't that far-fetched. I'm just surprised it took this long."

Ayanda smiled and leaned down to press a kiss to Danny's forehead. "Thank you."

"No problem. Think you'll be home for dinner?"

"I hope so. It's just three prisoners."

"Okay. I'll stop and grab some steaks on the way home."

"Sounds good. Love you."

"Love you, too," Danny said.

Ayanda teleported away, and Danny went back to working on her report.

***

Being a solo Superhero sucked. It wasn't that Danny minded helping out, or that the work itself wasn't important. She'd broken up two attempted bank robberies, four convenience store hold ups, and a mugging, rescued a cabin cruiser that had capsized when it got too close to a supercargo, and even popped over to Tampa to help put out a dock fire that was getting out of control. All a good day's work, especially considering it was barely 2:00 PM, but without Ayanda there to talk to and joke with, it was all a bit dull. She even found herself missing Lori, if for no other reason than Lori's constant running commentary kept things interesting.

After her last bit of supering, she grabbed a couple of gyros and some chili cheese fries at the mall and sat down on the edge of the roof to eat, but instead of thinking about rescues and how she could help the first responders, she just found herself looking forward to dinner. A nice salad, some clam chowder for a soup course, then steak, mashed potatoes with a nice thick gravy, some honey glazed carrots, and some peanut butter cheesecake for dessert. Ayanda would love it, and once they were done, maybe a quiet evening spent cuddled up in bed.

She sighed as she balled up the wrapper of the first gyro and dropped it in the sack her lunch had come in. She had to face it. She was lonely. Ayanda had been gone for less than six hours, and she was lonely. It was kind of pathetic, if she were honest. She'd thought about reaching out through the link, just to feel more connected to Ayanda, but the link was strangely silent. She could still feel Ayanda, knew she was okay, but she wasn't getting the normal ups and downs she usually got through the link. It worried her a little, but she figured it was probably just the tedium. She'd done fugitive retrieval, and unlike a certain pair of movies featuring Tommy Lee Jones, she knew that ninety-nine percent of a manhunt was pure boredom.

It weighed on her a bit more than it probably should, though. The loneliness. If she was like this after less than a day, then how bad would it be for Ayanda if she were gone for twenty-nine years? It hurt to think about, but then, every time she thought about what it would be like for Ayanda if she went back to her own time, it hurt.

When she finished her lunch, she looked out across the city. She could just see Sunrise Tower from where she was, and she thought about going back home and breaking out the physics books. She hadn't touched them in almost three months. Not since she and Ayanda had finally gotten together. When she'd arrived in the past almost nine months earlier, she'd thought she could find a way to get home faster. Now, she wondered if she could use the books to find a way that she could stay without disrupting the timeline.

"Control to Scatter," Cecile said over comms.

"Scatter here. Go ahead, control."

"We've got another one for you."

"Figures. What is it this time? A kid fell down a well?"

"Close. A truck lost control on the Wabasso Causeway Bridge. Cab's hanging over the side and the driver is trapped."

"Is that North or South?"

"North. Head that way, and I'll guide you in."

"On it."

Scatter picked up the sack with her lunch, and chucked it in the general direction of one of the trash cans below, using a bit of telekinesis to make sure it went in. Then she floated up and shot off to the North, following the Indian River. She passed Vero beach, then spotted the Wabasso Causeway Bridge and the truck hanging over the side. She floated down next to one of the officers on the scene.

"Get everyone back," she said.

"Yes, ma'am," he said. He started yelling and shooing everyone back from the truck while Danny turned towards it. She reached out, using her telekinesis to lift it up and gently set it back on the bridge. Once it was settled in place, she waved to the officer and the truck driver, then shot back into the air and headed back towards Pontian.

"All taken care of," she said.

"Good job," Cecile said.

"Thanks. You got anything else for me?"

"Not at the moment," Cecile said. "How are you holding up?"

Danny frowned slightly. "What do you mean?"

"I know you must be worried about Focus," Cecile said. "I don't blame you. If my girlfriend was going toe-to-toe with Chernobog, I'd be climbing the damn walls."

Danny stopped in mid-air. "Chernobog?" she asked. "She's fighting Chernobog?"

"She didn't tell you?" Cecile asked.

"She said that three prisoners had escaped from one of the former Soviet bloc prisons. She didn't say anything about Chernobog."

"Oh, shit," Cecile said. "Um…"

"Who else?" Danny asked.

"Chernobog, Baba Yaga, and Vodenjak were the three that broke out."

"Who is with her?" Danny asked.

"The Gentleman and The Alchemist went after Baba Yaga, and Clockwork, Red Flame, and Whitewater went after Vodenjak," Cecile said.

"Cecile, who is with Focus?"

"No one," Cecile said. "After what happened to The Gentleman and Dark Fire last time, she insisted on handling Chernobog alone."

"*Fuck!*" Danny said. "Take me off the board."

"Scatter, wait," Cecile said.

"No. Take me off the board," Danny said. Cecile said something, but Danny didn't hear her. She'd already reached out through her link with Ayanda, opening the connection wide enough that she could feel what Ayanda had been hiding. Pain, fear, and exhaustion flooded through the link. Danny ignored it and reached for Ayanda's location. She found her easily enough, and before Ayanda even realized that Danny had opened the link, Danny took hold of Ayanda's location and pulled.

***

No one knew where Chernobog came from. No one knew if he was a metahuman or something else. No one was even sure of the extent of his powers. Some people thought he was what he claimed to be. The Chernobog of myth and legend. The dark god who brought misfortune and hungered for human blood. Others believed he was a demon who'd adopted the myth and legend to frighten those he hunted. Still others believed he was a sorcerer or a wizard or a warlock who had twisted his own form with magic in order to gain power.

What people were sure of was that he was one of the oldest surviving Supervillains. That he was evil on a scale few people had seen. He had fought for the Nazis in World War II during the invasion of Russia, and legend was it took a hundred Soviet Superheroes to chain him. The Soviets had built the prison in Armenia for the sole purpose of housing him. The other cells came later. Chernobog was the first prisoner, and more than any other, the one they feared until the passage of time made them forget.

Danny knew all of that, but when she appeared in the night sky over Eastern Europe, none of it meant a damn to her. She saw the monster. Sixteen feet tall if he was an inch, with a wingspan of nearly forty feet. Goat legs, a barrel chest, arms thicker than Danny's entire body, and fingers tipped with claws that were the size of her forearm. Eyes that glowed an evil red, and razor-sharp horns.

He stood on a mountain that had been split open down to its roots and called up the molten blood of the Earth itself, hurling a stream of lava at Ayanda. For one brief, terrifying moment, Danny thought it would hit her, but Ayanda twisted, throwing her power out and grabbing the molten rock, bending the stream around herself and shaping it into a massive spike as she cooled it, then hurling the weapon forged from the blood of the Earth back at the demon.

Chernobog slapped the spike of stone aside and hurled another wave of lava at Ayanda, who flung it up into the air with a dismissive wave before blasting him with a beam of energy. Chernobog roared in frustration, clearly enraged that the lava was getting him nowhere. He leapt into the air and charged forward, murder in his eyes as he flew towards Ayanda, who braced herself for the impact.

It never came. Danny reached out and grabbed the ball of lava Ayanda had slapped into the air and cooled its surface while heating the inside, then dragged it down with as much telekinetic force as possible. She accelerated it well past terminal velocity, so much so the air around it started to burn before the stone sphere slammed down on Chernobog between his wings, slamming him into the ground as the rocky exterior shattered and the molten lava inside covered him.

Ayanda turned towards her, and Danny could feel the shock pouring through the link as Ayanda realized she was there, but Danny dismissed it. She didn't have time. Chernobog was already moving, trying to claw his way out from the lava bomb Danny had hit him with. Danny reached out and picked up the spike Ayanda had thrown at him, and lifted it up, then drove it down, pinning him to the ground.

Chernobog screamed, in rage or pain or both, Danny wasn't sure, but he flailed and writhed and tried to pull loose. Danny was having none of it. She reached out and called fire and earth, liquifying the ground around him, pulling it into a sphere with him at the center, and then commanding the fire to flee, cooling the molten earth into a solid sphere of rock in seconds with Chernobog trapped at its heart.

She felt power flare within the sphere, trying to wrest the earth from her command, but she fought it, holding on to every ounce of stone, holding it in place through sheer force of will as she lifted the sphere into the air.

"Containment?" she asked through gritted teeth. The effort to hold Chernobog was already making her sweat.

Ayanda touched her ear pierce. "Ich brauche den käfig!" Ayanda said. 'I need the cage,' in German.

Danny felt Ayanda reach out and add her power to Danny's. They poured in their elemental control, fighting Chernobog's magic. They wrapped the sphere in telekinetic power as well, using main force to bolster their hold. The fight stretched out, seeming to take forever before Danny heard the sound of a chopper coming in. She looked towards the sound and saw a massive helicopter with a German flag on it coming towards them, a huge cage hung from cables underneath as a pack of helicopter gunships flew alongside it.

"The cage is enchanted," Ayanda said. "If we can get him inside it, it should hold him as long as they can get him back to a regular cell before sunrise."

Danny looked at the cage, then the improvised prison she'd forged. "We'll have to peel away the rock," she said.

"Can you hold him on your own?" Ayanda asked.

"Yes," Danny said.

"I'll let go and get ready. When I tell you, peel the rock off of him, and I'll blast him into the cage."

"Okay," Danny said.

It took a few more minutes before the helicopter dropped the cage. Once it did, all the helicopters pulled back as Danny and Ayanda got the stone sphere in place.

"I'm going to let go in five, four, three, two, one, now."

Danny felt the strain increase, and Chernobog must have felt the change too, because he started struggling harder. It didn't matter. She held on as Ayanda moved into position.

"Let him go in five, four, three, two, one...*now!*"

Danny dropped the telekinetic hold and ripped the rock away from Chernobog, and for a moment, he was completely stunned. It was all the time Ayanda needed. She slammed a blast of telekinetic force into him that hit like a runaway train, knocking him into the cage. Danny flung the cage door closed, and it locked instantly, the magic runes covering the bars and the locks glowing a bright aquamarine as the spells trapped him.

"Got you, you son of a bitch," Ayanda said.

Danny turned towards her. Ayanda must have felt Danny's anger through their link because she turned towards Danny with a guilty expression on her face.

Danny held up a finger. "Not one word," she said.

***

Danny set a couple of plates on the counter, forcing herself to be careful with them when all she wanted to do was throw them. She wanted to throw everything. The pot full of pasta. The saucepan full of meat sauce. The table where the salad was already set out. The oven where the garlic bread was baking. The refrigerator where the grocery store tiramisu was waiting for their dessert.

The problem with being a Superhero was that if she started throwing things, she might knock over a building or hit a passenger liner or knock the International Space Station out of orbit. If it was even built yet, which she didn't know, which was another thing that pissed her off.

She heard Ayanda come into the kitchen, but she didn't turn around. Instead, she picked up a wooden spoon and stirred the linguine, making sure the noodles didn't stick together, and trying her best not to be pissed that she was stirring pasta instead of flipping a couple of nice steaks. The dinner she'd planned for them had gone the same way as the rest of her plans for the night, which made her want to scream and yell and stomp her feet.

She hadn't been this angry since the night she'd walked in on Claire fucking a member of the girls' basketball team her junior year of college. Though Amber had gotten her close a few times during their ill-fated relationship.

The link made it worse because she could feel everything Ayanda felt. She could feel the love and the worry and the longing coming through the link. Not that she needed the link to know Ayanda loved her. She knew that Ayanda had done it because she loved her. She could see the logic laid out in Ayanda's head. Chernobog's abilities were based in magic, and her and Ayanda's powers weren't great at protecting against magic. Her and Ayanda's powers worked within the confines of the laws of physics, whereas magic bent and twisted and sidestepped those laws. Chernobog was dangerous, and if Danny went with her to fight him, she might get hurt. It made sense. It made perfect fucking sense, which only made Danny angrier.

She felt Ayanda's hands settle on her hips, and Ayanda's breasts pressed against her back. Her body betrayed her and leaned into the touch. She wanted it. She needed it. She craved the comfort of Ayanda's arms around her. She wanted to curl up with her head on Ayanda's shoulder and cry away the hurt and fear and stress, which only made her angrier.

She felt Ayanda press a kiss to her shoulder and she wanted to melt. Another one a little higher up, and then another, and another, until Danny realized what was about to happen. She stepped away and turned around, pointing the wooden spoon in her hand at Ayanda like it was a dagger she was going to drive through her heart.

"Don't you fucking dare," Danny said.

"What?" Ayanda asked.

"Don't think you can come in here and kiss the magic 'get her horny' button and make me forget what you did!" she snapped. Danny slammed the wooden spoon down on the counter as the timer for the pasta went off. She waved her hand and the pasta rose up out of the boiling water and dropped into the sauce. Another wave of her hand and half a cup of the water from the pasta pot followed it, then the saucepan started moving back and forth, tossing the pasta with the sauce.

Ayanda at least had the decency to look guilty when she realized she was busted, but she didn't have the sense to shut up.

"I just wanted to apologize," she said.

"The fuck you did," Danny said. "Apologizing would mean you were actually sorry, and you're not. You're not even a little bit sorry about what you did. You're just sorry you got caught."

"Danny—"

"I trusted you!" Danny yelled. "You came to me this morning and I trusted you. I have trusted you every step of the way, and today, you broke that trust. You lied to me."

"I didn't lie."

"Yes, you did! Yes, you did. A lie of omission is still a lie, and you knew that if you told me you were going after Chernobog, I would want to go with you. So, you let me think it was a couple of second-string nobodies the locals were having trouble rounding up and I bought it because I trusted you."

"I just wanted to protect you," Ayanda said.

"I don't need your protection," Danny said.

"Yes, you do!" Ayanda said. She stepped forward and put her hands on Danny's shoulders. "You do."

"I can take care of myself," Danny said.

"I know, but...I don't know if we can die, love. I don't know. But if we can, Chernobog, or someone like him would be the person to do it.

His powers can get around ours. When Cecile told me he got loose again, all I could think about was that he might kill you." Ayanda pulled Danny into her arms and hugged her as tightly as she could without using her powers.

"I just found you. I never expected you. I thought I would be alone forever, but then you walked into my life, and you just stood there, demanding that I love you, and now the thought of losing you terrifies me. You're right. I'm not sorry for what I did, because I would do anything to keep you safe."

Danny slowly wrapped her arms around Ayanda and hugged her back. The rage she felt melted away, and she wanted more than anything to say it was okay. To pretend like nothing happened, but she knew she couldn't. She'd learned that lesson the hard way. They needed to settle this, or it would keep happening, and it would eventually tear them apart.

Danny turned and pressed a kiss to Ayanda's check. "I know, love, but you can't. We can't work that way."

Ayanda pulled back a bit so she could see Danny's face. "What do you mean?"

"I mean that if we're going to work, if we're going to be together, it isn't enough for us to love each other. We have to respect each other. Both of us have to let the other one make their own decisions. You said I could be out there with you if I wanted, and I decided that I did, and now you have to respect that decision."

"I do," Ayanda said.

"Only when it's not a risk," Danny said. "Ayanda, you are going to run out there and risk your life, and if you don't think that it would hurt me just as much to lose you, then you don't respect me at all."

"It's not that," Ayanda said. "I know how you feel about me. How could I not? With the link, I feel what you feel. But I was made for this. I was literally created to fight evil. Stopping monsters like Chernobog is the reason I exist, but it's different for you."

"No, it's not," Danny said. "Love, this is not what you were made for. Your people created you to stop Idimoni. To lock him in a prison. You did that. You fulfilled your purpose. You're allowed to have a life outside of being a hero. Being Focus is a choice. Not an obligation."

Ayanda stared at her as if she'd just said the sky was orange and the sun was purple. "A choice?"

"Yes," Danny said. "You don't have to be Focus, love. Not if you don't want to be. And even if you do, you're allowed to take time away.

Cops, firefighters, paramedics, and soldiers all get vacations. And I will respect whatever choice you make. Even if it's not being Focus anymore.

"But you have to give me the same respect. Being Scatter is a choice I made. Just like being a cop was a choice I made. I have been running towards danger since long before I met you, and I am not going to change anytime soon. I accepted the risk that comes with loving you. I accepted that you might die out there, being a hero, but if this is going to work, you have to respect me enough to accept the same risk. You have to accept that I might die out there, being a hero right alongside you."

"I don't know how to do that," Ayanda said.

"Then I'll help you figure it out," Danny said. "Because you're worth it. But the first rule is that you cannot lie to me again. Even by omission."

"Okay," Ayanda said.

"Promise me," Danny said. "This will not work if you use my trust against me." She felt a small moment of hesitation, but then Ayanda nodded.

"I promise," she said.

"Good," Danny said. She leaned in and kissed Ayanda. "I love you."

"I love you, too."

Chapter Fifteen

DANNY LET OUT AN amused laugh as Ayanda started kissing and licking her shoulders again. "You're going to be disappointed," she said.

Ayanda nipped at her collar bone. "What do you mean?" she asked.

"I mean I don't think I have another round in me," Danny said. "I'm pretty sure six times before breakfast is a hard limit for twenty-eight-year-old Danny."

"Well, first, you're the one who wanted to go to brunch for your birthday, and second, I believe you'll find that you stopped aging at twenty-seven."

"Well, thanks to all the time jumping shenanigans, I'm pretty sure my birthday isn't for another two and a half weeks, but it doesn't matter, because unlike you, my aging didn't stop when I was sixteen."

Ayanda made a disgusted noise. "I was twenty-four of your years old," she said.

"Yeah, well, unless you're planning on waiting until 2011 and having your way with sixteen-year-old Danny, you're still not getting a seventh round before brunch."

Ayanda laughed and pulled Danny close, wrapping her tail and wings around her. "That depends. Does sixteen-year-old Danny know how to do that thing with her tongue?"

"No," Danny said. "I learned that in college."

Ayanda gave Danny a quick peck on the lips. "I just want to make sure you have a good birthday," she said.

"I get to spend it with you, love," Danny said. "I'm pretty sure that makes it the best birthday I've ever had."

"Sap," Ayanda said.

"You're a sap," Danny said.

Ayanda settled her head on Danny's shoulder. "I wasn't trying to start anything," she said.

"Really?" Danny asked in a dubious tone.

"Really," Ayanda said. "I just...sometimes I want to touch it, just to remind myself it's real. To remind myself that you're real."

Danny leaned in and pressed a kiss to Ayanda's forehead. "Is it that hard for you to believe I love you?" she asked.

"No," Ayanda said. "No, I know you do. I can feel it. It's just, sometimes I wonder if this is all a fever dream. I was alone for so long, I never expected to be anything else. I never expected you. I never expected a human would ever look at my true form and see anything other than a monster."

Danny felt a surge of shock and anger go through her at Ayanda's words. "Did that happen to you, love?" she asked. "Is that why you were so afraid?"

Ayanda turned, hiding her face in the crook of Danny's neck.

"Love, talk to me," Danny said.

"Do I have to?" Ayanda mumbled into Danny's neck.

"No," Danny said. "But I want you to. I want to understand."

There was a long silence, and for a while, Danny was sure she wasn't going to get an answer, but then Ayanda shifted so her face wasn't buried in Danny's neck anymore.

"Her name was Harriet," Ayanda said. "I'd seen humans before her. Enough to be able to take a human form and make clothes for myself, but Harriet was the first person I spoke to on Earth. She was lonely, like I was. Her family had died, except for her brother, and he was…indifferent to her. She was kind to me. She took me in, taught me how to dress and behave properly, taught me human manners and how to make my way in human society.

"I lived with her for almost two years, and I fell in love with her. I thought she loved me back. She said she did, and I believed her enough to tell her the truth. Where I came from. What I was. I even showed her some of what I could do. She said I sounded like an angel. A champion doing God's work. And I thought maybe I wouldn't have to be alone anymore, but after a while, she asked to see what I really looked like, and I showed her."

"What happened?"

"She screamed. She called me a demon. Said the devil had sent me to tempt her into sin."

Danny hugged Ayanda tightly. "I'm sorry, love," she said.

"It's okay," Ayanda said.

"No, it's not," Danny said. "She was a fool not to see how beautiful you are. To not see that you're a gift."

Ayanda smiled at her. "You're the gift," she said. "Sometimes, I think you're the universe's way of apologizing for what happened to my people."

Danny felt her cheeks heat up and she had to look away, to take a breath and calm down. She didn't feel worthy of what Ayanda had just said. Who could, honestly? Ayanda had lost her people, her world, her culture. Everything that she had been born into and grown up with. All traded away to give her the power to stop a monster and protect the rest of the universe. How could any person be a worthy trade for that?

"Hey," Ayanda said. "Look at me."

Danny turned back to her.

"It's true," Ayanda said. "Being with you brings me peace. It makes me feel whole and alive in a way I haven't felt since I became Focus. Knowing that you love me is a miracle. One I never thought I would have."

Danny leaned forward and kissed Ayanda. "You're the miracle," she said.

Ayanda laughed and gave her a quick peck on the lips. "This may have to be one of those agree to disagree situations," she said.

"Oh, I have ways to persuade you," Danny said.

"Really?"

"Really," Danny said. She turned away and tilted her head just so, baring the back of her neck, and her mating mark, to Ayanda.

It turned out that twenty-eight-year-old Danny could manage seven times before breakfast after all.

***

"Reservation for Robinson," Ayanda said.

"One moment," the hostess replied. She looked down at her book while Danny wondered if she could get away with goosing Ayanda as a bit of payback. They'd ended up having to teleport in order to make their reservation, and Ayanda had kissed the mating mark right before they left, which made Danny want to climb her like a cat climbing a Christmas tree right there in the middle of the restaurant. The worst part about it was she could feel how smug Ayanda was about the whole thing.

"It looks like the rest of your party has already been seated," the hostess said. "Right this way."

"Rest of our party?" Danny asked.

"You'll see," Ayanda said as she took Danny's hand, and pulled her along.

The hostess led them across the restaurant to a private dining room at the back. She opened the door and led them inside, and Danny stopped dead as she saw who was waiting for them. Jia Li, Eurion, and Cecile all looked up from their drinks and smiled at her.

"Here's the birthday girl," Cecile said.

Danny cringed slightly and turned to the hostess. "You didn't hear that," she said.

"Of course," the hostess said.

"Seriously," Danny said. "If anyone sings…"

"Not a word," the hostess promised. "Your server should be here with your menus in a few moments."

"Thank you," Ayanda said.

"Enjoy your meal," the hostess said before closing the door on her way out.

Ayanda pulled out Danny's seat for her, and Danny sat down.

"I thought you might like your friends to be here," Ayanda said.

Danny smiled up at Ayanda. "Thank you," she said.

"See," Cecile said. "Heart Eyes, just like I said."

"I think it's lovely," Jia Li. "True love is so rare in this day and age."

"Guys," Ayanda said as she took her seat.

"No, Jia Li is quite right," Eurion said. "I haven't had anyone look at me that way since my last wife passed back in 1911. Perhaps I should have offered you more for her when I had the chance."

Danny laughed and shook her head. "Sorry to disappoint you, Eurion, but you're a little…male for my tastes."

"Oh," Eurion said. "I hadn't realized that would be a problem." Eurion waved his hand and a column of smoke rose up around him, swallowing him completely before dissipating almost as quickly as it appeared, leaving behind an absolutely gorgeous young redheaded woman in a white tuxedo with no shirt underneath. "Is this better?"

Before Danny could say anything, the sound of Cecile coughing filled the room. She turned and saw the poor woman turning an impressive shade of red.

"Are you okay?" Danny asked.

Cecile nodded and held up her water. "Wrong pipe," she said.

"Oh, dear. Did I do that?" Eurion asked in a voice that somehow managed to come across as both sultry and faux innocent at the same time.

"Eurion, behave," Jia Li said in a warning tone.

Eurion sighed in a way that somehow managed to make her breasts threaten to escape from the tuxedo jacket. Danny glanced over at Cecile, whose eyes were roughly the size of dinner plates at that moment and shook her head. She turned back to Eurion.

"Can you not give my friend a heart attack?" Danny asked.

"I was just trying to be accommodating, my dear," Eurion said. She waved her hand, and the column of smoke returned. It vanished again, leaving Eurion behind in the form Danny was more accustomed to. He turned to Jia Li.

"I must say, humans these days are so much pickier about gender than they used to be."

"I think you're simply noticing more, old friend," Jia Li said.

"Perhaps," Eurion said. "You know I have a hard time keeping up with the human world when I don't have a bride."

"So, how did you and Danny meet, exactly?" Cecile asked.

"Oh," Eurion said. "That is a fun story. Partinaci Ragusa sent his son to murder me, and Danny stumbled into the middle of their attack on my den in her quest for Tacos for Tuesday. She beat little Tony and his compatriots senseless, but then she objected when I tried to finish them off. We had a lovely fight. She punched me between the eyes, which I must say was quite the surprise at the time."

Cecile turned and looked at Danny. "You're the one who put Tony Ragusa in the hospital with a torn larynx?"

Danny shrugged. "I just wanted tacos."

"Uh huh," Cecile said. "Where is that waiter? I need a mimosa for this."

***

"So, let me make sure I have this straight," Cecile said, waving her mimosa in the air as she talked.

"Honey, ain't nothing straight about anyone at this table," Danny said, which earned her a glare from Cecile, and laughter from Jia Li and Eurion.

"She does have a point," Jia Li said.

"Let me make sure I have this correct," Cecile growled. "Eurion and Jia Li both offered to buy you for your weight in gold."

"No," Danny said. "Jia Li offered twice my weight."

"My mistake," Cecile said.

"A rather large mistake," Jia Li said, sounding slightly insulted. "I know something's worth when I see it."

"Right," Cecile said. "But you ended up with 'Kelly' here for free."

"I did," Danny said before taking a sip of her own Mimosa.

Ayanda reached up and slipped her arm around Danny's shoulder. "Some of us don't need to pay for our women," Ayanda said in a smug tone.

"Oh, please," Danny said. "I practically had to hit her over the head with a club and drag her back to my cave by her hair."

"Maybe we should have asked you to pay for her," Jia Li said.

"You wouldn't have gotten a very good price," Danny said. "I don't have any money."

"Just a superpowered sugar-mama," Cecile said.

Danny glared at Cecile. "I know where you sleep, La Saint," she said.

"Tell me it's not true," Cecile said.

Danny glared.

"Superpowered sugar-mama..." Ayanda said. "I think I can live with that."

"Are you interested in a similar arrangement, Ms. La Saint?" Eurion asked. "If you are, I can be quite generous."

"Uh...no thanks," Cecile said.

"Is it my current form?" Eurion asked. "I believe you were rather taken with the one I wore earlier. I can change back, if that's more to your liking."

"No," Danny said.

Eurion turned towards her. "I wasn't negotiating with you, my dear."

"No, you weren't," Danny said. "But she's taken."

"I am?" Cecile said.

Eurion looked at Cecile for a moment, then back to Danny. "She doesn't seem to think so."

"If you want Cecile, it will cost you that pretty blue gem you like so much," Ayanda said.

Eurion flinched and drew back from the table. He looked at Cecile. "I apologize. I had not realized that the price would be quite that high. I must decline."

Cecile looked back and forth between Eurion and Ayanda. "What just happened?"

"Our friend just reminded Eurion that there are other types of claims, beyond bride price," Jia Li said. "I don't think she wants to let you get dragged off to Eurion's new territory."

"I see," Cecile said.

"You know, that reminds me. Where did you end up? I'm guessing not Jacksonville, after what happened there."

"No," Eurion said. "I ended up in Sun City."

"I thought a dragon already had a claim on Sun City," Danny said.

"Yes. Rachel," Eurion said. "A lovely young dragon. Born in New York during all of that unpleasantness with King George a few centuries back. She's done quite well for herself for one so young, but young dragons aren't quite so territorial as us older dragons. She was willing enough to exchange claims. I dare say she was even eager, though I don't know why."

"Rachel?" Danny asked, trying her best to keep her voice neutral.

"Yes," Eurion said. "A bit eccentric, to be honest. She loves working with iron and steel."

"That's eccentric?" Cecile asked.

"For a dragon." Jia Li said. "Most of us are goldsmiths by trade, though silversmiths are a close second. Working base metals like iron and steel is seen as what your kind would call slumming it."

Danny laughed. "Okay, you have got to introduce me," she said.

Ayanda sighed. "Must they?" she asked. "I'm not sure I want to have to fend off someone else making offers to buy my mate."

"Can't handle the competition?" Cecile asked.

"There's no competition," Danny said. "She licked me, so I belong to her."

"I'll bet she licks you all the time," Cecile said.

"Damn right she does," Danny said.

"I'm beginning to regret ordering that third pitcher of mimosas," Ayanda said.

"I'm not," Jia Li said. "In fact, I think we need more."

"That's because you're a nosy pervert," Eurion said.

"And you're a prude," Jia Li said.

Danny turned back to Ayanda. "I've had very good luck at making friends with dragons."

"Yes," Ayanda said. "Only half the dragons you've met have tried to incinerate you."

"Right!" Danny said. "So, I want to meet Rachel."

"You're drunk, aren't you?" Ayanda asked.

"It's my birthday," Danny said. "I'm allowed to get drunk and meet dragons if I want to!"

Ayanda leaned in and kissed Danny on the cheek. "Yes, you are."

"So, you'll introduce us?" Danny asked.

Ayanda looked over at Jia Li.

"I'll make the arrangements," Jia Li said.

"Great!" Danny said. She turned to Cecile. "You have to come meet the dragon lady, too."

"I do?"

"Yep!" Danny said.

"Why?"

"Because reasons," Danny said.

"Because reasons?" Cecile said. "That doesn't make any sense."

"It doesn't make any sense now," Danny said. "But I will have you know that, in thirty years, that is an absolutely devastating argument."

"I weep for the future," Jia Li said.

***

One of the unfortunate things about having so much life stuffed inside her was that even though Danny was good and sozzled when she got into the cab, by the time they got to Cecile's apartment and walked her to the door, she was stone cold sober. It did make teleporting back to the apartment a lot easier, since she could teleport herself and Ayanda didn't have to carry her through the port, but she could have done with an afternoon spent pleasantly drunk.

It wasn't that she was unhappy. So far, her birthday had been lovely. Waking up, making love to Ayanda, getting surprised by her friends at brunch. Finding that she didn't even have to stretch the word friend to cover Eurion, who was actually charming when he wasn't trying to incinerate her.

It was more that there were things that weren't quite right. She missed getting a call from her mom and dad and her sisters. She hated that in eight months, she was going to have to leave Ayanda alone, and that for her, only a few seconds would pass, but for Ayanda, it would last almost three decades.

She twisted her hair up as she went into the kitchen. She'd let it grow out since she'd been in the past, which was convenient for covering the mating mark when she was out in public, but she knew how much Ayanda liked to be able to see it, so she always wore her hair up at home so the scar was exposed.

She grabbed a couple of glasses of water and headed to the bedroom, where she found Ayanda already stretched out in her natural form. She flushed a little as she felt Ayanda's eyes on the mating mark, but she played into it. She turned her back as she stripped down, letting Ayanda's eyes linger until she was ready to crawl into bed.

"You should get more furniture that fits you," she said as she climbed into bed.

"Is that your way of telling me you don't want to spend all your time naked in my bed?" Ayanda asked.

"No," Danny said. "I like that part, but you shouldn't feel like an alien in your own apartment."

"I'm used to it," Ayanda said. "And I have the bedroom."

"It's not enough," Danny said.

"How would I explain the furniture to anyone who saw it?"

"Don't," Danny said. "Love, this place is supposed to be your home, not a part of your disguise. How much time did you spend as yourself before I came along?"

"Just when I slept," Ayanda admitted.

"That's not right," she said. "You have the right to be yourself. You have to hide every minute you're out there helping people. You shouldn't have to hide at home, too."

Ayanda rolled on her side so she was facing Danny. "You know, sometimes I think you care more about me than I care about myself."

"That's because you had given up on yourself," Danny said. "You'd given up on Ayanda, let Focus and Kelly replace her. I don't want you to do that again while I'm gone."

"It might be easier," Ayanda said. "When I'm Focus, I don't have to feel anything. It's just the current problem, the current crisis. Being Ayanda means being alone."

"It doesn't have to," Danny said. "Cecile knows you now. And you have Eurion and Jia Li, and I'm sure Rachel will adore you."

"You know Rachel in the future, don't you?" Ayanda asked.

"If it's the same Rachel," Danny said. "I think it is. The timing would be about right. I didn't know she was a dragon, but then, I had never met a dragon before."

"I don't know about showing Cecile my true form," Ayanda said. "It's easier with the dragons. When they look at me, they see kin. I'm not sure Cecile would want to see the real me."

"Cecile isn't Harriet," Danny said. "And the world has changed a lot in the last two centuries. When you met Harriet, the dragons and the other magical races were all in hiding, metahumans were a lot rarer, and most people had never even heard of aliens, much less seen one. Now there's a derelict alien spaceship the size of Mount Kilimanjaro in orbit, there's a dragon with his own TV show, and metahumans are a dime a dozen. People know the difference between aliens and demons now."

"I think you're braver than I am," Ayanda said.

"Hardly," Danny said. "You're the one who lived through the end of her planet and kept going."

"It wasn't a planet," Ayanda said.

"What?"

"My home world Umhlaba wasn't a planet. It was a moon. We orbited a gas giant about the size of Saturn."

"Were there rings?"

"Massive ones," Ayanda said.

"It sounds beautiful," Danny said.

"It was," Ayanda said. "I can show you, if you like."

"You can?"

Ayanda nodded. "One of the side effects of becoming Focus. I'm surprised you haven't noticed yet. I have perfect recall of my entire life."

Danny frowned. Perfect recall of her entire life? Surely, she would have noticed something like that. She thought about it for a second, trying to recall some silly detail that she would never remember on her own. A math test from first grade maybe.

Sure enough, a picture of a test floated into her mind. She could see every detail. Even where she had erased an answer to correct it.

"Holy shit," Danny said.

"Yep. It's a blessing, and a curse."

"How so?"

"Try to remember the way you felt the first time you tried to talk to a girl you liked."

Danny promptly rolled over and buried her head in a pillow as she recalled the day in seventh grade when she'd tried to ask Olivia Preston to go to the spring dance with her. She'd spent the whole day trying to work up the nerve, only she'd made herself so sick with worry; she'd walked into her sixth period class, taken one look at Olivia, and promptly ran to the bathroom and tossed her lunch.

"I hate you right now," she said.

Ayanda laughed and pulled her into a hug. "You want to see Umhlaba?"

Danny looked up at Ayanda. "Yes," she said.

Ayanda pressed her forehead to Danny's. "Close your eyes."

Danny did as she was told, and she felt the link open wide. A moment later, she was surrounded by the sights and sounds and smells of Ayanda's world.

Ayanda was right. It was beautiful.

***

Danny slipped out of bed after Ayanda dozed off. She did her best to stay as quiet as possible as she made her way to the bathroom. Once there, she closed the door, and then turned and looked in the mirror. The woman she saw looking back at her wasn't half bad, if she did say so herself. Tall, lean, muscular. Not terribly curvy, but that was a side effect of her athletic build and the amount of time she'd spent exercising. Features that were a bit softer than she would have liked, but then, she'd always kind of wanted to go for a nice soft butch look, and she'd never seemed to get much past color-tinted Chapstick on the butch/femme scale.

When she'd gotten her powers, one she'd carefully avoided using was shapeshifting. She had seen way too many girls get caught up in makeup and fad diets and unrealistic beauty standards, and she didn't even want to think about the kinds of self-esteem issues something like shapeshifting could lead to, but tonight, she had come to a realization.

She'd made love to Ayanda in all three of her forms at various points over the last few months. She had tried to be good, to stick to making love to Ayanda in her true form, but Ayanda had loved Danny's reaction to her different forms. Tonight, seeing Ayanda's home world, she'd come to realize she'd been neglecting something her shapeshifting ability could let her do for Ayanda. A way to return some of what Ayanda had given her.

She looked in the mirror, and she thought of all the ways Ayanda had shown her how to use the shapeshifting ability when she had implanted the skills Danny needed to use her powers, and she thought about all the different members of Ayanda's species she had seen in Ayanda's memories. Then she began to reshape herself. First, she took away the hair. Then she made her ears grow. Then her legs became digitigrade, and her pinkie fingers became second thumbs. The wings were the hardest, but they sprang out of her back and took shape. She made her skin a bit redder than Ayanda's, giving her a bit of a purple hue instead of the blue Ayanda sported, but once all was done, she looked at herself in the mirror and saw her own glowing blood pumping through her wings and ears and leaving lines all over her body, and when she opened her mouth, she saw the fangs there.

It would take practice to learn to move right, to learn to use the extra limbs and deal with the different configuration of her body, but she had time. Not a lot, but it should be enough that at least one night before she went back to her own time, Ayanda would get to hold a member of her own species in her arms.

Chapter Sixteen

"ARE YOU SURE THIS is a good idea?" Cecile asked as they approached the restaurant.

"I'm positive," Danny said. "Besides, it took us nearly two months to set up, so if you even think of ruining it by running out on us, I can promise you that you will have an angry Superhero hunting you down and dragging you back."

"I don't see why you need me to go with you to meet this dragon lady," Cecile said.

"Cecile, a word of advice," Ayanda said.

"Yes?"

"Just let her have her way. You know she's going to get it in the end, and the less you fight, the less she gloats."

"That's not reassuring," Cecile said. "Especially since the last two dragons I met started arguing over how much gold I was worth."

"Cheapskates, both of them," Danny said. "You're worth at least three times your weight in gold, and not an ounce less."

"Is your girlfriend planning on selling me to the dragon?" Cecile asked.

"Maybe," Ayanda said. "I didn't think to ask."

Danny shook her head as she pulled the door to the restaurant open. Ayanda and Cecile followed her inside as she walked up to the maître d.

"Hello. We're meeting Rachel Levi," Danny said.

"Ah," he said. "Follow me." He led them towards the back of the restaurant to a door. He knocked, and after a brief pause, he led them inside, where they found Rachel and Jia Li waiting. Danny couldn't keep the smile off her face.

There was no wondering if this was the right Rachel. The woman before her was a much younger version of the short, stoutly built woman who had greeted her the night she'd gone to visit Cecile in 2021. The bushy hair was brown and red instead of brown and gray, and she lacked the glasses and the age lines on her face, but it was very much the same face. The big difference was what she was wearing. When she'd met Rachel in the future, Rachel had been wearing loose fitting clothes that mostly hid her physique. That wasn't the case here and now. She was wearing a clingy, blue off-the-shoulder dress that left very little to the imagination, instead showing that while she might only be five foot, three inches and thickly built, she was a solid slab of well-defined muscle.

"Ah," Jia Li said. "Here they are."

"Sorry we're a little late," Danny said.

"Don't worry about it," Jia Li said. "Please, have a seat."

Danny moved quickly, taking the seat next to Jia Li and leading Ayanda to the seat next to her, which left Cecile no choice but to take the seat next to Rachel. Danny had to fight down the urge to do a victory dance, because in the ninety seconds or so it took them to get seated, she caught Cecile sneaking glances at Rachel's arms three times and licking her lips twice.

"Your server should be in shortly," the maître d said. "I do hope you ladies have a lovely evening."

"Thank you," Rachel said. The maître d bowed and stepped out of the room, closing the door behind him, which Jia Li seemed to take as a cue.

"I suppose introductions are in order," Jia Li said. "Rachel, these are our local Superheroes, Focus, who goes by Kelly in her civilian life, and Scatter, who goes by Danny. The lovely young woman accompanying them is one of their Marshal friends, Cecile La Saint."

"It's a pleasure to meet all of you," Rachel said, without her eyes ever once leaving Cecile. It was all Danny could do not to squeal.

"Likewise," Cecile said.

"And thank you all for agreeing to my choice of restaurants. You have no idea how hard it is trying to keep kosher when you're eating out."

"I still don't know why you abide by those silly laws," Jia Li said.

"I'm Jewish," Rachel said.

"You're a dragon, dear. Your mother just happened to be married to a Jewish woman when you hatched."

"And she raised me to be a good Jewish girl," Rachel said. She turned to Cecile. "Some of the older dragons don't see the point in keeping the traditions we're born with, but I think it's important to remind ourselves of where we come from."

"That can be hard when the culture you come from rejects who you are," Cecile said.

"Or when it's gone," Danny added as she took Ayanda's hand. She gave it a small squeeze and felt a surge of warmth come through the link.

"I know what you mean," Rachel said. "Jewish culture didn't have a lot of places for a girl with two mothers a couple of centuries back. Reform Judaism is much more accepting these days, but the Orthodox community still looks at me as the product of sin."

"I'm sorry," Cecile said. "I didn't mean to bring up painful memories."

"Oh, no. Don't worry about it. It sounds like it's something we share. Where are you from, if I may ask?"

"Oh," Cecile said. "I'm a bit of a mix. My mother is Haitian, and my father is Cubano, so you've got all the tension of being a mixed child from two cultures that don't necessarily get along, and on top of that, I'm a lesbian."

"That does sound like a recipe for disaster," Rachel said. "Though I must say, a rather beautiful one."

Danny had to bite her tongue to keep from laughing at how deeply Cecile blushed, but she couldn't hold the laughter in anymore when Ayanda leaned over and whispered in her ear.

"She's better at this than Eurion and Jia Li."

Danny let out a loud bark of laughter. Jia Li scoffed and rolled her eyes. Cecile drove her elbow into Ayanda's side, while Rachel gave everyone a confused look.

"Did I miss something?" Rachel asked.

"No," Cecile said. "My friends here think they're funny, but they're mistaken."

"Cecile, don't be a spoil sport," Jia Li said. She turned to Rachel. "We had dinner with Eurion a few weeks ago, and there was some discussion of Cecile's worth, but you know how old-fashioned Eurion is. There was no preamble. It was right to negotiating price."

Rachel shook her head and turned to Cecile. "I apologize. Sometimes my fellows forget that we no longer live in a day and age where women can be bought and sold."

"It's okay," Cecile said.

"It's not," Rachel said. "But my kind are long lived and resistant to change."

"You don't seem that way," Cecile said.

"I'm very young by dragon standards," Rachel said. "I haven't even taken my first bride."

"You haven't?"

"No," Rachel said. "Though to be clear, bride is an antiquated term we adopted simply because it was easier for us to acquire women to fill the role. Dragons, despite the stereotype, only take what we earn or pay for. At least, most dragons. There are some thieves among us, but I'm getting off topic. Humans were more willing to part with daughters than with sons, so when we sought out companions, we could often only find women to fill the role."

"Would you prefer a man for your companion?" Cecile asked.

"Honestly, no. I don't want to paint the entire gender with a single brush, but I work in a craft that's dominated by men, and I must say, it's soured me a bit on them. I find the company of women far more pleasant."

"Really?" Cecile asked.

Before Rachel could answer, there was a polite knock on the door, and then their waitress entered the room. She took their drink order and disappeared, while everyone picked up their menu and tried to decide what to order.

"If you like lamb at all, I can't recommend the lamb with mint sauce enough."

"That does sound good," Cecile said.

"I usually get it with the olive oil and rosemary roasted potatoes, but if you're not worried about kosher, I understand the loaded mashed potatoes are delicious. If you do care, everything that is kosher on the menu is marked with a 'K'."

"I'll keep that in mind," Cecile said.

When the waitress returned a few minutes later, Cecile ordered the green salad, the stuffed mushroom appetizer, and the lamb with mint sauce with the olive oil and rosemary potatoes. Danny couldn't help but notice each item had a 'K' next to it on the menu. She went with the eggplant parmesan herself, while Ayanda got a porterhouse, and Jia Li ordered the Beef Black Mushroom.

"So, are you curious?" Jia Li asked Rachel as soon as the waitress disappeared again.

"About what?" Rachel asked.

"The price we discussed, of course," Jia Li said.

"Jia Li!" Rachel said before she turned to Cecile. "I'm sorry."

"You hatchlings and your ideas about romance," Jia Li said with a shake of her head. "Never taking the practical into account."

"Stop it," Rachel said.

"All I'm saying is that if you pay for what you take, no one can come along later and try to claim it for themselves," Jia Li said. "It's like that nasty business with that Helen woman. If Paris had paid for her, then Illum never would have been sacked."

Rachel looked at Cecile. "I'm sorry."

Cecile laughed and shook her head. "It's okay. We might as well let her talk. Otherwise, we'll never hear the end of it." She turned to Jia Li. "So, how much did you and Eurion decide on?"

"Oh, we never reached a consensus. Eurion is a bit of a cheapskate, to be honest. He said you were worth one and a half times your weight in gold. I said two."

"You're both cheap," Danny said. "She's worth at least five."

"Five?" Jia Li said. "Don't be ridiculous. My fourth bride was the daughter of the Emperor of China, and I only paid four times her weight in gold."

Rachel looked right at Cecile. "I don't know," she said. "Five honestly sounds like a bargain to me."

***

It was an odd thing, watching two people fall in love. It wasn't something Danny had ever seen happen in real time before, but by the time the appetizers appeared, Rachel and Cecile were off in their own little world, talking, laughing, flirting, feeding each other off their own plates. By the time the entrée arrived, Danny honestly wasn't sure if they even remembered there were other people in the room. She and Ayanda both kept quiet. It was easy enough to say anything they wanted to say to each other through their link. Even Jia Li, professional shit stirrer that she was, just sat there with a soft smile on her face as she watched.

They talked about everything. Growing up Jewish in the early 1800s. Growing up as a biracial child in the 60s and 70s. Blacksmithing. Police work. The fact that Cecile was into woodworking, but all her tools were in storage because she was living in an apartment. It was honestly adorable, the way they wandered from topic to topic, sharing what they loved and what they were excited about.

The check was paid, and they were all sitting around sipping coffee before Rachel said something that made Jia Li break her silence.

"You know, I just realized I haven't asked," Cecile said. "How are you liking Pontian?"

"Oh, it's wonderful. Don't get me wrong, I liked Sun City well enough, but there's so much more culture here. There's the Cuban quarter and Little Haiti, and Chinatown, and a big Jewish community, and Little Saigon, and South Shore, and the Russian neighborhoods. It reminds me a bit of New York, to be honest, though I like it better here. You know in New York there are five dragons?"

"Really?" Cecile asked.

"Yes. One in each borough. It's ridiculous. If I want to go visit my mother, I have to let four other dragons know, just to avoid starting a war."

"That sounds awful," Cecile said. "Are they really that territorial?"

"Yes," Rachel said. "I understand it's instinctual, but we're intelligent creatures. You'd think we could overcome our baser instincts."

"You seem to be doing well enough with that."

"I like to think so," Rachel said. "But I admit having that dreadful little dragonkin in my territory makes my scales itch."

"Dragonkin?" Jia Li asked. "What dragonkin?"

"Oh, that awful little man. What was his name? Partinaci Ragusa. Eurion warned me that there was a mobster who might try to make trouble, but I have to admit, if he'd told me Ragusa was dragonkin, I never would have agreed to the trade."

"Partinaci Ragusa?" Danny asked. She turned to Ayanda. "Captain Porkpie's dad?"

"The one and same," Ayanda said, fury in her voice. She turned to Jia Li. "Why didn't you tell me he was dragonkin?"

"I didn't know," Jia Li said. "He's not in any of the genealogies."

"I'm sorry," Cecile said. "What is a dragonkin?"

Rachel looked at Cecile. "I'm sorry. I should have explained."

"It's okay," Cecile said.

Rachel nodded. "Dragons are more magic than flesh," she said. "Obviously we are creatures of flesh and blood, but magic flows through us, makes us what we are. But one thing we aren't is particularly fertile. If we were, the world would be peopled with dragons instead of men. And given how territorial we are, that would be a disaster.

"Like humans, we crave physical companionship as much as we do social companionship. We have sex, but our breeding seasons only come once a century or so, and we lay two or three eggs at a time. But we can mate with humans in human form. We can sire children, or even bear them. Our physical nature is fertile enough to allow for that, even if our magical nature is not. Most children born that way are human enough. They might be imbued with a bit of magic. Merlin and Morgana Le Fey were the children of dragons, but if a child is conceived by a human and dragon couple while the dragon is in season, the child gets the full measure of our magical nature visited upon them. We call them dragonkin. They're half-breeds. They have our shapeshifting ability so they can hide their true faces, but they have a draconic form. They stand about seven feet tall, walk on two legs rather than four, have wings and a tail and a dragon-like head and breathe fire, and depending on their lineage, they may have other breath weapons."

"We keep track of them," Jia Li said. "They are our children, after all. We list them in the genealogies, and the council keeps watch; they make sure the dragonkin aren't hunted by dragon slayers or the Catholic Church, but also to make sure they abide by our treaties and don't stir up trouble with the humans."

"But Partinaci Ragusa isn't in your genealogies?" Ayanda asked.

"No," Jia Li said. "If he was, the council would have skinned him alive for what happened with Eurion." She turned to Rachel. "Do you know his ancestry?"

"One of his parents was a black dragon," Rachel said.

Danny turned to Ayanda. "One of the ones from Jacksonville?"

"They're a mated pair," Ayanda said. "Mated dragons don't take human brides."

"No," Rachel said, her voice filled with anger. "But they do sometimes take human slaves."

"What happened to the dragons in Jacksonville?" Danny asked.

"They're still there," Ayanda said.

"After they tried to burn the city?" Danny asked.

"They're still waiting for their trial in the council," Jia Li said. "Some of the dragons on the Council are stalling. They resent the involvement of human authorities in our affairs, and believe no crime was committed because the incident was precipitated by humans trying to force a dragon into another dragon's territory."

"And the treaties say we can't take any action until the Dragon Council reaches a verdict," Ayanda said. She turned to Jia Li. "One of yours is running an organized crime syndicate. And he's going after dragons with a dragon blade."

"I'll see to it," Jia Li said. She turned to Rachel and Cecile. "You have my apologies, both of you. I did not mean to spoil the mood of the evening."

Rachel reached over and took Cecile's hand in hers, threading their fingers together. "Do not apologize. What you've done will make the city safer, and for that, I am indebted."

Jia Li nodded, and Rachel turned to Cecile.

"If it's okay with your friends, would you allow me to escort you home this evening?" she asked.

"I would like that," Cecile said.

"We have no objections," Danny said.

"Then I think we'll take our leave," she said. She stood up and helped Cecile to her feet. "Good evening."

"See you at work tomorrow," Cecile said. "Jia Li, a pleasure as always."

Danny and Ayanda nodded.

"Just remember not to let her sample the wares until she's handed over the gold," Jia Li said, which made Cecile blush rather spectacularly.

"Mind your manners, old mother," Rachel snapped so harshly that Jia Li flinched.

"My apologies," Jia Li said.

Rachel nodded, and then she led Cecile out of the dining room.

***

"So, I'm guessing she was the right Rachel?" Ayanda asked as the limo pulled away from the restaurant. Danny laughed and leaned into Ayanda, who responded by wrapping an arm around her and pressing a kiss to her temple.

"Definitely the right Rachel," Danny said.

"That was a nice thing you did."

"I hope so," Danny said. "Cecile has been such a good friend the last few months."

"It was," Ayanda said. "I don't think I've ever seen her connect with someone like that."

"They were married in 2021," Danny said.

"I thought it was something like that," Ayanda said. "Now, do you want to tell me what's wrong?"

Danny sighed. "I'm going to miss all of it," she said. "Twenty-nine years of my friend's life. I'm not going to get to go to her wedding. At first, I thought this was just going to hurt because I would be leaving you alone for all that time, but the longer I'm here, the more I realize how much I'm going to miss."

Ayanda pressed another kiss to her temple. "I'm sorry, love. It's not fair."

"I feel guilty about it, too. That I'm feeling sorry for myself. That I regret all the things I'm going to be missing. I get to skip across twenty-nine years, but all the people I'm leaving behind have to live through it."

"You shouldn't feel guilty," Ayanda said. "Pain is not a competition. You're allowed to want to see all of those things, and you're allowed to regret that you'll miss them."

"I wish I could stay."

"I know. I wish you could stay, too."

"It's funny. When I got here, I spent so much time with my head buried in books, trying to find a way to go home sooner. Now I just wish I'd spent all that time with you."

"We have all the time in the world, love. Just on the other end."

"It feels unfair to ask you to wait that long," Danny said.

"I would wait forever for you," Ayanda said.

Danny smiled and snuggled in closer to Ayanda. "You know how to make a girl feel loved."

"Wait until I get you home," Ayanda said. "I'll make you feel very loved."

"Mmm...I like the sound of that."

"You better," Ayanda said.

They settled into silence for a bit, but before they got all the way home, something started niggling at the back of Danny's brain.

"What are we going to do about Ragusa?" she asked.

"I'm not sure," Ayanda said. "Dragonkin are legally under the jurisdiction of the Dragon Council. Right now, it's in their hands. The good news is, the council doesn't have quite the same standards of evidence as human courts, so if they decide he's endangering the treaty, they will smack him down with prejudice."

"I'm worried he'll come after Rachel. And Cecile is in the crossfire, too."

"I wouldn't worry too much. Rachel may be young, but a fight between a dragonkin and a dragon only ends one way. And after tonight, if Ragusa dares even look at Cecile, Rachel wouldn't need the approval of the council to squash him. Going after a dragon's bride isn't just suicide. It's begging for a slow, painful death."

"What would the Marshals do to Rachel if she did stomp him?"

"I don't know," Ayanda said. "They are big on relocation any time a dragon is exposed, but there are rules for when they can, and when the dragon has the authority to defend their territory, their den, their brides, and their hoard. Those rules are why we have to wait for the council before we can do anything about those two lunatics up in Jacksonville."

"If you had told me, before I got assigned to your detail, that dragon politics would be a major factor in my social life, I would have said you were crazy."

Ayanda pressed a kiss to Danny's forehead. "None of us ever get the life we expect, love. We just have to make do with the one we get."

"As long as the one I get has you in it, I can live with that."

Chapter Seventeen

DANNY SMILED AS SHE spotted Cecile in the hall and rushed to catch up with her. She was a little surprised that Cecile didn't notice her, because Cecile usually had good situational awareness, but as she came alongside, she realized Cecile's eyes were practically closed. If it wasn't for the huge smile on her face and the way she was humming some song Danny didn't recognize, she'd think Cecile just wasn't caffeinated yet.

When Cecile started to dance just a little as she walked, Danny was pretty sure Cecile still hadn't realized she was there. She watched in amusement as Cecile danced her way down the hall, humming the same song until they got to the door to her office. She reached down and grabbed the swipe card on her belt and ran it through the card reader next to the door, then turned and looked right at Danny.

"You coming in?" she asked, surprising Danny just a bit.

"Yeah," Danny said. She followed Cecile into the office and took a seat while Cecile settled herself behind the desk. Danny could feel the emotion pouring from Cecile. Happiness, joy, contentment, anticipation, and most of all, love.

"What can I do for you this fine morning?" Cecile asked.

"You saw Rachel last night, didn't you?" Danny asked.

"I did," Cecile said.

"I take it things are going well?"

Cecile blushed. "So well," she said. "God, I feel like a teenager. No, I take that back. I never felt like this when I was a teenager. I feel like...I don't know. I just know that when we're together, I don't ever want her to leave, and when we're apart, all I want is to be with her."

"You're in love," Danny said.

"Yeah," Cecile said. "But it's so much more than that. I've been in love before, but never like this. If you'd told me two months ago that I'd fall in love with someone the night I met them, I'd have told you you're fucking nuts, but then I met Rachel, and God, it's like I can only breathe when she's with me. I know it's probably crazy, but I think she's the one. I look at her, and all I can see is forever."

"I'm happy for you, and I promise the absolute minimum number of U-Haul jokes."

Cecile laughed. "I can't even be mad, because it's true," she said. "So, was there something you needed?"

"Not really," Danny said. "I just wanted to see how my friend was doing."

"She's doing very well," Cecile said. "And she's very thankful for what you did."

"What did I do?" Danny asked innocently.

"Don't think I haven't figured it out," Cecile said. "Seriously, I know that the whole time travel thing hasn't been the easiest ride for you, and I know what going back is going to cost you and Focus, but what you gave me...I don't think I can ever thank you enough."

Danny felt herself getting a little choked up, but she nodded.

"Now, seriously, did you need anything, or can I kick you out and get to work?"

"I was wondering if we'd heard anything from the Dragon Council about Ragusa and the Jacksonville dragons?"

Cecile sighed. "No," she said. "The official line is they are still conferring on the matter. Officially, Jia Li has talked to Ragusa on the council's behalf, and requested he present himself and declare his lineage, and a decision will be made after that has happened."

"Unofficially?" Danny said.

"Unofficially, the Dragon Council is near a deadlock. There are members of the council who see Jacksonville and Ragusa as an internal territorial dispute, and don't think the Marshals have any business interfering, which is a nightmare."

"If it's an internal territorial dispute, can't Rachel just squash Ragusa like the little bug he is?"

"I don't particularly want to encourage my girlfriend to commit premeditated murder, but in theory, yes," Cecile said.

"And in practice?" Danny asked.

"In practice, if Ragusa is acting as the agent of the Jacksonville dragons and Rachel ends the little fucker, she might find herself facing two much older, and very pissed off, black dragons. Rachel is young. She's a red, and reds tend to be the largest for their age, but she's not even two hundred years old. She's maybe half Eurion's size, and you saw the black dragons. Both are bigger than Eurion or Jia Li. Throw in their ability to control the weather when Rachel is just a pure fire breather and Rachel wouldn't stand a chance on her own."

"You know Focus and I wouldn't let that happen, right?" Danny asked. "You're family, and so is your girl."

"I know," Cecile said. "And that means a lot, believe me, but I don't want it to come to that."

"We'll figure something out," Danny said.

"I hope so," Cecile said. "And I hope it's soon. We only have four more months before we lose you."

Danny sighed. "Don't remind me," she said. "The closer we get to December, the more I hate the idea of going back."

"On the plus side, you know how all of this turns out," Cecile said.

"Yeah," Danny said. "Doesn't mean I wouldn't rather find out alongside you guys."

"I know," Cecile said. "We all do."

Danny reached out and squeezed Cecile's hand. "I better go find Focus before she gets in trouble."

"She does so much of that," Cecile said dryly.

"I know," Danny said. "I have no idea how you kept her in check before I showed up."

"Clinical depression," Cecile said. "Go, get. Go find your girl."

***

"You think Jia Li will be able to wrangle the Dragon Council before things come to a head?" Danny asked.

"I hope so," Ayanda said. "Things have been a bit tense between the Marshals and the dragons since the treaty was signed, but it's held up for thirty years."

"Not long for a dragon," Danny said as she looked around the city. They were out doing a post-lunch flyover, which the Marshals hoped would be a deterrent for petty crime. Danny wasn't sure how much effect it had, but breaking up the odd mugging or old-fashioned stick up was a good way to burn off some energy, so she never objected to doing the flyovers, but something felt off about today. Maybe it was her conversation with Cecile putting her on edge about the situation with the dragons, or maybe it was just the reminder that she only had four months until she was set to return to the future. Whatever it was had her on edge.

"You know how it turns out," Ayanda said.

"In a general sense," Danny said. "I know the treaty holds. I know you, Cecile, and Rachel make it through okay. I know Jia Li is alive and well. Beyond that, I don't remember any of the details. Eurion could die."

"Eurion will be fine," Ayanda said.

"I hope so," Danny said. "I just don't want to leave before all of this is settled."

"You mean you don't want to leave at all."

"That, too," Danny said.

"I wish you could stay, love. Believe me, more than anybody, I wish you—"

Danny looked over to see what had caused Ayanda to stop talking, but Ayanda was no longer flying next to her. Instead, she was hovering and staring off into the distance. Danny circled back and followed Ayanda's gaze, looking out over the city until she saw it. A dead zone where her perception couldn't reach.

"Null," Danny spat.

"Looks like," Ayanda said. "Call it in."

Danny reached up and tapped her earpiece. "Scatter to base, we've got a situation."

***

"Did you bring them?" Danny asked as she walked up to Cecile, who was standing at the back of one of the Marshal's SUVs, putting on her bulletproof vest. Cecile finished fastening the last Velcro strap and turned back to the rear of the SUV and pulled out a pair of Ithaca 37 Stakeout shotguns.

"Are you sure about this?" Cecile asked. "We can have our regular entry team take this fucker down."

Danny reached up and knocked on the hard armor plate that had been added to the chest of her uniform. "We're ready for this, and we owe this guy," she said as she took one of the shotguns. "Besides, even in his damping field, we'll get one or two shots with our powers before we have to wait for a recharge."

"Scatter's right," Ayanda said as she took the other shotgun. "We're your best bet for actually catching this guy before he escapes."

"Okay," Cecile said. "David's given the all clear for you guys to lead the breach, so if you want it, it's yours, but if either of you assholes gets yourself killed, I will personally raise you from the dead and kill you myself."

Danny smiled as she grabbed a pair of flashbangs. "Good reason not to die."

"Damn right," Cecile said. "Any idea what we're looking at inside?"

Danny turned and looked at the building where Null was. A warehouse full of digital recording equipment. She reached out with her empathic senses, getting a feel for everyone inside.

"No hostages this time," she said. "Twelve goons, plus our guy."

"How can you be sure?"

"Because our guy is the only one who's nervous," Danny said. "I felt it the last time. He's worried about his boss. Worried if he fucks this up, his boss will kill him."

"Well, let's make his fear come true," Cecile said.

***

At twenty-two and a half inches, the Ithaca Stakeout shotgun was one of the shortest production shotguns ever manufactured. It was also illegal as hell for civilian use. Fortunately, as Superheroes who worked with the US Marshals' metahuman responder program, both Danny and Ayanda carried badges as Special Deputy US Marshals, which meant that as they approached the open loading dock door, each of them had one of the short-barreled, five-shot shotguns holstered on their hip. Neither of them had the guns drawn. Instead, they each had a flashbang in hand, and Danny had her empathic senses extended, using them to keep track of where Null and his goons were.

She waited until Ayanda was in position on the other side of the open loading bay door, then she reached out with her empathic sense, and gave them just a little nudge. A little bit of worry that directed their attention away from the door. She felt them turn away and gave a small nod to Ayanda. Both of them pulled the pins on the flashbangs they were holding, and as one, they turned and tossed them in through the door.

She heard the sound of the grenades hitting the ground, followed by the characteristic firecracker-like bang. The two of them charged in before the echo had died away. Danny grabbed her batons and snapped them open. She hit her first target, kicking him in the back of the knee and then smacking him in the head with one of her batons. He went down as she stepped past him and drove a snap kick into the head of the next target, then moved on. The third target got a love tap in the temple with a baton before she slammed her heel into the back of the fourth target's knee. He dropped and she kicked him in the solar plexus as he fell.

By that point, the shock from the flash bang was starting to wear off, so the fifth target managed to turn in her direction, raising his gun. She hit him across the back of the hand with one of her batons, breaking the metacarpals before she kicked his feet out from under him, then kicked his gun aside. Her sixth and last target actually managed to get his gun up, and to take aim at her. A problem she solved by throwing the baton in her right hand at his face. He was either still too blinded to see it coming, or too stupid to dodge. Either way, he caught a pound of hard steel in the face and went down. Danny kicked his gun away as she passed.

She dropped her second baton as well and drew the shotgun from her hip holster. Unsurprisingly, Null was already reaching for his wrist and the escape teleporter he'd used to slip away from them before. Danny shot from the hip, just as she'd done two years before when facing an unregistered meta on her last fugitive retrieval. The short-barreled shotgun bucked like a mule, but the beanbag round flew across the distance between them and slammed into Null's gut.

Shooting someone with a beanbag might sound like a ridiculous idea, but even wrapped in cloth to keep it from penetrating, forty grams of lead shot hitting someone at ninety meters per second will make them aware they've been touched. Null staggered back under the force of the blow and dropped to his knees. Danny heard him gagging as he clawed at the mask, and he just barely got it off before he heaved, vomiting all over the floor.

"Don't move!" Danny shouted as she racked her shotgun, chambering another one of the beanbag rounds.

Null looked up at her and for a moment, Danny thought she was looking at Captain Porkpie again. That thought vanished as she got a better look past the red, swollen eyes, the tear covered face, the vomit covered chin, and the bleeding ears, and realized that however closely Captain Porkpie and Null resembled each other, Null was a woman.

She reached for her wrist again, and there was another boom as Ayanda fired. This time, the beanbag slammed into Null's left arm. The arm bent at a place where it wasn't meant to, and Null screamed as the teleportation device sparked and went dark.

Null reached up with her good hand and grabbed some sort of medallion hanging around her neck. She let out a roar that was all too familiar, and Danny dove out of the way on instinct as fire poured out of Null's mouth.

Ayanda fired again, but Null thrust out her broken arm, which snapped back into its proper shape with a sickening crunch, and the beanbag round bounced off an invisible shield. Null roared again and Ayanda moved out of the way just before Null spit a lightning bolt at her. Danny fired again, sending a beanbag round at Null's head. Not the way you were ever supposed to use them, but she was done fucking around. The round bounced off the same shield Ayanda's shot had.

Danny moved, already expecting the roar and the gout of flame that nearly incinerated her. She dropped the shotgun and pulled another flashbang.

"Fire in the hole!" she yelled, sending the same message over her link to Ayanda as she closed her eyes, opened her mouth, and covered her ears. There was a firecracker like bang, and for just a moment, the power dampening field vanished. Danny's healing abilities kicked in instantly, washing away the effects of the flashbang.

Danny looked up at Null, and she saw something with her powers that she hadn't seen without them. A faint glow came from the medallion as Null gripped it, and Danny felt the power damping field start to push down on her again. Before it could take hold, she reached out and pulled. The medallion jerked out of Null's hand, the cord around Null's neck snapped, and the power damping field vanished as the medallion sailed into Danny's hand. Null screamed and tried to stagger to her feet, but Ayanda was there, and put her down with a quick joint lock, and pinned her with a knee on her spine.

Danny looked down at the medallion. It was an intricate piece, covered in all sorts of runes and symbols, none of which she recognized, but what was impossible to miss were the two highly detailed, enameled black dragons which formed a circle on the face of the medallion.

She held it up, letting Ayanda get a look, and Ayanda uttered Danny's exact thought.

"Fuck."

***

"Here," Ayanda said as she set a cup of coffee in front of Danny, who had been staring at the medallion for the last twenty minutes. Danny looked up at her as she and Cecile sat down.

"Thanks," she said. She picked up the coffee and took a sip.

"Rachel, Jia Li, and Eurion are on their way up," Cecile said.

"Good," Danny said. "That's good."

"We got an ID on Null, not that there was ever much doubt."

"And?" Danny asked.

"Maria Ragusa," Cecile said. "Tony's younger sister."

Danny sighed and leaned back in her chair. "How the fuck did I not know Tony Ragusa has a younger sister?"

"It's not like either of them are exactly big names in organized crime," Cecile said.

"Not like you're in the organized crime unit, either," Ayanda said.

Danny shrugged and tapped the evidence bag with the medallion in it.

"How fucked are we?" she asked.

"I don't know," Ayanda said. "The obvious assumption here is that the Ragusa's are descended from the Jacksonville dragons, but we still don't know if Maria is the only Null or if there are a hundred of these damn medallions."

"I'm less worried about that than I am about the tech they've been stealing," Danny said.

Cecile and Ayanda both looked at her like she'd grown a second head. "You're more worried about a bunch of microchips than about necklaces that can render Supers powerless?" Cecile asked.

"I pulled the files for all the Null robberies," Danny said. "I..."

She trailed off as the door opened and David led Rachel, Jia Li, and Eurion into the room. David closed the door once they were all inside, and Danny watched as they all took seats. Rachel sat down next to Cecile, David sat at the head of the table, and Jia Li and Eurion took seats across from Ayanda and Danny.

"Okay," David said. "Now that we're all here, let's figure out just how far up shit's creek we are, and see if there's any chance we can find a paddle. Cecile."

Cecile nodded. "Rachel, Jia Li, Eurion, I'm not sure if you're familiar with the Supervillain called Null. If you aren't, she appeared on the scene about eighteen months ago, and organized a series of thefts of high-end technology all over the country. In all but three instances, Null's crimes were complete successes. The three failures all came here in Pontian. The first was a shipment of microchips, the second was schematics for some sort of fiber optic technology, and this afternoon a shipment of digital recording equipment. During the robbery this afternoon, Focus and Scatter were able to apprehend Null, and we discovered three things. First, Null is Maria Ragusa, the younger child of Partinaci Ragusa. The second is that Null's ability to suppress metahuman abilities is not an innate power, and third…" Cecile nodded to Danny, who slid the medallion across the table to Jia Li.

"Maria was using this to dampen our powers. In addition, it lets her breathe fire and lightning," Danny said.

"Obviously, we're concerned that there might be more of these medallions out there," David said.

"I think we should be more concerned about the tech thefts," Danny said.

David turned towards her. "Explain."

"The microchips were designed for phone routing. The schematics were for fiber optic switches. The digital recorders would be able to record phone calls. The hard drive would be able to archive the digital recordings. The list goes on and on," Danny said. "Whoever had Null pulling these jobs is looking to be able to tap and record phone conversations."

"What for?" David asked.

"I don't know. Blackmail. Insider trading. Industrial espionage. All of the above," Danny said. "It doesn't matter. That kind of capability is horribly dangerous now, but give it five or ten years, and the power someone with that kind of access could wield would rival most governments."

"She's right," Jia Li said. "Knowledge is power, and what she's talking about is unlimited access to knowledge."

"And dragons are masters of wielding that sort of power," Eurion said.

Jia Li held up the evidence bag with the medallion in it. "May I?" she asked.

David nodded, and Jia Li tore open the bag. She examined the medallion for a moment, then passed it over to Rachel with a growl and a hiss. Rachel took the medallion and turned it over in her hand a few times, then nodded and hissed at Jia Li with a thoughtful expression on her face. Jia Li growled back, and Rachel shrugged and hissed, then snorted and blew a smoke ring. Jia Li clicked her teeth, and Rachel rolled her eyes and wiggled a little in her seat before hissing again.

"You're sure?" Jia Li asked.

"As sure as I can be without having forged the thing myself," Rachel said. "The blood stink on it is hidden well enough that I'm not surprised you can't detect it, but the enamel has melted dragon scale in it. I've used the same trick to cover blood magic. Scale enamel is about the only thing other than gold that will hide the blood stink, and if you fully enclose the blood in gold, it binds the power in the blood."

Jia Li nodded and turned back to David. "We can be reasonably sure that the number of medallions is limited. If Rachel is right, the medallion is made using the blood of one of the dragons in Jacksonville. In order to tap that power, the person holding the medallion would need to have a touch of magic themselves, but no dragon would give that to anyone who wasn't of their own blood."

"Why not?" David asked.

"Blood magic is a two-way street," Rachel said. "You bind blood into an item so it can draw magic out of the donor, but once the blood is in the item, any magic put into the item can follow the blood path back to the donor. In fact, I would bet a bride price that Maria's blood is mixed in as well, as a safety measure. If they mixed her blood in, any malicious magic she tried to direct into the dragon through the medallion would strike her as well."

"Even with that precaution in place, the donor dragon would be paranoid about leaving themselves that exposed," Jia Li said. "My guess would be that this is a one-of-a-kind item. That Maria was a particularly trusted servant. More so than her father or brother."

"I wouldn't be certain of that," Ayanda said. "Tony had a dragon blade when Scatter fought him."

"Dragon blades are easy to come by," Rachel said. "A little unicorn horn, some griffin feathers, even a bit of dragon claw for the magical infusion. These things are not hard to find if you know where to look. Finding a smith who knows the spells isn't much harder. Dwarves and dragons have hated each other for so long that any dwarven smith will know how to forge a blade, and tensions between dragons and the other magical races have been running high ever since Jia Li outed our existence to the world."

"So Tony might have gotten the dragon blade on his own?" Ayanda asked.

"That, or Partinaci," Jia Li said. "Killing a rival dragon would elevate both Tony and Partinaci in the eyes of the dragons whose blood they carry."

"So, if we put all of this together, we have a pair of black dragons who are trying to build some kind of information empire," David said.

"But why are they so interested in Pontian? Why challenge another dragon for it?"

"Maybe they're not," Danny said.

Everyone turned to look at her.

"Pontian, on its own, isn't very interesting, but I-95 runs right through town, and I would bet good money that all of the phone lines from South Florida run right alongside it. We should check and see if there is a major telephone switching station here in Pontian. If there is, that's likely their target," Danny said.

"Why would South Florida be important?" Rachel asked.

"Drugs," Cecile said. "I-95 from Miami to Fort Pierce is a major drug corridor. If they can tap the information flow, they can turn the drug pipeline on and off at will, and effectively tax the cartels."

"That doesn't seem like something that would be stable," Eurion said. "The cartels could shift the traffic over to the Alligator Alley to I-75 to I-4 loop."

"It's a trial run," Danny said. "They see how effective the tech is, and once they do, they can move beyond the cartels."

"What about the dragon in Miami?"

"Haasi," Jia Li said. "He's an old, old dragon. Even older than the ones from Jacksonville. He mostly just sleeps on his gold and dotes on his wives. If the drug dealers came to him for help, he'd probably eat them."

"This can't go on," Ayanda said.

"Agreed," Jia Li said. "Partinaci and the Jacksonville dragons have got to go."

"Will the medallion make the Dragon Council act?" Ayanda asked.

"Perhaps," Jia Li said. "If not, then I will."

"You can't take on those two alone," Cecile said.

"I won't be alone," Jia Li said. "Will I?"

"No," Ayanda, Rachel, Eurion, and Danny said.

Chapter Eighteen

ONE OF THE HARDEST skills for Danny to learn when she became a cop was how to go from dead to the world asleep to wide awake and ready to shoot back in the span of a single ring of the phone. It was a skill she had eventually acquired, because one truism in the age of smartphones was that good news came by text. If the news was bad, people called. When she'd been thrown into the past and become a Superhero, she'd had to adapt a bit. Bad news no longer came in the form of a ringing phone, but in the form of a screaming pager and a squawking radio, but by now, the effect was the same.

Two pagers went off at exactly the same moment, and by the third beep, Danny and Ayanda were both on their feet and in their Super suits, picking up the radios they carried in the field.

"Focus…"

"Scatter…"

"…to base, go ahead."

"Gunshots at La Saint's apartment. We can't reach her."

"On our way," they both said, feet already off the ground. Neither of them bothered with anything so pedestrian as a door. Not when Cecile might be in trouble. They phased through the roof of the building as they shot up into the air, fixing their radios to their belts as they flew. It took them seconds to cover the distance to Cecile's apartment, rattling windows the whole way and not bothering with doors or windows on Cecile's end, either.

They phased through the wall and landed in her apartment, and Danny's heart sank the moment she saw it. The door wasn't just broken open, it was shattered. The whole room stank of gunpowder, fire, and ozone. The walls were charred and scorched and there were bullet holes everywhere. Cecile had hit someone, at least if the blood stain on the wall on the other side of the front door was any sign.

Danny reached out with her empathic senses, searching for the familiar feel of Cecile's mind, and felt a huge wave of relief when she felt it. She headed for the bedroom, Ayanda already moving with her. The two of them were in sync through the link between them, all senses open for signs of danger as they passed still smoldering bits of wall and carpet.

Danny touched her earpiece. "Possible dragon fire on sight. Send the fire department and call central and see if there's a mage available."

There was another splash of blood on the wall in the hallway that led to the bedroom. The splatter pattern looked like the shot had come from the bedroom, which was a good sign, but the pain and fear Danny could feel coming from Cecile wasn't. Every part of her was screaming to run to Cecile's side, but she held off, moving slowly with Ayanda in the lead. It wouldn't do any of them any good if she and Ayanda got themselves killed.

They stepped into the bedroom and it took Danny a moment to process what she was seeing. The bed had been flipped up and thrown against the wall so hard the frame was embedded in the sheetrock. There were two bodies on the ground that were effectively gone above the waist, filling the room with the sewer stench of ruptured bodies. A SPAS-12 shotgun lay in the middle of the room, bent at a forty-five-degree angle just forward of the breach.

She felt Ayanda's hand on her shoulder, and the final detail clicked into place. Cecile.

"She's alive," Ayanda said, already moving.

Danny went with her, dropping down next to her, fighting to get her brain to register what she was seeing. It was Cecile. She could see her face and her arms and her legs, but it took conscious effort to focus on her torso. There were three gashes that laid her open, shoulder to hip. Three gashes. Danny could see her lungs, struggling and failing to fill themselves, could see her frantically beating heart. Could see the blood leaking out of her. And worse, she could feel that Cecile was awake and aware.

"Danny, I need you to breathe for her. The pressure outside has collapsed her lung," Ayanda said. Danny nodded and reached out with her power, pushing air into Cecile's lungs, and then drawing it out again, breathing for her.

"Good," Ayanda said. "Keep going."

Danny felt Ayanda deepen the link, felt her push down Danny's own shock and panic and let calm flow in. As it happened, the scene became clear. She could feel Cecile's life slowly fading. She and Ayanda both reached for it, pouring their healing power into her.

The wounds should have closed easily, but that wasn't what happened. Something fought them, struggled and squirmed and wouldn't let them knit flesh back together. There was something in the wounds, something living, with a will to kill. Danny let Ayanda guide their healing abilities as she took a strand of power and channeled it into a different direction. Or three different directions.

She reached out, finding familiar minds and spirits. Ones that weren't quite human, but were still cherished, and she screamed for their help and felt their acknowledgement. She felt power stir and move. She felt ancient things uncoil and leap into action, and in her mind and her soul, she heard cries of rage.

"They're on their way," Danny said as she turned her attention back to Cecile. She didn't need to tell Ayanda who was coming. She knew. Instead, Danny took a bit of power and reached into the wounds, trying to find the enemy they were fighting with her senses. She could feel it, but not see it. There was no malice in it, just intent and purpose. It existed to end life. Blaming it for that would be like blaming water for being wet, so Danny didn't waste her energy. She just tried to catch it and pull it loose, but it was like trying to catch smoke.

There was a scream and a crash and a moment later, Rachel came running into the room.

She screamed when she saw Cecile, a cry of pain and rage which didn't slow her down at all. Rachel might seem gentle and kindhearted, but she was a dragon. She dropped down and Danny reached out, connecting to her empathically and telepathically. With Rachel in the link, Danny felt herself directed back to healing, while Rachel took over the hunt for the thing in Cecile's wounds.

Danny heard the beat of wings and then the crunch of feet on broken glass and felt, more than saw, Jia Li kneel beside them. She added Jia Li to the link, and Eurion in turn when he appeared only a few moments later.

Each of them, Rachel, Jia Li, and Eurion took a different one of the gashes, and each of them reached in with a bit of the magic that made them who they were. They grabbed the things, because there were three, living in Cecile's wounds and drew them out like poison. Tendrils of magic that had been wrapped around claws. Once they had the things, the magics, they held them away from Cecile, letting them choke and starve while Danny and Ayanda knitted flesh back together, and drew air out of places it wasn't supposed to be.

"It's done," Ayanda said. "She'll live, but she needs blood."

Danny reached up and touched her earpiece. "Control, I need an ambulance."

"Already in route, ma'am. ETA two minutes. David is right behind."

"Understood. Let the ambulance know we'll meet them on the street. We have a patient in hypovolemic shock."

"Yes, ma'am."

"Come on," Danny said. "Let's get her downstairs."

***

Rachel rode with Cecile in the ambulance, while Eurion followed in the air using a spell to hide him from the eyes of the public. Danny worried about whether he was enough to protect them, but she suspected that Eurion was less the guardian than the distraction to give Rachel time to get out of the ambulance. Dragons enraged over a threat to their mate were well known for punching above their weight.

That didn't stop Danny from wanting to climb into the ambulance or to jump into the air and follow. Cecile was her best friend, and watching the ambulance carry her away was one of the hardest things she'd ever had to do.

"She'll be okay," Ayanda said. "The dragons got the magic out of her wounds, so they won't reopen. She just needs to get her blood volume back up."

"How the hell did this happen?" Danny asked.

"I don't know," Ayanda said, "but this ends tonight."

"Damn right it does," Danny said.

"That's more accurate than you know," Jia Li said, making Danny jump. She hadn't noticed Jia Li and David approaching.

"What does that mean?" Ayanda asked.

"It means that the dragonkin attacked a dragon's promised bride," Jia Li said.

"Rachel and Cecile were engaged?" Ayanda asked.

"Yes," Jia Li said. "Rachel said they had planned to tell us at brunch this Sunday, but it doesn't matter who knows. Only that the promise was made. Partinaci Ragusa declared war tonight, whether he and his ancestors realize it or not."

"But why go after Cecile?" Ayanda asked. "Even if they weren't engaged, Ragusa and the Jacksonville dragons had to know this would provoke a response. Not just from Rachel."

"I'm not sure the dragons gave the order," Jia Li said. "This may be Ragusa acting on his own. I'm also not sure Cecile was targeted because of her connection to Rachel. I think this may have been because of her connection to you and Scatter."

"Because they arrested both his children," David said.

"Yes," Jia Li said. "I believe he went after Cecile to get to the two of them. The fact that it also meant striking a blow against Rachel would have been a happy accident as far as he was concerned, but as much as I hate to say it, it is a happy accident for us as well. He has stripped himself, and by extension, his ancestors, of their protection under the rules of the Council."

"They've done that before and the Council hasn't done shit," David said.

"Before, they'd only broken human law. Now, they've tried to kill a promised bride. No dragon on Earth will side with them. The moment Rachel is willing to leave Cecile's side, I will call an emergency council meeting."

Ayanda turned to David. "Sir?"

David turned and looked up at the apartment where Cecile had been attacked, then back to Ayanda. "Ragusa broke the rules. Finish it. Whatever it takes."

"Yes, sir," Ayanda said.

***

'Tonight' turned out to stretch into the next morning. After they left David at the crime scene, they went to the hospital. By the time they arrived, Cecile was in a private room, guarded by four Marshals. Rachel and Eurion were in the room with her, and Rachel wouldn't leave until Cecile woke up, which took about six hours, during which time the nurses hung three units of blood. The nurse had just left after hanging a fourth unit when Cecile came round.

It started with a slight moan, which was more than enough to get Rachel's attention, but then Cecile squeezed Rachel's hand and opened her eyes, slowly looked around the room, and surprised everyone by laughing.

"Cecile?" Rachel asked.

"Sorry," Cecile said. "It's just...three dragons, an alien, and a time traveler walk into a bar..."

Danny, who had spent the last six hours terrified that she'd fucked up the timeline somehow and gotten her best friend killed, completely lost it. She started laughing and couldn't stop, even when she fell out of her chair.

"Jesus, Danny," Cecile said. "It wasn't that funny."

Danny climbed up off the floor with Ayanda's help and walked over to the bed. "You scared the shit out of me," she said.

"You scared the shit out of all of us," Rachel added.

"I'm sorry," Cecile said.

"It's not your fault," Rachel said. She leaned in and pressed a kiss to Cecile's cheek. "We're just glad we got there in time."

"So am I," Cecile said. "Though I thought there would be more pain."

"You can thank Danny and Ayanda for that," Rachel said. "Once we got the magic out of your wounds, they were able to put you back together. The only thing they couldn't do was put the blood back in."

"I probably wouldn't have wanted it anyway. It's been a couple of weeks since I vacuumed the bedroom floor."

"How are you laughing at this?" Rachel asked.

"I just saw my own lungs," Cecile said. "If I don't laugh, I'm going to start screaming." She lifted Rachel's hand to her mouth and pressed a kiss to it. "I'm sorry if it upset you."

"You have nothing to apologize for, dear heart," Rachel said. She reached up and pushed Cecile's hair back out of her face. "You're alive."

"I am," Cecile said. "I hope this doesn't drive down the price though. Damaged goods and all."

Rachel made a sound that was halfway between a laugh and a sob and wrapped her arms around Cecile, lifting her off the bed into a tight hug. Cecile could only wrap one of her arms around Rachel because of the IV, but she did, and held her tight.

"I love you," Rachel said.

"I love you, too," Cecile replied.

Rachel lowered Cecile back down into the bed. "Who did this?"

"Partinaci Ragusa," Cecile said. "At least, I'm pretty sure. Will be hard to miss. I shot the bastard's eye out."

"Which eye?" Rachel asked.

"Right one," Cecile said.

"Okay," Rachel said. "That's good. That helps."

Cecile put on a forced smile. "You have to leave, don't you?"

Rachel nodded. "We all do," she said. "We have to end this."

"You come back to me," Cecile said. "You understand? You made a promise."

"I know, and I will be back. I swear," Rachel said. "I swear it on all my treasures."

Cecile turned to Danny and Ayanda. "You two, you take care of my girl. You hear me?"

"I promise," Danny said.

"We'll protect her with our lives," Ayanda said.

Cecile turned back to Rachel. "Don't take too long."

"I won't," Rachel said. She leaned down and kissed Cecile before standing up and looking at Jia Li and Eurion. "You two call the council. The three of us need to stop by my place, but we'll meet you there."

Jia Li nodded. "Be ready for a fight," Jia Li said.

"We will be," Rachel said.

***

"Death Valley?" Danny asked as she, Rachel, and Ayanda touched down near a cliff face.

"Where else would you put a meeting place for creatures who have fire in their blood?" Rachel asked.

"She has a point," Ayanda said. "Humans don't like it here."

"That's because it's 104 degrees in the shade and it's only 7:00 AM," Danny said.

"If it makes you feel better, the council's den is actually inside," Rachel said.

"It does, actually," Danny said. "Because nothing says a good time like being locked in a room with hundreds of fire-breathing dragons who don't like humans very much unless they're served on crackers with a bit of horseradish sauce."

"Well then, follow me," Rachel said. "And keep the dragon blades close."

Rachel led the way towards the cliff face and let out a gout of flame as they reached the rock. There was a brief shudder, and the rock split, revealing a massive tunnel that looked to be about a hundred feet tall and twice as wide.

"Stay close," Rachel said. Danny and Ayanda both followed her into the tunnel, which ran forward for at least a mile before it began to turn, slowly spiraling down into the Earth. If not for her powers, Danny was sure she would have lost track of how many circles they made, but with them, she knew it was ten full circles, and they ended up nearly a mile down before they came to a massive arch. Rachel stopped just this side of it and turned to them.

"I can't go any further like this," she said.

"We understand," Ayanda said.

Rachel blew out a stream of smoke. It wasn't a slow process like it had been when Danny had seen Eurion transform. Instead, she was enveloped in seconds, and then the smoke vanished, leaving a red dragon with a wide streak of purple down its back. It was a small dragon, but small was a relative term. In this form, Rachel was about forty feet long.

"This way," she said, her voice octaves deeper.

They followed her through the arch, and Danny was stunned by what they saw. They were in the middle of a massive colosseum. The central floor was surrounded by wide, flat tiers of stone, each of which had dozens of huge stone bowls set into them. Bowls lined with gold. Dragons were sitting in most of the bowls already, though there was a smaller one on the first tier that was empty.

As they crossed towards the empty bowl, they were met with hissing and growling, but Jia Li's voice rang out as she came flying down from one of the upper tiers in her dragon form.

"Enough!" Jia Li bellowed. "They have business here. The law of hospitality dictates we speak in a tongue they can understand."

"You called this session saying there had been a violation of dragon law," a deep, gravelly voice said from one of the upper levels. "Yet this whelpling brings humans into our midst?"

"Only one human," Jia Li said. She turned to Ayanda, who shape shifted in a blink, standing before the dragons in her true form. The chamber filled with hissing and growling and the clicking of teeth, and Danny could feel the surprise and knew the noises were gossip rolling up the tiers, but the same voice answered.

"Still an outsider," the voice said.

"An outsider who is a friend to us," Jia Li said. "But these two, human and alien, come to present evidence this day."

"Evidence of what?" deep and gravelly asked.

"Bring in the prisoner," Jia Li called.

A pair of dragonkin, one blue and one red, both dressed in silk robes, dragged a third out onto the floor. The third dragonkin, the prisoner, was of black dragon stock. He had a still bleeding wound where his right eye should have been, and he was wearing what looked like a ruined business suit. Danny took a step towards him, only for Ayanda to put a hand on her shoulder and stop her.

"What is this?" deep and gravely asked. Danny looked towards the voice and saw a pair of black dragons rise up out of their bowls and leap into the air, gliding down towards the coliseum floor. Both of them landed heavily near the prisoner. Danny spotted scars on the smaller one where someone or something had clawed its face, and she was sure that they were the Jacksonville dragons.

Jia Li nodded to Ayanda, who stepped forward.

"Last night, this dragonkin, Partinaci Ragusa, attacked Deputy US Marshal Cecile La Saint in her home."

"So?" deep and gravely asked. This time, Danny could place the voice. It was a dragon who had sat to the left of the Jacksonville dragons.

"So, this is a violation of the treaty you have with us," Ayanda said.

"Human law," deep and gravely said.

"Dragon law as well," Jia Li said.

Deep and gravelly rose up and leapt into the air. The massive dragon, green with a black stripe down his back, glided down to the coliseum floor.

"You, who is your ancestor?" deep and gravely asked.

Partinaci nodded towards the smaller of the two Jacksonville dragons. "Aurelia Ragusa."

"And did you attack this Cecile La Saint human?" deep and gravelly asked.

"I did," Partinaci said.

"Why?"

"She imprisoned my children," Partinaci said.

"See," deep and gravelly said, waving a claw dismissively. "A human matter. You waste our time, Jia Li."

"Ah, Tarantasio, always in a rush to finish things," Jia Li said. "It's no wonder you have trouble finding brides."

Deep and gravelly, Tarantasio, took a step towards Jia Li, a burst of fire shooting out of his nose.

"You forget yourself, whelp," Tarantasio said.

"And you forget yourself, old father," Rachel growled.

Tarantasio turned towards her. "What did you say to me?"

"I said you forget yourself. Your voice carries much weight here, but all dragons have a voice on this council. It is not for you to decide matters are finished, simply because you do not care about them."

"Perhaps not," Tarantasio said. "But perhaps I will teach you a bit of respect."

"You would be wise to stand away from her," Jia Li said. "She is the petitioner here."

"Then she should make this fast. Some of us have other things to do, besides be at the beck and call of humans."

Rachel turned towards Partinaci. "Why did Cecile arrest your children?"

"Does it matter?" Partinaci asked. "The human imprisoned my offspring. I took revenge."

Rachel turned to Aurelia. "Instruct your child to answer."

Aurelia growled at Rachel, and Danny tensed as lightning danced along her lips, but Aurelia turned to her offspring.

"Answer," Aurelia said.

"She arrested my son after he was caught trying to force Eurion to pay protection money. She arrested my daughter after she got caught trying to steal something for me."

"You ordered your son to extort money from a dragon?" Tarantasio asked, seemingly taking an interest for the first time.

"Pontian is my territory," Partinaci said.

Tarantasio gave a derisive snort. "Dragonkin can't claim territory for themselves."

"But they can claim it for another dragon," Rachel said.

Tarantasio looked at her. "True enough."

Rachel turned back to Partinaci. "Were you trying to claim Pontian for your ancestor?"

"What does that matter?" Aurelia asked.

Tarantasio's eyes narrowed as he turned towards Aurelia. "Answer the question, dragonkin."

Partinaci looked at Aurelia for a moment, which was apparently too much for Tarantasio's limited patience. Tarantasio turned and brought his snout down within inches of Partinaci's face.

"Answer, and answer true, whelp. I will know if you lie."

"Yes," Partinaci said.

"Was the robbery on your ancestor's orders?" Rachel asked.

Partinaci hesitated for a moment, but a growl from Tarantasio loosened his tongue. "Yes!" he shouted. "Everything was."

Rachel turned towards Tarantasio. "By the dragonkin's admission, the actions which led to the attack on Cecile La Saint were carried out on Aurelia's orders. Aurelia bears the blame for the attack."

Tarantasio turned towards Aurelia. "Did you actually order the attack? Speak true!"

"I did," Aurelia said.

Tarantasio gave a disgusted growl and slapped Aurelia across the face with a foreclaw, leaving three deep, bleeding gashes. "Stupid whelp." Tarantasio turned to Jia Li.

"How much gold will it take to settle this matter with the humans? Surely a bride price will be enough."

"It will not," Rachel said.

Tarantasio turned to Rachel. "Was this human some pet of yours?"

"Cecile La Saint was my promised bride," Rachel said.

Tarantasio hissed and took several large steps back, clearing out of the path between Rachel and Aurelia.

"This is ridiculous," the other Jacksonville dragon said.

"Silence, Gaius," Tarantasio said. "Your mate has filled her nest. Let her brood in it."

Gaius ignored Tarantasio. "You don't want this fight, whelp. You've barely started your third century. Let us make amends. We'll give two bride prices."

Rachel stepped forward. "You insult me. I paid a five weight for Cecile and called it a bargain, but I would not accept your entire hoard in recompense. I demand both their lives."

"Aurelia will kill you before they let you slaughter her offspring," Gaius said.

"True," Aurelia said.

Jia Li circled around and stood next to Rachel, and a moment later, Eurion landed next to them.

"I will not fight alone," Rachel said.

Aurelia looked at the three dragons now facing her, and Danny could practically hear Aurelia doing the math.

"I did not know the human meant anything to you," Aurelia said.

"Liar," Tarantasio said. "You speak falsehood."

"And I don't care," Rachel said. "Whether you knew or not, you tried to take her from me. You tried to kill my promised bride."

The entire colosseum filled with hissing and angry growls. Danny watched as dozens of dragons stood up in their bowls. Gaius and Aurelia looked around, and Danny could feel the panic coming from them.

"Wait!" Aurelia shouted. "I did know the human was Rachel's pet, but not that she was a promised bride."

"You speak true," Tarantasio said.

"And I don't care," Rachel said.

"But your promised bride still lives," Aurelia said. "You said she was attacked. That I tried to take her. That implies she still lives."

"She does," Rachel said.

"Your anger is justified but consider this. You are but a youngling, and I am old and powerful. Even with your friends, you may not overcome me. If you pursue your claim, you will risk throwing your life away."

"A risk I am willing to take," Rachel said.

"I offer a bargain," Aurelia said. "My offspring fights your alien. If your alien is slain, I will pay a five weight for damage done to your bride, a five weight for your alien, and I will forswear any further harm to your bride. If your alien wins, I will bare my neck, and you may have one blow undefended."

"No," Rachel said.

"Be still, young daughter," Tarantasio said. "It is a good bargain."

"I have right of vengeance!" Rachel snarled.

"Yes, you do," Tarantasio said. "But if you get yourself killed, who will protect your bride? Who will provide for her? Who will keep the promises you made? Would you risk her going to the victor?"

Rachel flinched at that, and Jia Li put a foreclaw on Rachel's shoulder. "Make the bargain."

Rachel turned to Jia Li for a moment, and then looked to Eurion. Both gave her small nods of the head.

Rachel turned back to Tarantasio. "Aurelia and Gaius must both forswear any claim on Pontian and sever all ties to the Ragusa family, regardless of the outcome."

Tarantasio turned to Aurelia. "A reasonable addition to your terms."

"Very well," Aurelia said.

"Does anyone here object?" Tarantasio asked.

"I do!" Danny said.

Everyone in the colosseum turned to her, and she could feel Ayanda's shock through the link.

"Silence your human," Tarantasio said to Rachel.

"Silence yourself," Danny said. "I introduced Rachel and Cecile. I named the price Rachel paid."

Tarantasio took two steps towards Danny and lowered his head until his snout was practically touching her nose. He sniffed, and then growled.

"She speaks truly. She has standing." Tarantasio lifted up his head and looked down on her. "What terms do you object to, little human?"

"I will fight the dragonkin, or there will be no bargain."

Rachel turned and looked at her. Danny gave Rachel a wink and mouthed 'trust me'.

Rachel turned back to Tarantasio. "I agree."

Tarantasio turned to Aurelia, who looked absolutely delighted. "And you?"

"Agreed," Aurelia said.

"Very well," Tarantasio said. "A bargain is struck."

Danny turned to Ayanda, and reached out through the link, so they could speak privately.

"Aurelia and Gaius see you as the threat. When I kill Partinaci, they will both attack you," Danny sent through the link.

"I know, but why did you take the fight?" Ayanda sent back.

"Because they'll use the power damping spell to try and rig the fight, but if it's focused on me, when he goes down, you'll be able to protect yourself," Danny sent.

"Unless they do an area of effect," Ayanda sent.

"It's not a perfect plan, but you can fly without powers," Danny sent.

"I don't like it," Ayanda sent.

"Are you ready to fight, little human?" Tarantasio asked.

Danny lifted the dragon blade in her hand. It looked like a simple cane until she pressed a rune carved into it, at which point it stretched out to a seven-foot-long spear with a nine-inch leaf shaped tip.

"I'm ready," Danny said. She stepped forward as the dragonkin guards released Partinaci. He reached up and tore away the top part of the suit.

"I'm going tear you open the same way I did the cop," Partinaci said.

Right on cue, Danny felt her powers pushed down. She stepped forward, spear braced and ready for the fight when she heard a hiss and a snarl and a shriek of agony, and suddenly her powers snapped back into place. She turned and saw that Tarantasio had driven a talon through one of Aurelia's forelimbs.

"You will not interfere!" Tarantasio said.

Danny smiled as she turned back to Partinaci. "Looks like you actually have to win this one on your own."

Partinaci let out a roar and spat a huge gout of flame at Danny. She just threw her arm out and raised a shield, blowing the fire back at him. The flame engulfed him and for a moment he disappeared into it, but then the flame gave out, leaving him standing there naked, clothes burned completely away. Danny frowned and shook her head as she got a far more detailed look at dragonkin anatomy than she wanted.

Partinaci jumped, giving a couple of flaps of his wings to try and get above her shield, but Danny leapt into the air to meet him. She thrust her dragon blade at him. He tried to dodge, but the spear was too quick and nimble for Danny to miss completely. The leaf shaped blade pierced his wing, and Danny swung down, slicing the wing membrane in half and causing him to fall.

Danny let herself fall after him, surrounding herself with a shield bubble. Partinaci turned as he fell and breathed a stream of lightning at her. The lightning hit her shield, dancing over the surface and creating a hemisphere of brilliant white light. Danny closed her eyes and used her powers to see past the lightning, guiding the tip of her blade.

Partinaci hit the ground, and for a moment, the wind was knocked out of him, robbing him of the ability to breathe fire or lightning. It was all the time Danny needed. She dropped her shield and hurled the dragon blade, using telekinesis to drive it right through his heart as she landed next to his body. Partinaci screamed in pain, and then fell silent, and when Danny looked over at him, the light had already gone out of his eye.

The entire colosseum was silent as Danny grabbed the spear and wrenched it from Partinaci's body. She conjured a cloth, and wiped his blood off the blade, then vanished the cloth before turning to Tarantasio.

"He's dead," Danny said. "And I believe Aurelia has a debt to pay."

"Indeed," Tarantasio said. "Aurelia, present your neck to the youngling. One undefended blow."

Aurelia, still bleeding from the three gashes on her face and the hole in her forelimb, looked at Rachel with contempt. "I will not."

"You will!" Tarantasio shouted. "A bargain was struck, and you will not break it."

For a moment, the span of two or three heartbeats, there was silence, and then there was utter chaos. Gaius leapt over Aurelia and went for Tarantasio's throat. Aurelia turned and breathed a stream of lightning at Ayanda. Ayanda teleported clear of the blast of lightning, and deployed her dragon blade as Eurion, Jia Li, and Rachel all leapt into the fight, and dozens of dragons from the tiers took to the air and descended into the fray.

The fight that followed was fast and decisive, and neither Danny nor Ayanda had any part in it. They watched from the sidelines as a massive dragon, bigger even than Tarantasio, removed Aurelia from the fight by the simple expedient of landing on her and crushing her under his bulk. Aurelia tried to snap at the dragon who landed on her, but the dragon caught Aurelia's neck in a foreclaw and pinned it to the ground. Aurelia, though, was the lucky one. Every other dragon from the stands turned on Gaius, and Danny watched as he was torn apart by tooth and claw.

The whole fight lasted perhaps two minutes, and when it was over, Gaius was nothing more than blood on the stone, hunks of meat, and broken bones. Aurelia lay pinned to the ground under the weight of a dragon twice her size. Tarantasio walked over, bleeding from several gashes where Gaius had bitten or scratched him. Tarantasio grabbed Aurelia by the neck, just behind the head, and the larger dragon lifted its foreclaw so Tarantasio could pull Aurelia's head forward, stretching out her neck.

Tarantasio turned to Rachel and said, "One undefended blow, young daughter. Strike well and true."

"Thank you, old father." Rachel stepped forward and looked down at Aurelia, who whimpered in fear.

"Please, have mercy," Aurelia begged.

Rachel lifted a foreclaw and swung, slicing clean through Aurelia's neck.

"There, old mother," Rachel said. "That is more mercy than you showed me and mine."

Tarantasio turned to Jia Li. "Is this business settled to your satisfaction?"

"Yes, old father," Jia Li said.

Tarantasio turned to Rachel. "And you, young daughter. Are you satisfied?"

"Yes," Rachel said.

"Then we are finished here."

Molly J. Bragg

Chapter Nineteen

"CECILE SAID YOU'D BE up here," Ayanda said from somewhere behind Danny. She turned and looked across the roof of the Marshals' station and saw her approaching from the access door. She gave her a smile and held her hand out, waiting until Ayanda took it before she turned and looked back out at the city. "Everything okay?"

"Yeah," Danny said. "I'm just thinking."

Ayanda let go of Danny's hand and stepped behind her, wrapping her arms around Danny's waist and pressing a kiss to Danny's cheek. "Penny for your thoughts."

"I'm not sure they're worth that. They're mostly self-pity."

"What's wrong?" Ayanda asked.

"It's the twenty-seventh of October," Danny said. "I've only got two months left."

Ayanda tightened her arms, squeezing Danny against her.

"I don't want to go," Danny said. "I know I should. My parents are back there. My sisters. My job. I have a whole life to go back to, but all I want to do is stay here with you and my friends."

"I know, love," Ayanda said. "I wish you could stay. Having you here, being with you, it's been the best time of my life. I'm sorry I wasted so much of it being afraid."

"You weren't the only one who was afraid," Danny said.

"But you never let that stop you," Ayanda said. "You just stood there, demanding to be loved."

"I had an advantage," Danny said. "I'd already seen how this ends. You had to take the long way around."

"I'll wait for you," Ayanda said. "My love, my mate." She pressed a kiss to the center of the mating mark on the back of Danny's head, and Danny let out a small moan.

"Not fair," she said.

"Who said I was trying to be?" Ayanda asked. "It's past six. Our shift is over. Let me take you home."

Danny turned around in Ayanda's arms and kissed her, nibbling at Ayanda's bottom lip, then running her tongue over it. Ayanda tightened her grip on Danny and lifted them both off the roof as she slipped her tongue into Danny's mouth. The kiss dragged on for what seemed like forever before Ayanda lowered them back down to the ground.

"Come on," she said. "Let's go let Cecile know we're going home."

"I like that plan," Danny said.

"I thought you would."

***

Normally the first thing they did when they got home was have dinner. Danny usually cooked, because she was better at it, and she enjoyed it. Ayanda had been a soldier on her home world, and her knowledge of how to cook had largely been limited to reheating field rations or finding the mess hall. She'd expanded her repertoire a bit since arriving on Earth, but it was still fairly utilitarian compared to Danny's.

That night, though, neither of them were interested in stopping in the kitchen. The kiss Ayanda had placed on Danny's mating mark back at the station had had its usual effect, and all Danny wanted by the time they got home was for Ayanda to take her hard and fast on the first convenient horizontal surface.

If she was honest, she'd admit she would have let Ayanda take her on the roof of the Marshals' station, but she fought the impulse to throw Ayanda down on the couch as soon as they were in the apartment. However much her body was screaming with need, she wanted the night to be special, not just frantic love making. So instead of the couch, or the dining room table, or the living room floor, she led Ayanda back to their bedroom.

Once they were in the bedroom, Danny turned to Ayanda and watched as she shifted out of her Focus persona and into her natural form. The sight always made Danny weak at the knees. Ayanda standing there, the glowing lines standing out wherever her circulatory system ran, the light blue of her skin, the tempting curves and sharp lines and the memories of all the times they'd been together made heat and desire pool between her legs.

Ayanda pulled Danny into her arms, kissing her, and backing her up to the bed. Danny felt Ayanda's wings bracing on the bed and knew what was about to happen. She wanted it. God, did she want it. Every part of her screamed to give in and let Ayanda take her and reduce her to a quivering pile of spent flesh, but instead, she put a hand in the middle of Ayanda's chest and gave a small push. Ayanda backed away, giving her a questioning look, but Danny just smiled.

"Back up for a minute, love," Danny said. "I have a surprise for you."

Ayanda smiled. "A surprise, huh?"

"Yeah. I think you'll like it." She bent down and untied her boots, then kicked them off. Socks were next, and then she stood up and looked Ayanda in the eye as she unbuttoned her shirt and tossed it aside. She watched Ayanda's eyes dilate just a bit as she pulled off her sports bra, but that wasn't too big a surprise. Ayanda was definitely a breast girl. Still, it was nice to be appreciated. She unbuckled her belt, then unbuttoned her jeans and slipped them and her panties down together and kicked them aside, leaving her standing naked in front of Ayanda, who had a slightly confused look on her face.

Danny took a deep breath and closed her eyes, concentrating. She'd done this countless times before at this point, but never with Ayanda watching, and she wanted to make sure, this time more than ever before, that she did it right. She reached inside herself, using her power to take hold and twist, bending and reshaping the very fabric of her physical self, adding and changing until she settled into a very, very different mold all the way down to the genetic level. Every cell, every strand of DNA was reformed, and when she opened her eyes, she saw in colors that didn't exist in her human form as she stood, looking back at Ayanda as a member of Ayanda's own species.

Ayanda stood there, staring at Danny with her mouth slightly open. Not quite the reaction Danny had hoped for. She'd wanted something a bit more enthusiastic.

"Is this okay?" she asked, suddenly wondering if she'd made an error in judgement. She'd wanted to do this for Ayanda, to make her happy, to make her feel less alone, but now she wondered if she'd made a mistake and hurt her, reminded her of what she'd lost.

Ayanda stepped forward, and Danny could see tears glistening in her eyes. She reached up and cupped Danny's face in her right hand.

"You did this for me?" Ayanda asked softly, reverence in her voice.

"I wanted to make you feel less alone," Danny said.

Ayanda moved suddenly, leaning in and kissing Danny, pulling Danny into her arms. She felt the smaller hands at the tips of Ayanda's wings grip the hands at the tips of her own wings, fingers lacing together. She felt Ayanda's tail wrap around her waist and she returned the gesture.

"I love you," Ayanda said between kisses. She pushed Danny down onto the bed, and it was awkward for a second, getting used to the feeling of her wing joints under her, but her body seemed to know almost instinctively how to position them, and when she felt Ayanda's lips and teeth on her jaw and then her neck, she had other things to worry about.

Her mating mark throbbed in time with the need she felt between her legs. She clutched Ayanda to her as Ayanda's hands roamed to places on Danny's body that matched places Danny knew Ayanda loved to be touched. The root of her wings, the wing membranes, the edge of her ears. Every touch was heaven, and every one made her want something she couldn't name.

She buried her face in Ayanda's neck and inhaled something she'd never smelled before. Something that smelled like love and sex and home and forever. She opened her mouth and lapped at the warm skin of Ayanda's neck like a kitten lapping at fresh cream. She opened her legs and rolled her hips, seeking contact, seeking relief for the burning, aching need. She felt Ayanda's right hand slide down between her legs as Ayanda's tail shifted.

"Please," she begged. "Please don't tease."

Ayanda didn't seem to have any intention of teasing. She pushed all three of her fingers inside in a single thrust. Delicious pain shot through Danny as she was stretched open, the thick fingers pushing her closer to the edge with each thrust as Ayanda pinched Danny's clit between both thumbs on her right hand. Ayanda's left hand slipped up Danny's back, and Danny couldn't help herself. The moment Ayanda's hand touched the skin between Danny's wings, they snapped open, spreading out until the left one hit the wall and the right one extended all the way out. Danny howled in pleasure as her fingers dug into the skin of Ayanda's back. She whimpered a moment later when she felt Ayanda's tail slide down between the cheeks of her ass.

"Yes," Danny hissed as the tip of Ayanda's tail pressed against her ass. Ayanda was gentler there than she had been with her fingers, slowly pushing her way inside, until Danny could feel fingers and tail rubbing against each other through the thin wall separating them.

"Fuck," she cried as each thrust carried her closer and closer to the edge, and as the unfamiliar craving in her grew stronger and stronger. She ran her tongue over Ayanda's neck again and again, drawing hisses and moans each time as she got closer and closer to her own release. She was close, so, so close, but she couldn't quite topple over the edge.

Not until she felt Ayanda kiss the edge of the mating mark. Then, with the blush of lips and the scrape of teeth, whatever wall had been holding Danny back broke and she screamed as she came.

Wave after wave of pleasure washed over her, but instead of leaving her sated, every spasm, every wave of release seemed to stoke the craving inside her, and as her orgasm ebbed, she looked up at Ayanda, not understanding what she wanted. Ayanda kissed her, which just stoked the hunger inside. She whimpered as she felt Ayanda's fingers and tail leave their places inside her, and then Ayanda was moving off of her. She wanted to grab her and hold her, but Ayanda was too quick, and was gone before Danny could make the grab. Danny turned to see where she was going, only to find Ayanda in the middle of the bed, on her hands and knees.

Something inside Danny howled in satisfaction and she stood up and moved around the bed. She climbed up onto it, coming at Ayanda from behind. Ayanda flicked her tail off to the left, out of Danny's way as Danny grabbed Ayanda's ass. She leaned down, scraping her teeth over the right cheek, pulling a purr of approval from Ayanda that made the craving all the more intense.

She licked and nipped her way up Ayanda's spine, and just like hers had when Ayanda touched her between the wings, Ayanda's wings snapped open when Danny dragged her tongue over the skin between them. She pressed her hips against Ayanda's ass and rocked slowly, grinding into her as she pressed the small hands at the tips of her wings into the mattress for balance. She wrapped her tail around Ayanda's waist, letting the tip slip down between her legs to find her clit.

This felt familiar, like she'd done it before, and it felt right, like this was the one place in the universe where she belonged. She pressed her nose against the nape of Ayanda's neck and breathed in the same perfume she had earlier. The sweet, musty scents of love and sex and home and forever filled her, and stoked the craving inside her as she slipped a hand down past where her tail was already teasing Ayanda. She parted sopping wet folds, drawing a sob from Ayanda as she ran three fingers over the wet flesh inside. She pressed a kiss to the nape of Ayanda's neck as she pushed a finger inside and started fucking her.

"Don't fight it," Ayanda said. Danny didn't understand what she meant, but it didn't matter. She knew what to do. She added another finger inside of Ayanda and picked up the pace. She pressed her lips against Ayanda's neck, but it wasn't enough. She wanted more. Needed more. More what, she wasn't sure, but she felt her lips pull back as she scraped her teeth over Ayanda's neck.

"Yes!" Ayanda hissed. "God, yes."

Danny ran her tongue over the spots she'd scraped with her teeth, soothing the skin as she drove her fingers into Ayanda harder and harder.

"More," Ayanda begged, and Danny didn't hesitate. She drew her fingers out and pushed back in with all three of them. Ayanda responded by wrapping her tail around Danny's waist.

"Take me," Ayanda begged. "Don't fight it. Take me. Make me yours."

Danny thought that was what she was doing, but she was too lost in the moment to care about the words. She could feel each thrust into Ayanda throbbing through the link, through the mating mark. Each thrust of her fingers, each swipe of her tail across Ayanda's clit drove them both closer. She lapped at Ayanda's neck, drinking in the taste of Ayanda's sweat and her need and something Danny could only identify as a hunger built inside her.

"Don't fight it," Ayanda said again.

Danny kissed her on the back of the neck.

"Don't fight it."

Danny opened her mouth, the craving, the hunger driving her mad as Ayanda hovered on the edge.

"Don't fight it."

Danny bit down, sinking her teeth into Ayanda's neck. She tasted blood and felt heaven flow through her as both of them came. The doors of the link between them broke open and there was no more Danny, no more Ayanda. There was only them. One being made up of two souls, so tangled together there was no way to tell where one ended and the other began. They flowed into each other, merged and melted into one singular existence full of memory and love and grief and longing and loneliness and happiness and joy and togetherness and fear and elation and a need to protect and to cherish and to love.

It faded slowly and all at once. They were one for an eternity and for just a few seconds, but even when it was over, they never quite separated. Not completely. The link was there, stronger, bigger than before. A power that flowed from both sides.

Danny opened her mouth, her needle-sharp teeth leaving Ayanda's neck, eliciting a whimper of protest, and on pure instinct, she lapped at the wound as it closed up before placing a final kiss in the middle of the newly-made mating mark.

She felt Ayanda's tail loosen around her waist, reluctantly pulled her fingers out of Ayanda, and uncurled her tail. Ayanda pulled in her wings and rolled over, pulling Danny down on top of her.

"I love you," Ayanda said, the feelings behind the words echoing in both of their minds.

"I love you, too," Danny said. She curled in against Ayanda's side, resting her head on Ayanda's shoulder.

"Thank you," Ayanda said, her voice cracking slightly.

Danny looked up to see tears rolling down her face. "What's wrong?" she asked, but immediately, she knew nothing was wrong. All that was coming through the link was happiness and joy.

"I never thought I would get to have one," Ayanda said.

The mating mark, Danny realized.

"I'm yours," Ayanda said, nearly sobbing. "I'm really yours."

Danny shifted, moving up so she could kiss Ayanda. "You always have been," Danny said.

Ayanda's response didn't involve any words.

***

Danny kept having to fight the urge to reach up and brush aside Ayanda's hair so she could see the mating mark. She was a little surprised that Ayanda kept it in both her Kelly and her Focus forms. Surprised, but not at all unhappy. She'd spent most of the morning forcing herself not to reach out and touch it, because as much as she loved wearing Ayanda's mark, she loved seeing her mark on Ayanda's neck that much more.

She wasn't sure why it got her motor running the way it did. She'd never even thought of anything like it before the night Ayanda had marked her. But something about the visible evidence of their connection, the reminder of what they were to each other, made Danny ache to touch Ayanda. Part of that could have been the link, too. The connection was stronger than ever, like the volume had been turned up. She could feel Ayanda's love for her and could feel the way her love made Ayanda feel. It was a weird sort of feedback loop that both of them were going to have to learn to manage.

She just hoped today was a slow one, because she knew she was going to be distracted all day, thinking about what had happened the night before.

"You with me?" Ayanda asked as they touched down in front of the Marshals' station.

"Yeah," Danny said as they stepped inside. "Just thinking about last night."

Ayanda flashed her a smile and caught her hand, giving it a small squeeze as they approached the security checkpoint. Danny caught a surge of disgust coming off the guard behind the desk and felt herself tense up. She looked right at him.

"Is there a problem, Deputy Marshal?" she asked, putting just a bit of frost in her tone.

"No," he said, and Danny could feel just a hint of fear, which was probably more satisfying than it should have been. She felt a little disapproval from Ayanda, but she ignored it and pulled her along as they passed the checkpoint. Neither of them said anything until they were out of earshot of the guard, but then Ayanda looked over at her.

"What was that about?" she asked.

"Guy was being a judgy asshole," Danny said. "So I judged him right back."

Ayanda lifted their hands and pressed a kiss to the back of Danny's. "I'm here," she said.

"I know," Danny said. She took a deep breath and let it out slowly, letting a bit of tension that had creeped up on her go with it. "It's just been a while since that happened, and honestly, I probably wouldn't have noticed if I had my empathic senses locked down. Sixteen months and you'd think I would know better than to read random people."

"I'm sorry."

"I'll survive," Danny said.

"Is it better, in your time?"

"Yeah," Danny said. "There are still a lot of people like that, but it's not nearly as safe for them to let people know it anymore. Anti-discrimination policies and laws have a lot more teeth than they do now."

"Good to know," Ayanda said.

"Come on," Danny said. "Let's go see Cecile before the morning briefing. I want to see if she and Rachel are going to make brunch on Sunday."

They turned down the hallway that led to Cecile's office, but before they could get very far, Jenkins, one of the Deputy Marshals from Beta Squad, came running up to them.

"Ma'ams," she said. "Moore wants to see you in his office."

Danny frowned, wondering what David wanted this early in the morning.

"Did he say why?" Ayanda asked.

"No, ma'am," Jenkins said. "But La Saint is with him."

"Thank you, Jenkins," Ayanda said.

The two of them turned around, and Ayanda dropped Danny's hand as they headed towards David's office, both of them putting on their work faces as they went. Danny could feel Ayanda's worry, and it matched her own. Usually if there was some sort of problem, David, Cecile, or one of the comm techs would call them over the radio. Sending a runner was odd, to say the least.

They reached David's office fairly quickly. It was in the same place as Perez's would be in the future, even if it wasn't the enormous, high-tech affair it would be twenty-nine years later. Instead, it was a small office, with a picture window that looked out over the situation room. When they got there, they found Cecile and Joann Walker, the station's media liaison, already inside.

"You wanted to see us, sir?" Ayanda asked.

"Yes," David said. "Close the door, then have a seat."

Danny closed the door while Ayanda waved a hand. Two of the chairs sitting under the window lifted up and floated over next to the desk. Ayanda and Danny sat down in them.

"What's going on?" Ayanda asked.

David picked up a picture off his desk and handed it over to Ayanda. Danny leaned over to look at it and couldn't stop herself from smiling.

"That's a terrible shot," she said, because it was. A photo that had to have been taken the night before of her and Ayanda floating in the air, kissing. There was no doubt of who it was. Focus' and Scatter's costumes were too distinctive for it to be anyone else, but that was just about all that could be said for it. The angle was weird, and the lighting was terrible, and overall, it was just a bad picture.

"Where did this come from?" Ayanda asked.

"It was delivered to the front desk via courier today," Joann said. "Along with this."

She handed over a sheet of paper to Ayanda, and again, Danny leaned over to read it. It was an offer from Nathan Price to sell them all rights to the picture, along with all copies and the negative.

"Who is Nathan Price?" Ayanda asked.

Danny, remembering a conversation with Cecile she wouldn't have for twenty-nine years, said, "He's a reporter with the Pontian Tribune."

"He's a stringer, technically," Joann said.

"I don't know what that means," Ayanda said.

"A freelancer," Joann said. "He sells most of his work to the Tribune, but he's not actually on payroll. That means he can sell elsewhere if he wishes, or if they don't buy a piece of his work. In this case, he seems to think it would be more profitable to offer the picture to us, thinking we would pay more to keep it out of the papers than any of the papers would pay for the right to run the picture."

"Why?" Ayanda asked.

"What?" Joann asked.

"Why would we pay to keep the picture out of the papers?" Ayanda asked.

Joann looked at her like she was crazy. Cecile just shook her head. David reached up and started rubbing his temples.

"You want to explain?" Cecile asked, looking at Danny.

"Me?" Danny said. "Nope. I say let the papers run it and prosecute the fucker for blackmail."

"Scatter," Cecile said.

"What?"

"Look, I get that it might not be a problem where you come from," Cecile said, "but I warned you this could happen, and it could damage Focus's credibility."

Danny had to bite her tongue to keep from saying something she would regret, but she couldn't stop herself from feeling a flash of anger at Cecile for wanting to keep them in the closet.

"You think people will care that the woman who is pulling them out of a burning building is involved with another woman?" Ayanda asked.

"Yes," Joann said.

"That's ridiculous," Ayanda said.

"It's also true," Cecile said. "Look, I know that before this past year, you didn't really spend a lot of time out in the world, so you might not realize how fucked up our culture is when it comes to this shit, but entire careers have been destroyed over just a rumor that someone is gay."

"But I'm not gay," Ayanda said.

"Gay, Bisexual," Cecile said. "People aren't going to care about the distinction."

"But…"

Danny reached out through the link and physically, resting a hand on Ayanda's wrist to stop her.

"Love, you're not going to win that argument," she said, ignoring the way Joann flinched slightly at the way she'd chosen to address Ayanda. "I understand the distinction, but the fact is, the vast majority of people on the planet are going to look at the picture, and they are going to label you as gay. If you say you're not gay, they either won't believe you, or they will assume you mean you're bisexual. Thirty years from now, it might be a lot easier for people to get the distinction through their heads, but right now it's just not going to happen."

"She's right," Cecile said. "If people see that photo, the headlines are all going to read 'Gay Superheroes' or 'Focus is Gay', or something similar."

"Honestly, I think the best thing would be to simply buy the pictures," Joann said. "Then the two of you can work on being a bit more…discreet about what you do in private in the future."

Danny felt her temper flare, and her anger reached her mouth before her sense did. "Or maybe David can hire a media liaison who isn't a small-minded bigot."

"Scatter," David snapped. "That's out of line."

"The hell it is," Danny said.

"Look," Joann said. "What the two of you do in private is your own business, but my job is to protect the reputation of this department, and of the Metahuman Emergency Response Team program. A scandal revolving around Focus' sexuality could damage that reputation. That's what I'm trying to avoid."

"This shouldn't be an issue," Danny said.

"You're right," Cecile said. "It shouldn't be, but it is. Look, you know I'm with you on this. People shouldn't have to hide who they are and who they love, and in the future, maybe they won't, but this is now, and we need Focus. Not just here in Pontian, but the whole world."

"That future you're talking about is only going to come if people have the guts to stand up and say 'We're here. We're queer. Get used to it.' And you're right, Pontian needs Focus. The whole world needs Focus. That's why she's the perfect person to come out. She's too valuable for them to kick her to the curb just because she's not straight."

"You can't be serious," Joann said. "There's not a single openly gay Superhero anywhere in the world."

Danny stared at Joann for a moment, and then looked at Ayanda. "Can I speak to you in private for a minute?"

"Of course," Ayanda said.

Danny stood up and walked over to the corner of the room, with Ayanda in tow. Once they were there, Danny raised a forcefield around them that blocked out all sound so no one else in the room could hear them.

"What do you think?" Danny asked.

"I think humans are ridiculous to care this much about something so trivial."

"I know, but they do."

"What do you think I should do?" Ayanda asked.

"I already know how this ends," Danny said. "Can I tell you?"

"Yes," Ayanda said.

"You call a press conference. You tell the media that the reporter is trying to blackmail you. You tell the world you're gay."

"How does that go?" Ayanda asked.

"It helps make the world a better place," Danny said. She reached out and took Ayanda's hand in her own, and let her own feelings pour into the link. "I've honestly had a crush on you since I was five years old. You were a big part of what made me realize I was gay. And your coming out gave other people the courage to do the same. Other heroes, other celebrities. You save lives every day just by letting the world know who you are. You let queer kids out there know they aren't alone."

"You knew this would happen," Ayanda said.

"Of course I did," Danny said. "The same way you knew when I pulled that lever, I'd end up here."

Ayanda smiled and blushed a little. "Touché," she said. "What do I say?"

"You tell the press that you're gay, that Nathan Price tried to blackmail you, and that you refuse to be blackmailed."

"And that makes that much of a difference?" Ayanda asked.

"More than you could believe," Danny said. "It makes you a hero to every gay kid out there."

"Okay," Ayanda said.

"Thank you," Danny said before she dropped the forcefield.

Ayanda turned to David. "Call a press conference," she said.

"Are you sure?" David asked.

"Yes," Ayanda said. She turned and looked at Danny. "I trust her."

"Okay," David said. He turned to Joann. "Make the call."

"One more thing," Danny said.

"What?" David asked.

"Who is the best photographer we have on staff?"

***

They scheduled the press conference for early the next morning. Danny and Ayanda spent the day out in the city being heroes, but came back to the Marshals' office before sunset and met one of the forensic photographers up on the roof. A woman named Crystal who shot the occasional wedding on the side. Danny had explained to her earlier in the day what they were looking for and she had her gear ready to go. When sunset came, she ordered them up in the air, and told them to kiss. Danny leaned in and kissed Ayanda like it was the last time she'd ever get the chance, and Ayanda kissed her back with just as much passion and intensity. They barely heard the sound of the camera shutter, and Crystal had to tell them she was done twice before they heard her and broke the kiss.

They stayed at the office for a couple of hours while Crystal developed the film, and then Danny selected which of the pictures she wanted to use. It was an easy choice. She picked the one that she'd had up on her wall for years. Once the picture was selected, they went home while Crystal started making prints.

They were back at the Marshals' office the next morning by 7:00 AM, and at 9:00 AM, they stepped out of the front doors of the Marshals' office along with David, Cecile, and Joann. Danny hadn't wanted Joann there given her attitude, but handling the media was her job, so there wasn't anything Danny could do about it. She just took up a position off to the side as Ayanda walked up to the podium that had been set up. Danny could feel Ayanda's discomfort as she looked out at the reporters and sent back love and reassurance through the link they shared.

As Ayanda took the podium, a handful of Deputy Marshals walked through the crowd of reporters, handing them each a manila envelope. She could feel the emotions from the reporters too. Her empathic sense was nearly overwhelmed by a feeling of hunger coming from them. They were all expecting something huge, and in a way, Danny thought they were going to get what they wanted.

Ayanda waited until the last envelope had been handed out, and the Deputy Marshals were out of the way before she spoke, but once they were, Ayanda took a deep breath, and Danny felt a calm spread over her.

"Good morning," Ayanda said. "As I am sure you are all aware, I am Focus. For the last three years, it has been my privilege and my honor to serve as the protector of both Pontian and the Earth. I have never publicly discussed my past, my private life, or how I got my powers, but today I will tell you that a great many people made enormous sacrifices in order for me to become what I am. I have tried to live up to those sacrifices, to be a champion for those who cannot protect themselves. For most of my life, I have done that alone, but a few months ago, I was very fortunate to have someone come into my life who brings me immense joy and comfort. Someone I love with all of my heart and soul.

"Yesterday morning, a picture of us sharing a private, intimate moment was delivered here to the US Marshals' station. Accompanying the picture was a letter, offering to sell all copies of the picture and the negatives, as well as all rights to the photo. This was done on the assumption that I would be so ashamed of the moment that I would do anything to keep the picture from the media. This was an incorrect assumption, because copyright law dictates that you could not run the photo without paying the individual in question for the rights to use the photo. I asked another photographer to take a similar photo that you could use. Each of you will find a copy of that photo, along with details on how to obtain the rights to run it, in the envelope you have received. You will also find a copy of the letter from the photographer who is attempting to blackmail me. I would like to make a simple statement to explain the contents of the picture and why all of you are here. After this statement, I will not be taking any questions.

"I'm gay. A reporter named Nathan Price with the Pontian Tribune took a photo of me kissing my girlfriend and tried to blackmail me with it. I refuse to be blackmailed, because I am not ashamed of who I am, or who I love."

With that, Ayanda turned away from the podium and walked over to where Danny stood. She took Danny in her arms and kissed her. Danny wrapped her arms around Ayanda and kissed back like her life depended on it. She could hear cameras going off, could hear reporters shouting questions, but none of it mattered. She was kissing Ayanda. The world could wait.

Ayanda broke the kiss. Danny saw the smile on her face and couldn't help but smile in return.

"Shall we?" Ayanda asked. Danny nodded and took her hand, and the two of them lifted up into the air, leaving the Marshals' station, the reporters, and the bigotry that fueled the whole situation behind as they took to the skies.

Chapter Twenty

DANNY SMILED AS SHE looked at the trays she'd put together. Big, thick, center cut porterhouse steaks, fluffy scrambled eggs, hash browns covered with chili and cheese, crispy bacon, big, fluffy pancakes smothered with butter, pots of warm maple syrup, a carafe of fresh brewed coffee and another of orange juice, a bottle of hot sauce, and salt and pepper shakers. A perfect breakfast, for what she hoped would be a perfect day. She waved her hand and the two trays lifted up and started floating out of the kitchen. She followed them, floating along at a walking pace until she came to the bedroom door. Another wave of her hand and the door opened, and she saw herself lying there in bed, curled up in Ayanda's arms. It was a picture of happiness and contentment, a big smile on her face. A perfect moment.

She carefully lowered the trays down onto the vanity, and then released her telekinetic hold on them before floating up over the bed and letting her astral self sink back down into her body. She lay there for just a moment, soaking in the warmth of Ayanda's body. She opened her eyes reluctantly as she felt Ayanda start to stir and looked up just in time to see Ayanda open her eyes.

"Do I smell bacon?" Ayanda asked. "And steak?"

Danny laughed and wiggled a little, letting Ayanda know she wanted to be let go. Ayanda moved her wing so Danny could sit up, and when she did, she waved her hand and the trays lifted up off the vanity and floated over next to the bed, waiting.

"What's this?" Ayanda asked.

"I made us breakfast," Danny said.

"But how?" Ayanda asked.

"A little astral projection, a little telekinesis."

Ayanda laughed as she sat up and scooted back against the headboard, tucking her wings down between the headboard and the mattress. Danny scooted back to sit next to her and waved the trays over. Legs folded down and the trays came to rest over their laps.

"You're amazing, you know that?" Ayanda asked.

"I do, but I never get tired of hearing it." She leaned over and pressed a kiss to Ayanda's cheek. "Merry Christmas."

"Merry Christmas," Ayanda said.

Both of them reached for their silverware and dug into their breakfast. They ate in companionable silence, enjoying the meal and each other's company. Danny spent every moment savoring the touch of Ayanda's mind and heart on her own, letting the warmth, comfort and companionship keep her darker thoughts at bay. It was Christmas morning, and she wanted more than anything just to enjoy spending it with Ayanda without worrying about the fact that she was going home in two days.

She realized she wasn't quite as successful at holding back those emotions as she thought she was when she felt Ayanda shift slightly, wrapping a wing around her shoulders, and sending a wave of affection and concern through the link.

"I'm sorry," Danny said.

"It's okay, love," Ayanda said. "You're here, with me. We still have time."

"I am," Danny said. "We do."

Ayanda leaned over and kissed her temple. "I love you."

"I love you, too."

They went back to their meals, and when they were finished, Ayanda waved her hand and sent the trays floating out of the room. Danny waited for a moment until the telltale look of concentration faded from Ayanda's face, then she shifted closer and snuggled in, resting her head on Ayanda's shoulder.

"Can we just stay here for a little while?" Danny asked.

Ayanda used a bit of telekinesis to lift Danny into her lap and wrapped both arms around her. "We can stay as long as you like," she said. "Though I do want to give you your present at some point."

Danny smiled and bounced a little in Ayanda's lap. "What'd you get me?" she asked.

"Nothing too exciting," Ayanda said. She pressed a kiss to Danny's temple. "After all, it had to be small enough for you to carry with you when you go back."

"Well..." Danny said. She reached out with her power, opened her drawer in the dresser, and pulled a small, carefully wrapped present into her hand. "I might have gone for something a bit small, too."

Ayanda smiled as she looked down at the box. "You didn't have to," she said.

"I know, but I wanted to." She held out the box, and Ayanda took it, but she didn't open it. Instead, she turned and gave a small wave of her hand, and the drawer in the nightstand on her side of the bed opened. A long narrow box floated out of the drawer and into her hand. She held it out to Danny. "Here."

Danny took the box and pressed a kiss to Ayanda's cheek.

"You want to go first?" Danny asked.

Ayanda shook her head. "You first."

"Okay." Danny took the box and tore off the paper. Inside were two thin, narrow gold bars, each maybe an eighth of an inch thick, three-quarters of an inch wide, and ten inches long with a sort of curving spiral on each end. The spirals curved in different directions from each other, and both bars were covered in some sort of script that Danny didn't recognize.

"They're beautiful," she said, trying to hold back her confusion.

"But what are they?" Ayanda asked, a teasing grin on her face.

Danny laughed and looked at Ayanda. "Yeah."

"Most of my world was destroyed," Ayanda said. "But after the fight with Idimoni ended, I went back home to see if there was anything left. I managed to save a few relics." She reached into the box and picked up the gold bar. "My people called these isongos. We gave them as betrothal gifts. I know it's a little late, since we already have each other's mating mark, but I thought, if you wanted, we could wear them."

Danny stared at the isongos, not quite believing what she was hearing. "Are you…" She stopped, choking on the lump in her throat. She took a deep breath and tried again. "Are you asking me to marry you?"

Ayanda grinned, and Danny could feel a mix of fear and excitement swirling through the link. "I guess I am," Ayanda said. "What do you say?"

Danny leaned in and kissed Ayanda, letting everything she felt pour out through the link. All the shock, the joy, the excitement, the love. Everything. She shifted, so she was straddling Ayanda, and deepened the kiss, moaning when she felt Ayanda's tongue slip into her mouth. She was getting lost in the kiss, wanting it to go on forever, until she felt Ayanda's hands sliding up her spine. She pulled back, breaking the kiss, knowing what would happen if Ayanda touched the mating mark on her neck. As much as she wanted that, wanting to spend the day getting lost in Ayanda, she wanted to answer her first.

"Yes," she said. She kissed Ayanda again. "Yes, of course I will."

Ayanda's smile got even wider than it had been, and she leaned in and kissed Danny again. "It's going to be so hard waiting for you," she said. "But knowing I have this to look forward to is going to make it so much easier."

Danny kissed Ayanda again, then reached for the isongos. "So, how do we put these on?" she asked.

Ayanda took one from her. "Hold your left arm out to the side." Danny did, and Ayanda pressed one of the spirals to her bicep. The rest of the isongo wrapped itself tightly around Danny's bicep.

"Won't it fall off?" she asked.

"Flex your arm," Ayanda said. Danny did, bending her arm at the elbow. She watched her bicep swell as it tensed, but the isongo changed shape to match. The band got narrower as it got longer to fit around the extra girth her arm had when she flexed. Then when she extended her arm again, the band got thicker as it shrank, tightening itself down. Ayanda reached up and gave it a tug, but it didn't move or slip, like it was attached to the skin.

"There's a safety mechanism built in that will make it release before it does any damage to the arm, but short of that, it's not going anywhere. It's got a power collector inside that pulls ambient energy to drive the mechanism, and the metal is about a hundred times stronger than steel, so you should even be able to wear it as Scatter if you decide to go back out in the field with me in the future."

Danny leaned in and kissed her. "Of course I will," she said. "If you think I'm letting you slip off to fight the Balrog of Morgoth or something without me, you're crazy."

"Balrog of Morgoth?" Ayanda asked, and Danny shrugged.

"I blame that one on my Cate Blanchett phase," she said. "Just read Lord of the Rings at some point, and you'll get it."

"Well, I will have a lot of free time on my hands," Ayanda said. "You're pretty high maintenance, you know."

"Me?" Danny said. "High maintenance? You take that back!"

"Never," Ayanda said.

Danny reached down and picked up the other isongo. "Take it back," she said.

"How about if I said I love you anyway?"

"Hmph."

Ayanda leaned in and kissed her. "Okay," she said. "I take it back."

"Good," Danny said. "Now, hold out your arm."

Ayanda did, and Danny pressed one of the spirals to Ayanda's bicep, just the way Ayanda had done for her, and the isongo wrapped around her arm.

"There," Danny said. "You're mine now."

Ayanda rested her hands on Danny's hips. "I already was," she said before leaning in for a kiss.

Danny pulled back when the kiss started to escalate. She didn't want to, but she did want to give Ayanda her gift before they got distracted, so she reached down and picked it up, offering it to Ayanda.

"Your turn," she said.

Ayanda took the present, smiling as she tore the wrapping paper off, then opened the cardboard box underneath, only to find a small jewelry box inside. She lifted it out and opened it, carefully. She looked at Danny, who gave her a small nod. Ayanda opened the jewelry box. Inside, there was a necklace with an oval pendant. A white opal set around the edge with gold. Ayanda lifted it up out of the box, and turned it over to look at the back, which had a black opal instead of white.

"It's a locket," Danny said.

"Oh," Ayanda said. "How do you open it?"

"You'll have to use your powers," Danny said. "Just reach out and touch it with your mind."

Ayanda stared at it for a second, then gasped as the locket swung open. Danny could feel her surprise as an image rose up out of the locket, taking on a full three dimensions. It was the two of them, Danny standing in front, with Ayanda in back, but it was Ayanda in her natural form, her wings half open. She had her arms around Danny's waist, and both of them were smiling.

"How?" Ayanda asked. She looked up from the image to Danny. "When I touched it, it felt like I was touching your mind."

"Eurion," Danny said. "He kind of owed me a favor for the whole trying to kill me thing, and he is a wonderful jeweler. He's also a dragon, so you know, the magic kind of goes hand in hand. He laid protective enchantments on it so nothing short of dragon fire can destroy it, and he took a drop of blood from the mating mark to fuel the magic, so as long as either of us are alive, the magic should endure, which means that the magic will last even while I'm not with you."

"Is that why it felt like you?" Ayanda asked.

"No," Danny said. "I didn't want to leave you alone, and Eurion knows that, so when I told him what I wanted to get for you for

Christmas, he made a suggestion. I'm not sure how it works, or even if I believe it, but he said he could take a fragment of my soul and bind it into the locket."

"A fragment of your soul?" Ayanda asked, and Danny could feel a bit of fear in her.

"A small one," Danny said. "Just a sliver. Like I said, I'm not even sure if souls exist. Maybe it's just a bit of my life force, or a telepathic impression or something, but Eurion swears it's harmless and Rachel and Jia Li agreed with him. I just didn't want to leave you alone, and this way, even when I'm gone, a piece of me will always be with you, and when you need me, you can reach out and feel me there, and know that I love you, even if I can't be with you."

Ayanda looked down at the locket, and Danny could feel a rush of emotion from Ayanda. There was so much there that she had trouble sorting the individual emotions, but she could feel so much love coming through.

"Thank you," Ayanda said softly. She looked up at Danny. "This is…I don't know what to say."

Danny took the locket from Ayanda, and closed it, then opened the clasp on the chain. Ayanda leaned forward, stretching out her neck, and Danny put the locket on her, careful to avoid touching her mating mark. Once the locket was hanging against Ayanda's chest, Danny covered it with her hand, and looked Ayanda in the eye.

"Say you won't run away from the world while I'm gone," Danny said. "I know Focus might not make friends, but you have Cecile, and Jia Li, and Rachel, and Eurion. Keep them in your life and find other people, too. Maybe David, or maybe other people you meet along the way. I know you'll wait for me, and I know I'll see you on the other side, but please, love, don't be alone for the next three decades. Find friends, build a family of people who love you. Be happy."

"I'll try," Ayanda said.

"That's all I ask," Danny said. She leaned down and kissed Ayanda, and this time, when things started to escalate, she didn't stop them.

***

Danny and Ayanda descended slowly towards building seven on pier fourteen. The warehouse. The place where her life had changed so drastically eighteen months earlier. The place where it was set to change again in less than an hour. It was an unremarkable building.

Steel reinforced concrete walls to make it proof against hurricane force winds. A peaked roof so rain would roll off it during the storms that came every afternoon in the summer months. Heavy insulation to protect against the subtropical heat, and massive air conditioning units to keep the contents from baking. All in all, just like the hundreds of other warehouses that littered the piers all along the bay. When she'd rushed inside that building eighteen months earlier and twenty-nine years in the future, she never would have guessed how different her life would be when she walked out of it.

"You all right?" Ayanda asked as they touched down.

"Is it okay if I say no?" Danny asked.

"Of course it is," Ayanda said. "Come here."

Danny took a moment to unsling the duffle bag that contained her gear from the future, then stepped into Ayanda's arms, hugging her tightly as Ayanda hugged her in return.

"I know this is hard," Ayanda said. "But I'll be waiting on the other side. I promise."

"I know," Danny said. She took a deep breath and let it out as she stepped back out of the hug. "And who knows? Maybe Archie won't let us in, and I'll get to stay."

Ayanda chuckled. "Not much chance of that. I bought the warehouse the day after you arrived, so Archie works for me now," she said.

"You know, sometimes I forget just how rich you are," Danny said.

"If that's your way of asking me to outbid Jia Li, you should have said something before we got engaged."

"Damn it," Danny said. "I guess Jia Li is right about giving the milk away for free."

Ayanda shook her head. "Come on."

"Where do you get all your money?" Danny asked as she picked up the duffle back.

"You do remember that one of our powers is being able to transmute matter, right?" Ayanda asked as Danny followed her to the door. "When I woke up, I transmuted a few dumpsters full of garbage into gold bars. These days, I mostly just live on the interest."

Ayanda gave a firm knock on the door. Danny waved her hand, vanishing the mask and the Scatter emblem from her suit as they waited. Archie the security guard opened the door.

"Ms. Focus," he said. "I've been expecting you."

"Thank you, Archie," she said. "Is everyone else inside?"

"Yes ma'am," Archie said.

"Everyone else?" Danny asked.

Ayanda gave her a mischievous grin. "You'll see."

Archie stepped back, clearing the way for them to enter the warehouse, and Danny spotted four people waiting for them. Cecile, Rachel, Jia Li, and Eurion all stood near the door, and Danny felt a lump in her throat at the sight of her friends.

"You guys came," Danny said as she dropped the duffle bag again.

"You didn't think we were going to let you go without saying goodbye, did you?" Cecile asked as she stepped forward and hugged Danny.

"I thought that's what dinner last night was about," Danny said.

"Don't be silly," Jia Li said. "Dinner last night was just an excuse to eat expensive food and spend time with good company. Today we're here to say goodbye and see you on your way."

Danny let go of Cecile and turned and hugged Jia Li. "Thank you," she said.

"Think nothing of it," Jia Li said. "After all, I'm just here to protect my interests. I still have an offer of a double weight if Ayanda ever gets tired of you."

Danny laughed and smacked Jia Li's shoulder. "If she ever does get tired of me, I'll be sure to put in a good word for you," she said. She let go of Jia Li and found Eurion stepping forward next.

"Young daughter," he said, and Danny found herself a little shocked that he would address her that way. A sign of respect normally reserved for others of his kind. "I am so glad I did not kill you that day."

Danny pulled him into a hug and was a little surprised by the strength he used to return it. "I'm pretty happy about that myself, old father."

He stepped back and rested his hands on her shoulders. "You have been a joy to me, and I will miss you terribly. I do truly hope I get to see you on the other side of your journey."

"Keep yourself out of trouble and I'm sure we'll meet again," Danny said. "Maybe if you stop being so cheap, you'll even have a bride to introduce me to."

"A single weight is not cheap," Eurion said. "There is a reason a bride price is a set weight of gold."

Danny laughed. "Keep telling yourself that, but you saw what Rachel had to pay for a quality bride."

"Indeed," Eurion said. "And I think our Rachel got a bargain at that. Be safe and be well, Danny Martin."

Eurion stepped back, and Rachel stepped forward with tears in her eyes.

Danny pulled her into a hug. "Thank you for coming," she said.

"I wouldn't miss it," Rachel said, squeezing with inhuman strength. "But I don't know what to say." She let go and stepped back so they could see each other's faces. "You introduced me to the first person I have ever loved. You brought happiness and joy and light into my life. You helped me avenge the wrong done to her. There aren't words to express my gratitude, or any way to repay the debt I owe you."

"There is," Danny said. "As much as you love Cecile, I love Ayanda. I can't be here to take care of her for a while. If you truly believe you owe me a debt, then all I ask is that you take care of her in my place. Don't let her brood, or wallow. Don't let her withdraw. Don't let her be alone. Give her the same friendship you gave me, so that she's happy and in good company while I'm away, and we can call it even."

"We will," Rachel said. "All of us. You have our word." Rachel leaned in and pressed a kiss to each of Danny's cheeks. "And you come back to us, as soon as you get home."

"You have my word."

Danny turned to Ayanda. "I should get changed," she said.

Ayanda gave her a shaky nod and turned to Archie. "Where's the restroom?"

Archie pointed to a door near the office. "Right over there."

"Thank you," Danny said. She grabbed the duffle bag and trotted across the warehouse to the bathroom. Once she was inside, she vanished her costume, and pulled on her old Marshal gear. It went fairly quickly. She'd taken the time to refamiliarize herself with it the day before. Once she had it on, she took a moment to look in the mirror, taking in a different look than she had when she arrived. Her hair was longer, to cover up the mating mark on the back of her neck. Her face and body were different, too. Leaner, more muscular from all the time she spent in the gym and from the caloric burn that came with using her powers and fighting Supervillains. The new look was good on her, and along with the mating mark and the isongo around her left bicep, proof that all of this had actually happened and wasn't just some fever dream caused by a shock from a superweapon.

She picked up her rifle and the now empty duffle and headed back out into the warehouse where her friends and her fiancée and one probably very confused security guard waited. When she got there, she laid the duffle on the ground with her rifle on top of it, then looked at Ayanda.

"What now?" she asked.

"Now, we wait," Ayanda said.

"I suck at waiting," Danny said.

"I know, love," Ayanda said. "And if you weren't bristling with weapons and explosives, I'd hug you."

"Hug me anyway," Danny said.

Ayanda held out her arms, and Danny stepped into them, resting her head on Ayanda's shoulder.

"Remember your promise," Danny said.

Ayanda pressed a kiss to Danny's temple. "I will."

No one else said anything as the minutes crawled past, waiting for a doorway to the future to open. Every minute, another memory came to Danny, another reason she didn't want to go, another reason to hold tighter to Ayanda.

"Will it hurt?" Danny asked.

"Yes," Ayanda said. "But when you get there, look for me, and when you find me, reach for me. The pain will stop as soon as our minds touch again."

"What about you?" Danny asked. "How will you stop it?"

"When our minds touch again," Ayanda said. "Until then, I can endure."

"I don't want to leave you."

"I know, but you have to. You have to go home."

"This is my home."

"Only for a little while," Ayanda said. She pressed a kiss to Danny's temple. "You've made my life so much better, and I am going to miss you so much, but I will be there, waiting on the other side."

"I know," Danny said. She pulled back from the hug, just enough to lean in and kiss Ayanda, pouring everything into it, letting every emotion flood through the link. She let Ayanda feel how much she loved her and how much she wanted to stay, and in return, she felt every bit of Ayanda's love, and how much Ayanda wanted her to stay. The kiss seemed to go on forever, until there was a soft cough from behind them.

"It's time," Jia Li said.

Danny pulled back from the kiss, and when she opened her eyes, she noticed a strange light filling the room. She turned and saw a glowing blue vortex maybe twenty feet away, and the reality of it sank in. She was going home. She was really going home.

Even the thought hurt, like she was being ripped in two, but there was nothing for it. Jia Li was right. It was time. She walked over and picked up her rifle and clipped it to the single point sling, and then, careful not to look back, she walked up to the portal.

"Ayanda," she said.

"Yes?"

"I love you."

"I love you, too," Ayanda said. "Always."

She took a deep breath, and before she could change her mind, she jumped into the portal.

Chapter Twenty-one

"WILL IT HURT?"

"Yes. But when you get there, look for me, and when you find me, reach for me. The pain will stop as soon as our minds touch again."

The words echoed in Danny's mind as agony took her. She passed through the portal, and it felt like her soul had been cleaved in two. For the first time in a year, when she reached into that place inside her where Ayanda lived, there was no answer, no warm, loving touch, no echo of the soul that was the other half of her. She reached out desperately, hunting for her other half. Ayanda wasn't gone. She couldn't be gone. They were one, together, forever.

An eternity passed in unimaginable loneliness as she searched, but then the eternity ended. She felt a shock run up her legs as they hit concrete and she realized she had stumbled out of the portal and into the future, the present. She wasn't sure what it was anymore. She knew only that it hurt. That she had lost something. A piece of herself so important that she couldn't go on until she found it again.

She felt herself falling, but strong arms caught her, and when she looked up, inhumanly blue eyes she knew better than her own looked down at her. She reached out, body and mind, hand touching face as mind touched mind. The link snapped back into place, thrown wide open by the force of the reconnection and love and longing and joy and relief and happiness poured through in both directions as they both stared into the eyes of the woman they loved.

"Gotcha," Ayanda said, and Danny somehow managed to laugh and sob at the same time. She moved the hand she had on Ayanda's face to her shoulder, and reached up with the other one, resting it on her back, then used both of them to haul herself up so she could kiss her. Strong arms wrapped around her as she kissed Ayanda and Ayanda kissed her back. Time, which still hadn't quite settled back into its usual flow, fell away again as the kiss stretched out, lasting seconds and eons at the same time. Every touch of the lips, every swipe of the tongue, every scrape of teeth tearing down another wall between them until there was no Danny and Ayanda, only a singular them. One being. One soul wrapped up into two bodies.

They heard someone clearing their throat and ignored it, lost in their own world, lost in themselves. The sound came again, and they ignored it again.

"Hey, you two!" someone yelled. The words were enough to drive the first wedge. They fought to hang on, but slowly and all at once the walls between them came back, and they were Danny and Ayanda again. Still connected but separated into their own bodies as the kiss ended. Ayanda lifted her up and set her on her feet.

"I've missed you so much," Ayanda said.

Danny reached up and brushed a strand of hair out of Ayanda's face. "I'm sorry I had to leave."

"I know," Ayanda said. "But I kept my word."

Danny smiled. "You did?"

"Brunch every Sunday. We invited David. Jia Li's wife. Hell, sometimes even old Tarantasio and his latest bride would join us."

"Tarantasio got married?" Danny asked.

"Yeah," Ayanda said. "A nice Italian girl named Sophia. You'll love her."

"It's like we're not even here," Lori said.

"I know," Perez said.

Danny laughed and leaned forward, resting her forehead against Ayanda's. "How long was I gone?"

"Two hours, give or take," Ayanda said.

"Two hours."

"I know."

Danny reached up, running her hand over Ayanda's left bicep. She smiled when she found what she was looking for.

"You're still wearing it," she said.

"Why wouldn't I be?"

"I was worried you'd change your mind," Danny said. "Twenty-nine years is a long time."

"I would wait for you forever."

Danny closed her eyes and took a deep breath, letting it out slowly. She straightened up, opened her eyes and stepped back, then turned and looked at Perez.

"Sorry about that, ma'am," she said.

"You want to explain what the hell is going on?" Perez asked.

"It's a long story," Danny said.

"Then we should probably get all of this packed up and debrief back at the station," Perez said.

"About that," Danny said. She turned and walked over to where the 'hostile' was sitting and knelt down.

"When were you trying to get back to?" she asked.

He twitched his antenna. "How did you know?" he asked.

"I had a long time to think about it," she said. "Tell me what happened."

"My name is Ren Bok," he said. "I'm a chrononaut. We come back and observe history. My temporal translator was damaged. Even the emergency beacon is offline. The technology to fix it won't exist for another two hundred years, but this century is advanced enough that I could build a temporal gateway."

"And when I tampered with it, the discharge knocked me into the past," she said.

"Yes," Ren said. "I only ever wanted to get home."

"The Kaiju lure?"

"A distraction," he said. "I thought if I could keep everyone focused on the bay, then there was no chance I would accidentally hurt anyone while I was getting the materials I needed."

"When are you from?" Danny asked.

"I left for this era on August 12th, 2759," he said.

Danny turned to Perez. "What time is it?"

"It's 12:47 PM."

"12:47 PM May 20th, 2021," Danny said. She turned back to Ren. "Who would you send a distress call to?"

"I work out of the Sun City University History Department."

"Right," Danny said. She looked over at Ayanda. "Say 12:50 PM, May 20th, 2021 for pickup."

"Sounds good," Ayanda said.

"What are you two talking about?" Perez asked.

"Just wait for it, ma'am," Danny said.

"I'm not in a patient mood," Perez said.

"Trust me," Danny said. "I am about to save you so much paperwork."

"Do I have a choice?" Perez asked.

"Not really," Danny said. "Just, nobody shoot anyone."

"You're not selling me on this," Perez said.

At that moment, another time portal opened, and six people stepped through. All the Marshals raised their weapons, but Ayanda threw a forcefield between the new arrivals and the Marshals.

"Easy, everybody," Danny said. "They're just here to help."

The time travelers all looked around curiously.

"Perez, trust me, please," Danny said.

Perez sighed. "Everyone, lower your weapons."

The Marshals all lowered their weapons, and Ayanda dropped the force field. Danny waved at the time travelers.

"Your missing historian is here," she said. "Time machine is over there."

One of the time travelers walked over to Ren. "How much damage did you do?"

"I think I created a class three predestination paradox," he said.

The time traveler groaned and looked at Danny. "Are you in charge?"

"No," she said. "That would be Deputy Marshal Perez."

"Then I shall speak with her," he said.

"You do that," Danny said. "I'm going to find somewhere to sit down. It's been a long couple of hours."

***

It turned out the 'somewhere to sit down' was a gurney. Perez insisted Danny ride back to headquarters in the back of an ambulance and that she get a full medical workup when she got there. Danny didn't actually mind that much since she got to leave the scene right away and Ayanda insisted on riding back with her. They just sat quietly the whole ride, Ayanda holding her hand, both of them submerged in the link.

The doctor tried to separate them when they got to headquarters, but she didn't have a lot of luck. The best she could do was get Ayanda to stand behind the radiation shield while they did a full body CT scan. She wanted to do an MRI, too, but Danny politely refused. By the time the doctor was done poking and prodding, it was almost 5:00 PM, and Danny was ready to go home, but they ended up waiting another half hour until Perez and Lori arrived before the doctor came in to give her final report.

Danny sat on the bed, still holding Ayanda's hand and ignoring the odd looks from Perez and Lori as the doctor put a couple of X-Rays up on the light box.

"So, for the most part, Deputy Marshal Martin is in amazing health. Her eyesight and hearing have substantially improved. All the fillings in her teeth are gone, replaced by natural bone and enamel. Her appendix scar is gone, and both her appendix and her tonsils have grown back.

The scar from the prior break in her leg is gone, as is the slight curvature in her spine that's been noted in her medical file since age twelve. However, based on the ID photo taken when she was stationed here, and footage from our internal security cameras, I'd estimate that she's experienced about eighteen months of hair growth since this morning, and has gained significant muscle mass since her last physical exam."

"Are you sure this is our Danny Martin?" Perez asked. "Not a clone, or a Danny from an alternate universe?"

"Definitely not a clone," the doctor said. "Clones and identical twins experience epigenetic variance, and we have ways to test for that. We don't have enough data on Alternate Universe copies to know if epigenetic variance would distinguish them, but..." She gestured to Ayanda.

"This is Danny," Ayanda said.

Perez looked at her. "You're sure?"

"Absolutely."

"How are you sure?" Perez asked.

"She's got my mark," Ayanda said.

"What does that mean?" Perez asked.

"If I may," the doctor cut in. She walked over to the light box and turned it on. "These are X-Rays of Danny's neck. I noticed that there was extensive scarring from some sort of bite mark on the back of her neck and wanted to check for spinal damage. Instead, what I found was a mass of nerve tissue clustered within the perimeter of the bite mark and attached to her spine."

"Some kind of tumor?" Perez asked. "Alien parasite?"

"It's not a tumor," Danny said.

"She's right," the doctor said. "And it is alien. Just not a parasite."

"It's a Umoya mating mark," Ayanda said.

"Okay," Perez said. "You're going to need to explain that."

"I'm an alien," Ayanda said. "My species were called the Umoya. When we take a mate, part of the process involves a bite applied to the back of the neck. When we bite our mates, it injects a soup of nerve cells and nutrients into the wound. The nerve cells absorb markers from our mate's genetic makeup, so our mate's body doesn't identify them as foreign tissue. The tissue attaches itself to the spine, and then sends runners up to connect to the brain, forming a telepathic link between the two people who are mating. That's what you're seeing on the X-ray. I marked Danny when I took her as my mate."

"And when was that?" Perez asked.

"Depends," Danny said. "By my timeline, 367 days ago. By the calendar, Christmas morning of 1991."

"So, while you were in the past, you two..."

"We lived together for almost eighteen months," Danny said. "I spent a year of that time working as the Superhero Scatter."

"So, you are a metahuman?" Perez asked.

"I wasn't when I went back in time," Danny said. "But a lot of shit happened."

"I'll look forward to the debrief," Perez said.

"I've already been debriefed on most of it," Danny said. "Just read the old reports from Scatter's time here. As for the rest, we're telling you what we're telling you so you believe I am who I say I am, but a lot of what happened in the past is personal. And I won't be returning to work as a Marshal."

"You won't?" Perez asked.

"No," Danny said. "But I will be coming back as Scatter." She looked over at Lori. "Sorry, but you're going to have to break in a new partner."

Lori shrugged. "Like I said, you'll last or you won't. This is better than you getting your ass killed."

"Hey, maybe my replacement will be bi, and you can finally fill out that softball team."

Lori laughed. "Maybe," she said.

Danny swung her legs off the exam table and stood up. "Come here."

Lori stepped forward, a little hesitantly, only for Danny to pull her into a hug.

"God, I've missed you," Danny said.

Lori hugged her back. "Your girlfriend isn't going to throw me into orbit for this, is she?"

"Not my girlfriend," Danny said as she let go of Lori.

"Really?"

"Really," Danny said. "She's my fiancée."

"Good luck with that," Perez said. "You'll probably die of old age before you finish the HR paperwork for a workplace relationship."

"Are we done here?" Ayanda asked. "We actually have somewhere to be."

"We do?" Danny asked.

"Yeah," Ayanda said.

"Do I get to know where?"

"Nope," Ayanda said. "It's a surprise."

***

Danny took the time to grab a shower before she changed back into her civvies just to wash the smell of the medical center off of her. Wherever Ayanda was taking her, she didn't want to spend the whole time smelling of antiseptic and cleaning products. Once she was done changing into her regular clothes, she met Ayanda outside of the locker room, and they headed out. They only got to the front steps before they found Lori waiting for them. She was standing at the bottom of the steps in her own civvies, looking up at them with a worried expression on her face.

"Hey, Lori," Danny said.

"Hey," Lori replied.

"Everything okay?" Danny asked.

"Yeah," she said. "I just wanted to check on you without Perez around. Make sure you're okay."

"I am," she said. She looked over at Ayanda and smiled. "Better than okay."

"You sure?" Lori asked. "I mean, no offense to Focus—"

"Call me Ayanda."

Lori's eyes bugged out as she turned to Ayanda. "Did you just tell me your name?"

"I did," Ayanda said. "It's not the name I use every day, but it is the name my parents gave me."

"Why are you telling me, though?" Lori asked.

"Because you're Danny's friend," Ayanda said. "I try, but I'm not used to making friends. Danny's better at it than I am, and even if she's going to be working here in a different capacity, I know she'll still want you in her life, which means that you're going to be a part of my life. I'd like for us to be friends."

Lori smiled. "I think I'd like that."

"You know," Ayanda said. "If you don't have any plans, you're welcome to come with us."

"I wouldn't want to get in the way," Lori said.

"You wouldn't be," Ayanda said. "There are a lot of people who have been waiting a very long time to see their friend again. The more, the merrier. And this way, you can see for yourself that Danny's really okay."

"All right," Lori said. "Lead the way."

Ayanda grinned at Danny.

"Don't," Danny said, but Ayanda turned back to Lori.

"You might feel a little disoriented."

"Ayanda!" Danny said.

"What?" Lori asked.

Ayanda waved her hand, and the teleport took them all.

***

Danny caught Lori as she stumbled coming out of the teleport.

"Are you going to be sick?" she asked. Lori shook her head, but she turned to Ayanda and glared.

"Consider it payback for giving my girl a hard time," Ayanda said.

Lori flipped her the bird, which only made Ayanda laugh and shake her head before she shifted into a form Danny hadn't seen before. This new form was actually taller than her Focus form and looked like a human version of her true form. She was wearing flat-soled ankle boots, black skinny jeans, and a long sleeved, blue silk button up, and instead of Focus's blonde hair, or Kelly's brown hair, this form had blue hair worn in a Pixie cut. The whole effect made Danny bite her lower lip and whimper slightly.

"Woah!" Lori said. "You're a shapeshifter?"

"Most aliens who look human are. Which reminds me," Ayanda said. She turned to Danny. "It's Amanda Williams now."

"I like it," Danny said. She reached out and took Ayanda's hand. "I like it a lot."

"Get a room," Lori said.

"I have several," Ayanda replied.

"Where are we?" Danny asked as she looked around. They were standing on the porch of a nice house that seemed familiar.

"Rachel and Cecile's," Ayanda said before Danny could place it.

"Really?" Danny asked, barely able to contain her excitement.

"Really," Ayanda said. She turned and knocked on the door, and it swung open immediately.

"I was wondering how long it was going to take you idiots to knock," Cecile said.

Danny stepped forward and wrapped her arms around Cecile, who hugged her so tight Danny's feet left the ground.

"God, you have no idea how hard it was not to just grab you and hug the life out of you the last time you were here," Cecile said. "I've missed you so much." She set Danny on her feet again and pulled back to look at her. "We all have."

Danny did her best to ignore the tears gleaming in Cecile's eyes. "Who all is here?" she asked.

"Come inside and see," Cecile said. Then she looked over at Lori. "Good to see you again, Ahmad."

"Likewise, La Saint," Lori said. "But please, call me Lori."

"If you'll call me Cecile."

"I think I can manage that."

"Then come on in, all of you. Otherwise, the HOA will be on my ass again, and Rachel might finally get mad enough to eat the nosy bitches."

"She'd be doing a service to humanity," Ayanda said as she stepped inside. Danny and Lori followed her, and once Cecile had closed the door, she led them through towards the back of the house to a large room that was filled with people.

"The guest of honor has finally arrived," Cecile said.

It took Danny a moment to take in all of the faces as they cheered, but there was Rachel at the front of the crowd. Jia Li with a gorgeous blonde on her arm. A curvy, dark-haired woman in suit pants and a matching vest over a green silk button down. The next few faces were all surprises. Her mother, both her sisters, and her father. The last person was a young woman with dark skin and bushy brown hair, about the same height as Cecile, but a bit on the plump side.

Before Danny could make sense of it all, Rachel wrapped her in a hug, picking her up off the floor easily and twirling her around, laughing the whole time.

"Welcome home," Rachel said.

Danny hugged her as tightly as she could. "It's good to be home," she said.

Rachel set Danny down on her feet, then smiled at Lori. "Good to see you again, Lori."

"It's good to see you too, Rachel," Lori said.

Rachel grabbed Danny's hand, and then waved the plump, dark skinned girl over. She was a bit shy as she approached, but she had a lovely smile.

"This is mine and Cecile's daughter," Rachel said. "Ruth Danielle Levi-La Saint."

Danny looked at her, but she didn't know what to say. Every time she tried to think of something, she just heard Rachel saying Ruth's full name again, and her mind went blank.

"It's a pleasure to meet you," Ruth said. "I've heard so much about you my whole life."

"It's nice to meet you, too," Danny managed.

Rachel patted Ruth on the shoulder. "Let's give her a minute. I think I just broke the poor dear, and I don't think you've met Lori, here, before."

Ruth looked at Lori, and the shy expression on her face changed to something that could only be described as hungry.

"No," Ruth said. "I would have remembered meeting you."

Lori, who had to have at least eight or nine years on Ruth, turned the approximate color of a tomato as Ayanda pulled Danny a bit deeper into the room.

The dark-haired woman in the suit pants and vest stepped forward next, and Danny looked at her for a moment, wondering who she was until she caught a faint whiff of smoke.

"Eurion?" she asked, surprise filling her voice.

"How did you know?" she asked.

Danny shrugged. "You're just so Welsh," she said, and Eurion's face lit up with delight.

"Oh, my dear, I am so glad I didn't manage to kill you," she said.

Danny hugged her. "How are you doing?" she asked.

"Quite well," she said. "Sun City agrees with me."

"I can see that," Danny said. "You know, if I weren't already taken, I'd be all over you. It's very Catherine Zeta-Jones."

"I'll take that as a compliment," Eurion said.

"You should. So, have you found a new bride, or are you still too cheap?"

Eurion blew a puff of smoke out of her nose. "Watch it, young daughter," she said, but there was no real rebuke in her tone.

"It's good to see you," Danny said.

"And it's good to have you home. We've all missed you terribly."

She stepped away as Jia Li approached, the gorgeous blonde still on her arm.

"Hello, Danny," Jia Li said. "I'd like to introduce you to my wife, Emilia Rose."

Danny blinked and turned to the blonde, looking her over, and sure enough, it was Emilia Rose.

"You're...you're Airheart," Danny sputtered. It was a stupid thing to say, because she'd known Jia Li was married to Airheart, but she'd never expected to actually meet her.

Emilia smiled at her. "Yes, I am."

"Breathe, love," Ayanda said.

Danny turned to Ayanda. "She's Airheart."

"Well, someone is clearly a fan," Emilia said.

"I don't think that's it, dear," Jia Li said. "Danny here is a healthy young lesbian. She would have been around twelve or thirteen around the time you did that photo shoot. The poor thing is probably remembering all the naughty thoughts she had about you."

That was exactly what was happening, and Danny very much wanted to die on the spot, or at the very least, teleport to the moon. Fortunately, Emilia seemed to take what Jia Li said in stride. She slapped her wife gently on the shoulder and shook her head.

"Ignore my wife," Emilia said. "Though, I suppose you should be used to her particular brand of shit stirring by now if you're as good a friend as Jia Li says you are, but there's no reason to be star struck. I heard how you helped Ayanda take down Chernobog, and how you took down Null without your powers. Those are quite the accomplishments."

"Thank you," Danny said. She took a deep breath, and she felt a wave of calm and support flow into her through the link, which was enough to ease her anxiety and let her think clearly. "And I apologize. Jia Li is right about one thing. I did grow up idolizing you. I mean, all of the Olympic Six, but I was a young teenage lesbian. You, Jia Li, and Ayanda were my heroes."

"Well, I'd say we're still just human, except that doesn't apply in Jia Li and Ayanda's cases, but you've been out there. You know what it's like, and you're every bit the hero we are, and I am honored to meet someone my wife thinks so highly of."

"Thank you," Danny said. "That means a lot." She turned back to Jia Li and was surprised to be pulled into a hug.

"We've missed you," Jia Li said.

"I'm sorry I had to leave," Danny said.

"Nonsense," Jia Li said. "You did what had to be done, and you are home now, with your family."

"I am," Danny said. "And speaking of family, it looks like someone brought mine. I should go say hi."

"Go on then," Jia Li said. "Leave an old dragon at the mercy of her cruel wife."

"Don't enjoy her mercy too much, old mother. I'm not sure your heart could take it."

Jia Li smiled and waved her away, so Danny reached down and took Ayanda's hand in hers. She felt a wave of nerves come from the other end of the link.

"They'll love you," Danny said.

"I hope so," Ayanda said. "I let Cecile make all the arrangements, so I haven't actually talked to them."

"Wait," Danny said, as a thought occurred to her. She used just a touch of power to conjure a simple pair of diamond solitaire engagement rings, one on her finger and one on Ayanda's. Ayanda looked down at her hand, and then up at Danny.

"You want to tell them now?" she asked.

"I do," Danny said. She gave Ayanda's hand a small tug, and led her over to where her mother, father, and sisters were waiting.

"Hey," Danny said.

"There's my little girl," her mother said, holding out her arms. Danny stepped into the hug, giving her mom a good squeeze.

"When your friend called and said they were planning a surprise party, I couldn't figure out what it was for, but they said it was important."

"It is," Danny said. "God, I've missed you." She pulled away from her mom.

"Hey, Dad," she said, giving him a quick hug, before moving on to each of her sisters in turn. When she was done, she stepped back and took Ayanda's hand. She looked at Ayanda.

"How long are they going to be in town?" she asked.

"They're scheduled to fly back on Sunday," Ayanda said.

Danny smiled as she turned back to them. "Amanda, this is my mom, Patricia, my dad, Carl, and my sisters Sam and Max. Mom, Dad, Sam, Max, I'd like you all to meet my fiancé, Amanda Williams."

She wasn't quite ready for the volume of her mother's scream of excitement.

***

Hours later, Danny stepped out of the bathroom in Ayanda's new apartment. Well, sort of new. She'd been there about ten years, but it was new to Danny. She loved it, though. All of the furniture was usable by humans, but it was obviously designed with Ayanda's true form in mind. To anyone not in the know, it would look like something out of some weird European furniture catalogue. Danny loved knowing that

Ayanda had a place where she could be her true self, but that was honestly a thought for another time. It had been a very long day, and Danny was more than ready to crawl into bed and drift off.

The problem was her favorite pillow wasn't there waiting for her. She reached out through the link, feeling her presence and letting it guide her out to the balcony. She found Ayanda there, staring out towards the bay.

"Is everything okay, love?"

"Come here," Ayanda said.

Danny walked over to stand next to Ayanda, but when she reached the railing, Ayanda moved to stand behind her. She wrapped her arms around Danny, and rested her chin on Danny's shoulder, letting out a contented sigh.

"Now, everything is okay," she said.

Danny leaned back into the embrace. "Thank you for the party."

"I like your parents, and your sisters," Ayanda said.

"They like you, too," Danny said. "Especially mom. She'll be after us to have babies the moment we're married."

She felt a twitch of regret through the link and squeezed Ayanda's hand.

"It's okay," she said.

"Are you sure?" Ayanda asked. "I know you said so that night, but…"

"I said it then, and I meant it. All I want is to be with you."

"Even after what I did?"

"What do you mean?"

"I sent you back," Ayanda said. "I knew what would happen if you pulled that lever, and I told you to do it."

"I had to go back," Danny said.

"I could have told you. I could have warned you."

"Why didn't you?" Danny asked.

"Because I was afraid you wouldn't go," she said. "I was selfish. You going back was the best thing that ever happened to me. I met you, I fell in love. But more than that, I opened myself up to real friendship for the first time since my world died. Jia Li, Eurion, Cecile, Rachel, David…a few others over the years. If you hadn't gone back, everything that makes my life worth living would just vanish. So, I didn't warn you, and now I can't help but wonder if I deserve any of it."

Danny turned around in the circle of Ayanda's arms and looked up at her new face. The human face that so closely resembled her true face.

"You did what needed to be done. I had to go back, not just for you, but for Eurion, for Cecile and Rachel, and for all the people we saved. Maybe the way you did it was selfish, but I don't care. Going back was the best thing that ever happened to me, too. All I've ever wanted to do with my life was help people, to do good, and you gave me the power to do that in a way I could never have imagined. Being with you means that I will always have someone there with me, someone I love, to help carry the weight. If you need me to forgive you, then I forgive you, though I don't think you've done anything that needs forgiving. And if you need to do penance, then love me and be with me, because being with you makes me feel happy and loved and cherished and safe."

Ayanda leaned down and kissed her, and Danny returned the kiss, slipping her hands up to find the mark she'd left on Ayanda's neck. The one the pixie cut showed off so well. Ayanda gasped as Danny's fingers touched the sensitive flesh, and Danny could feel the fire and the need she'd awakened.

"If you need to do penance, then take me to bed and show me how much you love me," Danny said.

Ayanda lifted Danny up into her arms easily, and carried her towards the bedroom, where she showered Danny with three decades worth of want and love, and where Danny returned every touch and feeling, and where they both swore, whatever the future held, they would never be apart again.

About Molly J. Bragg

Molly Bragg is an autistic trans woman with a degree in Astrophysics and a love of storytelling. She loves science fiction, superheroes, and giant robots. Her hobbies include collecting Transformers, watching way too many crafting videos on YouTube, playing Dungeons & Dragons, and complaining bitterly about the way a certain comic book company treats her favorite superhero.

Connect with Molly

Email mollyjbragg@gmail.com
Website http://www.themollyjay.com/
.Facebook https://www.facebook.com/themollyjay
Twitter https://twitter.com/themollyjay
Tumbler https://themollyjay.tumblr.com/

Note to Readers

Thank you for reading a book from Desert Palm Press. We appreciate you as a reader and want to ensure you enjoy the reading process. We would like you to consider posting a review on your preferred media sites and/or your blog or website.

For more information on upcoming releases, author interviews, contests, giveaways and more, please sign up for our newsletter and visit us at Desert Palm Press: www.desertpalmpress.com and "Like" us on Facebook: Desert Palm Press.

Bright Blessings

www.ingramcontent.com/pod-product-compliance
Lightning Source LLC
Chambersburg PA
CBHW052021020726
47501CB00004B/1174